Darkstone's Asylum

The Hatchetman

By Adam Kass

For Tami, whose insight, love, support, and patience has made this book possible.

"The void cannot be reasoned with
Its will is absolute
A desire harder than diamond.
Clad in the most brilliant light
And deepest black
It will promise all you desire
Wealth beyond imagination
Power over all.
Do not be fooled, young ones
For the darkness gives nothing
And will take all that you hold close to your heart.
The sweetest fruit shall turn to ash in your mouth
Jewels shall turn to coal in your hands
And in the end your very soul will wither and die."

Esagila Scrolls, Book of Fei Long 5:25:4 – 5:25:17

Inhale. Exhale.

Fear became anxiety.

Inhale. Exhale.

Anxiety became apprehension.

Inhale. Exhale.

Apprehension became concern.

Inhale. Exhale.

Concern became determination.

Sonja Verztuk jerked her head up. Her heart pounded in her chest. Groggy, thoughts mired in a fog of confusion, she desperately tried to recall what had happened to her. Dizziness punctuated the aching in her head. She felt as though she had been drugged, felt a nagging sense she was forgetting something important. No matter how hard she tried, no memory would come.

The rough cloth of a blindfold scraped on her eyelids as she blinked. Abyssal darkness greeted her opened eyes. Focus came in spurts but would not stay. Even the all-encompassing darkness seemed blurry to her eyes. Sonja shivered as cold swept over her. Trying to cover herself, she discovered that she could not move. Her chest felt tight, her heart raced as awareness penetrated her disjointed mind. Panting, feeling as though she were unable to get enough air, fear attempted to reassert itself. She closed her eyes, concentrated on her breathing. Concentrated on staying calm.

Inhale. Exhale.

Sonja gagged on the putrid stench wafting through the wet, stale air. A perfume of rotting garbage, human waste, and other unidentifiable yet equally grotesque smells. Humidity exacerbated the olfactory assault. Bearing down like a lead weight, the heavy air pressed its noxious stew into her. She shuddered. Goosebumps raised on her arms as intermittent, slow currents of air caressed her skin, covering her in a thin, sticky film. The stench helped focus her mind and distracted from the fear attempting to take hold. She needed to get a handle on her situation. Twenty-four years of wheelchair-bound life had prepared her for challenging situations. This was not a challenge she had ever considered.

7

Her arms were stretched upward at forty-five-degree angles, tight bindings around her wrists holding them in position. Numbness was creeping into her hands. Pins and needles of half-awake nerves sent fire through her as she flexed her fingers. She knew the diminished blood flow meant it was just a matter of time before she wouldn't be able to feel anything from her hands at all. The tight, slick weave pattern cutting into her wrists told Sonja that the restraints were made of nylon. She instinctively jerked her arms forward. Her forearms snapped back, slamming into the edges of rough wood. Pain radiated through her. She hissed a breath.

Though she could not feel them, Sonja assumed her legs had been similarly bound. She was upright, of that she was certain. Hung and splayed open like some twisted piece of wall décor. Rushing blood pounded in her ears as her heart rate spiked again. A lone bead of sweat wound its way down her neck, sending convulsive shivers through her.

Inhale. Exhale.

Motor functions in her arms were limited. She had no fine control in her hands, and intense concentration was required to get a desired result out of them. From the chest down, her body was beyond her. A surreal, existential dream. She could feel the pressure, the sensation of being stretched out. That inexorable downward pull of gravity. Though her movement may have limitations, her senses were keen. Taking a breath, she wished she could turn her nose off. Her stomach churned. Intense nausea threatened to force her gastric contents into the light. She retched. The sudden taste of acrid bile added to the offensive, grotesque perfume. She sucked in a breath through her mouth. It did little to help. Her throat burned from the stomach acid, and she could taste putrescence in the humid air.

As she slowed her heart rate, a barely discernible tapping in the darkness grabbed her attention. Sonja let her ears take the place of her eyes. A low electrical hum gave a baseline to the soft cavalcade of sound in her darkened world. The rhythmic dripping of unidentified liquid. An intermittent on/off thunk of some motor-driven piece of machinery. Whooshing of forced air blowing. The quiet roar of far-off traffic.

The increasing volume of footsteps approaching.

Sonja winced as the darkness exploded with the sound of shrieking metal. Her heart pounded against her ribcage in a desperate attempt to free itself from the fleshy prison of her body. She panted, trying to catch her breath. Her arms involuntarily jerked. Her head buzzed from the adrenaline hit. Bursts of light danced in the black of her vision.

Inhale. Exhale.

The smell of fresh air mingled with the rancid fragrance permeating her sightless void. She surmised the blasting shriek was a door that had been opened. Calming herself, she heard the footsteps again. They were close, but not coming toward her. The hair on her arms stood, a shiver of dread swept through her. Somehow being alone in the putrid darkness was preferable to having another invisible person in the room.

The footfalls were light, the steps of stealth. Sonja turned her head, directing her ears toward the sound. The unseen person kept a consistent distance. They were walking around her. She suddenly felt like a small fish being circled by a hungry shark.

Another bead of sweat wound its way down her neck. Her skin tingled as the point of liquid slowly crept across her clavicle and down her sternum. She could pinpoint where nerves stopped sending sensory signals. Halfway down her chest, the bead of sweat just disappeared. The remnant of its passing itched. A torturous line of fire.

Inhale. Exhale.

The footsteps completed one circle, began another; their owner walked in silence. She did not understand what the point of this was. Intimidation? Was the shark waiting for her to speak? Was it trying to figure out its next move? No, that couldn't be it. Whoever the person was, they had clearly done this before. They had a plan.

Sonja mustered all the confidence she had. "Hello?" Her high-pitched voice echoed in the world beyond her blindfold.

"You're really awake," a pleasant male voice returned. "That's awesome, 'cuz I need your help."

His footsteps changed direction, swiftly coming at her from behind. Sonja froze. Her breath caught in her throat; her heart pounded out of control. She felt like she was having a heart attack.

A swift tug jostled her head as the blindfold was removed. Her blue-grey eyes saw only more darkness. Confusion overtook her once again, a confusion quickly replaced by dreaded curiosity as ten red dots appeared, hovering in the air before her. Her mind reeled for a moment. What were they? Drones? Bats? Cyclopean lab rats? Sonja's mental confusion started taking her down a rabbit hole of ridiculous answers. Then it struck her.

Cameras. They were the recording lights on cameras.

A shudder ran down her spine. Nausea reared its ugly head. She involuntarily gulped a heaping load of fetid air, gagging on her exhale. The smell clung to her mouth. Sonja scraped her teeth over her tongue in a futile attempt to remove the disgusting flavor. She tried to spit the rancid taste out. Her mouth was a desert, the only wetness coming from the putrid humidity and the bile that insisted on creeping up her throat. She hadn't noticed it before, but she was parched.

Inhale. Exhale.

Pain shot through Sonja's eyes as ten computer monitors sprung to life. Dots of sparking, blinding light intruded on her vision. She blinked furiously, trying to exorcise the bright spots that infected her eyes. She heard movement, her captor making his way around her. As her eyes cleared, a lump formed in her throat. Fear threatened to take her sanity.

The cameras were affixed to the top of each computer monitor arranged in the form of a person with their legs and arms outstretched. A digital Vitruvian Man. What was on those monitors sent an uncontrollable spasm through her. She was looking at herself.

The digital mirror brought unwanted awareness. She was naked. She already knew her shirt was missing. She could feel that much. Sonja had not allowed herself to think beyond that. Now, she had no choice but to confront the totality of her situation. Bound to an elongated X-shaped crucifix, she saw that her previous assumption was correct. Her ankles were bound the same as her wrists, holding her legs apart. She retched at an intrusive thought. A thought she did not want to consider. A thought she did not want to voice.

Each monitor held a portion of her body. One for each forearm. One for each upper arm. One displayed her head and chest. One gave a view of her abdomen. One for each thigh. One for each lower leg and foot. Her mirror image was bathed in the green high-contrast of night-vision optics. Her eyes appeared a demonic black, a side effect of the image enhancement. She watched the rapid rise and fall of her chest as panic tried to set in. Her lungs burned from exertion, and she felt lightheaded. She was hyperventilating. Sonja shoved the fear aside, forced her breathing to slow. She would not give in so easily.

Inhale. Exhale.

"Who are you?" Sonja breathlessly whispered into the void, trying to maintain some semblance of confidence in her voice.

A face intruded into her vision. Goosebumps covered her as she felt the tip of his nose brush across hers. Her heart punched the inside of her ribcage. She instinctively jerked her head back. The backlit head cocked sideways, as if posing an unspoken question. Impressions of his features came as Sonja's eyes adjusted to the change in light.

The face of her captor appeared to be that of a handsome sixteen or seventeen-year-old boy. She thought he must be older, the low light or genetics making him appear younger than he really was. A wide, comforting smile graced his countenance. A smile that said, "Come on in, get comfortable, stay a while." The green glow of the computer monitors made it hard for Sonja to tell if his shaggy hair was light brown or blond, and the dim light made his skin tone impossible to determine.

"Who are you?" she asked meekly. The confidence she strove to exude had abandoned her.

"Oh, the question isn't who I am." His pleasant, silky voice was hypnotic. "The question is: What can you do for me?" He leaned into her ear, his breath an unwanted caress. Every hair on the back of her neck stood. "I need you," he whispered. Sonja's blood turned to ice.

Terror gripped her. She felt as though all the air had been sucked from the room. Her lungs refused to work. Panic sent her heart racing once again.

Calm down. She needed to calm down.

The Boy disappeared back into the darkness. She took in a deep breath of the noxious air. This time she didn't gag.

Inhale. Exhale.

Deep breaths calmed her heart. Terror retreated into the recesses of her mind. As rational thought returned, confusion washed over her. What would be the point of raping her? Having brought her into this abyss, her captor must know she can't feel anything below the

11

shoulders. She recognized the emotional violation she would feel, the mental trauma. But physically, the actual act would be one she could not feel. The muscle memory of violation, that visceral feeling of physical intrusion, was simply beyond her body's ability to process. If it was a show of dominance he was after… She lived in a state of physical powerlessness to begin with. Standing over her with clenched fists would be far more effective.

Sonja could hear the Boy's footfalls again. He had resumed his sharking circle. She winced at each footstep as though they were seconds on a clock ticking down to her demise.

The monitor's monochromatic night-vision green prevented Sonja's eyes from adjusting to the darkness of the room. The effect was the same as a blindfold. She could hear him, but she could not see him. A chill gripped her. She broke out in a cold sweat. The fear refused to keep at bay.

Inhale. Exhale.

"You don't—" Her voice broke. She took a deep breath, summoning all the courage and defiance she had cultivated over her lifetime. "You don't have to do this," she said, her words calm and commanding.

"Yeah," his soft voice answered from the darkness, "I do have to do this. How can I be whole if I don't?"

Sonja opened her mouth to speak. No words would come. His response had puzzled her into silence.

A loud clack ricocheted through the room, followed by the buzz of electricity. Pain seared Sonja's eyes as a single bank of fluorescent shop lights sprang to life. She blinked furiously as tears of pain blurred her vision. Blood pounded in her ears, a vise of pressure that interrupted her mind. She vigorously shook her head, eyes squeezed tight, attempting to shake out the pain and relieve the pressure.

Inhale. Exhale.

As the headache subsided, Sonja's vision cleared. A lump formed in her throat. Terror returned to her.

Her prison was a mid-sized concrete room. Water stains dripped Jackson Pollock lines across mottled walls. An unidentifiable, shiny black substance obscured the joints where floor and wall met. Covering the ceiling, aluminum, PVC, and copper pipes led to a partially open, heavy-looking green door at the far end of the room. The concrete floor was a galaxy of multi-colored stains, rancid puddles, and what appeared to be dark mold.

Sonja saw that she was on a small, raised wooden platform. An armature holding the computer monitors was bolted to the custom piece of flooring, as was the S&M crucifix that held her upright. Power cables for the monitor setup snaked their way through the floor-level universe of filth into the world beyond the green door. She sucked in a sharp breath as she looked at the monitors. Her heart froze. The digital mirror had switched to full color and the true condition of her body was now on display for her to see.

Inhale. Exhale.

Darkening, hand-shaped bruises encircled both her forearms. Her distended abdomen, atrophied lower legs, and knees held angry-looking, red scrapes. A black substance was smeared around the wounds and across her stomach. She had been dragged, face down, through that putrid floor. For the first time she felt hot. Anger boiled through her at the indignity. How dare this cretin treat her like an oversized bag of garbage. Something shiny caught her attention. A sight that robbed her of anger.

Sonja's chest tightened, her breathing strangled by fear. Situated on its side to the right of the door, her specialized wheelchair bore evidence of an encounter with a sledgehammer. The wheels were now an M.C. Escher sculpture. Wires and broken pieces of circuit board dangled from the black plastic encasement on the back of the chair. She stifled a sob, blinking furiously to keep tears at bay.

Inhale. Exhale.

Finding her voice, Sonja said, "You're a good-looking boy." Her sincerity was genuine. Were the situation different, she probably would have found the Boy desirable.

Sonja could now see the Boy's hair was a dirty blond. His pale skin indicated he avoided sunlight. He stood a modest five feet, nine inches, wore a dark blue three button polo shirt, khaki dress pants, and scuffed black loafers.

"I'm sure you wouldn't have a problem finding a girl to be with you," she said, studying the Boy's face, trying to divine the magic words

13

that would transport her from this dark world of filth back to the land of light and people.

His emerald-green eyes widened, eyebrows raised to their limit. The pleasant, welcoming smile contorted into an expression of disgusted horror. Sonja could see a hint of emerging anger.

"What kind of monster do you take me for?" His insulted, indignant tone indicated this was not a question he wanted answered. "I am not a rapist," he sneered. "That's disgusting!"

Sonja recognized the burgeoning rage that was replacing the Boy's initial good cheer. She had seen it before.

Inhale. Exhale.

Her heart raced. Sonja knew violence would come if her words failed. "I'm sorry if I offended you," her tone infused with as much syrupy submission as she could stomach. She coyly tilted her head. "I am naked."

"Oh, that." The Boy's building anger instantly evaporated. "Well, that's how it's supposed to be when you prostrate yourself before a God, right?" He flung his arms out, putting his grandiosity on display. The warm, inviting smile returned. "Everything is supposed to be laid bare."

Inhale. Exhale.

Sonja felt lightheaded again. Nausea returned to her with the realization that the charming and handsome young man before her was batshit crazy in a Charles Manson meets Ted Bundy fashion.

"A God?" She choked out the question.

"Of course! You know this already," he stated factually, his cadence that of a carnival barker. "You are one of the Goddesses." An unmistakable sense of pride permeated his words. "We are the Gods of old reborn!"

Inhale. Exhale.

Sonja's face flushed, her eyes flashed anger and hate. Rational thought would have told her to play along. Rational thought would have told her ingratiating herself was the best course for survival. Rational thought had left the building.

Her whispering voice trembled with anger. "What kind of Goddess is confined to a wheelchair?" Hate filled her voice, her volume increasing with each syllable. "What kind of Goddess can't move HER

OWN FUCKING BODY?" Her words ricocheted off the walls of the small room. The Boy winced at the sonic assault.

"Jeeze, keep your voice down," the Boy stated as he furiously vibrated a finger in his ear to cull the aural pain. Ignoring her emotional state, he paced in short strides. "You are incomplete, like me." He momentarily stopped pacing to give an infomercial point of his finger toward Sonja. "But also like me, you have a gift."

Inhale. Exhale.

Goosebumps raised on Sonja's forearms, the hair on the back of her neck stood in warning. She did know what the Boy was talking about. Every fiber of her being said he could not know that truth. She looked at the Boy with scathing incredulity.

"I have no gift," she angrily blurted out. "I'm just a fucking cripple."

"Don't," he said. "Don't you ever say that about yourself again." He seemed insulted on her behalf. As he walked toward her, his body language was one of genuine concern.

Sonja was perplexed by his reaction. She was adept at reading people, a skill developed from a lifetime of disadvantage requiring her to determine friend from foe. This paradoxical nutball was an enigma. One moment he bore the hallmarks of a dyed-in-the-wool sociopath, the next he displayed empathic awareness a sociopath could only dream of mimicking.

"You are an Oracle." The Boy's eyes sparkled at the declaration; he gingerly brushed an errant lock of dark brown hair from Sonja's face.

Jerking her head away from his touch, Sonja closed her eyes. She winced as pressure gripped her head. Her heart pulsed in her ears; its pace had quickened upon hearing the word "Oracle." Fragments of memory came flooding back to her. Disjointed shards of forgotten time attempted to reassemble themselves. Their revelation sucked the air out of her. She worked her jaw, her teeth grinding as she tried to slow her heart once again.

Inhale. Exhale.

The memories came to Sonja in still images. Her grandmother lay motionless in the foyer of the psychic shop she had run for fifty years. Wet crimson blood seeped into the Turkish rug that greeted customers. A dark figure stood over the old soothsayer's shattered body. A

15

cheerful, "I've been looking for you," and the prick of a needle before everything went black.

Hot tears of anguish fell over Sonja's cheeks. Inhales caught in stuttering sobs. The Boy's inviting smile churned loathing within her. Grief mutated. Rage and hatred drove all remnants of reason from her mind. Her grandmother was the only family she had. She was raised by the wise woman when Sonja's parents abandoned her. Now she was alone. The only person who had shown her true love, the only person who truly cared for her, was gone. For Sonja, this was a death sentence. White hot rage brought her thoughts into sharp focus. She cast her survival instincts aside. She didn't need them anymore.

"You killed her, you sick fuck." The calmness in Sonja's voice surprised her. "You took away the only person who ever loved me."

"Who was that?" the Boy asked. Rubbing his temple, he appeared genuinely confused. He leaned in, nose to nose, as sympathy washed over his face. "I'm afraid I don't know who you're talking about."

"YOU KILLED MY NANA, YOU BASTARD!" Sonja screamed as she lunged her head forward, her teeth catching the tip of his nose. He reeled back, pain evident on his face as he held his ear. A flash of murder reflected in the Boy's eyes. Recovering his composure, the comforting smile now appeared tight, forced.

A miniscule bead of blood oozed from a scratch on the tip of his nose. Touching the injury, the Boy looked at a blood smear on his finger. He let out a little chuckle. "Neat," he said with measured control. An icy chill ran through Sonja as he wiped the blood on her nipple and chuckled again. "You can't feel that, can you?" She couldn't, but the digital mirror allowed her to see every second of the violation.

Inhale. Exhale.

Standing at the edge of the wooden platform, the Boy snapped his fingers. "Ah," he clipped, "now I remember. That old gypsy bitch." Sonja felt her face flush, the comment served to stoke her anger. "She was a fraud." He nodded his head as if the gesture confirmed the veracity of his words. "She didn't care about you, the old twat just wanted to use you for your gift."

Sonja's jaw clenched. Tears of anguish and tears of rage mingled on her cheeks. Staccato convulsions jolted her with each breath. Silent sobs she could not contain.

"And she was just a human anyway." The Boy turned toward her, flashing his smile of lethal charm. "Gods and Goddesses shouldn't be so attached to such worthless creatures." His brow scrunched as he stared at Sonja, an expression of worry overtaking his features. "What's wrong? There's no need to cry. This will all be over soon."

"She was—" A sob strangled Sonja's words. "You didn't know her. She was every—"

"Holy fuck, are you still going on about that? You need to move on. Accept what you are."

"And what am I?" she growled.

"You are a seer," he said. "The tales of your accuracy abound on the Goddess Message Board."

She felt a lump in her throat. The message board.

Three years ago, she had been invited to join an online community accessible only on the dark web. It was an internet forum for disabled women possessed of varying gifts, all branded with the same birthmark. Sonja had made friends through the site, shared stories of her gift. The message board was invite-only. There was no way this man was on the invite list. That meant…

Inhale. Exhale.

A fatalistic calm overtook her. The smiling wretch before her had ripped all she held dear from her. He would get no more.

"I'm not who you think I am. I cannot help you. I have no gift." Her voice was measured, emotions under strict control. "I'm just a disabled woman whose family you kill—"

"Don't be like that. You're simply incomplete." His voice was calm and reassuring. Flashing his charismatic smile he said, "You and I are the same."

Sonja's arms shook uncontrollably, adrenaline-fueled anger coursed through her. The sheer notion of them having the slightest bit in common broke her calm. She gritted her teeth.

Inhale. Exhale.

"I am nothing like you," Sonja stated. A sardonic smile crossed the Boy's face, and he nodded as if considering her words.

"Ah, but you are," he said. She flinched as he reached out, caressed her face. "And I need you to tell me the name and location of the one who can make me whole. I need you to guide me to the one who can make me perfect."

"How am I supposed to know that?" she asked.

Cracks formed in the Boy's gentle expression. Convulsive sneers interrupted the smile he tried to maintain. "Tell me what I want to know," he demanded.

"How am I supposed to know that?" Sonja repeated.

Starbursts of light flashed in Sonja's eyes as the Boy wrenched her head back, a bushel of her hair gripped in his hand. She winced, feeling her scalp being pulled to its limit. Her head pounded to the rapid beat of her heart. The Boy dropped all pretense of congeniality, his smile disappearing into a bestial sneer.

"Tell me!" he snapped, his face distorted by barely controlled rage. "Tell me where she is!"

"I— I don't understand." Sonja couldn't keep the fear out of her voice.

She let out a pained cry as the Boy tightened his grip, ripping a significant portion of hair from her scalp. He yanked her left ear forward, revealing a perfect infinity symbol behind it. Most people mistook the dark brown birthmark for a tattoo, its form an exercise in perfection. Sonja had always felt it was a lucky mark, one that made her special.

The Boy sneered at the infinity symbol, disgust written on his face. He violently pushed her head, releasing his grip. He paced for a moment. His arms gestured wildly as if he were having an animated discussion with someone who wasn't there. Sonja took a panicked breath when he barreled toward her, stopping just short of collision.

His breathing was ragged, spit flew from his mouth as he spoke. "You don't understand? YOU DON'T FUCKING UNDERSTAND?" He grabbed his left ear, yanking it forward, and shoved his head toward Sonja. "TAKE A LOOK, YOU STUPID BITCH! TAKE A LOOK AT MY DEFORMITY!"

His birthmark stared at her. Unlike the perfection of Sonja's biological brand, his infinity symbol was misshapen. Its diffuse edges were ill defined, its color a haphazard collection of blotchy reds and browns.

Anxiety churned within Sonja. Every hair on the back of her neck stood up once again.

Inhale. Exhale.

The Boy stared intently, his eyes seeking signs of revelation. Sonja cocked an eyebrow. Illumination had come to her, but it was not what the Boy sought. She accepted this was her end. Resignation washed through her. There was no getting back to the world of people and light. For all his talk of her being some sort of Goddess, in his eyes she was nothing more than a talking corpse. The only thing she could do was ensure he did not get what he wanted. If her death was to be drawn out, she would draw out his desperation before her end.

"That's it?" Her voice was flat. A Mona Lisa smile formed on her lips. "You brought me here to find someone to fix your ugly tattoo?"

Her teeth slammed together, pain radiated through her jaw. She tasted copper. Mingled with the blood in her mouth, Sonja felt a small, hard object. Moving her tongue across her teeth, she found its source. The object was a piece of an incisor. She hadn't seen the Boy's hand move, hadn't felt the strike. In the background of compiled pain, she could feel the sting on her lips from the point of impact. Bloody spit oozed from the corner of her mouth, snaking its way down her chin.

Inhale. Exhale.

She locked eyes with the Boy, a wide grin overtaking her face, daring him to end this. His twisted expression turned to disgust at her blood-streaked teeth. This wasn't how it was supposed to be. She was supposed to be crying. She was supposed to be screaming. She was supposed to be begging for her life.

She was supposed to be giving him everything he wanted.

His face was flush, a rage-induced red. Sonja could see his hands shaking under the strain of self-control. An itch flared up behind her left ear, the sensation like that of an insect crawling the figure eight path of her birthmark. A shudder ran through her. She knew what this itch was.

No.

Not now.

Not for him.

A foreboding sense of doom tore through Sonja as her birthmark, her birthright, asserted itself.

Inhale. Exhale.

Legs jerking, Sonja winced as she felt the ankle restraints bite into her. Rivulets of sweat sent tingling chills through her. She felt her stomach muscles clench, her thighs tighten, her toes curl and flex. Her mind was momentarily overwhelmed by the sensory input of every nerve within her waking up at once. The existential dream that was her body came to life. The surreal experience that was her body now entirely under her control.

Staring into her eyes, the Boy found confirmation of what he desperately sought. Adrenaline coursed through him. His rage turned to excitement as he watched Sonja's pupils dilate, devour her blue-grey irises, then snap into vertical slits. He thought her eyes were like those of a cat. A deranged, toothy grin overtook him.

Clamping her eyes shut, Sonja's brow furrowed as a series of images assaulted her mind.

Dismembered body parts lay in a shallow grave.

Luminous blue eyes, hardened and ready for violence.

Men in black, guns blazing.

A woman with dark blonde hair, half of her neck torn away, eyes glazed and lifeless.

Insectile creatures, glistening mockeries of nature.

A featureless black silhouette standing upon a hill of rotting corpses.

Green, cat-like eyes framed in heavy eyeliner, sadness and determination held within them.

Her name.

Sonja's body shook in convulsive waves, explosive sobs escaping her lips. She did not cry for herself. She cried for those yet to meet their end. For the pain and anguish yet to come. She tried to calm herself.

Inhale. Exhale.

The Boy slowly backed away from the bound, crying woman. Apprehension filled him. This was a new emotion. He did not understand. Why was she crying? What did his future hold that would cause her to weep so freely for him? This was wrong. This wasn't progressing like the others. This wasn't...

Sonja opened her eyes. She could feel that something about her vision had changed, she just couldn't place it. The room appeared the same, her effigy in computer monitors hadn't changed. She looked to the Boy and saw it. She retched, choking on a scream.

A flickering light in the shape of the Boy stood. Twenty-nine black voids were riddled throughout the dim light, slowly growing like cancerous tumors. She instinctively knew what this was. She was looking at the Boy's soul.

"It's dying." She had not intended to speak the words, but they refused to remain an unspoken thought. Compassion flashed through her. She could not shake the feeling that the world was going to lose something precious, something that could never be replaced. She blinked furiously, trying to stave off welling tears.

"Who's dying?" The Boy's confusion was evident. Sonja's sight had returned to normal, seeing the insane young man's pale countenance.

"You are."

"No I'm—" The Boy stopped himself. His sense of apprehension evaporated. His face felt hot as frustration and anger gripped him. Turning from her, the Boy threw up his hands. He took a few steps onto the grime-covered floor. "Fuck this shit," he declared through gritted teeth.

Inhale. Exhale.

Sonja's altered state had muted her fear. Her heart did not spike when the Boy turned toward her. The violence in his eyes did not phase her. She was going to die here. She accepted that. Something in her welcomed death. Something told her that death was not the end. Something seemed to be pressing into her mind, trying to get her attention.

"Give me what I want," he growled. "Tell me the name of the one who can make me whole."

"No."

Sonja's calm demeanor, the confidence in that single word, unnerved him. None of the others had stood up to him, the threat of assault enough to ensure compliance. Now this woman, this bitch, would deny him his perfection. She would deny him his rightful godhood. He could feel his control slipping, the red trying to invade his vision. Rage wanted its turn.

Not yet. The rage would have to wait until he had what he wanted.

The slit-pupils of Sonja's eyes taunted him, withholding the knowledge he so desperately sought. Defiantly, she cocked her head to the side and smiled. She was done with this game. She was ready to go.

Inhale. Exhale.

"Fuck. You," she stated as her smile widened.

The Boy's eyes went wide. Unintelligible snarls escaped his face of malice.

"Have it your way, bitch." He extended his arm toward her and gave a flick of his wrist.

She heard the cracking of bone, the subtle, wet sound of slicing flesh, and the following pouring of liquid. Her thigh swung down as though her leg had been freed from its binding. Her eyes widened. Sonja realized what the digital mirror was for.

On the bottom left monitor she could see her lower leg, dangling off-axis and still bound at the ankle. Sparkling crimson blood poured over the detached appendage. The cut was clean, sliced straight through the kneecap. She hadn't felt the assault; there was no impact. Instant shock.

Cold sweat broke out over her body, and she clenched her teeth as searing pain began to register. Every single nerve ending in her leg screamed. Her heart pounded, lungs tightened. With a strangled wheeze she gasped for air. The fear her change had so deftly suppressed flooded back into her. Through the pain she tried to regain her composure.

Inhale.

She had dared him to kill her. He wasn't going to make it quick or painless. There were still nine monitors with uninjured body parts to be mutilated.

"Shall I relieve you of your other leg?" The Boy chuckled.

Exhale.

Sonja grunted through clenched teeth. Pain wracked her as exposed nerves caught every movement of her untethered thigh, the air like sandpaper on the wound.

"Or are you going to give me what I want?"

She winced as her body convulsed; electric agony pierced her, robbed of her breath.

Inhale.

Dizziness overtook her. Thoughts were muddled, moving at odd angles. She couldn't escape the feeling that she was not alone in her own mind. Sonja's head felt heavy. She put her chin to her chest, lolled her head side to side, trying to clear her mind.

Losing blood. She was losing blood too quickly. A lopsided smirk crossed her face as she realized her death would likely come before the Boy could inflict much more damage. In his haste, the killer had managed to nick her femoral artery. Fatigue set in, the desire to sleep clawed at her. Confusion washed through Sonja, she momentarily wondered where she was. She hissed as another wave of pain tore through her.

"HEY!" the Boy shouted. "ARE YOU LISTENING TO ME?"

His voice sounded distant.

Exhale.

"Keep your voice down," she said. "I'm trying to sleep."

The Boy's eyes widened as he realized what was happening. His heart spiked as he moved to his bound victim. He lifted her head, firmly patted her cheek.

"No," he said. "No, no, no, no, no."

Inhale.

She tried to pull away from him, face scrunched in defiance. Her words slurred, "Hey, stop that." She shook her head, eyes closed. "Turn off the light."

The Boy gripped her chin. "Tell me!" His anger had turned to desperation. He was close. So close. "What is her name?"

Exhale.

Sonja lazily opened one eye; the vertical pupil stared at him, death-intoxicated amusement shone through. Her lips curled into a lopsided smile. A silent chuckle shook her.

"No."

Her chin struck her chest as the Boy released his grip. Her brow furrowed on impact. "Ow."

Inhale.

23

Frustrated anger overtook him. He resumed his agitated pacing. He had acted too hastily, did too much damage in his anger. He was going to lose his best chance at finding the one who could make him perfect. Make him whole. Make him a god.

This wasn't fair.

Pounding tore through Sonja's mind, as if the police were at the door trying to get her to open up. She groaned. "Ugh," she uttered, her words almost unintelligible. "Come in already."

Her words stopped the Boy in his tracks. He looked at her in bewilderment. Who was she talking to?

Exhale.

He stared expectantly at her motionless body. The blood river from her amputated leg stopped as if the wound had been cauterized. An uneasy stillness hung in the wet, putrid air.

The Boy's eyes narrowed. He had questioned nine other Goddesses. They always broke. They always gave him what he wanted. First in information, and then in screams. But this one was different. Why? Had she foreseen this with her gift? Did the knowledge of her end provide some preternatural strength? Was she a masochist with suicidal tendencies? The questions unnerved him, and that made him angry. He was a god in waiting, a being of near perfection. Unease, self-doubt, would not do.

Her body jerked; her arms pulled at their restraints. Her bound leg tried working its way up. Her free, amputated thigh kicked forward. Sonja's head wrenched violently. The Boy jumped back.

The crucifix rattled under the barrage of movement. Hard clacking echoed around the small room, the wood of the giant X groaned under pressure. Then it stopped. Sonja was still.

The Boy took in an expectant breath as the bound woman rolled her head side to side as though she were working a kink out of her neck. Her hands flexed; fingers worked individually from clenched fists to open palms. The toes on her remaining foot curled and spread.

Confusion written across his face, the Boy opened his mouth to speak. The voice that cut him off shocked him into silence.

"Release me." A chorus of voices emanated from Sonja's mouth. The voice sent a tremor down the Boy's spine. She lifted her head, her eyes clenched tight. "You will release me."

Gathering his confidence, he reminded himself that strange things always happened in the presence of the Goddesses when their gifts rose to the surface. This was no different, it was simply stranger than the other nine.

"No." The Boy gave a sadistic smile.

"Then you will get nothing."

"Look, bitch." His smile faltered as anger bubbled to the surface. "I'm in control here." His pale skin flushed. His reddened, contorted face was that of an enraged demon. "This is my show, you got that? You do what I say!" He felt his self-control slipping with each word. The rage beckoned him to set it free. It wanted its turn to play, and there was so much damage to be done. He held fast to his control.

Sonja smirked as the chorus spoke. "The price for the knowledge you seek is releasing me."

"No."

"Then I shall do it myself," the chorus declared, "and you shall receive nothing."

Sonja snapped her eyelids open to reveal black chasms where her eyes had been. Empty sockets stared at the Boy. Light caught on the deep red of the exposed muscles that had granted control over her eyeballs and held them in place. Glinting crimson reflections highlighted minute movements of her exposed anatomy. He recoiled in disgust, stumbled over some of the computer cables as he stepped back.

This wasn't just new. This wasn't just different. This was wrong.

"What's the matter?" Sonja's chorus asked. "Do you not like my perfection?" A teasing smile crossed her eyeless face. "Is this not what you seek?"

The Boy retched at the sight of her limp eyelids stretching and flopping as she spoke. In his quest for perfection, he had found perfect imperfection.

"I will give you one last chance. Release me."

"No," the Boy vomited out. A lump caught in his throat, his Adam's apple bobbed up and down. His confidence, his anger, his rage, all

25

replaced by something he had never felt in the presence of any Goddess. For the first time he felt fear.

"Then you shall not receive the answers you seek."

Sonja gave a lopsided smirk as a high-pitched whine filled the room. Starting softly, the sound quickly ramped up, a banshee shriek that forced the Boy to cover his ears. He watched, transfixed as the very air around his bound captive vibrated with the appearance of heat distortion. The rattling of wood, the sound of cracking boards, blasted through the small space. He squeezed his eyes tight and dropped into a crouch as the screaming tone reached a crescendo.

The Boy gritted his teeth, rocked by a concussive shockwave as the giant crucifix exploded. Showered in splinters and a few chunks of wood, the smell of sawdust filled his nostrils. Standing, he looked toward his captive. Cold sweat formed on his brow. His heart pounded a warning in his chest.

Sonja stood amid the ruins of his restraint system, some unseen force having replaced her amputated leg. She began walking toward him, her stride slow and measured, her atrophied legs moving with the efficiency of a runner.

Hurriedly backing up, the Boy lost his footing. He let out a pained grunt as his tailbone made hard contact with the concrete floor. He awkwardly scrambled backward, unable to take his eyes off the nude, eyeless woman approaching him. Back pressed against a wall, he felt like a caged animal. The only difference was that the thing walking toward him had sucked out his will to fight.

"STAY BACK!" Terror permeated his words. "DON'T COME NEAR ME!"

Sonja's eyeless, beatific smile widened as she slowly closed the gap between them. She raised her arm, reaching toward the Boy. Instinctively he flailed a defending arm, flicking his wrist. Her hand dropped to the floor, a clean slice through her wrist. The chorus emanating from her mouth chuckled.

"That tickles," the cacophony of voices playfully stated as she continued uninterrupted toward the Boy. His arms flailed in a desperate attempt to stop her from reaching him, his mind too mired in the chaos of fear to aim.

Sonja's right arm split into three pieces. The remainder of her left leg dropped to the floor with a fleshy thud. Her right foot stayed planted to the ground as she took a step toward the Boy. No blood spewed from her injuries, and the loss of her extremities did nothing to slow her advance.

Her flesh appeared as little more than a meat covering for some unseen body that refused to be damaged. As she reached the Boy's scrambling, kicking feet, a final flick of his wrist heralded the removal of her head. Sonja's eyeless countenance unceremoniously dropped to the floor at his right side, swayed for a moment, and came to rest, the gaping voids of her eye sockets staring directly at him. Her body crumpled into what he would have called a kneeling position had both her legs been intact. The headless remnant was still.

Ragged breathing echoed in the room as the Boy tried to catch his breath. His heart raced. The sound of rushing blood filled his ears. He had a headache. His hands shook as the fear-driven adrenaline surge began to wear off. Leaning back into the wall, the lunatic killer began laughing uncontrollably.

"The head," he breathlessly said. "That's how it always works in zombie movies. Take the head and the body dies. I forgot that rule."

"This isn't a movie," the chorus of voices stated.

The Boy stiffened as another spike of adrenaline hit him. His heart pounded in his ears. His chest felt tight. His whole body was shaking. Slowly he turned to look toward the voice. Sonja's decapitated head wobbled slightly. She was grinning. The black, eyeless voids bore into him. The skin around her empty eye sockets sagged, gravity pulling the loose flesh toward the ground. Disgusted fear was written all over his face.

This wasn't a Goddess. This was a devil.

He jerked as Sonja's head flexed its jaw, opened and closed its mouth. She smiled wide at him, her teeth streaked with bright red blood. He recoiled from the sight, shuffling to the left.

A hard impact bounced the Boy's head off the concrete wall. He felt a hand gripping his throat, pinning him to the grimy bulwark. His vision tunneled. All he could focus on was the handless arm stretched before him, the ghost of her missing appendage clamped around his neck. He

27

was dimly aware of her body—its blurred form leaning toward him, its weight poured into the arm that trapped him. Out of focus, his mind registered the points of her dismemberment. Red, striated circles of muscle dotted with the off-white of bone and dark brown of the marrow. Acid burned the back of his throat as he retched; the taste of acrid bile lit a fire in his nose as he exhaled. He squeezed his eyes shut.

This wasn't happening. This couldn't be happening.

The remnants of Sonja became statuesque, unmoving and unyielding. Time warped for the Boy. His tailbone ached. He could feel a lump forming on the back of his head where it had struck the hard wall. In the stillness, his breathing slowed, his heart rate calmed. But the anxiety, the fear, remained. His eyes darted around the room, desperately looking for something, anything, with which he could pry himself loose from Sonja's unnatural grip. Nothing was within reach. He twitched, body moving slightly to the left. In response he felt the unseen hand tighten its grip on his throat.

Stillness.

What was she waiting for?

His breathing calmed as the minutes ticked by. Fear was replaced by incessant questions, his mind reeled with possibilities. Would his quest end here? Would she slowly pull his arms and legs off? Would she let him go and leave him back at square one? The Boy felt the entire situation was patently unfair. That someone would do him such a disservice was unconscionable. Her disrespect stoked the dim fire of anger still smoldering within him. He closed his eyes, worked his jaw.

He looked at the motionless head on the floor beside him. His earlier disgust morphed into hate. He was done sitting quietly.

"Tell me, bitch," he hissed, "tell me what I want to know. Tell me what I need to know."

He twitched as Sonja's decapitated head playfully smirked.

"SPEAK!"

A sense of dread crowded out his anger as the chorus of voices spoke.

"In the city that stands as one, in the towers guarded by the woman of green copper, Raven makes her nest," the voices stated dispassionately. "She hunts for the one who has harmed her charge. She is coming for you."

The corner of the Boy's mouth lifted in a smile. A flush of hope overwhelmed him.

"Who is she?" Eagerness filled his voice. "Who is the Raven?"

"She is the Key, the Crossroads," the voices answered. "The one who binds the damaged, the suffering, the lost. She is the one who makes them whole."

His body buzzed with excitement. He had spent so long searching for the one that would elevate him to his rightful godhood, to make him the perfect being he was meant to be. Now he had a definitive clue to her identity. The internet message board for the Goddesses stated that she would find them, that she knew where they were and knew their suffering. And there were those whom she had anointed, those who had become whole. They urged all to have patience. But he had realized she wasn't coming for him. Just to join the message board he'd had to pose as one of the Goddesses. The Raven had no interest in helping Gods, so he had to resort to finding this "Key" and forcing her to help him.

He felt the grip around his throat release, and the remnant of Sonja's body leaned back. Rubbing his neck, he said, "I thought you said you wouldn't give me what I wanted." A taunt was hidden in his tone as the Boy's warm, inviting smile returned.

"We gave you nothing you wanted," the chorus stated. A wave of anxiety coursed through the Boy as he registered the change in pronoun. "She will not give you what you seek. She will bring you misery and pain for what you have done."

"I'm sure she and I can come to an understanding just as you and I have."

The detached head smirked knowingly. "She is coming for you, and with the death of Sonja Verztuk she knows where you are."

Confusion crossed the Boy's face. "Your death?" He thought for a moment. "So, as long as I keep you alive she won't know my exact location, right?"

Disbelief splayed across Sonja's face. "You misunderstand," the chorus of voices said. "Sonja Verztuk died on the cross." The eyeless head chuckled. "She found you at the moment of death."

29

He felt like an idiot. Sonja's body in pieces, her head lying next to him on the floor, and it never occurred to him that she had died. Fear teased him as the question formed in his mind.

"If you're not the Goddess," his chest tightened, "who are you?"

The head gave a slight chuckle. "Centuries ago we were asked that same question by a so-called Holy Man," the chorus began.

The Boy watched, disgust pressing bile into his throat as Sonja's eyes grew back into their sockets. The dead, blue-grey oculi moved to look at him. Her lifeless face smiled.

"We are Legion. We are many." The chorus giggled.

Sonja's headless, dismembered body toppled backward, a fleshy thud echoing as she hit the concrete floor. With a whisper, the chorus spoke one last time. "Raven is coming for you."

Chapter 1

I looked at the check with a mixture of awe and disbelief. There were more zeros printed on the green slip of paper than I had seen in my entire life. My excitement was tempered by a parade of red flags marching through my mind. Wrenching my vision from the check, I looked across my cluttered desk to the man who had presented the lottery-level amount. He was a man who appeared out of time. His drawn face was rimmed with finely trimmed 19th century-style mutton chops and he wore a three-piece charcoal grey suit, complete with a watch fob resting in the pocket of his waistcoat. He had identified himself as Mr. Strickland. No first name given. Looking pensive, holding a thick file folder, he cleared his throat.

"Mr. Hayes—" he began. I cut him off.

"It's Jonathan," I stated curtly. "Mr. Hayes was my father." I didn't bother to complete the thought that I wanted as little connection to that drunk asshole as possible.

"My apologies. Mr. Jonathan—" he began again. And again I cut him off. Handing me a check of this size with nothing but a company name put my guard on high alert.

"I noticed that the name on this check is the Dunbar Association," I stated, as if telling him something he didn't already know. "The check itself was issued by Deutsche Bank and the authorization signature is printed directly on the check, not handwritten." A thought occurred to me as I spewed these details out, and without thinking the thought passed my lips, "A black-ops slush fund?"

Mr. Strickland raised an eyebrow and smirked. "Very close, and all that with only a simple piece of paper." His accent was just as out of time as his clothing, giving him the air of an aristocratic butler. He stood from the chair and placed his file folder in a small clearing on my desk. "Your reputation appears well deserved."

"I have a reputation?" It was a joke. From the look on Mr. Strickland's face, the joke clearly had not landed. I had been in the private investigation business for over a decade. If I didn't have a reputation, I would be worried.

"The check," Mr. Strickland said as he sat back in his chair, "is from one of my master's shell companies." A battalion-worth of red flags joined the waving cavalcade of suspicion in my mind. "He wishes to keep this assignment away from prying eyes."

"That's great and all," I couldn't help suspicion creep into my voice, "but I'm not going to take a case without knowing who's hiring me. The last time someone tried a third-party hire, it turned out to be a damn drug cartel."

"Of course." Mr. Strickland sounded reluctant. He paused for a moment, appearing to contemplate who he should say his employer was. He sighed, apparently deciding the truth was his best option. "Joseph Handler," he stated. Mr. Strickland's face seemed to grow even more dower than it already was.

Without thinking, I pulled a silver cigarette case from the breast pocket of my black, button-down shirt. The case was etched on one side with a pentagram, the lines of the five-pointed star designed to appear as if they dipped and rose under and over each point of contact, the circle a simple weave of Celtic knotwork. A small button on the side of the case activated a spring-loaded mechanism. Popping open with a quiet *snik*, the inside of the case was lined with cigarette-sized sticks of cinnamon. I quit smoking a few months back; this was my coping mechanism. I placed a piece of the spice in my mouth, holding it between my lips as though it were a cigarette, then closed the case and returned it to my pocket. This garnered no reaction from Mr. Strickland's stoic face.

"Never heard of him."

"I should think not." Mr. Strickland's voice had a slight quiver; I could tell he feared repercussions for saying too much. Another platoon of red flags joined the parade. "Master Handler keeps a very low profile. His wealth would make his family a target for nefarious persons." Mr. Strickland paused, measuring his words.

"If he can cut a check like this," I said, "that's quite understandable."

"Staying out of the light did not afford him complete protection," Mr. Strickland said. "Three months ago, his daughter was murdered."

I glanced down at the folder he had placed on my desk. Mr. Strickland continued, "Her name was Rita Vineland." I looked back to the man out of time. "Her mother's maiden name," he said, answering the unasked query.

"A protective measure, I assume?"

"Yes, but it is unlikely that her murder had anything to do with her parentage."

My eyebrows raised at that. Not so much out of surprise as it was confirmation that the feeling in my gut was potentially correct. Mr. Strickland's tale struck me as similar to the backstories undercover police officers create. Enough truth to be believable, but on the whole a tapestry of bullshit.

"Okay, so what can I do with this case?" Murder investigations weren't my thing. Missing persons? Yes. Missing pets? You got it. Think your house is haunted? I'm all over it. But murder? I'd take my chances with a pissed-off poltergeist over a human killer any day.

"My master would like you to identify the culprit and, if possible, his or her location."

I absent-mindedly stroked my chin. "So treat this like a missing person case," I said to myself, my thought process passing through my lips. "Only I also need to figure out who the missing person is."

I glanced up at the man; his eyes seemed apprehensive, hoping I would take the case. I would have loved to believe that the reputation he mentioned imparted his hope that I would agree to it. I'm just not that full of myself. I'm good at what I do, but people come to me as a last resort.

"The file I gave you is a comprehensive—"

"Why me?" I asked.

Mr. Strickland appeared taken aback by the question.

"Well," he started, fumbling to find the words, "as you have probably surmised, you were not Master Handler's first choice."

I nodded. "Nor his second, third, fourth, or fifth choice, I assume?"

"Quite," he stated. "In fact, we've had six other private investigation firms work this case so far." Mr. Strickland motioned to the folder that lay in front of me. "That is the sum total of six top-notch investigative agencies' progress."

"Well, that's just sad," I blurted out.

"Yes." He dismissed my statement. "As your firm, this Darkstone's Asylum, has a nationwide network—" I cut him off again.

"I think you may have the wrong impression about Darkstone's Asylum," I stated flatly. My office, located in downtown Los Angeles' rundown industrial district, was a single shoddy room. How one could get the impression a "firm" was attached to my operation eluded me.

Mr. Strickland's eyebrows raised. "Then please disabuse me of my ignorance."

"DA operates much like a guild. It was founded to ensure that members would not have to fight tooth and nail to get cases, it provides benefits and members share resources." I could see Mr. Strickland's disappointment at this revelation. "Each member operates independently within their own regions."

"I see," he said. His tone belied a mind furiously working through some unknown machinations.

"As I'm sure you're aware, Darkstone's Asylum members generally take cases no one else will. Those cases most firms deem beneath them or stray too far from the norm." I couldn't help letting my distaste for those big firms slip. "From missing pets to paranormal investigations, the methods we use range from standard investigative techniques to employing psychics, witches, occultists, and the occasional politician."

"This does mean that you have resources all over the country, does it not?"

"Yes, it does. However, you should know that if I must cross DA boundaries, I will have to involve at least one of the investigators of that region. As such, while I can provide assurances of client privilege toward the outside world, client information may have to be disseminated to any adjoined investigators."

"If that is the case, it is acceptable," he said approvingly, "as the most recent murders by this suspect appear to be in Las Vegas."

"Um…" The plural concerned me. "Multiple murders?"

"Yes. As of this moment, we are aware of thirty-five dead by this culprit."

"How do you know they are all the work of the same individual?"

"The modus operandi. You may have seen an article or two in the news. They are calling this killer the Hatchetman for…reasons." Mr.

Strickland paused. "You will find such distasteful details in the documents provided."

I had heard tell of this Hatchetman, but didn't know too much about the case. I avoid mass media like the plague. Not because I am some weird conspiracy theorist who believes the nightly news is run by shape-shifting corgis with a cankle fetish. If that was the case, I'd be glued to the tube all day. I just find every news outlet to be depressing as hell.

"Okay." I had made up my mind. "Let's get the paperwork out of the way."

I thrust my hand purposefully into one of the piles of paper chaos on my desk and pulled out a contract.

"All contracts come with a twenty-four-hour cooling period," I explained. "This means that if you or I decide not to pursue this case within one day, you'll get all your money back and any information you have provided will be shredded."

"That is acceptable."

For the next twenty minutes I went over the contract line by line with the man out of time. Both of us signed on the dotted line and bade our farewells. This business end had always been the one part of my job I hated. I sat for a moment staring at the folder, contemplating whether I should open it now. I decided against, opting to get a second opinion about the case before availing myself of any more information. My wife had a sixth sense about these kinds of things.

I opened the small office closet and pulled my black leather trench coat off a hook on the back of the door. The coat was an inheritance from my mentor, who had made modifications to the garment. Protective sigils had been stamped into the interior of the coat's leather, running around the entire perimeter of the body's edge. Wide leather cuffs had been sewn on; words circled each wrist-cover, stamped into the leather and dyed an electric blue against the black. The words were written in Theban script, sometimes referred to as the Witches' Alphabet. It looked like varying permutations of the letters Y and M. When translated, the right cuff read, "My Eyes Divide the Sky as Sirens Sound in Heaven," and the left cuff read, "My Will Brings Down the Moon and Shatters It to Pieces." They were lines from a song entitled "Divide" by Assemblage 23, one of my favorite bands. My mentor, who also happened to love the song for its message of self-realization and empowerment, chose those words as reminders of how much power is truly in each of our hands when we quit getting in our own way. Donning the coat, I placed a black 1940s-style fedora on my head. Catching my reflection in the long mirror that hung on the door, I paused.

For a moment I took in my own visage, thinking I looked like a goth Sam Spade. In my best Bogart impression, I pointed at my reflection. "Here's looking at you, kid." I chuckled softly, but no real humor passed through me. Staring back at me from the mirror, I saw him. I saw my mentor. I had adopted his look, right down to the rectangle-lens glasses.

The man most people only knew as Darkstone had been gone for five years. Four people knew his real name. Three of them were dead. The Atsuko Takanashi case had claimed their lives. That case had almost claimed his.

The founding members of Darkstone's Asylum had been brought in on a human trafficking case by an LAPD detective. In the end, I was summoned to the hospital where Darkstone lay severely injured. Detectives dissuaded me from seeing the other three due to the condition of their bodies.

As I said my goodbyes to my mentor, promising to come visit the next day, he said, "Monsters are real." It was the last thing he had said to me before disappearing. The next day I found that he had checked himself out of the hospital. His personal items were largely absent from his home, as was his car. Only a note remained. A single haunting sentence: "Don't look for me."

I shook my head to bring me back to the present. I needed some happiness. I needed to smile. I needed my wife.

A testament to the atrocious taste of my landlord, the apartment building my wife and I lived in was a large, turd-brown, two-story rectangle with pale olive-green trim. Twin, barely living palm trees bracketed a short staircase leading below sidewalk level and to the front door of the building. It was an eyesore, especially in the noon sun.

Situated one block north of Hollywood Boulevard, the location was ideal for walking access to restaurants, convenience stores, the Hollywood Police Division of LAPD, prostitutes, and any kind of drugs you could want, legal or illegal. Our apartment was the first unit on the ground floor, the only one-bedroom in a building full of studio flats.

Our unit's layout was simple. One entered into a combination living room/dining room. Large windows occupied two walls; cheap, white vertical slat blinds covered them. A black leather couch sat under one of the windows against the right wall. A circular IKEA dining table was situated at the far end of the room, next to our woefully undersized kitchen. To the immediate left, a short hallway led to the bedroom and bathroom.

We had lived here for two decades and have wanted out for nineteen years and six months. Plumbing problems were constant. The landlord, who was just a hair above being legally declared a slumlord, required numerous orders from the Los Angeles City Housing Department to get anything fixed. If he wasn't ordered to do it under threat, it wouldn't get done. The building's wiring hadn't been updated since the 1970s, and multiple units shared breakers. Power going out due to someone using their microwave was common, and on two occasions the breaker boxes began spewing smoke when the outdated, cloth-wrapped wires started smoldering. On the plus side, it was rent-controlled and had parking.

I entered the apartment with the stealth of a ninja. My wife was seated at the table, her back to me. I slowly, silently took a few steps toward her.

"Welcome home," she said without turning around. Sneaking up on her was impossible.

Clearing the rest of the distance, I slid my hands under her chin and pulled her head up to look at me. Bending over, I planted a long kiss on her soft lips. In that moment, connected to her, I felt the world melt away from me. As our lips separated, I reminded myself that it was not the time to get worked up. I had responsibilities, I had a schedule, I had… I had to let my desire out in a long exhale. I would much rather have spent the rest of the day in bed with the beautiful woman sitting before me. I hate being a responsible adult.

Without a word I reached around her and placed the impossibly large check on the table, then took a seat in the empty chair to her left. She picked up the rectangle and did a double-take. In silence, her mouth opened and closed, words failing her.

Tara's deep blue eyes were wide as saucers, sparkles of withheld tears evident. She was shaking, staring in disbelief at the check I had presented. She gingerly placed the slip of paper down on the dining table, a space that doubled as her office. My wife was the regional manager of Darkstone's Asylum, overseeing the various Southern California regions. Her domain was one of processing benefits, arranging for legal representation, facilitating investigation resources, and much, much more.

"Ho-ly. Shit," she whispered. I smirked at the exclamation. Tara rarely ever cussed, and when she did it was advisable to seek shelter. But not this time.

"So, you think I should take the case?"

Her deep blue portals regarded me with an "Are you stupid?".

"Okay," I said, "We're going to Vegas then."

Tara let out a long sigh and ran her hand through a tuft of shoulder-length dark blonde hair. Turning to her laptop, she began typing furiously.

"What are you doing?" I asked.

"Emailing Mike Turnbal." She looked up to me. "We've been wanting to move to Vegas anyway and I've been training him to take over for me."

I nodded. "Hamish Callaway is retiring soon, which will open a spot for me in the Vegas region."

"I have three applications for your slot here."

"New or transfers?" I asked. Tara completed her email and leaned back in the chair.

"All new investigators. I'd like you to take a look at them, see if we come to the same conclusion."

I nodded. "Sounds good. But now I need to get that check into the bank."

"Let me hold it one more time." Tara picked up the check and stared at it. "So many zeros."

"Well, due to DA bylaws, we're gonna have to say goodbye to twenty-five percent. I'm going to have to pull one of the Vegas investigators, it's their turf."

Tara frowned, sighed in resignation. "So long as it's not Harrison."

"I was thinking Stephanie Gonzalez." Tara looked to me. "She's a solid investigator, we've worked together more times than I can count, has sources in every law enforcement agency and—"

"Is the first person you'd want next to you in a fight," she completed my thought approvingly. I gave her a mischievous smile.

"Yup. Though in a fight I'd probably just stand on the sidelines feeling sorry for the poor bastard on the receiving end of her fists."

Tara gave a soft chuckle. "Go to the bank. I'll make reservations at the Cosmo."

I got up and walked around the table.

"Okay." I bent over and kissed my wife's forehead. "I have to meet with Tim at two o'clock. One of his paranormal investigations apparently needs my particular talents."

Sighing, Tara shook her head. "I had forgotten about that."

"It's okay." I chuckled. "You're my wife, not my secretary."

"I'm also the regional manager—"

"Exactly," I said. "You're not everybody's appointment book."

Tara sighed, and as suddenly as her feeling of responsibility for my schedule had come, it went. Turning her attention back to the computer, she raised a hand in farewell.

"Just hurry back," she said. "I don't want to be arriving in Vegas at three in the morning."

I snorted, smirked, and walked out the door.

Chapter 2

The Boy stood outside Starbucks, absently staring toward the distant mountains west of Las Vegas Boulevard. The swinging of his laptop bag brought awareness back to him as hot, high winds blew his blond hair in a frenzy. He rolled his head, neck muscles stretching with the movement.

Pulling a cell phone from his pants pocket, he scrolled through the contacts and hit the dial button. Five rings and the call went to voicemail. That was normal. She never answered her phone. At the beep, the Boy spoke.

"Hey, Mom, it's me," his voice cheerful and artificially sweet. "I just wanted to check in. My journey is going great, I feel like I've almost found myself." He paused, letting out a sigh. "I should be home soon. Say hi to Dad for me. Love you." He hit the end call button.

Looking back to the western mountains, he unconsciously pursed his lips and pressed them to the side. Momentary calm washed over him; the fast currents of air felt like a massaging caress blowing all his cares away.

The roaring of a black, ridiculously lifted truck starting its engine broke his moment of existential abandonment. Looking to the source of the sound, he sneered at the customized pick-up. Tinted windows gave him no view of its driver. The truck squealed out of the parking lot and onto Las Vegas Boulevard. The Boy caught a glimpse of a bumper sticker as it passed him, something about using swords if guns are outlawed. It made him snicker. Turning from the view, the Boy entered the purveyor of liquid life and made a beeline for the cash register to order his coffee.

Sitting in the back corner of Starbucks, he opened his MacBook Pro. Hitting the laptop computer's "On" button, the Boy turned to his phone. Plugging headphones into the device, he opened an app connecting to the Wi-Fi camera he had set up in his now-compromised kill room. He had hoped to use the location again, but the thing speaking through Sonja's animated corpse made it evident that was not wise. From the camera angle, he could see the platform he had held Sonja on. The remnants of her cross could be seen strewn about. After disposing of her piecemeal corpse, he took the cameras and monitors to a storage unit near Harry Reid Airport. No sense in losing expensive hardware.

He turned his eyes to the computer. Opening a TOR browser, he proceeded to type in a numerical web address, taking him deep into the dark web. A simple white page with a username and password prompt loaded. As she had shown him the site, the young psycho had taken Rita Vineland's username and password for himself. To his knowledge, no one had found her butchered body yet. While not his first kill, she was the first of the Goddesses he had come across. He took a sip of his soy latte as the screen changed. "Welcome SunshineFlower97" flashed briefly on the page before switching to a list of chats.

Each chat had a subject line, most of which were mundane help and motivational chats for various physical ailments. The top subject today caught the Boy's attention. "My Wait is Over! She Came to Me Last Night!" The username, WheelchairWarrior, pulled on something in his memory. He had a long chat conversation with her just one week ago. She was suffering from severe cerebral palsy; or as he knew, a condition that mimicked cerebral palsy. He had considered taking her but found that her gift was telepathy. Useless for his purposes. But it was she that pointed him in Sonja's direction, and he was grateful to her for that. He was so close to being made whole. Being made perfect. The Raven was coming for him, and he was sure he could convince her to give him what he wanted.

He clicked on the subject line and the page switched to a chat screen. A flurry of questions and well wishes filled the chat. He paid them no mind. There was only one question he wanted answered.

"What does the Raven look like?" he typed into the message line. He hit the post button. Nothing happened. His face scrunched. Confusion played over his youthful features. He hit the post button again. His question remained in the type box. Deleting the words, he retyped his question and hit the post button. Again, nothing.

"What the fuck?" he whispered through clenched teeth. His confusion quickly turned to frustrated anger. In a moment of realization, he looked around the coffee shop. Three people stood by the pick-up counter, noses to their cellphones. The green-aproned employees behind the counter were busy filling orders for those in the store and drive-thru. He took a deep breath, calming himself. A wave of obsession was building in him. He had to know. He needed to see her coming. He needed the Raven. He needed to be perfect. He needed to be God. He hit the post button again.

He fought his frustration, grinding his teeth as other questions popped up in the chat. Obviously the site was working for these other people. He tried the button one more time. A small chat box popped up. In the header bar the Boy read that it was an administrator messaging him.

"Who are you?"

"My name is Rita," he replied. "I just want to know what the Raven looks like, so I know her when she comes for me."

"How do you know that name?" The message stuck in his eye like a splinter.

The Boy quickly realized the massive blunder he had made. No one said her name. Those who had been made whole just referred to the Raven as "Her." Those waiting did not say, and likely did not know, her name. It appeared they all simply knew the Raven when they saw her. Would he recognize her? Would she be obvious to him? Or has he already passed her countless times on the street without a clue?

"Shit," he muttered.

His mind reeled for an answer to the question, a thousand different lies, each more outlandish and ridiculous. He opted for simplicity.

"A friend told me."

"Who are you?" the message asked again.

"Rita," he typed. "Rita Vineland."

"Liar. I can see you."

He felt his stomach bottom out. Bubbling acid threatened to reach up and burn his throat as a wave of anxiety overtook him. His eyes came to rest on the integrated camera lens of the laptop. The piece of black electrical tape he used to cover it had peeled up in one corner, partially exposing him to the camera.

His eyes narrowed as he flattened the tape back down. He knew that, at best, the administrator could only see an out-of-focus sliver of his face.

"Rita gave me access to her account since I never received the invite," the Boy replied.

"No. No she didn't."

Something in the message made his blood run cold, his body involuntarily shook as a chill ran down his spine. They were just words on a screen, text from anonymous fingers somewhere in the world. His heart dropped as the next line of text appeared on his screen.

"Rita is dead. You killed her."

He sat back for a moment, contemplating his rebuttal to the accusation. His response formulated, he reached for the keyboard. He was too slow.

"Goodbye now," the message box read. The Boy moved to close out the message box and browser. The computer was frozen. A painful shock blasted his eyes as the screen flashed bright white. A high-pitched crack of an electrical zap pierced his ears and the laptop died.

Leaning back, the Boy let out a measured sigh. An explosive expression of anger would only serve to call attention to himself, not that anyone here knew who he was or what he had done. A small measure of paranoia helped keep his emotions under control when out in public. Grinding his teeth, he looked at his disabled computer, now a very expensive Apple-branded paperweight. Another setback on his road to perfection. Mired in torturous frustration, he became aware of a soft sound emanating through his headphones. The sound of light footfalls. Bolting up, fumbling for the phone, he expected to catch the Raven searching that dingy room. His heart leapt, confronted with an eye covering the screen.

He studied the oculus for a moment. Framed in black eyeliner, hints of tears forming at the rim, the eye's dark green iris was speckled with gold and hints of red. From the pupil he knew he was looking at her. The vertical black line staring into the camera induced a rush of excitement. The Boy couldn't decide if the eye reminded him of the inscrutable glare of a feline or the cold, hungry stare of a reptile. He might not know her face, but now he knew her eyes.

"I found you," he said in a sing-song whisper, a disturbed smile twisting his face. Dark machinations churned through his mind at light speed. He knew how to draw her to him, but how to convince the Queen of the Goddesses to give him what he wanted?

"So…" Her words broke the Boy's train of thought. "You're the one who has been harming my charge." Her voice was cold, a subtext of rage radiating from each syllable.

Staring at the eye on his phone, an icy chill ran down the Boy's spine. His smile faltered. He couldn't shake the feeling she could see him through the Wi-Fi camera. Reason told him that was impossible, but he had seen the power held by the incomplete Goddesses. The power he had at his command. She was the penultimate Goddess. He did not know how far her power extended. A sharp breath in his ears drew his attention.

"I will find you," she hissed, "and when I do, you will suffer, you will scream, you will beg for death."

The Boy heard a loud pop, the cracking of plastic, and the video went black. He switched off the app connecting the phone to the camera, leaned back, and smiled broadly. He would draw her to him like a moth to a flame. He would get what he wanted, then he would kill the queen. He would become perfect. He would become the ultimate God.

Raven surveyed the grime-covered room. With emerald eyes rimmed in black kohl, a claw-like branch pattern extended from the outer corner of her left eye, the delicate lines reaching halfway down her cheek. Black hair, high cut in the back, angled to sharp points at her jawline. Brushing her purple Bettie Page-style bangs aside, she rubbed her forehead.

Standing five feet, six inches, Raven's slight build belied her strength. She had mangled the Wi-Fi camera with the swift closing of her hand, its black plastic case crumpling like tissue paper. The silver and green of its internal circuit board had become a splintered mess in her fist. Opening her hand, she let the remains of the surveillance device fall to the filth-covered ground. Clad in a simple black t-shirt and black tactical cargo pants ensemble, half-calf combat boots completed her look and kept her feet safely isolated from the universe of putrescence that covered the floor. Taking in the room, Raven's gaze settled on the raised wooden platform.

Situated about a foot off the ground, the platform had the perplexing appearance of being hastily put together, and yet signs of professional craftsmanship were evident. A discolored square with four large holes marked the place where something had been removed, consistent with the nine other death chambers Raven had been led to. This time, the X-shaped crucifix was absent, though pieces of it remained. Two shredded stumps remained bolted to the platform. One piece of the splintered wood was discolored with the reddish black of dried blood. Raven took in a deep, troubled breath. Choking down the urge to collapse into a ball and cry, she walked to the edge of the platform, reached out to the bloody stump.

"I'm sorry," she whispered. "I'm sorry I couldn't get to you in time."

The psychic tether that linked her to the women bearing the infinity birthmark, women known as Caretakers, had its limits. She knew all their locations, she knew their names, but their thoughts and experiences were beyond her until she made them whole. In extreme circumstances, an urgency, a sense of danger, could be transmitted through that unseen connection to those Raven had yet to visit. It was how she had found her way to each of this killer's murder chambers, how she was tracking him. And each time she was too late. He was always one step ahead of her.

Sonja had been a part of the group Raven referred to as "the Waiting," those whom she had yet to visit and ask them to make a choice that would determine the path of their lives. Determine their destiny. It was a simple choice: join the ranks of Caretakers or become fully human. One choice would grant them the ability to use the randomly activating abilities they possessed at will. The trade-off was that they would sacrifice everything a human life had to offer. They would live a life driven by the inherent desire to protect others from the brutality that is Nature, the malevolent things hiding in the dark…from the entity known only as the Dark Man. To choose a human life would take away the ailments the Waiting were afflicted with, the world of a so-called "normal" life would be wide open to them. It would also

45

remove the gifts that would randomly manifest, never to be seen again. The change was permanent, the choice was an absolute.

Raven scanned the room, noticing the pattern of wooden shrapnel. She had seen this kind of debris dissemination before, though it was the first time she had seen it in wood. Blast patterns hold a fairly standard appearance. It doesn't matter if one uses dynamite, C-4, ammonium-nitrate, or any other explosive, the pattern at the blast point is the same. And that pattern of shrapnel was present here. She let out a melancholic chuckle.

"You did this, didn't you?" Lifting her head, Raven felt some pride among her sadness. "You didn't give in. So much strength. I wish I could have met you."

Her gaze cast down to the floor, Raven noticed the shoe prints scattered throughout the grime. It was clear from the lack of overlapping prints that the room was visited rarely. Time quickly erased the passage of visitors. The footprints of a single, small bare foot caught her attention. Following the trail, Raven saw the one foot had taken a few steps forward, then abruptly stopped. A portion of the trail had been smudged by shuffle marks. A sad smile crossed Raven's face; she had a good idea of what happened. The dragging trail was short, leading up to a butt print on the floor at the base of the wall. A circular mark, probably a knee, provided a slight cleaning to the world of grime on the floor.

"I hope he learned fear," Raven said to the darkness. "I hope he begged."

Raven turned to walk toward the green steel door. She noticed the remains of Sonja's wheelchair. The violence evident in its condition inspired a swell of rage within her. Turning to the wall, the slim goth slammed her fist into the concrete. A booming crunch exploded from the impact, a spider-web pattern of cracks emanating from the point of contact. Small pieces of cement crumbled to the floor. Raven sneered, grit her teeth, growled, and bit her tongue. Pain to assuage the overwhelming sadness, pain to hold back the torrent welling in her eyes. She could hold back her tears no more.

Cutting rivulets of glinting silver down her pale face, the sadness and rage housed within her would not be exorcized by tears alone.

Drawing in a deep breath, she let out a roaring scream. Her sonic blast hurled the remains of the wheelchair into the wall, the force of the impact decimating what remained of the mobility device and cracking the concrete. Her body shook as Raven felt her rage diminish into anger.

"No more," she promised herself as she turned back toward the exit. "No more of us will die."

Chapter 3

The house looked like it had been assaulted by a roaming gang of house painters with bad taste and a feng shui excuse. Two stories of garish red, the home was a square block with forest green faux-storm shutters bracketing two large living room windows. A long driveway on the left side of the house led to a detached garage situated on the back of the property. On the right, a concrete path cut through a verdant lawn, stretching about twenty feet from the sidewalk to the front door. The neighborhood, sandwiched between Sunset Boulevard and Hollywood Boulevard, appeared to have cropped up in the 1950s or 1960s, and likely had been occupied by affluent people at the time. No two houses were alike. A two-story, sky blue ranch-style home sat to the right of my target. A brick, stucco, and timber English manor-style home to the left. The residential block had a few English cottage-inspired homes and one that looked to be the work of Frank Lloyd Wright Jr.

Pulling to the curb, I saw Tim Darby standing on the long walkway speaking with a man I knew to be his client. As I parked, a clunky 1985 Honda Civic pulled up behind me. Looking in my rearview mirror I could see the massive black, Aqua Net-drenched hair of Moira Harris behind the wheel. Exiting our cars in unison, Moira gave a huge smile. Despite a tiny stature that barely broke five feet without her hair, everything about the woman was big. Big hair, big smile, big sunglasses, big nose, and a personality that couldn't fit into a warehouse.

"There's my boy!"

I snickered. She always greeted me like this. With enough makeup to plaster a wall, the sixty-five-year-old had been both a friend and an amazing resource for the past four years. A veteran of the CIA's "Stargate" program, the U.S. government's psychic research and defense project, Moira was possibly the best empath and medium I had ever encountered. She aced every test of Darkstone's Asylum's psychic vetting process, and I had worked with her numerous times on cases that went down the paranormal rabbit hole.

"Good to see you," I said, making my way over to her.

She looked at me sideways. "Still have those walls up, I see."

Anytime I vetted someone claiming to be an empath, my first request was that they read me. If they gave any answer other than, "I can't," they were a fake. I have spent a lifetime building up defenses against unseen threats; the result is that every proven psychic I know is blocked from reading me. It makes for a good baseline of honesty.

"Why take down what works?" I asked rhetorically. She laughed as I opened the trunk of my car.

Taking off my coat, I reached into the trunk and pulled out a shoulder harness. Most PIs would have gun holsters attached to a rig like this. I had two knife sheaths. With the gun laws in California, unless a private investigator is ex-law enforcement or military, discharging a firearm comes with more paperwork and possible jail time than it's worth. Opening a large metal carrying case, the knives to be holstered sat before me. Another item I had inherited from my mentor. As the knives had blunt edges and were clearly ceremonial in nature, I had petitioned the government for the right to carry them. It took a while, but I managed to force the issue on grounds of religious freedom. Besides, they were about as dangerous as a large serving fork. Sure, the tip could stab someone, but a spoon would be better suited to slashing a person.

Each knife was identical. Single-edge eight-inch blades that were etched with Celtic knotwork. At the hilt, extending approximately two and a half inches, an ovoid recess in the blade held a single large sapphire. A portion of the recess exposed what looked like gold wires extending from the stone into the blade's interior. Oddly technological looking. Circumnavigating the flattened blade edges was a gold wire that entered the brass hilt on the top and bottom. Carvings on the blackwood handles mirrored the Celtic knotwork of the blades. Finger grooves had small, smooth metal studs slightly poking out of them. Something about holding the knives with those little bumps in the handle was more comfortable to me than a normal knife. I sheathed both my sidearms, grabbed a black leather shoulder bag, and closed the trunk.

Looking toward Tim, his conversation did not seem to be going well. Tim Darby was the founder and lead paranormal investigator of the San Angeles Paranormal Investigators Coalition. They were a non-profit group who both sought out evidence of the paranormal as well as tried to debunk it. I had associated myself with them after going through the three-hundred investigation videos they posted online. In only three percent of the cases did he declare something paranormal was going on. The man was a true skeptic. While many claim to be skeptics, they are not. A true skeptic seeks verifiable evidence, and when they get it they accept the result. Many people use the term "skeptic" to justify a hardened disbelief that cannot be changed regardless of the evidence presented to them or experienced by them. Tim was a debunker, not a hardened disbeliever. Most of his investigations found unsecured floorboards, poor insulation, bad wiring, plumbing issues, or a furnace on the verge of exploding to be the culprits for claims of paranormal activity. In one case, crossed signals on a baby-monitor was to blame for a family hearing disembodied voices. Video coverage in his investigations was over the top, having thirty-six cameras at his disposal. He required floor to ceiling coverage of any event. Without full coverage, Tim felt there was too wide a margin for a hoax, or claims of a hoax, to be possible. And he never charged those who requested him. In this case, I didn't charge either.

The client Tim was speaking with, Harold Forne, had an eight-year-old daughter that was of primary concern. From the videos Mr. Forne had provided, she appeared to be in very real physical danger. He had handed over seventeen videos of scratch marks forming on the little girl's arms, face, and back. Not simply the girl with the marks on her, but the scratches actively forming. When Tim contacted me a month ago, my first order of business was to verify the videos' authenticity and briefly investigate the source. If children are involved, I do two things. The first is waive my fee. The second is to ensure that the parent's interest is keeping their child safe. Both Harold and his wife appeared to be good parents trying to save their daughter from what Tim had determined to be an honest paranormal threat.

Moira and I approached the two men. Tim was a lanky sort. Tussled brown hair and oversized round glasses with the demeanor, and wardrobe, of a college professor. Five feet, ten inches, Mr. Forne was dressed in casual business attire, balding with a comb-over, and clearly loved food. His body language said he was at the end of his rope, as did the frustration in his voice.

"Look," Harold said, pointing an exasperated finger at Tim. "We've done it all at this point. We got the psychics to come out here, and they didn't work. We got three priests and a damn rabbi to bless the house. Nothing. We've spent way too much money on trying to get rid of this thing—"

"You spent money on psychics?" Moira asked incredulously.

Mr. Forne turned to look at her. After a momentary sizing up of both Moira and me, he let out a deflated exhale.

"Yeah." He nodded, almost ashamed. "I didn't know what else to do."

"That's easy," Moira said. "You wait until Tim calls in someone who isn't a fraud. Any real psychic worth a damn, even those who might normally charge, will help a family for free."

I nodded in agreement. Among the paranormal community and those associated with them, there's an unspoken rule. Never charge for services when a family in distress is involved, doubly so when a small child is in the mix. This is true for investigators, psychics, occultists, and witches. Any who do charge are either fakes just looking to prey on the desperation of others or morally corrupt trash.

"As for the holy men," I piped up. "In cases of real hauntings, they're useless."

"Who are you?" Harold asked. His tone indicated that I had somehow offended him. I figured he might be the religious sort.

"I'm the guy that gets called in when the priests fail. I'm the nuclear option."

Moira gave the brown, heavy oak door a squinted look of suspicion. I could see a rare hesitation in her movement, a sign that she was able to feel whatever occupied the house from the outside. Pursing her lips and jerking them to the side, she turned to look at Harold Forne.

"When did everything start?" she asked. He had already answered the question a few times on camera during Tim's investigation. The only videos Moira had seen were of the attacks on the little girl, and all the audio had been removed from those. It was a way of ensuring she would not be tainted by outside information, something the psychic insisted on.

"There's always been strange things going on in the house," Harold said. "Items moving, sounds in the night, doors opening and closing on their own. The occasional shadow-person. The basic stuff you see in movies about hauntings."

"But it was never dangerous," Moira stated.

Mr. Forne nodded. "Not until six months ago," he filled in.

"What happened six months ago?" I asked. I knew the answer, the question was for Moira's sake.

"We started looking to move," Harold stated, "and my wife had one of her New Age friends bring in a Ouija board. She wanted to contact her dead father to get some real-estate advice." Mr. Forne chuckled at the thought. "It didn't go well. The board wound up flung into our fireplace. That was the first time we had actually seen anything move on its own."

Moira nodded sagely.

"That's when I knew we had a demon."

Moira winced at the word and I gave a little chuckle. I was interested in seeing her reaction to the term "demon" being used. Many use it as a catch-all for any non-human spiritual entity. I held a great distaste for the word. It was a loaded word. A religious word. And it was an overly simplistic word used by those who could not grasp that the spiritual realm was comprised of many different types of spirits. An entire ecosystem made of pure energy. There were almost as many known species of spirit entities as there were living species. Some had been catalogued and named throughout human history in what we now call Mythology and Fairy Tales. More historically recent religions had dumbed down the spirit world into a binary worldview.

"Demons don't exist," I stated flatly.

Harold looked at me as though I had just kicked his puppy. "Then what the hell is in my house? And why is it trying to force us out? Why is it hurting my daughter?"

"That's why I'm here," Moira said as she placed her hand on the door.

She stood still as a statue for a moment, allowing her senses to absorb all the information the house had to offer. Moira sighed as she pulled her hand back.

"What did your paid psychics tell you?" I asked Harold.

"They said we had an angry demon," he began. "They called it Zozo—"

I let out an explosive laugh. Mr. Forne looked at me in confusion.

"Zozo is a common name for demons in the movies. There's a little folklore attached to it, but it's all crap," I said.

"Well, they said this thing wanted the soul of my daughter." He paused. "I used three psychics and they all said the same thing."

"Same as in there was a common theme, or as though they were reading from the same story?"

This gave Harold a moment of pause as his memory worked through his encounters. His face dropped as he said, "They were reading from the same script."

"Well," Moira chimed in, "the good news is it ain't Zozo. The bad news is that you have a Red Hag that's on the verge of going poltergeist."

My eyebrows raised at Moira's identification.

"You're sure about that?" I asked. Moira nodded.

"What—" Mr. Forne stuttered. "What's a Red Hag?"

"Something that is normally harmless," I answered. "Red Hags are entities that feed off the energy of living things." I paused for a moment. "Generally speaking, a Red Hag will vow to act as a guardian for those they feed from. It is their way of paying for dinner."

"That sounds disturbing," Mr. Forne said. I nodded. I wished there was some other way to characterize the situation, but no alternatives came to me.

"They can be a nuisance, as they sometimes scare people with the classic haunting phenomena. This causes the body to amp up its energy output. Usually fear is a last resort for them. A happy household is an energetic household, it is in their best interest to keep their housemates happy, not fearful."

"It knows you're looking to leave," Moira continued my line of thought. "A few months ago it was probably just scared of losing its food source, now it appears to be on the verge of insanity. If that happens, it will become a poltergeist."

"I thought poltergeists were just angry spirits," Harold said.

"That is just one part of it," I chimed in. "In some ways, the word poltergeist is a psychological diagnosis. It means that a spiritual entity has mentally broken." I paused, seeing more questions in Harold's face. "These entities aren't that much different than humans from a psychological standpoint. Each one is an individual. Each has its own personality. Some are kind, some are cruel. Some are mentally unbalanced, and some are psychologically fragile."

"Your unseen housemate seems fragile," Moira said, sadness in her voice. "It likely has no idea that more people will come in to fill the space you will be leaving, so it is trying to gorge itsel—" Moira stopped, putting her hand to her chin. It was an idiosyncrasy she displayed when an epiphany steamrolled its way through her mind. "When your daughter has been scratched, was this always in your presence, or did it happen when she was alone?"

Harold appeared puzzled by the question, taking a moment to think about it. "It always happened when my wife or I was around. She was never attacked when alone."

"I don't think she's being attacked," I stated, also seeing Moira's revelation. "I don't think it's trying to hurt her. Not yet anyway."

Agitation spilled over Mr. Forne's face. "Then why the hell is it hurting my daughter?"

"It's frustrated," Moira said.

"It's trying to tell you something, trying to get your attention," I informed him.

"What?" Harold demanded. "What could it possibly be trying to tell us?"

"That is something I intend to find out. With a little luck it is still sane enough to reason with." I shook my head, letting out an uneasy sigh. "I would rather not have to kill it."

"How do you kill what's already dead?" Incredulity dripped from Harold's words.

"These entities aren't dead, *per se*." I looked to the worried father. "They exist as coherent energy. That energy can be disrupted and dispersed. In essence, killing them. I prefer to avoid such a thing as I see these entities as living beings."

"Can't they simply put themselves back together?"

"How?" I asked. "When the will is erased, there is nothing left to draw the energy back into any semblance of coherence." I gave Harold a sideways smile. "Religion and movies tell people these things are unkillable. I find that idea absolutely adorable."

"Why can you kill them but other people say it can't be done?" Skepticism infused Mr. Forne's question.

"Simple," I said as I walked up to the door. "I know what I'm doing, I have the skills, the power, and the will to use them. Other folks, well… They're afraid of the dark."

I looked at Tim, who had been auspiciously silent throughout the entire conversation, to find him pointing a camera at all of us. The man's tongue was poking out from the corner of his mouth. I gave a groaning chuckle. This case would likely be a huge boon for the San Angeles Paranormal Investigation Coalition.

"From what I've seen in the case so far," I looked to Tim, "a lot of the activity has been in the kitchen?"

"Yeah," Tim affirmed. "Still have eight cameras in there and one S-FLIR camera."

The S-FLIR was a Tim Darby special. He had taken a standard thermal imaging video camera and outfitted it with some extra optics that enhanced any moving form. When pointed at a person, the thermal differentials were overlayed on a reconstruction of the individual's visage. This appears to work for spiritual entities as well, giving the few he had captured on it a reconstruction of their unseen form. Most of them looked like blobs with tentacles.

I sighed. Kitchens were dangerous places in the presence of a desperate spirit. A lot of ammo to throw around. My techniques, while effective in shielding against spiritual attacks, were entirely useless against a flying wineglass.

"I recommend you all stay out here," I said. "I know the effect my techniques have on these non-corporeal types, but I don't know what it might do to the soul of a living person." I looked directly into Tim's camera. "That's one of the reasons why I don't deal with possessions."

"What are the other reasons?" Harold asked.

Turning back to the door, I said, "Most cases of possession are a kind of religious-inspired psychosis. It's why you never find so-called demons possessing people of faiths different from the possessed. When's the last time a Hindu demon possessed an Evangelical Christian?"

"I'll take my chances," Tim said.

I knew he would say that. I had control over the radius of my spirit-killing technique. From a few inches to engulfing the entire house. I was going to have to try for close quarters with Tim tagging along.

The house was eerily quiet. We stood in a small, hardwood-floored foyer, the living room on our right and a door to the kitchen on our left. A carpeted staircase sat squarely in front of us.

"When I start," I said, turning toward the kitchen door, "keep your distance. No matter what." Tim nodded.

A rectangular, raw wood dining table greeted our entry into the kitchen. A large room, the floor was covered in maroon vinyl tiles with walls painted to match. White moldings and a white ceiling broke the sea of off-red. One wall held a white, twin-door refrigerator that looked as if it had been there since 1980, as did the gas stove on the left side of the adjoining wall. White wooden cupboards were situated about a foot and a half over grey, faux-marble countertops. A white swinging door on the far side of the room swayed slightly. I assumed it led to a real dining room. Stainless steel, and looking relatively new, a farmer's sink sat beneath a large window that gave a view of the property's back yard. Midday light filtered through the window, giving a rather homey feel to what should have been a garish eyesore. With the cameras rolling I couldn't say it out loud, but damn these people needed an interior decorator.

Standing at the edge of the dining table, I could see all the cupboards had been cinched closed with twine around their handles. The counters lay bare except for a single white coffee mug. I frowned at the scene. It felt off.

"What time does most of the activity take place?" I asked Tim.

I had seen the videos, I saw the time stamps, I knew the answer was somewhere in my head. It refused to reveal itself.

"7pm to 10pm," he responded. "Why?"

"Was that coffee mug here earlier today?"

"I—" Tim looked at the ceramic liquid holster in confusion. "I really don't know. I haven't been in the house today."

From my vantage point I could see this heavy cup could do some damage. I silently indicated for Tim to wait by the door. Taking a deep breath, I let out a controlled exhale, centering my mind. I have always been able to see non-human entities. I have never seen the ghost of a person, but I've seen a variety of the inhuman unseen. From nightmare-inducing to adorable, I had known these things were among us ever since I was a child. It was that realization that set me on a path to learning how to get rid of those that were problematic or harmful. Darkstone was like me and had taught me the technique I now use to coerce, force out, or kill these non-corporeal creatures. For now, the kitchen appeared empty, though it was possible for these entities to remain hidden from my sight if they chose to.

"Let's do this."

I took two steps into the room and my expectations were met. The coffee mug shot off the counter. Cocking my head to the side, I felt the bottom edge of the cup graze my cheek. The sound of shattering ceramic heralded the end of the cup's existence, and the creation of potentially deadly shards.

"You know what I am," I said to the unseen entity in the room. "You know what I can do." The cupboard doors violently rattled in response, fighting against their twine restraints. I stopped in the center of the room. "I know it is fear and sadness that has brought you to this."

Sitting on the floor, I placed my shoulder bag next to me and drew my knives from their underarm sheathes. Placing one knifepoint down in front of me and one behind me, I swung my arms, cutting a circle in the vinyl. Some occultists and witches use words in what most call "magic." I use what could best be described as vocalizations of intent. Unintelligible sounds that express the energy I harness and the purpose I am using it for. My voice brought forth the intent of protection. In my mind's eye a wall of white light surrounded me, its radius the circle I had cut into the floor.

Reaching into my bag, I pulled out a five-inch by three-inch black plastic box; flicking a switch on the side of the thin rectangle, a short chime indicated the device was on. This was a specially constructed spirit box. Normally spirit boxes were used by paranormal investigators to help amplify the "voices" of spirits. They are, quite frankly, annoying. Most spirit boxes cycle through radio frequencies, generating the most irritating white noise in the process. If any response from a spirit comes at all, it is difficult to decipher amidst the mass of crackling. The question of whether one is truly getting a response or simply having a moment of auditory pareidolia makes the validity of the equipment questionable. The spirit box before me made no noise, it did not function by radio signals and did not pick up audio.

Spirits, being creatures of energy, have no vocal cords. The amount of energy required to produce a sound wave is more than one might think, and is a massive drain on such entities. It is one of the reasons Electronic Voice Phenomena, or EVPs, come out as barely perceptible whispers. My spirit box functions by direct contact. A spirit could touch the interior circuitry and, with minimal energy output, speak clearly and loudly. The device was the brainchild of one extremely talented, techno-savvy witch named Vickey Turnbael.

From a small town in Idaho, the locals just referred to her as the Green Witch of Hawthorne. Few were willing to say her name out of superstition. She thought this was hilarious. Vickey had a PhD in Electrical Engineering. Placing the spirit box just outside my protective circle, I brought out one more device. A five-inch, deep-green cube with gold pentagrams on each face. I placed it at my side. This item was also made by the Green Witch. It was one I hoped to use. Its necessity would mean there would be no killing here today.

I drew in a deep breath. "Show yourself," I said calmly.

Tim gasped. I knew he was looking at the S-FLIR camera feed and was able to see what I saw. The Red Hag thrust into my sight, stopping at the edge of my protective shield. Her face bore a twisted visage worthy of a horror movie. Contorted, deep black holes engulfed her eye sockets, her gaping mouth a screaming void of emptiness. Red hair franticly blew in all directions, moved by unknown currents. The expression on the spirit's face was one of profound sadness, anger, and frustration. Her silent screams bore evidence she was on the edge of sanity. My heart dropped. I felt nothing but compassion for this creature.

"Oh, sweety," I whispered. "What happened to you?"

I have seen three Red Hags in my life. Despite the name, they are luminous, beautiful creatures. Normally they have large black eyes, a small nose and mouth, bordering on the look of a Japanese Anime character. The red hair is what gives them part of their name, and the term Hag appears to have been assigned by those who crossed them and refused to take responsibility. "Red Lady" would be a more appropriate moniker.

I pointed to my spirit box. The Red Hag's abyssal gaze followed my finger.

"Touch this," I said. "You can speak through it."

She moved a sharply pointed finger. Hesitating, her finger hovered over the box. The voids of her eye sockets turned up at me as she thrust her finger through the black plastic case and into the spirit box.

An ear-piercing scream blasted from the device. Wincing, I gave the spirit a sideways look.

"No need to scream," I said. "You already have my attention. Do you have a name?"

"Thassa," a staccato female voice came from the box. "I. Thassa. Help."

"How can I help you?"

"Help," the voice repeated.

"Are you trapped here?"

The Red Hag slowly shook her head.

"My. Family." The voice paused. "Need. Help."

I felt confused. Harold Forne didn't appear to be in any sort of trouble, and my brief investigation of the family did not reveal anything that would pose a danger.

"Why does your family need help?"

"*Nianam*," the voice stated.

I felt confusion wash over my face. "Who is *Nianam*?"

I could see the black circles where her eyes should have been darken in frustration.

"*Nianam.* Terrance. No. Soul." The voice paused again; Thassa seemed to be searching my face for understanding. "Danger."

"Okay." My tone was calm, soothing. "Someone named Terrance is a danger to the family?"

"To. The. Girl." I could feel a sense of urgency in the digital voice. "Keep. Girl. Away."

"I think I understand."

With that simple acknowledgement I watched the Red Hag's gaping, abyssal maw change, retract into a small, pensive mouth. She was clearly still worried, but no longer needed to scream.

"I will make sure the family knows about this Terrance. Will you move with them?"

"No." In spite of the monotone voice produced by the spirit box, I could feel a sense of melancholy in her words. "Broke. Trust. Unworthy."

As she spoke through the spirit box, her eyes returned from the voids that had consumed them. Deep black, expressive and full of regret.

"You did what you needed to do, didn't you?"

She shook her head.

"Does. Not. Matter." Her face told the story of a final decision regarding the Forne family. "Unworthy. Others. Will. Protect."

She had made up her mind, so had I. Picking up the cube at my side, I opened it, a hidden hinge splitting the box in half. A small globe of rose quartz crystal sat on three metal struts. Clicking a button on the bottom, an electric current flowed through the mounting. I placed the device next to my spirit box.

"Kill. Me."

"You did what you needed to. You acted in the best interest of your family," I said. "If exile is what you choose, I understand. But you have shown honor in this. You risked your own existence, your own sanity to call for help. You deserve more than being cast to the wind. I refuse."

Thassa looked at me, her head cocked to the side. Spirits are fairly black-and-white creatures. A good end result does not mitigate any damage done in the pursuit of said result. Her face clearly showed that she did not agree with my assessment of her actions. I pointed to the crystal.

"Let me help you find a new family," I said. "This is a spirit crystal. In it you will sleep, the current flowing through the device will keep you fed. When I find a prospective family for you, one that will accept you, I will wake you."

She gave what I interpreted to be a doubtful look. I leaned forward. The past four paranormal investigations I had been called in on ended in the destruction of the spirits involved. I was starting to feel like a murderer. I needed to have a win.

"Please, come with me. Let me help you."

Thassa pulled her finger from the spirit box and nodded. She moved her finger to the crystal orb quickly. I gave the Red Hag my most comforting look as her form dissolved into the device. A small green LED light came on, indicating the crystal was now occupied. I lowered my shield, pulling the white light back within myself. Picking up the spirit box, I turned it off, and placed the spiritual translator back into my satchel. Standing, I slung the bag over my shoulder and gingerly picked up Thassa's slumber chamber.

"This vid's probably going to go viral," I said to Tim, who was frozen at the kitchen doorway.

"That—" he stuttered, his hands visibly shaking. "That was fucking amazing."

I cocked a sideways smile, indicated to the Ghost Hunter that it was time to leave. Exiting the house, we found Harold and Moira where we left them.

"So, she decided to go quietly," Moira said, her voice unusually somber.

"Yes." My hands cradled the box containing the sleeping spirit. I turned to Harold. "Who is Terrance?"

Harold's face turned a combination of shocked and confused. "He's a handyman we hired to fix up the house before we put it on the market. He does pretty good work."

"Let me guess," I said. "You hired him six months ago?"

"Yes." Mr. Forne's brow furrowed.

"Did anything odd happen in his presence?" I asked.

"A few things here and there," he said as his eyes darted back and forth, searching his memory. The portly man's eyebrows lifted as something struck his memory. "Right before the scratching on my daughter started there was an incident. He was working on something in her room while she was there watching him. I didn't see it, but according to Terrance, a porcelain pony flew off a shelf and hit him."

"What was he working on?" I asked, suspicion flowing through my mind.

"I—" Harold hesitated. "I honestly don't know."

"Listen to me carefully." I looked the worried father dead in the eyes. "What you've been experiencing, all of it, has been this spirit trying to protect you. Specifically, your daughter. It was almost driven insane by the frustration of it." Harold nodded as I spoke. "Keep this Terrance away from your daughter, keep him away from your family."

"Did," Harold began, his voice catching in his throat. "Did he do something to her?"

"I don't know," I answered honestly. "Ask your daughter exactly what happened when the pony hit him."

I could see every worst-case scenario running through Mr. Forne's mind, a swell of anger in his face.

"We will provide you with the videos," Tim told him. "That way you can see the conversation for yourself."

Harold drew in a deep breath, clearly trying to calm his mind. Nodding, he said, "Thank you for your help."

I gave him a head tilt. "My pleasure."

From the corner of my eye, I noticed Tim had brought his camera back to filming height, recording this as part of his after-action report. Turning toward the Ghost Hunter, I looked directly into the camera.

With dramatic flair, I pulled my glasses off, pushed away a non-existent lock of hair, and proclaimed, "This house is clean."

A muffled, hissing snort exploded from Moira. Tim desperately tried to hold his camera steady as his body convulsed in silent laughter. Mr. Forne looked at the three of us with profound confusion. Apparently the man had never seen the movie *Poltergeist*.

"That's supposed to be my line, kid," Moira stated, patting me on the back. I gave her a mischievous smirk.

"You gotta be quick with these things," I quipped. Turning back to Harold, my demeanor returned to one of serious professionalism. "You will have no more paranormal events for the remainder of your time in this house." I gave Mr. Forne a knowing smile. "Just…be open to those things in your new house that are there to help you."

I turned, headed toward my car.

"Wha—" Harold fumbled as I walked past him. "What does that mean?"

"Moira can explain it to you," I called back to him.

Opening my car trunk, I stowed my bag and placed my knives back in their case. Hearing fast footsteps, I looked up to see Tim standing by my car.

"Just a quick in and out, eh?"

"Sorry, man," I said. "Got a case this morning that's having Tara and me heading to Vegas for a bit."

Tim's eyebrows raised in surprise. He had never known me to leave town on a case, be it paranormal or mundane.

"That's—"

"Have you heard of this Hatchetman killer?"

Tim gasped. "Oh fuck, please tell me you're not going after that maniac."

I was a bit taken aback by his response. Aside from a few mentions in the nightly news, I really knew very little about the case I had taken up. Then again, I avoided watching the news. It should be called the *6 O'Clock Depression Hour*. Or *60 Minutes of Despair*. There's enough depressing shit to deal with. It's my job to help people resolve some of those things. I don't need Fox News to highlight the dumpster fire that we call humanity.

"I've been seeing it all over my social media," he said. "The guy's cut a swath up Cali, people found in pieces, and no one knows how he's doing it."

I groaned as an army of happy faces energetically waving red flags ran through my mind, all of them laughing at me. Giving Tim a nod of confirmation, the lanky man's face grew more serious than I had ever seen it.

"Just—" He paused. "Just watch yourself."

"Fortunately, I don't have to ever confront the guy, just find him."

"Still, someone psychotic enough to turn a person into spare parts—
"

"I'll be fine," I said to Tim, placing a hand on his shoulder. "It's a simple locate job. Nothing to worry about."

Tim let out a long sigh. Half smiling, he said, "Famous last words."

Chapter 4

The Boy opened his eyes. Lolling his head side to side, he realized he was on the carpeted floor of his Travelodge motel room. The illuminated digital clock on the nightstand told him it was 7pm. The dream was still clear in his mind, the faceless void he called the Dark Man imparting divine instructions.

Three years ago, the Boy's power had manifested while playing fetch with his beloved dog Dunkin. Making the standard false throw that got the husky worked up and ready to "get it," something had switched on in his mind. A dizziness overtook him, the world blurred, and he stumbled. As his vision cleared, he saw that Dunkin had been cleaved in two, nose to tail, blood and entrails splattered around him. He didn't know why, he didn't know how, he just knew he had done this. He had been a lover of animals. Something broke inside him that day.

For six months he attempted to control his new ability, the local wildlife suffering in the process. Empathy was something the Boy had always struggled with. He cared little for humans, his sympathy reserved for the animal kingdom. With each bird, each cat, each racoon and dog he slaughtered, that sympathy, his capacity for empathy, died. The death of his capacity for emotional connection begat the revelation that he did not belong in this world. A deep depression had taken hold, and he could see only one way out.

It was a Tuesday when he dragged the small folding knife up his arms, opening his veins for the world to see. He lay on the restroom floor of a 7-Eleven, his blood filling the grooves between dull grey tiles. Consciousness abandoned him quickly, and he found himself before the angel he had come to call the Dark Man. Standing upon a hill of rotting corpses, the entity appeared as a shadow that had been ripped from a wall, the substance of it a void from which no light could escape. At first the Boy thought he stood before the gates of hell, but when the Dark Man spoke, it spoke of him needing to live. It spoke of his destiny to become a living god. It gave him instructions to control his power.

The Dark Man came to him every night, the dream that was not a dream. Evidence of the encounters always followed him back into the waking world. As he lay on the hotel room floor staring at the ceiling, the fetid stench of rotting flesh filled his nostrils; the fading perfume of the Dark Man's abode. He rose from the floor. Crimson stains on the knees of his pants caught his eye, a tell-tale sign that the dream was real. Brushing his fingers over the wet marks, the Boy brought blood-smeared fingers to his nose, inhaling the copper aroma. Shuddering with pleasure, he slyly grinned and examined his red-tipped fingers. One by one he sucked the blood off them. Looking back to the crimson soaking through his pants, aggravation overtook him.

The Dark Man's holy instructions were not what he had wanted to hear. He was told to find the Raven, he was told to bait the line, he was told to have patience. He could not fathom why his messenger of the Most High refused to simply tell him where she was or show him what she looked like. It was in the killing of Sonja that he had discovered a name for the one who could make him perfect.

He let out a long sigh. "God helps those who help themselves."

Gritting his teeth, a realization hit him as he stared at his blood-stained pants. "Fuck," his voice louder than he had intended. "Gonna have to get a whole new wardrobe soon. Should send him a bill."

The Boy moved himself to a round, wood table situated next to the front door of the room. Falling into a matching wooden chair, he grunted in pain. His encounter with the thing that spoke through Sonja's corpse had left him with a bruised tailbone. He pulled open his laptop bag that hung from the back of the chair. The laptop itself had been rendered useless. The sight of the fried hardware brought a flash of anger. Tempering his emotions, he pulled a small notebook from an interior pocket. He smiled to himself.

Pragmatism was key in his pursuit of perfection. As such, the Boy did not trust critical information to digital storage. Opening the notebook, he navigated to a page titled "Nevada." Twenty-five names and addresses he had obtained in private conversations on the Goddess Message Board were neatly printed. He strove for perfection in all aspects of his life. Handwriting was a reflection of mental perfection. Two additional entries garnered his attention, both titled "Support Meeting." The next meeting was in two days. He would observe the attendees. Perhaps one would suit his purpose.

Hard as he tried, patience was not in him. He felt the need for the adrenaline rush, the power he felt when he took a life. He needed to hunt, he needed to exercise his power. He would be patient with gathering a Goddess; to capture the Raven he needed strategy. Normal humans, however... Normal humans were playthings to be used and abused.

"Fuck this shit," he muttered, rising from the desk to don a pair of clean trousers.

Peeking around the motel room's dirty window curtains, the Boy winced. Pain shot through his eyes as bright sunlight cut into them. He had forgotten that the summer sun drew out its exit. Hard to kill under the cover of darkness when an angry ball of fire hung in the sky. With an aggravated sigh he threw himself onto the uncomfortable bed. It smelled like dust and old socks. Maybe he could take a nap without the Dark Man interfering in his sleep. People would still be here when the sun took its leave.

Raven stood, unseen, in the corner of Rachel Hawkins' bedroom. A single lamp illuminated the brightly colored pink walls. Shelves filled with happy stuffed animals bracketed the hospital-style bed in which Rachel lay on her side, her mother attempting to feed the twenty-four-year-old.

Afflicted with a condition that medical professionals had diagnosed as severe cerebral palsy, Rachel's body was crumpled into a permanent fetal position. Her thin arms and legs were curled into her, muscles atrophied from lack of use. The smooth brown skin of her face stood in sharp contrast to the bleach white of her pillow. Her large, fearful brown eyes darted around the room as her head moved erratically, trying to evade the spoonful of poison.

"You need to eat," Rachel's mother belted out, exasperation bleeding from each word. "I already pushed dinner back way too far. I'm not letting you go to sleep hungry."

Rachel let out a disapproving, guttural sound. Her body might not have been cooperative, but her sense of smell worked just fine. The strong odor of bleach was unmistakable. Her mother stood, grabbed the helpless young woman by the chin. Forcing Rachel's mouth open, she shoved the spoon into her mouth. The woman held her hand over Rachel's mouth until she choked down the poison-laced food.

"If you would just eat, I wouldn't have to do this every day."

Raven wanted to intervene. A split-second look from Rachel stayed her hand. A defiance that said, despite her fear, she knew what she was doing.

Standing between the light, Raven was invisible to the two women. She could feel light bend around her body, the soft caress of photons gliding over her was normally pleasant. Not this time. Each brush of light felt like a timer ticking down, an anxiety amplifier. Raven altered her vision to see within.

Rachel appeared to Raven as a bright, angelic light. A soul that was strong and healthy. Rachel's mother was a different matter entirely. She appeared dim, Raven counting fifty-nine black, cancerous voids eating away at her. She was infected by unnatural purpose and had acted on it. By the small pinpoint void that appeared to be recent, Raven surmised that each void represented an attempt on her daughter's life.

"There. All done." Rachel's mom feigned satisfaction. "Now you try to get some sleep." She pulled a blanket up to Rachel's neck, kissed her on the forehead, and closed the door on her way out.

Raven watched as Rachel took several deep breaths before the convulsions began. She could do nothing for the girl beyond conversion, and as a rule Raven refused to make the choice of conversion for her charge. Before she could complete her mental debate on free will versus rule breaking, Rachel demonstrated why she had survived fifty-eight previous attempts on her life.

The convulsions abruptly stopped, Rachel's deep brown eyes now sporting the cat-like vertical pupils of her birthright. Rolling onto her back, Rachel straightened her limbs, stretching every inch of her body. She clenched her jaw, hands closed into white-knuckled fists. Raven understood. She was neutralizing the poison, healing any damage and resetting the health of her body. The process only took a few seconds. Rachel lay stretched out on the bed, her breathing calm and measured.

She raised a hand above her, watching her fingers flex and move. She put her arm by her side.

"I know you're there." Her voice was rough from disuse. "Please don't hide."

Walking out of her space between the light, it appeared to Rachel as though Raven was stepping out from behind invisible curtains.

"It's you," Rachel said with a warm smile. "I didn't know if you heard me."

Raven had felt an urgency cross the psychic tether linking her to Rachel. She was linked to all those who bore the infinity birthmark, the Caretakers, but she knew only basic details about those who had yet to be activated. Those she referred to as the Waiting. Though no information was transmitted, an intense need was made obvious. With someone out there killing her charge, Raven thought this could be them. She was simultaneously relieved and disappointed it wasn't the case. Raven took the young woman's hand.

"Yes, I heard you." Raven smiled. "I must admit, your speech—"

"I used to be able to speak. I lost my voice six years ago," Rachel said. "I started losing everything. I used to be able to walk with crutches, you know. But when I turned thirteen, things just stopped working. One by one, my body just stopped doing things."

"I'm sorry," Raven whispered.

"Nothing to be sorry for. It is what it is." Rachel smiled. "I'm more worried about Mama. When I stopped talking, something in her broke. I could see it in her eyes, like her life was slowly fading away."

Raven nodded in understanding.

"What happens now?"

"You have a choice." Raven's voice was soft, soothing. "You can choose a human life. The power you possess will be gone, but all the experiences and possibilities of a body without impediment will be open to you."

The expression on Rachel's face told Raven that the human option was less than desirable. A note of sadness tinged Raven's smile. She knew too well the hardships that come with owning that birthright, the sacrifices that are made.

69

"Or you can embrace the power you feel in this moment, shed the possibility of a fully human life."

"I want to be what I was meant to be." Rachel's hoarse voice expressed a desire she had longed for her whole life. "I already know what it is to be powerless. Even if I could move without restriction, as a human I would still be powerless. I know I am meant to be more than that."

Raven nodded as she felt Rachel's hand curl. The young woman's body slowly began to revert to a fetal position. Her mouth moved, tried to form words, but her voice had been silenced. Bright brown eyes, pupils round once again, pleaded. Raven wrapped her hand around the back of Rachel's head, her index finger coming to rest on an infinity-shaped birthmark behind the left ear.

Raven's pupils contracted into their feline appearance, the green of her eyes became luminous as she connected to Rachel's DNA. The young woman's body stopped its regression, relaxing. Raven looked into Rachel's expressive eyes, now calm and accepting. She took a deep breath.

"This is going to hurt like hell."

Chapter 5

As Tara bolted around the apartment in a packing frenzy, I perused the dossier Mr. Strickland provided. I was in disbelief that any private investigation firm had done such shoddy work. Once again, the multinational army of red flags paraded through my mind in a long succession.

Consisting mostly of coroner reports, police reports, and photographs, conspicuously absent were the investigation reports from both law enforcement and private firms. Four investigation summaries from big name firms were included, but these amounted to little more than cover letters offering no more insight than the police reports. The photographs included were a different story. It was the photos that had given the folder the appearance of being packed full of information.

Thirty-five victims were included, their bodies found all over California and the most recent in Nevada. San Diego, Los Angeles, Bakersfield, Oakland, Yreka made for what should have been an easy track of movement. A skip to Las Vegas put the line of movement into question. And then there was the M.O.

The bodies of each victim had been dismembered using, according to the coroner reports, unknown methods. The cuts were clean, no tool marks. The Yreka coroner had suggested that a laser cutter may have been used, or possibly a custom bandsaw. The victims were buried in shallow graves, their locations not far from major roads and tourist viewing overlooks. This Hatchetman didn't seem too keen on doing the heavy labor of digging suitable graves. More than half of the burials were found because wildlife had dug them up. With the unidentified subject, or unsub, crossing to Nevada, the disposal method drastically changed.

Eight days ago, three bodies were found in the Valley of Fire State Park in Nevada. The police report stated that, once again, they had been dismembered using unknown means. However, this time they were on display. Using duct tape, the perpetrator fixed the body parts to giant Xs made of large wooden branches. The heads of each victim were suspended above their torsos using an oversized wooden dowel, sharpened at both ends and impaling the points of severance. Each victim was an attractive prostitute, most likely picked up at one of the casino bars in Las Vegas. Two more bodies, also young women, had been found in shallow graves ten feet from the macabre display. These two had been local girls, but not working girls. I tried to reason out why the two had been buried. Were they test subjects? Did they not meet some criteria for public display? A coroner's report was missing from this most recent set of murders. Where was that?

With questions ringing in my head, I turned my attention to the photographs. The victims were of all ages, genders, races, and social statuses. They were also found in various stages of decomposition, ranging from a few days to a month before being found. Predation had also made the identification of some remains rely on dental records. Spreading the afterimages of life over the kitchen table, lightning struck my mind.

Of the thirty-five victims, only nine had more than two photographs. Most of the attached images consisted of one family-provided photograph and one autopsy photograph. The nine also included crime scene photos. Strangely, these nine corpses displayed no sign of predation, even when buried next to victims murdered at approximately the same time. The most striking photographs of the nine were autopsy shots of infinity symbol tattoos behind each woman's left ear. I took in the sum total of what I had been provided.

There was no attempt to hide the manipulation. The lead placed before me was not just painfully obvious but insulting in the extreme. I didn't need Mr. Strickland's editing of information to figure out that the tattooed girls were the killer's focus. I had quickly surmised that all others were either incidental, got in the Hatchetman's way, or satiated a desire to kill. Perhaps they served to point him toward his true targets. With so little investigative information to go on, it seemed I would have to discover that answer using my own shoe leather.

A sense of annoyance, bordering on anger, gripped me. Not even one day into this case and I already felt like I was being played. Pulling out a slip of paper, I looked at the deposit receipt. The number of zeros in my bank account reminded me why I took this job when every ounce of reason had told me not to. To those who don't know me, this would appear as a decision born of greed. Maybe that is how this started. The family photos of those nine young girls, photos of the women alive and happy, granted me a reason beyond money. As it was with helping the Forne family, I felt duty bound to help these women. Letting out a long exhale, sound from the bedroom door grabbed my attention.

"Aw, man," Tara's disappointed words found their way to my ears.

"What happened?" I asked. Tara appeared in the doorway, her wheeled luggage in one hand, cell phone in the other.

"We missed Fat Vince Neil playing Fremont Street again," she pouted. Her referring to the former lead singer of Mötley Crue as fat wasn't meant as a pejorative. She just could not accept that the heroin-chic Vince Neil who had sung "Dr. Feelgood" and the kind, good-natured guy who showed up on reality television a few years ago were the same person.

"Damn," I responded with a chuckle. "We need to get his itinerary."

"I'm almost done." Tara smirked as she placed her suitcase by the front door. "Go get yourself ready."

I gathered the dossier back together, centered it neatly on my side of the dining table/desk, and headed into the bathroom.

Jumping through a quick shower, the images of death washed into the back of my mind. The general disquiet I felt about this case did not. Red flags. All I could see were red flags as unease raged through me. And the questions. So many questions. Who was this Joseph Handler? Where was the rest of the investigative materials? Why was I so blatantly being pointed toward nine of the victims? And why did this killer kill so many that didn't seem to fit with their presumed target group? Why the change in M.O.?

Shaking my head, bringing myself back to the present, I stood shirtless before the bathroom mirror. Scanning my pale form, I frowned.

In college I spent a year sporting a mohawk as my hairstyle of choice. My hair has never forgiven me. With my receding widow's peak hairline, it appeared the brown hair on my head was relocating to my chest and stomach. I looked down. It had been well over a decade since I had been in shape. Well, good shape. Now I had what was referred to as a "dad bod." Not fat, *per se*, but definitely not thin. I winced as a pain

73

shot through the lower left side of my abdomen, a torn muscle that had never properly healed.

"Damnit," I hissed. A deep breath and the pain subsided. Looking back to the mirror, I did a quick inspection. My skin was its usual ghostly white, not so different from the appearance of the Red Hag Thassa, who currently slumbered in a crystal chamber on the kitchen counter. I had no blemishes. I'm not particularly vain about my appearance, but I'm not unaware of it.

Looking down again, I unceremoniously shoved my thumb into my belly button, and with my index finger took hold of the fat that began above my pubic bone, approximating my current size. I hadn't gained any weight since I checked last.

"We need to get—" Tara's words broke off as she poked her head through the open bathroom doorway. She looked me up and down, then erupted into laughter. False indignation crossed my face.

"What?" Sarcasm dripped from every pore in my body. "How else am I supposed to know if I'm expanding?"

"Just—" She interrupted herself with another burst of laughter, only able to complete the statement by disappearing into the bedroom. "Just put yourself together, we need to get going."

I threw on my favorite t-shirt. Black with the words "Death Note" written in a white, horror-themed font, the shirt's graphics were from arguably the best Japanese Animation, or Anime, in existence. A white silhouette of the main God of Death that featured in the show hung below the words. Donning my coat and hat, I grabbed my go-bag. It was off to Sin City.

While I had been playing with the paranormal, Tara had taken care of the paperwork. Contracts, payment for the additional investigator…all the boring stuff. When I told Stephanie Gonzalez what her cut was, she went silent for thirty seconds and sputtered for a good two minutes. A former Marine sniper and FBI agent, Stephanie had law enforcement and government contacts equal to none. I had extensive contacts within the Psychic, Occult, and Pagan communities. I doubted we'd be relying on my personal network with this case.

During the car ride I bounced what details of the case I had gathered from my perusal of the dossier off Tara. Though not an investigator, she had a sharp mind, and her logic was beyond reproach. This made her an invaluable companion, and really frustrating in arguments.

Having flipped through the folder, many of the same thoughts came to her.

"What the hell is this?" she blurted out. "Where's the rest of it?"

"I know." My voice was flat. "I can't figure out what Mr. Strickland or this Joseph Handler is after."

"They're definitely leading you toward these girls with the tattoos behind their ears." Tara paused. "Do you think they could be part of some sort of cult?"

"The thought had occurred to me." I nodded. "But why kill so many others?"

"Forensic countermeasure?"

"Possibly," I said. "They could also be the people who led our killer to his true targets."

"His?" I caught Tara's questioning look from the corner of my eye.

"Playing the odds. Men are far more likely to engage in physical violence. That violence is usually pretty brutal."

"Lizzy Borden would disagree."

"Lizzy Borden was acquitted," I countered with a mischievous side glance.

"I know," she said chuckling. "I know. Statistically, women are far more likely to be poisoners. Though when they do get physical, women are far more brutal in their killing than men are."

Nodding in agreement, I said, "We're still left with one pressing question."

"Where is the rest of the investigation?" Tara completed my thought.

"I hate to ask you to do this, but could you—"

"Call all the police agencies handling these cases?" Tara asked, cutting me off.

"Yes." I smirked.

"I didn't come with you to gamble." Tara's tone bore the trappings of indignation. "Mike has the regional crapola handled. I'm being both the dutiful wife and faithful assistant." A wide smile crossed her face. "And we're buying a house before you close this case."

"Sounds like a plan." I chuckled, but humor would not stay as my mind drifted back to the seemingly insurmountable task that lay before me. Glancing at Tara, I saw her smile had vanished. She held her bottom lip between her teeth, an expression that always indicated her mental wheels were turning at full speed.

We drove in silence for ten minutes, contemplating what possible reason there could be for withholding information. Tara groaned. The noise generated by California's decaying roadways did not make for adequate auditory stimulation.

"Music?" I asked.

"Music quiz," Tara responded.

Chuckling, I nodded. During the great COVID-19 Lockdown of 2020, Tara and I signed up to drive for a gig-delivery company. It was a way to keep some money coming in and one of the few jobs that were considered "essential," not that you'd know it from the lack of recognition by either politicians or the companies themselves. We found a plethora of trivia videos we could stream online while we worked together. Many were general knowledge, some music. Tara loved the music quizzes. We noticed a lot of repetition between different quiz makers. Some of these content creators didn't seem to know the band Guns N' Roses had more songs than just "Sweet Child O' Mine." Tara had an unspoken standard with the quizzes and would turn off a quiz in protest should they not meet her expectations.

"Okay," she said, "here's one we haven't done yet."

Playing the audio through my car's speaker system, an overly happy 1920s piano-bar tune indicated the introduction to the quiz. Tara watched her phone as instructions neither of us paid any attention to flashed on screen. The piano music abruptly ceased, and a digital voice chimed in saying, "Number One."

Tara and I groaned as the vocal stylings of Bon Jovi informed us that he was "halfway there". Tara shut off the video. The song "Livin' on a

Prayer" was so ubiquitous on these quizzes that, like Guns N' Roses, you would think it was Bon Jovi's only song.

"Rejected," Tara declared, and promptly began seeking an alternative.

"I'm thinking I may need to check in with Bon Jovi," I said. "The dude's been halfway there for thirty-six years. I think he might be stuck."

Tara gave a polite snort to the joke I had made hundreds of times. Sighing, she put her phone down.

"Nothing new?" I asked.

"No. And I'm not comfortable enough with my knowledge of 1940s music to put time into a twenty-minute quiz on it."

"Fair enough."

As we approached the 210/15 freeway interchange, I threw on my favorite Assemblage 23 album, *Failure*. With the music playing, Tara and I were silent, half listening and half mulling through nagging questions and possible answers.

Cresting the Cajon Pass, Tara placed her hand over mine.

"I love you," she said.

Smiling, I said, "I love you too." I felt my face relax; until then I had not noticed that every muscle had been tense. A slight ache came from my jaw. It had been clenched tight for our entire ascent into the high desert.

Chancing a sideways glance at my wife, she was smiling. I brought her hand up to my lips and gave it a kiss. I needed a break from thoughts of killers and corpses, and she knew it. I heaved a deep sigh.

Taking her hand back, Tara turned off the music and scrolled quickly through her phone. "We have a *Trash Taste* talking about ghosts." She gave a slight chuckle.

"Sounds good."

Trash Taste was a podcast by three online content creators living in Japan. We had found the small discussion panel by way of a creator calling himself "Joey the Anime Man." The half-Japanese, half-Australian twenty-seven-year-old apparently got his start creating videos about Anime in the early 2010s. By the time Tara and I had started watching him, much of his content revolved around the adjuncts to

Anime and the subculture surrounding it. A fellow creator and staple member on the podcast was CDawgVA, A.K.A Conner. A Welshman, and quite likely the whitest man living in Japan, Conner appeared to make his mark by eating and drinking the contents of Japanese convenience stores and testing out cheap cosplay costumes. Nothing scars the mind quite like a pale Welshman wearing a knock-off Sailor Moon costume that is two sizes too small. The third of the trio, collectively calling themselves "the Boyz," Garnt was Thai by way of Britain and an ex-Buddhist monk. Of the three, he was the only creator whose content was still entrenched in Anime movies and TV series, and he always had Tara and me laughing our butts off on the *Trash Taste* podcasts. Especially when his very proper English accent performed sponsor advertisements ranting about "Ball Wash" and manhood grooming appliances.

Tara and I settled in, letting the Boyz take our minds off the thoughts and images of death and murder. Laughter is the best defense against the horrors of the world.

It was midnight when we pulled into the Cosmopolitan valet. I had made arrangements with Stephanie Gonzalez to pick me up at the ungodly hour of 9am, well before my usual business hour of noon. I have never been a morning person.

One of our favorite rooms, the Terrace Studio was designed to be walked from the door to the balcony in a straight line. Entering the room, a doorway to the right led into a large bathroom, a full-length mirror embedded in a sliding restroom door. An L-shaped, plush purple-grey couch pointed guests toward a flat-screen television mounted to the left wall, and two trendy cylindrical coffee tables sat in the middle of the seating arrangement. A sensual picture of a half-naked woman looking over her shoulder was painted on the wall behind the comfortable seating.

Situated in an alcove next to the TV, a marble-topped dark wood cabinet housed the mini-bar, mini-fridge, and some extra drawers. Five small circular pictures were arranged on the wall of the recessed snack area. Four of the pictures held with the sensual, almost erotic, nature of the wall-sized painting behind the couch. Two of the photographs were artistic shots of a woman's breasts, one of a man's naked chest. The last of the four was the face of a woman who looked like she was either Siouxsie Sioux, lead singer of the early gothic rock band Siouxsie and the Banshees, or, as Tara interpreted the picture, Tim Curry's rendition of Frank N. Furter from *The Rocky Horror Picture Show*. The fifth photo, centered among the others, looked like a still shot from a shampoo commercial. If said commercial was for dogs. A white, elegant canine with flowing auburn hair, its eyes closed and wearing what appeared to be a twice-wrapped pearl necklace and S&M collar with multiple O-rings. I figured the collection of pictures were intended to appeal to all sexual orientations, furries included.

A half-wall with integrated desktop separated the seating area from the fluffy, white-topped king-sized bed. Tara and I stowed our luggage in a closet situated across from the bed. Another flat-screen TV was wall-mounted to the left of the closet. While we probably wouldn't have time for much television, our habit was to watch *Forensic Files* when staying in Vegas. It was the only show in town that appeared to be on 24-7, and our visits never felt complete without seeing at least ten episodes. At this point I think we've seen the entire series at least five times. The room terminated at a sliding glass door that led to the balcony. A small, two-person wicker couch and a single-person wicker chair were backed up to the window, providing a private outdoor seating area.

Stepping onto the balcony of our 23rd-floor room, Tara and I looked across the neighboring Bellagio Resort to the glittering lights of the Las Vegas Strip. The Bellagio's famous fountain show was done for the night. It was one of the few things in Vegas that had start and stop times. At this height there was almost always wind. Tonight it was a soft, warm breeze. Tara's hair gently swayed with the light air current as she took in the view.

As she turned from the Strip, I wrapped my arms around her, kissed her neck. Smiling, she held my chin, pulling my lips into hers. I briefly forgot why we had come to Las Vegas. In Tara's own mystical way, she managed to go from passionate to business in the blink of an eye.

"I get the feeling we're going to need on-site tech support," she said. "I've already messaged Brianna Smith through the DA site."

"Considering she's impossible to track, never stays in one place more than three days," I pulled back to look into Tara's deep blue eyes, "and she makes paranoid schizophrenics look downright rational, do you really think she'll be willing to come here?"

"It's already arranged." Tara gave a mischievous smile. "Turns out she's in Vegas."

"Is she sure 'they' aren't here?"

"Whoever 'they' are, she's pretty confident it's all good."

"Cool," I sighed. "It'll be nice to finally meet the tech wiz who provided us with cyber-security the NSA would be jealous of."

Tara nodded, then looked back to the glittering lights of Las Vegas. She pulled her shoulders up, stretched, yawned, and moved toward the balcony door.

"Come on. I hear the Sandman calling."

"I'm not feeling all that tired yet," I said.

Tara drew in next to me, drawing my ear to her lips. "Come inside and I'll help you with that."

Chapter 6

The Boy had managed to nap without a visit from the Dark Man.
The nap had lasted longer than he intended, but by Vegas standards the
night was still young. The pulsating signage of casinos and LED
advertisement screens turned night into day. Even in the midnight hour
on a weekday, Las Vegas Boulevard had tourists rushing about in
various stages of inebriation, and a diverse array of obnoxiousness.

"Too many people," the Boy muttered as he scanned the sidewalk
for a suitable toy.

His mood soured, seeing no easy way to grab someone from the
throngs of drunkards, Bros, Woo-girls, and card-slappers. Two feather-
tailed, scantily clad showgirls walked past him. Their thonged butts
swayed in an accentuated runway walk designed to get men to stop,
stare, and give a crotch salute. An anonymous individual clad in a purple
dinosaur costume stumbled down the sidewalk. A drunk Barney the
Dinosaur for all the kids to be horrified by. Following the weaving plush
sauropod, a green-haired and purple-suited, heroin-chic rendition of
Batman's arch-nemesis, the Joker, periodically stopped, offering magic
tricks to the crowd. The Boy felt his stomach turning. He wanted to kill
them all. He wanted the streets to overflow with the blood of these
pedantic, useless, infantile wastes of oxygen.

Stopping at the corner of Flamingo Road, his gaze moved across the
street to the Bellagio Resort. The impressive Italian-inspired hotel
seemed to stand in judgment of him. He thought he could feel eyes
peering directly at him from every window. A shiver ran through his
entire body. The sound of roaring engines filled his ears as a rainbow of
Lamborghinis cruised down the Vegas Strip, followed by a cavalcade of
ridiculously lifted pickup trucks, most with multi-colored lights
illuminating their undersides. Shaking his head, movement in the crowd
caught his attention.

A slim figure in a dirty hoodie quickly turned to inspect a tree as
soon as the Boy's eyes passed over him. It seemed he wouldn't need to
grab someone after all. A twisted smile slowly formed on his face, then
contorted into a sneer. The audacity of this guy to think that he, a god-

in-waiting, was an easy victim made his blood boil. Running his hand though his dirty blond hair, a plan formed in his mind.

Turning away from Las Vegas Boulevard, the Boy moved to the east of the Strip. Leisurely strolling down Flamingo Road, he periodically glanced back to make sure his pursuer hadn't lost interest. Crossing onto a side road that ran behind the Cromwell Hotel, he walked into the low light of hotel service roads. The green-eyed killer turned down a delivery driveway and walked just far enough to be out of sight.

The hoodie-clad man followed his prey around the dark corner and stopped abruptly. Standing silently in the dim light, the neatly dressed Boy now made the man nervous. An underlying threat the man had not noticed in the pursuit of his intended victim. His instincts told him to run. He produced an eight-inch folding knife and flicked it open, ignoring his instincts.

"Wallet and phone," the man demanded. "Now."

The Boy didn't move. He felt this whole confrontation was a bit anticlimactic and using his abilities would be a waste of energy. He also had no car to transport pieces of the mugger's body once he was done. It was an oversight he cursed himself for. Next time he would have to make sure to keep his impulsive choices in line with some tactical thinking. He could tell the thief was nervous, the blade of the man's knife was unsteady.

"I said—" the hooded figure began.

"Yeah, yeah. I heard you the first time. Have you ever done this before?"

"What did you say, you little shit?" The mugger advanced on his target, stopping just out of reach. "I've killed men for less."

The Boy let out a sarcastic, snorting laugh. He couldn't tell if his mugger was full of false bravado or drug-induced confidence. He figured it was both. Footsteps caused the thief to pause, look over his shoulder. Walking on the dimly lit street connected to the delivery drive, the Boy recognized Junkie-Joker, who had been offering magic tricks on the Strip. His green pompadour bounced with each step. The Batman villain glanced toward them, chuffed, and kept walking. Clearly, he had no interest in getting involved. The blond-haired killer let out a sigh of relief. He didn't want any interruptions, and he didn't want to deal with any well-meaning "saviors." The fact that someone had seen the two of them made the mugger impatient.

"Wallet and phone," the man repeated, impatience and nervousness turned to clenched jawed hostility. "Or I take them off your fucking corpse."

"Fine." Exasperation filled the Boy's words. He reached into his back pocket and withdrew a black steel cylinder. Clutching the piece of metal, the Boy swung a wide arc in the thief's direction.

As he swung the collapsible baton, two nested steel bars extended, covering the gap between his fist and the thief. The end of the weapon caught the mugger on his jaw. A spray of blood and teeth arced with the turn of his head, painting the dark delivery driveway in spatter. His would-be assailant slumped to the ground, screaming in pain. The metallic clink of a knife hitting concrete signaled his disarmament.

"My teeth," the thief gurgled out. "You knocked out my teeth, you fucking—"

The Boy brought the baton down on the prone man's left knee. A mixture of rage and sadistic glee inscribed into his face as the crack of breaking bone echoed through the darkness. The thief cried out. The Boy giggled. Taking hold of his hood, the Boy sharply yanked the man's head up.

"You should've been a little more discerning with your choice of victim," his voice an eerie calm. "To prey on a God is to become prey."

"Wha—What are you talking about?" Bloody spit flew from the man's mouth as he gurgled the words. How had his judgment of this Boy been so wrong? He had thought the Boy would be an easy mark. He thought the Boy would piss his pants and beg for his life.

"You should be happy," the Boy said gleefully. "You have the privilege of being sent to the afterlife by God himself!"

Before the man could reply, the Boy released his grip on the hood and brought his foot down on the man's face. Torquing the helpless thief's jaw off-angle, he took a deep breath, slowly bearing down on the man's covered head. The sound of ripping flesh and cracking bone was a symphony to him. A shudder of pleasure ran through the Boy as he felt the thief's jaw rip from the man's head.

83

Blood spread through the hood, the dirty fabric soaking in the crimson liquid. The mugger's body convulsed. He looked down at the dying creature and suddenly found himself disgusted. Noticing blood spatter on his clothing, the Boy flew into a rage. Drawing his foot back, he let loose a barrage of kicks upon the shaking, crumpled form.

"This," he kicked, "is why," he stomped down on the dying man's ribcage, "I don't," switching feet, he nailed a headshot, "do close-quarter work."

The Boy stopped his assault, panting. His shoes and the cuffs of his pants were now a nebula of red stains. He screamed at the still, fetal form on the ground. Bending over with his hands on his knees, the Boy tried to slow his breath.

"Second time tonight," he muttered. "Second time I need a change of fucking clothes."

Senses coming back to him, he scanned his surroundings. No one was in sight. The overwhelming sound of the Las Vegas Strip hid the altercation from prying ears.

"Guess I'm gonna have to take the long way back."

Stepping over the lifeless body of his would-be mugger, the Boy headed back to his hotel. He hadn't received the catharsis he had hoped for, hadn't had the opportunity to exercise his power. He decided he would visit Sonja's resting place in the morning; perhaps epiphany would come to him there.

Remembrance flashed green fire in the Boy's eyes, having been forced to change his graveyard since some pretender had turned the Valley of Fire location into an art installation. A false god creating grave markers with random women unworthy of such veneration. The thought of someone trying to recreate his power, trying to replace him with such imperfection, made him furious. He would find the pretender, and their screams would be the stuff of legend.

Raven stood between the light, watching Rachel's mother. The haggard woman sat at the kitchen's island counter mumbling, head bowed down and a large knife gripped in her hand. Moving closer,

Raven realized that she was praying. Lifting her head, the woman's dark brown, unfocused eyes stared into an unseen void as she completed her prayer. Tear-stained cheeks quivered as a sob wracked her body, a momentary convulsion as she tried to steady her breathing.

"I'm sorry, baby," the woman croaked. Raven felt a spike of anxiety at those words. She had seen variations of this scene play out before.

Rachel's mother drew in a sharp breath, turned the knife upward in a two-handed grip. Closing her eyes, the broken woman brought her body weight down on the knife. Her head bounced off the countertop. Her body settled. Her head lolled side to side. She was still.

Her eyes snapped open to the sound of aggravated tapping.

Lifting herself off the counter, her dark brown eyes looked at her bloodless, knifeless hands. Tracking the sound, the woman let out a stifled cry. She stumbled back into the opposing kitchen counter.

The woman was presented with an angry looking goth, one hand on her hip, the other forcefully tapping the flat of the kitchen knife against her thigh. Purple Bettie Page-style bangs swayed above the kind of scowl mothers reserve for children whose stupidity scares the shit out of them. Rachel's mom was frozen, suddenly feeling like a child waiting for punishment.

"What did he promise you?" Raven's question came out as a whisper, voice quivering with anger.

"What?" the woman said weakly, her wide-eyed stare that of a deer caught in a car's headlights.

"What did that fuck promise you?" The words exploded out of Raven. "What could he possibly give you for killing your own child?"

Rachel's mother convulsed in a wrenching sob. Falling forward, she grabbed the island counter, her arms shaking uncontrollably as tears streamed unabated.

"He said I could end her suffering." Her voice was rough, infused with guilt. "He said she would go to a better place."

Raven would have doubted the sobbing mess, accused her of acting in selfishness, were it not for her attempt at suicide. She didn't need extra-human abilities to recognize soul-crushing guilt.

"I tried, you know," the woman said. "Fifty-eight times I tried to poison her food. Lethal doses of everything. She refused to die. But

85

tonight—" Her words were interrupted by another wave of sobs. "I forced her. I forced my baby to eat rat poison and bleach." Her tired face contorted into one of self-loathing.

Raven stood still, listening to the confession. Her feelings toward the woman were torn. She wanted to hate her, she wanted to divest her of humanity. Raven wanted that righteous anger that gave her the authorization to kill. But her heartfelt sympathy toward her, a woman pushed to the brink of insanity. Unable to understand that her love for Rachel was enough. A woman whose will had eroded into a weakness the Dark Man had exploited.

"Her suffering is over," the woman said, "and I don't deserve to live for what I done." A pleading emerged in her wide brown eyes. "Kill me. Please, end it."

"Oh, Mama," a hoarse voice carried into the kitchen. "You were the one suffering, not me."

Raven stepped aside as Rachel walked into the kitchen. Gone were all physical impediments, her atrophied limbs now toned and full. She smiled at her mother, a genuine smile filled with affection and love.

"Wha— How?" Rachel's mother sputtered, awe in her voice as the sobs began again. Arms failing her, Rachel moved as lightning, catching her mother. She pulled her into a tight embrace.

"It's me, Mama."

The bawling woman clutched her daughter. Raven watched as Rachel softly whispered affirmations to her mother, her mother responding with a muffled string of apologies and "I love yous." Curiosity gripping her, Raven changed her sight to look within. Something was different about Rachel's soul, an intensity to the bright light Raven initially didn't understand. Then she saw it.

Those fifty-nine voids in the mother's dying soul began to shrink. Awe overtook Raven, the extent of Rachel's ability surpassing all expectations. The capacity to heal was clearly Rachel's gift, but it never occurred to Raven that her ability could extend to the healing of another's soul. As the last of the cancerous voids disappeared, Raven felt a profound sense of hope.

A sorrowful smile crossed Rachel's face. She whispered, "I love you, Mama. Find happiness, find joy."

Her mother looked at her, a question she didn't want to ask written in her eyes.

"I have to go, Mama." Rachel's smile faltered. "I have always loved you."

Rachel's mother opened her mouth, but unconsciousness overtook the apprehensive woman before she could speak. Keeping hold of her sleeping mother, Rachel picked her up, cradling her. Raven followed as Rachel walked out of the kitchen and into the living room.

Gingerly laying her mother on the brown, plush sofa, she grabbed a blue knitted blanket off a chair. She draped the blue wool over the sleeping woman and stared at her face. Leaning over, Rachel kissed her mother's cheek. Raven stood as witness to this farewell.

"I've replaced the past three years of her memory," Rachel said. "She won't remember what she had done in her desperation."

"I see," Raven responded.

"In the morning she will believe I had died in my sleep years ago, and she has been in mourning all this time." A melancholic smile crossed Rachel's face as she looked to Raven. "She will believe that her daughter's spirit visited her tonight, granting her peace and the strength to move forward."

"I wish there was another way," Raven began.

"I'm sure you always do. This is best." Rachel looked at her sleeping mother one last time. She drew in a deep breath.

"Okay," she said. "I'm ready to go."

Chapter 7

Nothing gets the adrenaline pumping quite like rapid pounding on your hotel door at 5am. The booming sound had me up and out of bed at inhuman speed. I looked over my shoulder at the sound of a yelp to see Tara sitting bolt upright, her eyes wide.

"What the hell?" she blurted out.

"I'll take care of this," I grumbled. Buck naked and annoyed, I stomped toward the door. "Someone better be dead," I said loudly.

"Three someones, actually," Stephanie's muffled voice penetrated the door. Stopping at the closed portal, I let out an exasperated sigh.

"Give me a minute."

Throwing on my clothes, I looked to Tara. If looks could kill, the scowl on her face could have taken out a small village. I gave her a kiss on her forehead.

"I'm sorry, honey." I felt guilty for having her sleep so rudely interrupted. "Hopefully you'll be able to get back to sleep."

She gave a derisive snort. "Yeah, like that's gonna happen."

A sympathetic sigh escaped me. I kissed her goodbye and moved toward the door. This was not how I wanted to start our first day in Vegas. Opening the hotel room door, I was greeted with a cup of coffee shoved in my face. Styrofoam container in hand, I took in a deep breath of the brew. I looked up at the purveyor of ambrosia.

Stephanie Gonzalez was the world's largest leprechaun. Standing six feet, three inches, her skin was smooth and pale, creating a stark contrast to the dark sleep circles around her bright hazel eyes. Her naturally frizzy, long orange-red hair was pulled into a hasty ponytail. She had a fighter's build: broad shoulders and veritable tree trunks for arms. Looking at her, it came as no surprise when I learned she had done six tours in the Middle East with the Marine Corps. Stephanie's face was one that normally spoke of good humor. Today she looked like a train ran over her.

"Jonathan, this is FBI Special Agent Brock Allen." Stephanie gestured to a black-haired megalith of a man towering behind her. Despite being a good six feet tall, I felt really short.

Special Agent Allen stood an imposing six feet, seven inches, and wore a custom-tailored black suit. Stephanie had mentioned he was Native American, though she failed to include the tribe from which he hailed. It really didn't matter, but I was curious as hell as to how he wound up with such an Anglicized name.

I estimated the towering man to be in his early fifties. Subtle crow's feet at the edges of his dark brown eyes indicated a smile was his most common expression, though his deep frown lines disagreed with that assessment. A white scar horizontally stretching from the bridge of his nose, under his right eyelid, and terminating at his ear stood in stark contrast to his deeply tanned complexion. The bottom of his left ear was covered in what appeared to be scar tissue from a burn. Being shorter than the G-Man, I could see the burn scar extended onto his neck, but I could not tell how far down the damage went.

"Ah, the famous Agent Allen," I said, extending my hand. He looked at it, not moving. I lifted an eyebrow, questioning.

"You get a handshake when you've earned it." The low, rough sound of the agent's voice took me aback. I could have sworn the man had a built-in subwoofer.

"Okay then." I lowered my arm as he turned and walked down the hall.

"Don't take it personally," Stephanie advised. "He gave me the same treatment for six months after I joined the Bureau."

"With that attitude he's going to have to earn my respect," I muttered, following the two giants toward the elevators.

The stereotypical black Escalade was parked at the end of the Cosmopolitan's passenger drop-off area. Agent Allen half turned his head toward me as I reached the vehicle.

"You're in the back," he said.

I climbed into the back seat of the vehicle, muttering under my breath. The adrenaline hit that had brought me to full waking focus less than half an hour ago had worn off; grumpiness was all that remained. Agent Allen pulled two laminated ID badges from his coat's inside pocket. He handed one to Stephanie and passed one over his shoulder to me. From my back seat vantage point I could see the extent of the burn I noticed earlier. Mottled red and white scar tissue covered the entire back of his neck and into his scalp. It almost appeared to have the shape of a hand. Speculation on the events he had been through to receive such an injury raced through my mind. The agent's deep voice knocked me back into the present.

"As of now you're both official consultants for the Bureau," he said. "All I'll say is I'm glad to have one of you here."

"Okay," I began as he started the SUV. "So can we put the whole superiority complex aside and actually get some work done?"

In the rearview mirror I caught a flash of annoyance in Agent Brock Allen's glowering eyes. Stephanie tried to cover a laugh with a cough. The crotchety FBI agent let out a sigh.

"You're going to be a pain in my ass, aren't you?"

"That, my dear agent, is entirely up to you."

I had no desire to antagonize this man, who had clearly gone above and beyond for an old colleague, but I would assert my right to be shown basic human respect. Stephanie had spoken about the agent on multiple occasions, often referring to him as her mentor and as a top homicide investigator. I didn't see it. I took a swig of my coffee, the taste and feel of the warm liquid bringing me focus beyond the testosterone-laden tension in the car.

"So," Stephanie's voice filled the silence, "now that we have established absolutely nothing, shall we deal with something that matters?"

"Indeed," I said. "I really want to know what happened that required a 5am wake up." I took another swig. Agent Allen let out an exasperated sigh as he piloted the Escalade out of the Cosmopolitan's car park, turning us toward the western mountains.

"At 3:30am a park ranger discovered three bodies in Red Rock Canyon," Agent Allen began. "The bodies were—"

"Dismembered and their pieces attached to X-shaped crucifixes," I cut him off. Agent Allen again shot a glare through the rearview mirror. "Same as the three found in the Valley of Fire."

"Yes," Brock hissed. "Don't ever interrupt me again."

"What I don't quite get is how you got involved," Stephanie chimed in.

"I was contacted by detectives from both the San Diego and Los Angeles sheriff departments." His deep voice was oddly soothing as he spoke. "Between the two counties they had twelve dead. I have to hand it to those departments, they have a couple detectives who saw the potential for a larger kill zone relatively early and were able to connect with each other." He paused as we came to a stoplight. "They had hit a wall. The cause of death, methods of dismemberment, and the seemingly random disposal sites were leaving them a bit dumbfounded. They contacted the Bureau hoping to get a consult from the Behavioral Analysis Unit. The BAU declined the invite, but one of their agents recommended me."

"Why you?" I asked.

"I was part of the BAU."

"Yeah," Stephanie interjected, "for a week."

The driving behemoth shot her a disapproving glance. From my vantage point in the back seat, I could see the evil smile plastered across her face. Agent Allen gave a "Why me?" grunt.

"Anyway." With the exasperation in his voice, I was beginning to think the agent existed in a permanent state of annoyance. "I was between cases and my involvement was unofficial. The Bureau did not assign me to the case, but I was given clearance to take it as an expert consultant. I felt that this was an unsub I needed to find." He paused again. He seemed to be lost in memory.

"Why?" I asked.

"Don't know," Agent Allen stated bluntly. "Gut feeling, I guess. I just felt drawn. And after seeing the pictures of the victims…" He paused, trailing off for a moment. "While the method of dismemberment disturbs me, it's the apparent fixation on—"

"The women with the infinity tattoos," I completed his thought.

"Yes." He passed over my interruption. "To make matters worse, each woman with the infinity symbol was disabled in some way. Cerebral palsy, MS, severe sensory sensitivity, and a few that I can't pronounce."

"The why doesn't matter," Stephanie stated. I nodded in agreement.

"Well, you two are hired guns." The agent's flippant tone indicated he felt we weren't invested in the same way he was. Brock wasn't entirely wrong in that assessment. His involvement was one of honor. He lived to find justice for those who had been wronged. For us, this investigation began as a paycheck.

The moment I opened that folder, the moment I looked at the photos of the victims, I felt a duty to them. Money was what got me to take the case. It was those photographs, the afterimages of lives stolen, that made it personal. Tara always said I'm a softie at heart, and she's right. I've taken on cases pro bono just because a child's fear or an abused animal was involved. It did not take much for me to become emotionally involved.

"To be clear," I said, "being a hired gun doesn't make us any less invested."

"Damn skippy," Stephanie agreed as she gave Agent Allen a protracted cartoonish stare. "You know me. I do not walk in the company of Death so lightly."

"Ah, yes." The agent sounded uncomfortable, almost apologetic, toward my cohort. "I know. I meant no disrespect."

"The crucified women," I asked, "are they the work of the Hatchetman?"

"Two things," Agent Allen said, his tone even more irritated. "He's an unknown subject or an unsub. It's policy that we do NOT give these guys superhero names."

"Noted. And two?"

"The crucified women don't appear to follow our unsub's modus operandi," he stated, using the full words as if he thought I didn't understand what M.O. meant.

"An accomplice?" Stephanie suggested.

"Doubtful," the agent responded. "Our guy has never appeared to have a partner. The victims are local prostitutes, another deviation. Our unsub seems to be focused on getting to the women with the infinity tattoos. Most of the other victims can be traced to each of those women. Our crucifier doesn't appear to be dealing with that fixation."

"An admirer?" I asked.

"That," Agent Allen said, "is a possibility. And if that is the case, he knows who our unsub is."

"Where does that leave jurisdiction?" Stephanie asked.

"Because our unsub crossed state lines, I've been handed control of the case in an official capacity," Agent Allen stated. "This did not go over well with the detective initially called onto the Nevada leg of the case. One Detective Marcus Hanson."

Stephanie groaned. She had contacts all over the Las Vegas Police and Sheriff's Departments. She counted many of those officers as friends. This afforded her a wide range of knowledge and gossip. If she didn't know an officer, she likely knew of them.

"He could...be a problem," she stated.

"What's the deal with him?" I asked.

"He's a good ol' boy kind of cop, his mind stuck in the 1950s and his head lodged firmly up his own ass," she said. "I've had a few run-ins with the guy. He is racist, homophobic, sexist." I could hear aggravation rising in my friend's voice. "If there's something negative and it ends with '-ist,' that's him."

"Great." The word came out flat.

"Just be prepared for a verbal beating," Agent Allen said. "The guy screamed at me when I relegated him to the sidelines. He's not going to take kindly playing third fiddle to a couple private dicks with special privileges."

I cocked an eyebrow. If Special Agent Brock Allen, a man who appeared to resent my presence on this case entirely, was telling me this Detective Hanson would be resentful, this could not be good.

Chapter 8

Warm wind whipped through Red Rock Canyon, the early morning light dancing across the mountain tops. At one of many lookouts around the canyon, the Boy stood, his hands resting on a low rock wall. He was hoping to be alone at this time of day. He wasn't. Five leather-clad bikers taking a scenic ride stood twenty feet away from him. Everyone's attention was focused on the same point.

One hundred yards away, people dressed head to toe in white were erecting a large sheet: a privacy screen to shield the public from a gruesome scene. Three large wooden Xs stood facing the lookout. From this distance the dismembered bodies attached to the structures appeared to be little more than mannequins. The Boy knew better, and he struggled to keep his seething rage contained within.

The false god. The false god had done this. Beyond the sheer gall of the copycat's attempt to emulate his power, the Boy was incensed by the imperfection of the crucifix arrangement. It was uneven. The bodies were distributed in a haphazard manner. The first two women appeared to be thin, but the third was overweight. She should be between the two thin girls. The crucifix on the left side was closer to the center than the crucifix on the right. Each of the displays were slightly off-angle, not in a uniform line. Symmetry was one of the hallmarks of perfection. This display was from an imperfect mind. The Boy bit his lower lip, attempting to stem the rage that this imperfection evoked.

"Fuck," he muttered. "Fuck, fuck, fuck." His angry exclamations caught the attention of the bikers.

"You okay, man?" a portly biker with a beard reaching down to the top of his gut asked. He made his way over to the Boy.

"I'm fine." The Boy tried to sound cheerful. "I just forgot to feed my cat."

The man nodded, a skeptical expression crossed his face. The Boy stood straight, his arms at his sides, fists balled tight. He wanted to kill this man, rip off his face and wear it like a Halloween mask.

"Any idea what's going on?" the bearded man asked. His voice sounded like he ate gravel for breakfast.

"Some weird art installation, I guess." The Boy shrugged.

The man nodded thoughtfully, turned, and pointed toward the activity.

"Doesn't really explain the cops though."

The Boy hadn't even noticed four police cruisers sitting fifty feet away from his dump site. He didn't need to have seen them to know all the activity was law enforcement. He let out an exasperated sigh. Despite his growing anger, he did his best to remain amenable.

"No clue," he said. "I mean no offense to you, sir, but I would like to be alone."

The biker gave him a warm smile, nodded, and turned back to his comrades.

"I hear ya. Whatever's going on, I hope it gets better."

In the briefest moment of human connection, the Boy felt his rage lift at the man's kindness. The macabre scene in the distance obliterated the moment from his mind.

High winds making the erection of law enforcement's privacy screen a struggle, the Boy spotted the two graves he had dug being excavated. He let out a defeated sigh, expelling his building anger.

"Oh well," he quietly said to himself, "I'm not going to need any more graves when I ascend."

The overwhelming rumble of a truck entering the parking lot caught the Boy's attention. The obnoxious pickup came to a screeching halt facing the desert beyond the outlook.

Modified to the point of looking ridiculous, the chassis of the Dodge Ram was lifted six feet off the ground. Trying to see the driver, the Boy's eyes could not pierce through any of the heavily tinted windows. Something about the truck set the Boy on edge. He couldn't quite put his finger on it.

A glint of reflected light shone through the windshield as someone moved in the cab. Crossing the front of the truck, the Boy was able to make out binoculars pointed toward the police activity. As he moved to the driver's side of the ridiculous mechanical behemoth, the Boy saw the binoculars shoot down. He caught sight of dyed green hair as the driver noticed him. The truck roared to life. Tires screamed as the vehicle listed to one side in a tight turn toward the parking lot exit.

His gaze registered a bumper sticker he recognized, asking the question: "If guns are outlawed, can we use swords?" The green hair, the ridiculous truck. He stopped in revelation.

"That fucker's been following me."

He ran to his rented silver SUV. In a single fluid motion, the Boy was in the car, had it started, in gear, and in pursuit before the car door closed. Adrenaline pumped through him, excitement at the prospect of the chase…and the kill.

Tearing out of the lot, turning wide and crossing into oncoming traffic, the Boy swerved hard to avoid a black Escalade. Momentarily fishtailing, he brought his vehicle under control and hit the gas, reaching a pursuit speed that could have been interpreted as suicidal.

Comforting rage took hold of him. He had some questions for the driver of the truck, and a pound of flesh to take.

Raven stood on the side of the road, the warm wind whipping her black and purple hair in a frenzy. Her attention was momentarily distracted by two lunatic drivers tearing out of the observation point's parking lot. She shook her head in disapproval, returning her gaze to the police activity in the distance. The gothy girl would have preferred to observe from the designated viewing area. The small number of people there quashed that desire. She did not want to be in the presence of strangers. This was a solemn viewing, not to be shared with entities unknown.

Her keen eyes instantly recognized that the crucified, dismembered corpses were none of her people. The archeological-style dig around the two graves, however… She was certain one of those was Sonja. Whoever her killer was, he had either developed an artistic streak or there was a copycat on the loose. And that copycat knew who her target was.

Raven's attention shifted to a black SUV parking alongside two police cruisers near the crime scene. From the driver's side, a giant stepped out of the vehicle. His suit and aviator sunglasses marked his association better than a twenty-foot sign could have.

"FBI," she said to herself. "He looks familiar." She couldn't place the agent, but felt like she had crossed paths with him.

Emerging into view from the passenger side of the vehicle, a tall linebacker of a woman with a red ponytail emerged. In a short sleeve, dark grey button-down shirt, black jeans, and combat boots, the imposing figure was an enigma. She only knew that the tall redhead wasn't FBI. Exiting the rear driver side, a man clad in all black hit the ground. He took a moment to don a black leather trench coat before closing the door. Raven wondered how the man could wear such a garment in the Las Vegas summer heat. As the three conferred, she found their power dynamic to be inscrutable. The FBI agent clearly thought he was in charge, the man in black obviously disagreed, and the red-haired woman appeared torn between them.

Raven shifted her sight to look within. Though the distance was too great to see details, she could get a sense of the trio's souls. The taller two shone as bright humanoid silhouettes of white light. The man in black gave her pause.

A white line encased the soul of the trench coat wearing man, an afterimage of his form extending beyond the limits of his body. Raven had seen it once before. It was a kind of spirit shield, a rare attribute of a soul that had trained in what laymen would call magic. Useful for those who dealt with the non-corporeal, worthless in the physical realm.

She turned her gaze to the bikers on the outlook. Four of them appeared as human-shaped bright lights. Her eyes darkened seeing the fifth biker, a black void in place of a soul.

"You boys better watch out for that one," she said softly. "Nothing good will come of him."

She let out a sigh, returned her sight to normal. Closing her eyes, Raven lifted her head toward the sky. Hair jostling in the wind, a serene smile formed on her face. It was a rare experience of existing in just that moment. Opening her eyes, Raven studied the blue sky. A wispy cloud here and there gave a visual break to the blanket of blue. Another sigh escaped her as she turned away from the scenes of beauty and death. There was work to do. There was a killer to catch.

Chapter 9

I always liked a nice breeze. A light tossing of the hair, the soft caress of air on the skin. This was not a light breeze. My coat whipped around like the cape of a superhero, what hair I had felt as if the atmosphere was trying to pull it all out, and I was forced to lean into the hot gale to remain upright. With a temperature that had already topped 90 degrees, I reevaluated the wisdom of wearing full body leather. I opted to put the trench coat next to my hat in the SUV. No sense in getting heat stroke at my first murder scene.

The crime scene was a mess. Police tape was shredded by the winds, the privacy screen wouldn't stay put, and dirt blew everywhere. Agent Allen flashed his badge to a profusely sweating Clark County sherrif's deputy as we approached the police line, indicated Stephanie and I were with him. The young deputy gave a nod.

"Is Detective Hanson here yet?" Agent Allen asked the deputy. The officer snorted.

"He's not coming," the deputy responded flatly. "Please excuse my relaying this word for word. The detective said, and I quote, 'Let me know when that redskin Fed figures out the hookers are my case.'" A look of extreme discomfort overtook the deputy's face, clearly reiterating the racial slur did not sit well with him.

Agent Allen sighed. "At least that means we won't have to deal with him."

I had run across some bad cops in my career. Some had anger issues, some had drug issues, some soaked in alcohol, and some had problems understanding where the line between law abiding and criminal sat. It was the racist cops I had the most problem with. The ones that couldn't comprehend the simple notion that ethnicity isn't a personality trait.

"How is that douche still on the force?" I asked.

Agent Allen looked over to me. "Someone is protecting him."

"Who?"

The agent was about to answer my question when another gale-force gust of wind ripped through the crime scene, a blast of dust hitting everyone in the face.

"So much for footprints," I said.

"Maybe our killer is four hundred pounds," Stephanie postulated. "At least they'd have left a lasting print that way."

The crucifixes coming into view were larger than they seemed from a distance. Standing about nine feet tall, what appeared to be randomly bound wooden trunks were not so random. These had been constructed off-site, and not simply bound together. Large bolts and metal struts secured the structures against the wind.

Something about the bodies looked strange to me. Affixed to the large Xs with duct tape, the dismembered pieces looked as though they were made of plastic. As I stood before one of the victims, various scenarios ran through my mind. She was a pretty twenty-one or twenty-two-year-old blonde with a bob haircut. It appeared that her make up had been refreshed before the pieces of her thin body were attached to the wooden X. However, the dust kicked up by the unrelenting wind had dulled her glossy, bubblegum-pink lipstick. As my gaze met the lifeless grey eyes of the girl, a cold chill ran down my spine. Something about the stare of this corpse filled me with fear and dread. Thankfully, hiding my emotional state was one of my talents.

"So, Mister Private Detective." Agent Allen's deriding voice cut through the wind. "What do you see?"

I turned toward the FBI agent, eyebrow raised and ready to express displeasure with his attitude. Something in the distance caught my eye.

"I see someone who's about to get themselves into a world of trouble."

A momentary look of confusion crossed his face. He followed my gaze. Just past the parked vehicles, a woman dressed in a dark blue windbreaker walked confidently down the dusty access road. To combat the wind, her hand gripped the brim of a hat, pulling it low and obscuring her face. The initials FBI printed in bold yellow on the face of the headwear was in clear view.

Over the periodic howling of the wind, I heard Stephanie quickly approaching us.

"Were you expecting backup?"

"No." Agent Allen's voice and face might have indicated annoyance. At this point I couldn't be sure, annoyance seemed to be his default state of existence.

"Well, someone thinks you need it," Stephanie blurted out.

The towering man gripped the bridge of his nose, scrunched his eyes, and let out an audible moan. He said something unintelligible.

"You two stay here," he barked. The agent began walking toward the approaching woman. I caught up to him, trying to match his long stride.

"Like hell." I really didn't like taking orders from this guy. "You seem to have it in your head that I need to earn some basic respect." We passed the deputy standing guard at the police line. "How about I deal with this woman, and you keep your mouth shut."

Agent Allen stopped. His face was inscrutable yet oddly calm. I couldn't tell if he was going to punch me or hug me. Cocking his head to the side, an unnerving smirk rose at the corner of his mouth. His massive arm lifted, and I mentally prepared for a damaging impact. To my shock, he smacked me on the back and let out a laugh. Somehow, I didn't stumble from the impact.

"I like you," he said. My eyebrow raised in reflexive doubt. "Okay, if you want to show me what you've got, then you're on." We walked past the parked vehicles and stopped.

The woman couldn't have been much more than twenty-one or twenty-two. Standing around five feet, five inches, the windbreaker added some bulk to her slight build. Pale skin, hazel eyes, and blonde hair escaping her headgear, she stopped about five feet from us. She held up a badge that hung by a chain around her neck.

"Special Agent—" she began. I held up a hand to cut her off.

"Don't," I said. "If you finish that sentence, this man," I gestured to Agent Allen, "will arrest you for impersonating a law enforcement officer."

"Why would you think—" Feigned offense resounded in her words. Agent Allen looked expectantly at me. I sighed, incredulity creeping into my face.

"Your hat and jacket were purchased from a gift shop on Freemont Street," I stated. "You have no firearm, at least not one anywhere

Bureau protocols allow. You're wearing designer jeans and Doc-fucking-Martins."

The woman's confidence crumbled before my eyes. Her face and body language became that of a scared little girl.

"And to top it all off, your badge is a spray-painted LAPD replica. It's almost as if you wanted to be caught."

"But I can help you," the woman pleaded, stifling a sob. "I have—"

"What is your name?" My voice softened. I wanted to impress that she wasn't fooling anyone, not make the poor thing cry.

"Mary," she said as she struggled to regain her composure. Pulling herself back into a posture of confidence, she removed the hat. A cascade of shoulder-length blonde hair whipped into the wind and around her face.

"Mary what?" Agent Allen's deep voice broke in.

"Mary Thompson." She locked eyes with the agent. "And I have information that can help you."

"Call the FBI tip line and report it there." The words came out harshly. He let out a small sigh, softening his tone. "You don't want to be involved here. There are sights beyond these cars you don't want to see."

"Go home, Mary," I told her. "Pass along your information and spare yourself."

Agent Allen and I began to walk back toward the crime scene, but three words stopped us in our tracks.

"They're not tattoos," Mary yelled out.

I looked at the towering agent. "Was that ever—"

"No," he said. "That was a detail we never released."

We turned in unison to look at Mary.

"There's more," she said, "but you need to bring me in on this."

Once again, Agent Allen had the bridge of his nose held tight. I was fairly sure he was weighing his options. With his unreadable face, however, he could have just been deciding what to have for dinner. With dramatic flair, he swung his hand down, grabbed the key fob for the Escalade. An explosive sigh escaped him. He looked at me. I nodded, hoping I had properly read his decision.

"I'm going to get fired for this," he said with resignation, "or reassigned to the ass-end of Alaska."

Agent Allen motioned for Mary to follow us as we made our way over to the Escalade. Opening the rear passenger door, he held a hand toward the confused woman.

"Your hat, jacket, and that insult you tried to pass off as a badge."

She handed the items over to him. Unceremoniously tossing the items in the SUV, Agent Allen turned to me and slammed the door. He poked a massive finger into my chest.

"She's your responsibility," he bluntly stated. "She fucks up and I'm taking it out on you." The giant started walking back to the action. "Come on, you two."

I turned to Mary, giving her a smile.

"I'm Private Investigator Jonathan Hayes, that walking wall is Special Agent Brock Allen," I introduced. "I really hope you haven't eaten yet."

For seven hours crime scene techs scoured the grisly locale for evidence. The two graves had been painstakingly excavated in defiance of the wind. It was almost 2pm when the Clark County coroner carefully cut down the three dismembered victims and placed their pieces in body bags.

Something about the twisted display didn't sit right with me, and not just the fact that I had been staring at disarticulated corpses for a few hours. As I sat under a sun shelter that had wisely been erected after two hours of everyone being exposed to the bright sun, Stephanie and Mary walked up. Stephanie poked my furrowed brow.

"You're gonna get old man lines doing that," she stated. My eyebrow popped up. I stuck my tongue out at her.

"I was just trying to resolve some questions in my head."

"Like," Mary piped up, "why none of the dismembered bodies appear to have any visible evidence of insect activity?"

Stephanie and I both looked at her. When Mary had first caught sight of the three crucified corpses, she ran to the nearest bush and promptly threw up. Now she was examining the dead as though she'd done it all her life. My eyes narrowed at the behavioral inconsistency.

"What?" Mary said. "I watch a lot of crime shows."

I reluctantly took her answer.

"I'm way out of practice," Stephanie said. "I hadn't even noticed that."

"Do we know if the previous crucified and buried bodies have been autopsied yet?" I had heard nothing about a coroner's report on the previous Nevada victims.

"Brock said the coroner's office is a bit backed up," Stephanie replied. "Supposedly they're scheduled to do it today or tomorrow. I wouldn't hold my breath though."

"So, is this normal for you two?" Mary blurted out. "Like, does your job have you constantly looking at dead bodies and trying to find killers?"

I chuckled, shaking my head. Stephanie groaned at the memory of her former career in the Bureau.

"Not for me," I said. "More often than not I'm looking for a lost child, a lost cat, or trying to convince a poltergeist to vacate someone's home."

"I'm sorry," Mary said. "People pay you to get rid of poltergeists?"

"Yup. Though if it's a family in clear need, I'll happily waive my fee."

"And you believe in those things?"

"When a kitchen table spontaneously flies through the air aiming to take your head off, it's really hard not to believe." I folded my hands behind my head. "But it's not my job to convince people. Clients in those situations seek me out."

"So it's like that *Ghost Hunters* show?"

I let out an audible laugh; Stephanie shot me a disapproving glare.

"No," I said, "I get called in once a group like the ghost hunters determine those weird sounds in the middle of the night aren't just a busted furnace or shitty plumbing. Though there have been more instances than I'd like where the paranormal investigation teams have missed the mark and I'm the one doing a home inspection."

"How do they miss something like that?" Mary asked.

I let out a sigh. "Many of these so-called Ghost Hunters have such a hard-on for proving spirits are real that they lose sight of investigative integrity. They assume a door opening or closing on its own is a sign of a ghost. They don't really bother to investigate odd noises and just jump to the paranormal as a conclusion." I thoughtlessly pulled a stick of cinnamon from my cigarette case as I spoke. "They put far too much trust in equipment like spirit boxes and EMF readers. There's no evidence that those items are detecting what ghost hunters think they are detecting. I once was a part of an investigation where the EMF detector was going off the charts. Turned out, the wiring for the entire house was unshielded and primed for fire. It was kind of a miracle the homeowners didn't electrocute themselves while making toast."

"High electro-magnetic fields can also result in feelings of being watched," Stephanie chimed in.

I gave her a questioning eyebrow.

"I do my research." She smirked.

I nodded sagely at this. "Very true." Holding the stick of spice between my fore and index finger like a cigarette, I continued, "As I said, some of these investigators walk into a situation with the idea that there is something paranormal involved. This creates false assessments, and then I get pulled in just to tell the poor people that the ghost hunting team they hired are a bunch of delusional ninnies." I let out an exasperated sigh. "Those kinds of investigators, and all the videos they post online, make presenting real, solid evidence difficult. But like I said, it's not my job to convince anyone. People either believe or they don't."

"I see." Skepticism dripped off Mary's words. Stephanie cleared her throat.

"I take on more Earthly work," Stephanie said. "Missing persons, financial impropriety, infidelity."

"I don't get how you can take those cheater jobs," I told her, my words slightly muffled from holding the cinnamon stick between my teeth. "Someone tells me they think their spouse is cheating, I just tell them to get a divorce. If their trust is already that broken, no point in wasting money on a PI."

"I never could figure out why people did that," Mary said. "Seems like a waste of money."

"Depends on the state," Stephanie informed the young woman. "In at-fault states, having proof of infidelity changes how much community property each spouse gets."

"Which is why it'd be pointless for me," I said. "California is a no-fault state."

"Oh please," Stephanie chastised. "You just don't like stakeouts."

Mary watched our back and forth like a dog watching a tennis match.

"Well, duh." I chuckled under my breath. "There's nothing more boring than staring at a window hoping to get a picture of some privileged douche schtupping the help."

Mary stifled a laugh. Stephanie gave me a sideways smile and shook her head. Our banter was interrupted by Agent Allen's booming voice.

"You three may want to see this." He was standing at the grave excavation site.

The first thing I noticed was the disparity in the victim burials. In one grave, body parts were tossed in like pieces of garbage. The other grave was reverent, almost ritualistic in presentation. A white sheet had been placed to ward off dirt, body parts arranged as though they were the pieces of a doll that could be put back together. I was about to ask a question when I saw the head of the cruelly cast away body.

"Oh no." I felt my heart sink. "Madame Toulah."

"You know her?" Agent Allen asked.

"Yes," I said solemnly. "She is— was part of DA's extended network."

"What did she do?" Mary asked, looking a little green.

"A psychic," I stated. "One of the best. In our vetting she had a ninety-eight percent success rate, and in practice she hit one hundred percent. Forty-seven missing persons found with her help."

"And she was a total sweetheart," Stephanie added, her voice tainted with sadness.

"This means that the other body is…" I took a deep breath, not wanting to look. I forced my eyes to the sheet and felt my throat catch.

"Fuck!" Rage, hot and barely contained, struggled to release itself. I wanted to hit someone. I let loose a short, incoherent, anger-riddled scream. Taking a breath, calming myself, I noticed all eyes had turned on me. Stephanie put her hand on my shoulder, a low growl shuddering through her.

"You done?" Agent Allen asked. "Mind filling me in here?"

"This is Sonja Verztuk, Madame Toulah's granddaughter." My voice shook as I sank to the ground. "She was wheelchair bound, I never had the courage to ask why. Sweet, soft spoken, but a strong will and smart."

Stephanie turned to Agent Allen. "We need to send a CSI team over to Madame Toulah's shop."

The large man nodded in agreement. "If this runs the same pattern as the others, that's probably where your psychic was killed." He paused.

"Check behind her left ear." The words came in stereo as Agent Allen and Mary uttered them in unison.

One of the white-clad techs checked Sonja's head.

"She has a tattoo." The tech's voice was muffled behind his mask. "It looks like an infinity symbol."

"Like I said before," Mary stated, "it's not a tattoo."

Chapter 10

The sun hung low in the sky as the Boy entered an unusually crowded Starbucks. His mind spun with loathsome revelation and great aggravation. Earlier in the day he had stayed his hand, something counterintuitive for him. Perfection requires follow-through. When the act of killing begins, it is imperfect to change course.

He had chased down the ridiculous-looking truck in Red Rock Canyon, catching up to the black monstrosity at 110mph. There was an intense rush of adrenaline when he reached his left arm out the window, flicked his wrist, and cut through the speeding truck's rear tire. A shower of rubber had exploded over the highway.

In what looked like a scene out of an action movie, the truck's bare rim hit the blacktop, letting sparks fly. Acting like a pivot, the spinning metal of the wheel mount caught on the asphalt and violently wrenched the truck 90 degrees to the left. Traction abandoned the foolishly modified Dodge. Inertia and gravity exacted their revenge for its hubris. The deafening screech of grinding steel, smash of shattering glass, and crunch of splintering plastic accompanied the first roll of the truck. Halfway through the second roll, a cloud of dust engulfed the vehicle as it left the blacktop.

Only able to see a moving wall of dust and smoke, the Boy could not tell how many times the truck had rolled. Seeing where the wall of dust stopped, he pulled off the road. Hopping out of his SUV, he made his way through the stiff desert scrub brush toward the smoldering remains of the Dodge Ram. Having come to rest upside down, the massive struts that once held the vehicle at a ridiculous height now reached for the sky like the legs of some vanquished mythical beast.

Finding the driver-side door missing and the cab empty, the Boy surveyed the area. A cruel smile crossed his face.

"Where are you?" His voice held a sadistic sing-song temper. "I know you're here, you fuck. I know you've been following me."

He spotted footprints, one foot clearly dragging. The Boy knew the driver could not have gotten far. A rush of exhilaration overtook him. The thrill of the hunt.

"I'm gonna get you." He felt a surge of anticipation, a childish glee in this game of hide-and-seek. "And when I do, you'll be sorry."

The Boy tracked his victim like a lion stalking its prey through the African savanna. Coming upon an impassable wall of thorny brush, the tracks split in two directions. Looking to the left, then to the right, he ran a hand through his hair.

"Now where could you have gone?" Looking down, he saw drag marks leading under the wall of branches. He tuned his ears to filter out the wind. The wall of thorns sounded like it was out of breath.

The Boy swiped his arm in an arc parallel to the ground. Exploding on an unnaturally straight line, the wall of bushes was reduced to a low hedge-line. In the center of the clipped shrubs, a shock of green hair marked his target.

Fear and awe were written on the man's face. Wiry, face gaunt with dark circles around his deep blue eyes, the man had the look of a meth addict. His straight, healthy teeth were the only proof he was not a habitual drug user. Hands shooting up in supplication, he moved to an upright, seated position. The Boy raised his hand, a bestial smile plastered on his face.

"Please, oh great one, don't kill me." The man's voice was hoarse. "I have only done what our master commanded."

The Boy's smile faltered. He slowly lowered his hand.

"What did you say?" He could feel his anger shift away from this man. "I have no master."

"Really?" The man let out a nervous chuckle, eyeing the Boy mischievously. "The Dark Man would beg to differ."

An angry sneer warped the Boy's features, an unintelligible growl passing his throat.

"He is the messenger of the divine. He merely imparts the wisdom of the Most High," the Boy began. "He is not my——"

"Is that what he told you?" The green-haired man laughed. "Or is that what you're telling yourself?"

The Boy put a fist to his temple, shaking his head.

"No," he said. "No, no, no." His denials came rapid fire. "He told me what to do. He told me how to become the perfect god I am meant to be!"

The man smirked, nodding. "He told you what you needed to hear." The man's voice was sympathetic. "He guides us to what we want. But make no mistake, we are his. We cannot go against his will. He is our God."

The Boy felt something in his mind shift, his thoughts moving off-angle, contorted and muddled. He and his divine messenger needed to have a little chat.

"I am not unlike you," the man declared. "I am just doing my part."

The Boy had decided to spare the man...for the moment at least. Now, standing in line at Starbucks, he felt the need to complete the kill, to ease the anxiety that stopping mid-course generated. He despised imperfection, both in form and in action. Taking a step as the line moved inexorably forward at a snail's pace, he gritted his teeth.

"Caleb," a woman's voice rang out. "Caleb Voss?"

The Boy's head snapped toward the source of the voice. A young woman, about his age, stood next to him. With a warm smile, she was clad in a loose-fitting blue shirt and yoga pants. Long blonde hair framed her heart-shaped face.

"It is you," she said with excitement. "I haven't seen you since graduation."

He recognized the woman. They had gone to the same high school. Her name eluded him. He did not realize the depth of confusion plastered on his face until the woman placed a hand to her chest as if she were trying to communicate with Tarzan.

"Kelly," the woman said. "Kelly Talbott."

A beatific smile overcame Caleb's face, charisma radiating from every pore in his body.

"Ah, yes," he said. "I remember you. I'm sorry, my mind has been a little preoccupied."

He did remember her now. In high school she had been his shadow, following him everywhere. He never understood why she had been so insistent on being his friend. The girl was popular and upbeat, he had been broody and moody.

"It is so good to see you," she said. "I don't know if you remember this, but I had the biggest crush on you in high school."

His smile faltered as a wave of discomfort pulsed through him. Her admission of romantic feelings evoked an angering disquiet. He held no romantic desires. The thought of sex, all those fluids sloshing between two people, mingling in a frenzy of adrenaline and bacteria, made the Boy sick. He subtly inhaled, reinforced his charismatic smile.

"Maybe we could go somewhere and reminisce?" Caleb asked.

Kelly nodded. "I'd like that. I don't have anywhere to be tonight."

Caleb's smile widened as Kelly turned to the coffee shop's menu screen. He had found his object of relief.

Raven stood in the doorway of Sunrise Hospital room 242. Four women flanked Harriet Sorson, who lay unconscious in the hospital bed. Long, grey hair flowed beneath the tubes providing oxygen to her. A waxy pallor indicated the end was near. The warm cream walls of the private room held no comfort in their color. Any semblance of soothing was interrupted by the rhythmic beeping of a heart monitor, which provided little more than accompaniment to the clicking and whooshing of a respirator that imbued Harriet with borrowed life.

"Her body has five minutes left," one of the women stated in a thick Southern accent. With two fingers pressed to Harriet's forehead, Savannah Wilson was dressed in nurse scrubs, her eyes shut, her tightly curled black hair pulled onto an equally tight bun.

"I'm not too late," Raven said, her tone both reverent and relieved.

Savannah opened her eyes to reveal vertical pupils set within golden irises. "You're just in time," she answered, a sad smile greeting her compatriot.

Raven looked at the other three women. Standing sentry, Denise Olay, a tall chestnut-haired bronze-skinned woman of thirty, and Mai Xaio, a short twenty-eight-year-old with black hair and a physique that spoke of her love of food. Between them, seated and holding her dying mother's hand, Tippy Sorson looked up at Raven.

With shoulder-length reddish-brown hair, Tippy bore the smooth forehead, flattened nose, and heavy-lidded hazel eyes that told the world she was a Down's syndrome child. Even at the age of forty-three, she still appeared to be in her early twenties. She mustered a weak smile for Raven, then looked back to her mother.

"Mommy, Raven's here," Tippy's thick-tongued voice said softly, wavering in her determination not to cry. "You see? I'm gonna be all right. You can go now, Mommy. I'll miss you." Her voice cracked.

As Tippy paused, Raven placed comforting hands on her shoulders. Tippy took a deep breath.

"I'll see you again. It might not be for a bit, you know we have a lot of work to do." She brought her mother's hand to her lips. "But I'll see you again."

Tippy felt her mother's hand lightly squeeze hers, the last of Harriet's strength used to let her daughter know she was loved.

"I love you too, Mommy." The words came out in an explosive sob.

Denise and Mai followed Raven's example, placing hands of support on Tippy's shoulders. Savannah sighed, sadness permeating her exhalation. She turned off the alarms on the monitoring medical equipment and shut down the respirator.

"It's time."

Savannah moved to stand beside the four women. One by one their eyes changed, pupils growing to their limits then snapping to vertical slits, allowing the women to see beyond the mere physical. In her mind, Raven connected to the psychic web that linked her consciousness to the minds of all she had activated, allowing the thirty-five hundred Caretakers to see what she saw.

"We stand as witness," Raven sent the words across the psychic network. "Witness to the passing, the transition of the mother to one of our own. She may not be a Caretaker by blood, but by virtue of her daughter, by virtue of her kindness and caring she is still one of us." Raven took in a ragged breath, stifling her own sadness. "We all stand witness to remind us that death is not the end, but more importantly we stand witness to remind ourselves. Remind ourselves why we fight…and why we are."

Raven solemnly watched as the heart monitor silently flatlined. She lightly squeezed Tippy as a humanoid silhouette of light emerged from Harriet's body. Standing next to the hospital bed, the five women could see the face of Harriet within the light.

Smiling, Harriet's spirit blew Tippy a kiss. Tippy snatched this final gift from the air, holding it to her heart.

"I love you, Mommy," she said, her voice breaking.

The being of white light regarded the remaining women with a smile. Her gaze came to rest on Raven. Harriet's afterimage nodded to her. Raven returned the gesture. As if pulled by some unseen force, the soul of Harriet Sorson moved to the east in a flash, leaving the five women alone. Tippy stood and turned to Raven.

"I'm okay." Tippy's voice was unsteady, her eyes blinking, face scrunching with each close of her lids. "I'm okay, I'm okay, I'm okay."

Raven enveloped the girl, her arms wrapped tight. Kissing Tippy's forehead, Raven shoved aside her own desire to collapse into a sobbing ball.

"Sweety." Raven's voice was soft. "I know you are strong. We all know you are strong." Tippy wrapped her arms around Raven. "There is a time for that strength. Right now, right here, it is time to let us be strong for you." Raven felt Tippy's body shudder as she lost the fight to keep her sorrow at bay. "Let go. Now is the time to be sad. So let it out."

Tippy's arms tightened around Raven as wracking sobs tore through her. Muffled by Raven's body, her wails of grief cut through the small room. Behind Tippy, Savannah put her arms around the grieving daughter. From the left, Denise embraced the trio, Mai from the right, completing the circle. A shield against the outside world, the four women became a safe space, a home, for Tippy to release her sadness and begin to heal.

Chapter 11

"Birthmarks? How is that even possible?" Disbelief was etched onto Tara's face.

"I keep trying to wrap my head around it too." My words belied my exhaustion. "Agent Allen is ordering the coroner to test the symbols and determine what they are."

The day had been long. I felt wind-burned, wind-blown, and just plain winded. Tara's face appeared stuck in a state of confusion. I could see all the wheels she had in her head running to make sense of what Mary had told Agent Allen, Stephanie, and me. I let out a slow, calming exhale. Cutting the silence, Rammstein's "Du Hast," my ringtone, blared from my pants. I quickly fished the android from my pocket to see it was Stephanie on the caller ID. I slid the answer button.

"What's up?"

"Fingerprints!" Stephanie's excitement blasted through the phone. "We got fucking fingerprints."

As she spoke, I heard Tara's phone ring. She walked into the bathroom to talk.

"Let me guess, our installation artist left them on the duct tape."

"Yup." I could hear her smiling. "The Vegas crime lab is already running them through AFIS. Thanks to the priority nature of the case, we should have a list of possible matches within two hours."

"Well, at least we'll have some real leads. Going to be useless if our guy isn't in the database though."

Tara emerged from the bathroom.

"I don't think that will be a problem," Tara said. I looked at her quizzically.

"What was that?" Stephanie's voice came through my phone loud enough for Tara to hear the question.

"I'm putting you on speaker," I stated.

"I just got off the phone with Brianna Smith," Tara began.

"Holy shit, you actually talked to her?" Stephanie sounded genuinely impressed. "Most I've gotten from her has been text chats through the DA messenger."

"She's a bit—" I paused, trying to find tactful words. I failed. "Paranoid."

"Yes," Tara said, annoyed at the interruption. "She said she had detected the AFIS submission, snagged a copy of the prints, and is doing an expanded search, including DMV records."

"How the hell did she do that?" Stephanie asked. I could hear concern about the legal ramifications in her voice. "I know she's good, but—"

"Two words," I said. "Plausible deniability."

"Yeah." Disappointment snuck into Stephanie's tone. "I'm just curious as all hell. And I'd rather not blow this case due to…questionable evidence gathering."

"So," Tara interjected, "she said we'll have results in about thirty minutes."

My eyebrows raised. None of my cases had ever required a fingerprint search for an unknown subject. I usually had fingerprints identifying a known person. To my knowledge, an AFIS search could take anywhere from hours to days. Thirty minutes was TV crime drama speed. The two hours promised by the crime lab struck me as overly optimistic to begin with.

"She figured out how to turn real life into an episode of CSI?" Stephanie was genuinely impressed. "Okay, call me when you get her results." I could hear the start of a laughing fit. "The guys at the crime lab are going to be so pissed."

We briefly heard Stephanie's ever-intensifying laughter before the call ended. Tara sat on the bed as I slipped my phone into my pocket.

"Brianna said she'd be willing to meet in person tomorrow night."

I nodded, absent-mindedly clasping my chin.

"Were you able to get anywhere with—"

"No." Tara plucked the rest of the question from my mind. "All the law enforcement agencies told me that everything had been handed over to the Feds."

"I guess that's to be expected." I was disappointed, but not surprised. While I had no reason to distrust Agent Allen, I did not believe he would give us full access to all the case files.

"Detective Blaine said something interesting."

Cocking an eyebrow, I looked at Tara. I hadn't heard that name in five years. It was Detective Ryan Blaine of the LAPD that had requested help from Darkstone's Asylum in a human trafficking case, specifically trying to find a child by the name of Atsuko Takanashi. The girl was never found. Of the four Darkstone's Asylum members involved in the investigation, the man known as Darkstone was the only survivor. Following that incident, the LAPD investigation was mysteriously quashed, and all the case files seemed to disappear into thin air. With Darkstone in the wind, Detective Blaine was the last person with knowledge of that case. And he wasn't talking about it.

"What did he say?"

"He wasn't assigned to the Hatchetman case." Tara's voice carried the cadence of a storyteller. "Because of his history with us, he offered to look into it for me. He quickly hit an aggressive roadblock. The detectives assigned to the case told him in confidence that they were told to drop the case and remove any reference to their involvement."

"Weird." I raised an eyebrow. "Was it the FBI making demands?"

"No." Tara shook her head. "Blaine said it was someone with considerably more power. The detectives told him the demands inferred non-compliance could be fatal."

Drawing a hand across my mouth, I couldn't help wondering if detectives from all law enforcement agencies received the same veiled threat. Tara's expressive blue eyes seemed to read my thoughts.

"I wondered the same thing," she stated, "and I think the answer is yes. Both the abruptness by which they shifted jurisdiction and how quickly they tried to get off the phone—"

"Someone wants all information consolidated in an easy to erase position." I felt like some tinfoil-hatted conspiracy theorist. "At least, that's how it looks to me."

It occurred to me that the information Mr. Strickland gave me really was everything he had. Without an ace like Brianna Smith backing them up, those big-name PI firms were utterly useless. Could it be that some unknown player was intercepting information? I felt deflated at the thought. How the hell was I supposed to do my job when someone with priority access was gate-keeping the evidence?

115

Tara saw the doubts and frustration etched into my visage. She stood, walked over to the desk attached to the half-wall that separated the seating area from the bed.

"Fear not, intrepid detective." Her jovial voice brought me out of my self-indulgent pity party. "All is not lost."

From under the half-wall mounted desk, Tara lifted a large file box, a loud *thud* booming when it hit the tabletop.

"Let's just say we have a goddess of the digital realm on our side." Tara's smirk could light up a room. I was amazed.

"Okay, I know Brianna's good, but—"

"Oh, she's not just good," Tara cut me off. "She's damn near inhuman. If I hadn't actually spoken to her, I'd have thought she was an Artificial Intelligence program."

"So, this is…" My question trailed off as Tara lifted the box lid.

"Every piece of each investigation that had been entered into a computer."

"But how—"

"I don't know what kind of witchcraft Brianna uses, but it seems whoever is trying to redirect the information isn't as good as they think they are."

I smiled. Damn, that techno-wizard was good. I looked into the box. As with everything Tara did, it was superbly organized.

"Color-coded and everything." I held her face between my hands and kissed her.

With a mischievous smile, Tara produced a stack of colored three-ring binders. "Since you're the one who needs to go through these, you get to stick them in the binders."

"Fair enough." I sat down, pulled the first collated stack of information. "Thank you for doing this."

Without a word, Tara smiled, kissed my temple, and grabbed her laptop off the desk. "I'll leave you to it."

Pulling my phone out, I connected my ear buds and began studying the case to the musical stylings of Funker Vogt.

"We got results!" Tara exclaimed as I put the last of the case files into a colored binder. I had quickly skimmed each document before placing them in their assigned folders. A thorough examination of the information would have to wait.

"That really was fast," I said. Tara was sitting on the bed, laptop in her crossed legs. I stood, raising my arms into a deep stretch.

"She did promise results in thirty minutes," Tara stated. "Brianna's making AFIS and the crime lab look bad."

"So," I said with sarcastic elongation, "don't make me wait."

"We have one Scott Boyd," she began. "A.K.A Simon Tippett, A.K.A. Henry Holstein, A.K.A. Marion Birch, A.K.A Regis Philbin—"

"What?" I laughed at the usage of the deceased game show host as an alias.

"Yeah, I know, right?"

"I need to let Stephanie and Agent Allen know." Grabbing my phone off the desk, I walked to the bed, sitting beside Tara.

With the phone on speaker, each ring felt like an eternity. I held tempered excitement, knowing full well that no police agency would act on the information we had gathered. Hacking government agencies on a nationwide scale was generally frowned upon. Even if it could save lives. But it would put the hounds on the right scent. Stephanie picked up on the fifth ring.

"What's up, Jonathan?" Her tone was paradoxically good spirited and disappointed at the same time. "You must be psychic, I was about to give you a call."

"Our installation artist's name is Scott Boyd," I blurted out.

"Okay," Stephanie responded. "Well, that beats my news of having an independent coroner being brought in." I could hear her sigh over the phone. "I'm with Brock, putting you on speaker."

"You got something?" Agent Allen's voice came over the phone; in the background I could hear traffic.

"Yes. Where are you?"

"We're heading to the coroner's office," Stephanie said.

"Ah," I said, "gotcha." Tara turned her laptop to face me. On the screen, a mugshot of our green-haired suspect stared at me. I scanned the information.

"Well?" Agent Allen abruptly said.

"Our fingerprints belong to one Scott Boyd," I said. "The guy looks like a junkie's interpretation of the Joker."

"Like from a deck of cards?" Agent Allen asked. In unison, Tara and Stephanie let loose a howling laugh. I couldn't help but snicker.

"Not *a* joker, THE Joker." I was trying to keep my cool; it wasn't working. "You know, from the Batman comics. Green hair, purple suit, obsessed with killing a Halloween-costumed orphan."

"Oh." The G-Man's voice had gone soft. "That Joker."

"Anyway, this guy's got enough aliases to fill a phone book. Originally from Chicago, he's wanted in twelve states under his various names. Charges include everything from petty theft, assault with a deadly weapon, child molestation, and murder. The guy's a regular criminal jack-of-all-trades."

"And do we know where he is?" Agent Allen's voice was back to its confidently annoyed posture.

"Brianna is running a search now." As Tara interjected, her phone pinged. "I just got a text from her. The vehicle he had been using was a customized, jacked-up Dodge Ram, but that was found earlier today out by Red Rock." Tara's eyebrow lifted as she examined her phone. "Not much left of the truck, looks like it rolled a few hundred times."

"That bastard was at the crime scene today." The explosive words vibrated my phone. I could hear the frustration in the agent's voice, and the impact of his hand on a steering wheel.

"Not surprising," Stephanie said. "This kind of a killer wants to know his work is being appreciated. And there were a few people at that viewpoint looking right at the crime scene."

"I suppose," Agent Allen grumbled, growling under his breath.

"Anyhoo." I tried to steer the conversation back on track. "We've got the digital goddess on it. Knowing her it'll just be—"

A ding from Tara's phone got my attention. She looked at the text and let out a small chuckle.

"Well," she started, "Regis Philbin rented a silver Nissan Kick four hours ago from the Hertz at the airport."

"Wow," Stephanie said. "Impressive for a dead guy."

"What's the plate number?" the G-man asked. "We can put out a BOLO."

"Texting it to you now, Agent," Tara said. "And thanks to the cameras all over Vegas, Brianna is doing a traffic-cam search for the vehicle."

"I'd really like to meet this techno-wiz of yours."

"As long as you promise not to arrest her," I said flatly.

"Arrest her? I want to recruit her!"

"Not going to happen," Tara said. "She's former NSA and has made it abundantly clear she wants nothing to do with the government."

"Damn," he said. "Former NSA, huh? That explains a lot."

"I'll let you know when we have more info," I said. "So what's this about an independent coroner?"

"Her name is Mai Xaio," Agent Allen began. "Quite possibly the best there is. From Hong Kong, she's young for a coroner. A child prodigy, she graduated med school at nineteen. Top of her class—"

"You don't need to sell me, Agent. You say she's good, I'll take your word for it. But why do we need an independent coroner?"

"The medical examiner's office is backed up," Stephanie chimed in, "and apparently they don't consider either a federal request or potential serial killer to be grounds for prioritization."

"You're joking," I groaned. "The crime lab will fast track this case, but the M.E.'s office won't?" Out of the corner of my eye I saw Tara shaking her head.

"Too many cooks in the kitchen," Stephanie said, as if that was an explanation.

"I got a call from Mai fifteen minutes ago," Agent Allen stated. "Apparently she's bored and wants to get to work. We're just going to make sure she's properly situated."

"It's unlikely she'll have anything for us tonight," Stephanie said.

"If she does find anything, let me know. I'm going to give Mary a call and fill her in."

Agent Allen groaned at the mention of our tag-along's name.

"Hey, it's only fair," I said, responding to his unintelligible disapproval.

"Do what you want," he growled. "Like I said, she's your responsibility. And don't forget, tomorrow, 9am at the M.E.'s office."

"Oh, how could I possibly forget an appointment to watch disassembled corpses get even more disassembled?" I rolled my eyes as I spoke. I heard a change in the background noise as Stephanie took her phone off speaker.

"Okay," she said. "We'll see you tomorrow."

"Don't do anything I would do," I told her.

"Meh, Brock's not my type. You know I like the little guys."

With that she hung up. Letting out an exasperated sigh, I pulled up Mary's contact in my phone and hit the green button.

"Hey there, stranger," Mary answered the phone as if we were long lost friends. "What's up?"

"We know who one of our killers is," I said.

"Let me guess. You found your installation artist." I could tell this wasn't the news she wanted to hear.

"Yup."

"Well, getting one killer is nice and all, but that's not the one I'm after."

"Truth be told, me either." I had been contracted to find the man whose swath of murder had stretched the length of California and into Nevada, not some wannabe copycat with an artistic streak. "It's my hope that this guy will lead us to our killer."

I could almost hear the nod of agreement on the other end of the phone. "That makes sense," she stated. "By the way, I'm having a friend scan all the info I promised you. They should have it emailed to me by tomorrow."

"Exactly what is this information you are so certain will help our case?"

Mary paused, letting out a slow breath. I wasn't sure if she was mentally preparing or simply being dramatic.

"One of my best friends in the entire world was Victoria Flat." The name rang a bell. "We met when we were both five. We grew up as veritable sisters."

I recalled that Victoria Flat was one of the Los Angeles victims. Her remains had been discovered by hikers in Angeles National Park.

"That explains your insistence to join this case," I said, moving back toward the hotel room desk.

"I also felt very protective of her." There was a melancholy behind Mary's words. "She had spinal muscular atrophy."

"What is that?" I had never heard of it before.

"The short answer is that some issue with her nervous system caused muscle weakness and degradation. By the time she was sixteen, Victoria was using a wheelchair to get around."

"Okay," I said. "I don't mean to sound insensitive, but how does this help our case?"

"Victoria had the infinity symbol birthmark behind her left ear," Mary declared. This wasn't news to me. I had just finished scanning through all the case files and had separated those with the infinity symbols.

"Yes, I know."

"Well," she began, seeming a bit annoyed, "did you know that everyone born with that birthmark is disabled in one way or another?"

"I was informed that all our birthmarked victims suffered from a variety of ailments. As far as I can tell, it had just made them easy targets."

"There is a website on the dark web, it's a forum for women born with this birthmark," Mary stated. "Victoria showed it to me once. Literally thousands of members."

I grabbed my notepad and a pen, poised to write down what actually looked to be a promising lead.

"What is the site?"

"I don't know the address. Like everything on the dark web, the addy is just a numerical sequence."

I groaned and started bouncing my head against the table. A hollow thud quietly resonated with each strike of my forehead.

"What's that sound?"

"Nothing," I said. "Brianna might be able to track down the site."

"Bad idea." Her voice took on a warning edge. "From what I understand, the site has some nasty protective software. It's invite-only, and if you do manage to get in the admin can fry your computer."

"How does one get an invite?"

121

"Email. I have no idea how the person running the site finds the right people, but they do. That's not even the curious part."

"And that is?" I said, wondering why everyone I knew had a pathological need for dramatic pauses.

"Victoria told me that there is one person everyone on the site is waiting for."

"Ugh. Do not tell me this really is some sort of messiah cult."

"No, this actually appears to be a real person." Mary chuckled. "No one says her name. Even those claiming to have been visited, and those kinds of posts are generally good-byes before they stop posting."

"What does this unnamed person do?"

"Victoria said that she makes them whole." Skepticism rang through Mary's words. "She does something that takes away their disabilities. More to the point, they claim their disabilities are all caused by the birthmark not properly integrating into their genetics, whatever that means."

"Oh God. Not aliens. Please tell me it's not aliens."

"Aliens are not mentioned." Mary laughed. "No, they just say the disabilities are mimics, all the effects of these conditions without having them. Whoever this person they're all waiting for is somehow corrects the problem."

"Again," I said, "how does any of this help us find our killer?"

"It doesn't," Mary admitted. "But I think I know how he finds his victims, and I think I know how he kills."

Chapter 12

Cold.

Kelly Talbott felt unnaturally cold. Slight air currents in the room brushed against her body, sending shivers through her. Mind hazy, her memories were trapped in a fog. She felt she had been awake for the better part of an hour. What happened in that time? She did not understand why she was so cold, or why she could not remember.

Her head was bent forward, a screen of blonde hair obscuring the world around her. She felt tired, she wanted to go back to sleep. But the cold.

Another wave of convulsive shivers tore through her, and with them the rattling of metal. Looking down, she saw her clothes were missing. Instinctively she tried to use her arms to cover herself. More rattling of metal, and she found her arms would not budge from their outstretched position. A flash of memory emerged in her groggy mind. The charming face of Caleb Voss.

The memory was fragmented, short clips Kelly couldn't quite follow. She had left Starbucks with Caleb. As they walked toward her car, she began feeling lightheaded. Her chest had tightened, she stumbled, gasping for air. She felt as if her oxygen supply had been cut off. Caleb helped her to his car. He was going to take her to the hospital. The pain of a needle pricking her neck. Everything went dark. A flow of disjointed images followed. She could not move, her hands and feet bound to a rusty shelving unit. Caleb stood across the room. His arm was raised like some Harry Potter reject, finger pointing toward her. He ordered her to raise three fingers.

Staring down, she could see a crimson puddle on the ground. The sight made her stomach wrench, the hair on the back of her neck stood on end. Another shiver ran through her, this time not from the cold. She fought the urge to vomit as she raised her head. She did not want to look, but knew she had to see.

Rapid, shallow breathing echoed above the drum beat of her heart. A bead of cold sweat wound its way down her forehead and into her eye. The ocular intrusion did not register to Kelly; her mind was fixed on the sight before her. She could see that her wrist was bound by a wide, black Velcro restraint. Her eyes could not decipher the object poking from the top of the binding. A mass of bright red, crimson, and rust brown. Small patches of pale, untouched skin and the involuntary jerking of her thumb and pinky finger were the only indication that this was what remained of her own hand. Acid burned her throat, her abdomen violently convulsed. She turned her head back toward the ground as her stomach exorcised its contents, the brownish spew mixing with the crimson puddle on the floor.

Another wave of nausea passed through her. Violent metallic rattling blasted out as her bound appendages momentarily fought to be free. Though the vomiting had subsided, her throat burned with lingering acid. In the multicolored mess of fluids on the ground, she saw three fingers laying in the grotesque stew. Her perfectly manicured nails with their bubblegum-pink polish stared back at her. Another wave of gastric convulsions wracked her body. She shivered. The cold had returned. Through her ragged panting, she realized what that tormenting cold was. She was in shock.

Her epiphany came at a price. Pain suddenly tore through Kelly's body, searing every nerve. As if a switch had been flipped, her mind began registering the damage she had taken. Hissing breaths, stifling the urge to scream, she could feel every exposed nerve on the stumps where her fingers had once been. Slight movements of air sent waves of agony through her. But there was something else; that same nausea-inducing pain radiated from below.

Her breathing was unsteady, a fast-galloping series of clenched-teeth hisses. She desperately clung to what little rational consciousness she had as her eyes moved to survey her right foot. Panic gripped her as she saw two cheerfully painted toenails, and three blood-oozing stumps. Her detached toes lay in the puddle on the ground. Her chest rose and fell uncontrollably, hyperventilation bringing wave after wave of dizziness. Hot tears of fear and pain ran rivers down her face. She could make no noise. Her voice had been stolen by terror.

Kelly's head jerked up. Where was her captor? Where was the source of this evil? In her terrorized state, all she could hear was the pounding of her heart. A wave of dizziness overtook her. Her head lolled. It felt heavy. Sleep beckoned her. As her eyes lazily passed over the room, she spotted Caleb on the ground toward the back of the room. He was sleeping.

At one time, the dream had inspired a sense of wonder for Caleb. The paradox between the gentle breeze, bright sunlight, and the clear azure sky versus the horrifying image that stood before him now invoked anger. The Dark Man had lied to him. The young killer wished this place, this thing he had put his faith in, really was just a dream.

Shifting his body, Caleb felt his feet sink into the blood-soaked mud. Rotting, blackened stalks of reeds protruded from the sticky crimson-brown swamp, appearing as fleshless fingers reaching for the sky. The fetid stench of rotting meat filled the air, a sharp hint of excrement and bile punctuating the grotesque perfume. He closed his eyes and took a deep breath, savoring the putrid air. A momentary shiver of pleasure replaced his anger, an anger that returned as he regarded the foul mound before him.

Rising from this swamp of death, the hill of piled, writhing corpses emanated moans of pain and pleasure. Glinting in the sunlight, a black viscous fluid oozed from the decomposing remnants of life. With each undulation of the hill, the thick substance seemed to be squeezed from the rotting bodies. The black sick that spilled from the writhing figures mingled, combined into slow cascades feeding the swamp. Caleb raised an eyebrow as he watched a corpse pull itself halfway out of the hillside. Skinless, its muscles were the mottled grey of rancid meat. A mindless smile crossed the escaping body as its decaying countenance was lit by the sun. Caleb watched the pathetic thing as its expression turned to one of pure horror. The side of its head swelled as something beneath the surface writhed and pulsated, an unknown entity pressing for its own release. A loud pop echoed through the dreamland as a mass of maggots exploded from the skinless head. The body slumped down on the undulating surface of the corpse hill, the remnants of its head detached from its body, unceremoniously bouncing like a soccer ball down the hill and into the bog.

Casting his eyes up, Caleb spotted his object of anger. Atop the mound of rot, a black figure stood. The Dark Man appeared as a shadow that had been ripped from a wall and given substance. His featureless

125

form absorbed all light; as he shifted, his arms and legs appeared to fuse and detach from the void that was his core. Despite having no eyes, Caleb could feel the Dark Man's gaze upon him.

His resolve slipping, the angry killer drew in a deep breath to steel his nerves.

"You lied to me, you bastard." Caleb's voice broke with anger. "You told me you were a messenger of God."

A deep, guttural laugh came from all around him. An involuntary shiver ran down Caleb's spine. The damp, putrid air grew heavy. A wet miasmatic blanket pressing down on him, the fetid air forced into his nostrils.

"I said no such thing," the deep, unearthly voice declared. "That was an assumption you had made."

Caleb's anger faltered. "Why didn't you—"

"Many come to me and many call me to them." The voice held no point of origin, as if it were part of the very air that surrounded Caleb. "What they think I am does not matter. You all become mine in the end." The faceless figure standing upon the hill of writhing bodies gestured to its grotesque perch.

Caleb felt hot, his boiling anger asserted itself in a low growl.

He was to be perfect.

He was a god in waiting.

He was the be-all, end-all.

Rage coursed through his veins. How dare this faceless thing claim ownership of him?

Fear sharpened Kelly's mind. Her blurred vision came into crystal-clear focus, looking toward the source of a low growling. The stillness of Caleb's body had momentarily assuaged her terror. The noise now coming from the unconscious killer sent a chill through her. She held her breath, waiting for him to move. Waiting for him to sit up. He remained still. He was not waking up. At least, not yet.

She felt the mental fog trying to overtake her consciousness again. Her thoughts drifted to her mother, currently asleep in their hotel room. What would she think when Kelly failed to return in the morning? Would the police believe she had gone missing or brush her disappearance off? A wave of despair swept through her. She had watched many cop shows, she knew how often police tried to claim missing people had run off on their own, delaying investigations for days or months.

A sharp twinge of pain shot through her arm as she subconsciously tried to break her bindings. The pain brought focus, pushed back the drowsiness that threatened to drown her in permanent slumber. Her heart punched at her ribcage. The adrenaline spike caused her blood pressure to skyrocket. She felt the scabs that had formed on her hand and foot break open. Bright red rivers flowed down her arm, overtaking the brownish crimson rivulets of dried blood plastered to her skin.

Looking at Caleb, Kelly's body convulsed in fear and revulsion. Her mind could not reconcile the sight. Blood-drenched mud grew onto his feet, dark crimson liquid oozing from the preternatural substance, pooling on the concrete floor. Another adrenaline hit heralded a shockwave of pain through her body. Heart beating fast, Kelly couldn't catch her breath. Her head pounded with each push of blood through her veins. Vision blurring, she had to do something if she was to survive.

Hoping her blood had provided the necessary lubrication to slip from her wrist restraint, she pulled her arm down. Kelly retched. Her body shook with pain-induced convulsions. She slowed her breathing, desperately clinging to as much reason as she could. An analysis of the situation revealed a fatal flaw in her plan, and an insidious calculation in Caleb Voss' methodology. Though nylon on the outside, these restraints were designed to absorb liquid. They soaked up her blood, expanding and creating a tighter lock on her wrist. Her own mutilation made escape impossible.

Looking at her undamaged hand, she pulled down. The Velcro restraint held fast. Pain tore through her head, pounding pressure from an adrenaline spike that sent sparkling dots into her vision.

In a whisper of encouragement, she said, "I can do this."

Panting in staccato inhales, Kelly relaxed. Shock had once again dulled the pain into a manageable state. Fatigue once again threatened her consciousness.

"Okay," she said quietly, noticing her speech was beginning to slur. "Let's try a different approach."

She pushed her arm out from the shelving unit she was bound to. The wrist restraint felt like a solid lock on her arm. She relaxed, calming her breathing as best she could, letting up on the pressure. Sucking in a deep breath, Kelly violently wrenched her arm forward. The zipper-crunch of Velcro teeth separating registered in her ears; her arm felt a slight give in the restraint. Relaxing once again, she eased up the pressure, preparing to continue until her arm was free. An angry, guttural grunt from across the room caught her attention.

Caleb's head moved side to side. Agitation permeated his unconscious body. The pool of muddy blood at his feet had grown, brownish crimson mud reaching to his ankles. On the verge of hyperventilating, Kelly pressed her arm out again. Another line of Velcro teeth separated. The binding loosened slightly, but not enough for her to free herself from its grasp. Her stomach convulsed as nausea hit her. Her entire body shuddered as a wave of intense pain broke through her shock. She hissed through clenched teeth, trying to breathe through the pain. Caleb's voice drew her attention as his unconscious body spoke.

"FUCK YOU!"

Caleb could not disguise his hatred for the faceless void standing atop its throne of decay. Rage had gripped him. In the dream he could not use his power. Once the Raven made him perfect, the game would change.

"YOU THINK YOU OWN ME?" Caleb gave a sardonic laugh that blasted through the blood-swamp. "I AM NOT YOURS, YOU FACELESS FUCK! I WILL NOT BE—"

A blasting wave of pressure stole Caleb's breath. The Dark Man's bemused voice came from all around him. "You think you have a choice?"

Panting, Caleb sneered at the figure who crowned the undulating hill of rotting bodies. "I am a god," he snarled, "and once the Raven makes me perfect, I will kill you just like all the others."

A deafening laughter enveloped the defiant killer. Pressure bore down on Caleb, an overwhelming force that pressed his chin painfully into his chest. An involuntary bow of supplication. The putrid stench of fecal matter and rotting meat intensified as the wet air surrounding the

Boy thickened. Every muscle in Caleb's dream-body screamed in pain as he fought against the ever-increasing force pressing down on him.

"I will not bow to you," his voice strained. "I bow to no one."

Caleb's chin separated from his chest. He felt his neck muscles rip. A crunching pop reverberated in his head, yet inch by inch he lifted it. A defiant smile of victory crossed his lips as he straightened into a full upright position.

"I told you," he said. "I will not be—"

Caleb collapsed onto his knees. In an instant, the pressure bearing down on him had increased a thousandfold. He could not fight it. For all his power in the waking world, here, against this faceless void with the shape of a man, he was utterly powerless. As if a giant hand pressed upon his back, the killer lurched forward. He caught himself before his face hit the bloody bog. Fear gripped him as he watched his hands disappear into the crimson mud. The pressure slowly forced his body down into the noxious stew.

Kelly was frozen, her mind unable to comprehend what she was seeing. Caleb's body twitched and jerked erratically, then settled into eerie silence. Deep red stains grew on his pants' knees. The wet crimson quickly moved down his pant legs to meet the blood-soaked mud covering his feet. That same bloody mud grew on the Boy's hands, slowly inching its way up his arms. Hair on the back of her neck stood on end; she felt as if there was someone else in the disheveled storage room Caleb had bound her in. Someone far worse than her former classmate. She squeezed her eyes tight.

"This isn't happening. This isn't happening. This isn't—"

A shockwave of pain broke her mantra. Proof she was not dreaming. Proof she was not hallucinating. As the blood spread to Caleb's shirt, Kelly convulsed with silent sobs. Tears ran down her face, her mouth agape, lips silently flexing. She could taste the salt of her sadness mixed with watery mucus from her runny nose. The stench of rancid meat and fecal matter penetrated her obstructed nostrils. With her mouth open she could taste the fetid miasma. It was a blight on her tongue. A soundless scream passed her lips. Noiseless sobs wracked her body. Her voice had abandoned her.

Groaning from Caleb drew her eyes, his head slowly rolling side to side. Her paralyzing fear transmuted into terrorized motivation. With her good hand she frantically resumed her pull on the restraint. Loud bangs echoed through the storage room with each pull of Kelly's arm. Each pull of her arm was rewarded with the sound of another line of Velcro teeth separating. Keeping her eyes on Caleb's sleeping form, she froze as he twitched, his eyes fluttering.

Kelly's voice quivered as she managed to whisper, "Not yet. Not yet."

The wrist restraint had loosened significantly. Just a few more lines of separation and she could slip her hand out. Just a few more lines.

Caleb struggled to free himself as the bloody mud reached the middle of his forearms. Gone was the pressure forcing him down. The bog had him now, a hungry stew pulling him down to be devoured. With each attempt to free himself, the grip of the swamp grew stronger. Laughter came from all around him as he jerked and pulled. Panting, he looked up at the featureless void that stood in judgement of him. His eyes yearned to kill the source of this humiliation.

The Dark Man's rough voice asked, "Do you understand yet?"

Caleb sneered, but his slow, inexorable descent into the gory swamp chipped away at his arrogance. He felt the sticky, cold muck wrap around his elbows as the bog slowly enveloped him, his hips already beneath the surface. Wet crimson tendrils snaked their way up his shirt, staining yet another piece of his clothing.

"Who am I?" the Dark Man asked.

Conflicting emotions rose in Caleb. He hated this thing that had lied to him, the sight of it inspiring disgusted rage. At the same time, he was immersed in self pity. This was an unconscionable disservice to a god-in-waiting. He should be venerated by the Dark Man, not treated like a disobedient mutt. Caleb did not answer.

"Who. Am. I?"

The pressure returned, forcing Caleb further into rancid mud. Focused on his lower back, a kidney punch of pain wracked his body, stealing his breath. He felt the cold wet on his chest, and his head moved erratically, trying to keep its distance from the putrid ground.

"You," he spat out, "are my god."

For a moment Caleb felt the pressure lift, his descent into the bog halted.

"What—" Caleb began. "What do you want me to do?"

Pressure slowly built as the Dark Man spoke. Caleb's descent into the muck resumed. He turned his face to the side as the swamp enveloped his chest. The scent of copper and feces assaulted his nostrils. Mud forced its way into Caleb's ear, leaving him with only one aural receiver in working order.

"Draw her to you, take what you want, and scatter her flesh to the wind."

Caleb remained silent, his acquiescence to the Dark Man's authority a tenuous display. A battle momentarily raged in his mind. He was the master of his own destiny. He was a god. He needed no god or master. And yet, in this place, he was powerless.

"What do you say, little god?"

Opening his mouth to speak, Caleb spat as bloody mud slipped in. Choking on the unholy stew, he gasped out.

"Yes, Master."

Adrenaline pumped through Kelly's body as she watched the bright red and dark crimson blood appear on Caleb's twitching body. Her mind could not process the sight. She felt her sanity slipping. As his movement increased, so did her sense of urgency. She was close, she could feel the give in the Velcro strap that bound her undamaged hand. Hearing unintelligible muttering from her unconscious captor, she frantically pulled at the binding. Her vision blurred as she wrenched; with each pull she felt weaker. A mental fog threatened to drag her into the endless sleep. Shock and fear had made the bound woman oblivious to the blood now flowing freely from her dissected hand and foot. The terror induced an adrenaline spike, her blood loss increased exponentially.

Her senses muted.

Her struggle slowed.

She heard Caleb say, "Yes, Master."

As consciousness abandoned her, Kelly's chin fell to her chest. Her undamaged hand slipped from its Velcro binding, bouncing limp on her hip.

Raven white-knuckled the steering wheel of her modified '64 Mustang, racing south on I-15 at 120 miles per hour. A psychic tether to one of her charge screamed alarm bells in her mind. She knew the name of the young woman in peril, she knew precisely where her charge was. She did not know if her prey was the cause. Part of Raven hoped it wasn't him. If it was, this time she would not be too late.

Exiting the highway, Raven turned southeast toward the site of a home development under construction. Pulling up on the maze of streets, she flipped a switch on the back side of the steering wheel. All engine noise ceased as a custom sound suppressor kicked in. The device was the brainchild of a Caretaker who went by the simple moniker "Technomancer."

Light shone in the second-story window of an unfinished house. A black sedan with an Uber sticker was situated in front of the building. Parking behind the ride-share vehicle, Raven silently made her way to the front door. Finding the entry unlocked, she slipped between the light and entered the home.

Immediately Raven heard movement from the second story. Muffled cries, scraping on wood, and the unintelligible voice of a man reached her ears. She darted up the stairs and instantly zeroed in on the sounds. Light pouring through an open doorway provided the bull's-eye. She silently made her way and peered into the room. Raven's stomach churned; she felt the urge to vomit as disgust and rage battled for supremacy within her.

Christina Dorn was strapped to a dirty mattress on the floor of the unfinished room. Her hands were bound at the wrists, arms held taut above her head by a rope tied to a floor-mounted mooring. Her lower legs were folded into her thighs, wide black Velcro strips holding each of them in position. Leather straps wound around each knee. Bolted to the floor, steel O-rings provided tie-off points for the ropes that forced the young woman's legs apart. Her feet jutting out at odd angles, Raven could see the mobility issue that had likely made her a target. In a pile on the floor, Christina's blue denim jeans, white blouse, bra, and panties all bore evidence of an encounter with a pair of scissors.

The bound woman violently shook her head. Her dark brown hair flailed as she bucked against her restraints. A piece of her blouse used as a gag, Raven realized her ears had been mistaken. Christina's muffled voice wasn't crying out. She was cursing. Tears streaming down her face seemed paradoxical as vitriolic words spewed from the bound girl, muffled by the cloth in her mouth. Righteous hatred in place of fear. The target of her loathing: a shirtless man whose head was buried between her legs.

The loathsome creature lifted himself to his knees. A mess of faded tattoos covered his tan, bloated form. From behind, Raven could see his hair was jet black with slices of grey creeping in. Another wave of nausea hit her as the man's hand came into view. His index and middle fingers were held together, light reflecting off a slick, crimson-tinted coating.

A shuddering inhale let Raven know the half-naked beast was sniffing his fingers. She silently retched upon hearing an exaggerated slurp.

"Damn, you taste good." The low baritone voice sent shivers down Raven's spine. A reinvigorated string of muffled curses blasted at the man. "Don't be like that, baby." The man stood, unbuttoning his pants. "You're gonna love it. All the girls love it."

Raven's patience ran out as the violator's baggy jeans hit the floor. Casting aside stealth, and with lightning speed, she grabbed the naked creature by the neck, slamming him against the wall. The bare drywall buckled under the force of impact.

Under most circumstances, Raven would wait, let the birthright of her charge assert itself so they could prove to themselves they were not victims. It was a calculated risk. But the green-eyed Caretaker had her limits. Under no circumstance would she allow further violation by this cretin to be the catalyst for Christina. If she had only arrived a few minutes earlier…

Dazed, the man's empty brown eyes stared at Raven, trying to comprehend what happened. In her rage, the cat-like pupils radiated a predatory, reptilian aura. The man tried to move, finding himself pinned against the wall by Raven's grip on his throat.

"What the fu—"

"How many?" Raven demanded. Her voice felt raw, acid-burned.

"Who the hell are—" His question was interrupted by crushing pressure on his windpipe.

"How many, you piece of shit?" She tried to calm herself.

"What?" The man's voice shifted to an unnerving calm. "You mean these cripple bitches?"

Raven fought the desire to crush his neck like a piece of tissue paper, her body shook in restraint.

"I dunno." The man's tone was nonchalant. "Must be fifteen by now. Cripple bitches are only good for their holes anyway." His mouth formed a perverse smile. "In the end they all begged for more."

"You. Sick. Fuck."

"Hey now, gothy girl, I know you want it too. But you're gonna have to wait your turn." Amusement flashed in his eyes, a joke for which only he knew the punchline.

Raven lowered her head, gritted her teeth. She couldn't put her finger on why she didn't simply kill this thing. It had no business existing. It had forfeited its right to live.

"Nice contacts, by the way. Really digging the cat-girl thing you got going." As he spoke, his fist arced upward, the blow landing on Raven's chin.

The crack of bone produced a high-pitched yelp from the man, two of his knuckles breaking under the force of his own punch. He felt as though he had hit concrete. Lifting her head, a rage-induced smile upon her face, Raven chuckled.

"Feel better now?" Her grip on his throat tightened. "Feel like a big man?"

Fear finally registered in his eyes. Staring into the vertical pupils, witnessing their minute adjustments to the light, it dawned on the man that Raven wasn't wearing theatrical contact lenses. She cocked her head, smile broadening.

"Ah, so you're finally figuring out just how fucked you are."

Looking away from her penetrating gaze, the man's eyes widened in horror. Christina stood at the foot of the mattress, her bonds shredded. Long hair obscuring her face and head lolling side to side, a low growl escaped the girl's throat. Raven turned her head to see the naked woman swaying slightly.

"Bad news," Raven said to the man. "I'm not killing you today."

Taking her hand off the man's neck, Raven turned. She heard the violator exhale a misguided sigh of relief. Passing Christina, she put a hand on the girl's shoulder, pausing, uttering the only advice that mattered.

"Take it back. Take back what he took from you."

Christina appeared before the man in the blink of an eye. One hand shoved him back against the wall, the other hand grabbed onto the base of his slowly deflating erection. Her nails dug into him, seeming to grow sharper as she squeezed his weapon of choice. The man let loose a pained cry.

"Where are they?" she hissed through gritted teeth.

"The hills," he spat out, his fear lay bare. "The hills to the east of Lake Mead. A quarter mile past the last parking lot, just off the turnout on the right. Please don't kill me."

Between locks of hair, the man caught a glimpse of Christina's hazel eye, its pupil a vertical slit. She sneered at him.

"Look, I'm sorry," the man pleaded. "I'll make it up to you, I can make it all good."

"What I do now," Christina stated, "is give a voice to those you have silenced. In this moment…" As though they were spring-loaded knives, Christina's fingernails spontaneously grew, piercing the flesh behind the man's penis and scrotum. "I am retribution."

With a deft twist of her wrist, the man became a eunuch. Blood poured from the gaping hole his genitals once occupied. His scream was stifled by Christina as she rammed the partial erection down his throat, her palm ensuring his whole dismembered package fit in his mouth. She forced his chin upward, closing his mouth.

"Do you like it, motherfucker?" Her voice was eerily calm. "I know you want it. Tell me how much you want it."

He weakly clawed at her arms, the few inhales he managed serving to suck his shaft deeper into his esophagus until it cut his air supply entirely.

"Come on, you sick shit." Christina's words took on a sharp edge. "Tell me how much you love it."

A sick, muffled retching came from the man's convulsing frame, his body desperately trying to expel his own weapon, failing miserably.

"Tell me, asshole!" Hate flooded her voice. "COME ON, YOU FUCKING PIECE OF SHIT! TELL ME YOU LOVE IT!"

The man's body spasmed in the throes of death. Christina let him go, backed away. The creature slumped to the floor with a wet thud. Blood and excrement spread from beneath his crumpled form. The violator's head lolled to one side. His mouth hung open, a single bare testicle hanging from the stuffed orifice.

Looking at her blood-soaked hands, Christina's body shook with an explosive sob.

"Let it out." Intimate understanding permeated Raven's voice.

Staring at the remnants of her attacker, Christina opened her mouth. Loosing a roar, her anger, her sense of violation, the helplessness she had felt, were all focused into the scream. Raven lifted an eyebrow at the sound of splintering bone and ripping flesh. Christina's voice was a weapon in its own right. The slumped corpse crumpled and twisted under the sonic assault. An unrecognizable mass of flesh, splintered bone, and ichor were all that was left of her violator.

Raven stood behind the shaking girl, a mixture of awe and sadness replacing the rage she had felt. "Christina," she said softly, "look at me."

Christina slowly turned, revealing a torrent of tears streaming down her face. Her body convulsed with each inhale as she tried to stifle her sobs. Recognition emerged in Christina's hazel eyes as she took an unsteady step toward Raven.

"It's you." Her voice wavered. Raven moved to meet her.

With a piece of Christina's shredded blouse, Raven wiped the blood off the young woman's hands. As she did, Raven noticed Christina's legs slowly twisting back into the skewed angles she had been born with.

Looking into the traumatized woman's face, she watched as Christina's pupils rounded. Wiping the tears from her eyes, Raven moved her hand to behind Christina's neck, her index finger resting on the infinity birthmark behind the young woman's left ear. Establishing a connection, Raven halted Christina's reversion.

"You have a choice," Raven said as she gingerly brushed a lock of brown hair from Christina's face. "I can remove the genetic interference, your body will correct itself and you can live a fully human life—" Raven cut herself short. She could see the decision in the hazel eyes staring at her.

"I choose to fight," Christina said with finality. Raven's smile held a tinge of sadness, knowing what Christina's choice entailed.

The hazel-eyed woman's body stiffened as Raven asserted control, connecting to a single strange cell in the nexus of Christina's infinity symbol birthmark.

"Steel yourself," Raven said, "and don't forget to breathe."

Chapter 13

It was the ungodly hour of 8am when I pulled into the passenger loading area at the New York-New York Hotel and Casino. Mary stood amid a bustling crowd of tourists. Dressed in a matching tan jacket and skirt combo with an off-white blouse, she was sending the message that she took collaboration with law enforcement far more seriously than I did. I honked to get her attention. Getting into the passenger's seat of my sedan, she smiled.

"Good morning." Her cheerfulness cut through the car, her voice a tad bit loud for my groggy, coffee-less mind. I winced.

"It's way too early for that much happiness," I grumbled. "Need coffee."

"Ah," she said, "you're one of those people."

I shot her a disapproving glare. She responded by sticking her tongue out at me. I shook my head as I pointed us toward the nearest Starbucks. The drive-thru was blessedly empty. With my wake-up juice in hand, we headed toward the medical examiner's office.

"You really don't have to go through this." I was worried at the speed with which this seemingly good-natured young lady had acclimated to examining corpses in the field. "Too much exposure and you'll wind up like Agent Allen. Or worse, like me."

I mindlessly reached into my coat pocket, pulled out my cigarette case. One hand on the wheel, I deftly opened the spring-loaded case, placed it on my thigh, grabbed a stick of cinnamon, and closed the case. The object of hand-to-mouth fixation jutting from the right side of my mouth, I placed the case back in my coat pocket. Lightly biting down on the reddish-brown stick of spice, the flavor of cinnamon mixed with the taste of coffee lingering in my mouth. The effect was better than a cigarette, pretty close to sex, but not as good as chocolate.

"I do need to do this." Her jovial tone was gone, sharpening my focus on the conversation. "I need to find out who killed Victoria. I won't be left behind."

"Okay then, about what you told me last night."

"I figured you'd be the right person to mention it to." She looked out the window. "It's an impossible idea, and it sounds insane—"

"Are you trying to convince me or talk me out of it?"

"Fair point," Mary said. "Since we were kids, Victoria had this way of knowing things she shouldn't."

"Such as?"

"She knew her parents' fights were always about her, even though they never fought in front of her. She knew a boy who lived three houses down that she never spoke to was being molested by a priest—"

"Was that priest—"

Mary cut me off, anticipating the question. "The guy was arrested two days after she told me about it. Apparently, Victoria made an anonymous call to the police." Mary looked at me. "There's more. A lot more."

"Did she tell you how she came by all this information?"

"She said the plants would talk to her."

"Is that so?" I raised a skeptical eyebrow.

"I know how it sounds," she said, "and I had a hard time believing it until I slept over at her house when I was sixteen. By that time, Victoria couldn't walk on her own." A touch of melancholy tainted Mary's voice. "I was awakened in the middle of the night, Victoria's voice calling me, saying she wanted to show me something. I remember being shaken awake and finding her squatting next to me. She looked at me with these strange eyes. Her pupils were vertical, like the eyes of a cat. And I was stunned when she stood up. I thought I was dreaming."

"You're sure you weren't?"

"Absolutely. She walked without any problem over to a potted plant on her windowsill she called George." Mary let out a slight chuckle at the name. "She touched a leaf and started telling me all about the neighbors. Who was up, who was drunk, and who was screwing."

"How did she—"

"I'm getting to that." Her clipped tone made her annoyance with my interruptions clear. "According to Victoria, plants are all connected by a kind of energy. An invisible web created by life. It was through this network that she was able to take on information. She wasn't really

139

talking to the plants so much as reading what information the plants carried."

"So how was she able to walk?"

"According to her, this gift, as she called it, would randomly become accessible. When it did, all her symptoms would vanish. She could move like nothing was wrong."

I nodded, encouraging her to continue.

"Victoria said all those with the birthmark had gifts, all seemingly different. Telekinesis, telepathy, matter manipulation. Victoria said one girl could have real two-way conversations with her dog."

"That," I said with envy, "would be pretty cool."

"I thought so too." Mary nodded. "From what I gathered, it's as though the powers of a god had been divvied up, people with this birthmark receiving one or two of its abilities."

"Okay, so where does your theory come into play?"

"Victoria told me that there were no guys on the online forum."

"Well, that's kind of odd." Speculations quickly raced through my mind.

"I think our killer is an anomaly," Mary interjected before I could say anything else. "I think he was born with the birthmark and for some reason it is fully active."

"I'm following you so far."

"What if he's able to control air?"

"Seriously?" I groaned. "You have no idea how many Airbender jokes are going through my mind right now." I surprised myself by referencing the *Avatar: The Last Airbender* cartoon. It wasn't one I had ever paid much attention to. The number of references I had come across on the internet had passively put information about the show into my head.

"I'm amazed you're an actual PI with how easily distracted you get," Mary chastised. "A bad guy could dangle something shiny in front of you and get away."

"Hey now, do not underestimate the capacity of someone with ADHD when they get hyper-focused," I countered. "Besides, humor is the only thing keeping me sane with this case. We all have our coping mechanisms."

"Fair enough," Mary conceded.

"So, if our killer's able to control the air—"

"Grabbing his victims becomes an easy feat," Mary stated with certainty. "He could cut off their available oxygen, rendering them unconscious in seconds. It would preclude the need for an element of surprise, or the use of drugs."

My mind stopped on the words. Something, an amorphous concept, took shape in my mind. "Unconsciousness due to asphyxia normally only lasts for a short period of time. He would need drugs to keep the girls asleep until he was ready for them."

Mary nodded, considering the possibility. "I guess so. To be honest, I don't know much about it. On TV, choking someone seems to lead to instant death."

Being rendered unconscious by strangulation is not inherently a death sentence. The body knows how to breathe, and so long as the airway is cleared before a certain amount of time passes, chances of survival are high. However, someone with the capacity to cut off airflow from a distance and with precision does have quite a formidable weapon.

Thoughtlessly I said, "He could suffocate them to death." Catching the unintended verbal expression, I qualified, "I doubt that is the case though."

"Why do you doubt it?" Mary looked at me expectantly.

My mind flipped through the coroner reports I had perused before falling asleep last night. "No petechial hemorrhage in any of the victims. All the coroner reports seem to conclude blood loss was cause of death. Judging from the state of Madame Toulah and Sonja's bodies when we saw them—"

"Yeah. That brings me to my second thought on this," Mary said thoughtfully. "What was used to cut up the bodies with such precision?"

I had a good idea where she was going with this.

"Imagine a blade the width of an oxygen molecule traveling close to the speed of sound with some psycho at the helm." Her description hit home as I turned the car into the medical examiner's parking lot.

"If that's really the case, we are kinda fucked."

Stephanie and Agent Allen greeted us in the lobby of the ME's office. Well, Stephanie greeted us. Agent Allen grunted. As a point of honor, I chuckled in his general direction.

"Any word on Madam Toulah's shop?" I asked.

"According to the officers dispatched to the location," Agent Allen responded, "the place was an absolute mess. One of the officers described it as looking like a tornado had torn through the place."

Stephanie chimed in. "Blood-stained pieces of the floor were discovered."

"Wait, the floor was torn up?" I couldn't quite visualize it.

"Apparently our killer went to town on the entire place," the G-Man's deep voice cut back in. "Floors, walls, ceiling, all the contents of the store smashed or shredded. Got a CSI crew out there now digging through the mess. They estimate at least a week to complete sifting through that wreckage."

I shook my head in dismay. The store was a quaint little shop with a homey feeling and always smelled of eucalyptus. I sighed in resignation. "Damn. Well, let's get this over with."

The large FBI agent gestured for us to follow him. Leading Mary, Stephanie, and I through the maze of corridors, we stopped outside an exam room. Agent Allen knocked on the door. A small, pudgy, pretty Asian woman around five feet tall partially opened the door. Dressed in blue plastic protective gear, she scowled at Agent Allen.

"What you want, tall man?"

"Good morning to you too, Mai," the G-Man responded.

"Wait." She seemed momentarily confused. "It is morning?"

"It's nine." Agent Allen now seemed confused. "Have you been working all night?"

Looking over her shoulder at a wall-mounted clock, she said, "I guess so."

"I'd like to introduce—"

Mai held up a latex glove covered hand, cutting the FBI agent off. She pointed down the hall. "Get changed, then introductions." Mai promptly turned around, disappeared back into the exam room.

"So," Mary's chipper voice piped up, "is she always like that?"

"With me," Agent Allen looked at my helper, "yes."

Mary opened her mouth, I assumed to make some snippy remark about Agent Allen's barely there personality. I cut her off.

"Ya'll heard what the lady said," I declared. "No use lollygagging in the hallway." I started walking toward the changing room Mai had indicated.

"Did you just say *lollygagging*?" Sarcastic incredulity permeated Stephanie's question. The kind of tone that told a person they'd spend the rest of their lives hearing about it.

"We shall never speak of it again," I responded, waving for them to get moving.

Geared up in what looked like thin blue rain suits, we returned to the exam room. The antiseptic smell hit me like a freight train. Two metal autopsy tables sat in the center of the room, occupied by piecemeal cadavers. Sonja Verztuk was placed on one, her body parts placed in the anatomical arrangement they had in life. The other slab held one of the crucifix Jane Does, similarly reassembled.

"Ah," Mai exclaimed, seeing the four of us in our protective garb. "Much better."

"Now then," Agent Allen began, "Mai, this is Private Detective Jonathan Hayes and his sidekick Mary."

"Wow." A mischievous smile crossed Mary's face. "You made a funny. I hope you didn't hurt yourself."

The giant let out a grunt, shook his head in disapproval.

Mai bounced her finger at Mary, a broad grin on full display. "I like this one. She has got spunk."

I held out my gloved hand. As Mai took it, I noticed the remnants of dried tears at the corners of her eyes. "Are you alright?" I asked. Her grin faltered at my question.

"Odd question," she simply stated.

"I can see sadness in your eyes."

Mai took a deep breath, and her grip on my hand tightened. She met Agent Allen's gaze. "I like this one too. He gives a shit." Mai let go of my hand and gave me a head nod. "Thank you for asking, but I am fine," she said as a mischievous smile of her own came to bear. "I do

143

have one request that a man of your sensitivity might be able to accomplish."

"If it's possible," I said, a little taken aback, "I'd be happy to help."

"If it is at all possible," Mai pointed to Agent Allen, "please help this man extricate the telephone pole he has lodged up his ass. The guy has no emotions."

I couldn't stifle the laugh, which exploded out of me. Mary snickered uncontrollably, Stephanie snorted, and Agent Allen growled. Pushing stragglers of red hair into what she called a "glorified shower cap," Stephanie cleared her throat.

"Isn't this a little disrespectful?" she asked.

Mai waved her off as she moved into position beside the body of our Jane Doe. "The dead do not care," Mai stated with finality. "They are dead."

"Can we get to work?" Agent Allen's pleading, deep voice seemed to boom throughout the exam room. "Please?"

Mai let out an exasperated sigh. She and the agent had clearly played this game many times. Mai took her pen, tapped it against the dismembered thigh of the Jane Doe's corpse. I remembered this woman. It was her lifeless eyes that had unnerved me at the crime scene right before Mary had so foolishly arrived under the pretense of being an FBI agent. The sound of plastic hitting plastic quietly echoed through the room with each tap Mai gave the dead woman's leg.

"What do any of you know about plastination?"

Looking like an idiot, I raised my hand. Agent Allen rolled his eyes.

"For fuck's sake, this isn't middle school," he said. "Just spit it out, lest we get a bunch of technical terms I need a dictionary to decipher."

"It's the process of preserving tissue using polymers to effectively turn a cadaver into a mannequin," I said.

"In a nutshell, yes." Mai nodded. "All of the crucified bodies underwent the plastination process. The dismemberment occurred after their tissues had undergone preservation. I believe they were alive when this process occurred."

"You believe?" Agent Allen raised an eyebrow. "That's not like you."

"Well, tall man," Mai looked indignant, "they are basically blocks of plastic now. Besides some petechial hemorrhages, outward signs are inconclusive. They all asphyxiated; without opening them up I cannot really determine much else."

"Well, that explains the lack of predation," I said. Mai gave me a knowing nod.

"What about X-rays?" Mary chimed in.

"Useless. Unlike the preserved anatomical dissections of that Bodies exhibit at the Luxor, these bodies have been turned into solid blocks. No density differential for the X-rays to image."

"Okay," Agent Allen began, his eyes shut tight, fingers gripping the bridge of his nose. Stephanie took the frustration in his voice as a cue to step in.

"What have you been able to determine?" Her voice was diplomatic.

"I can tell you that the dismembering cuts on the crucified women are trying very hard to mimic the cuts our friend on the other table suffered." Mai gestured to Sonja's disarticulated remains. "However, our chemist here was unable to get purely clean cuts."

"Can we tell what he used?" The G-Man perked up at the possibility of concrete answers.

"Not without some serious experimentation," Mai stated. "My best guess is a custom cutter, probably using a small gauge wire running between ten to twenty thousand rpms."

"How did you come to that conclusion?" I asked.

Mai pointed at the cut edge of a dismembered arm with the butt of her pen. "There are microscopic strata throughout each cut."

"What about the cuts on Sonja?" I asked.

"Yes," Mai said, "she and her grandmother are a bit different. The cuts are clean, no tool marks. Absolutely nothing to indicate what was used."

"A coroner's report of a previous victim speculated a laser could have been used," I said.

"That person is an idiot," Mai stated with disgust.

"How so?" Agent Allen asked.

"A laser would leave obvious evidence. Specifically burst cell membranes and microscopic burns."

145

"Any theories?" I asked.

"All I can tell is that it looks like something that had to have been thinner than the width of a hair traveling at impossibly high speed made cuts that clean. Outside of some very expensive laboratories, nothing has such capability."

"Okay," Agent Allen said. "We're going to have to table that mystery until we either have our unsub in custody or find a device that fits the criteria."

"I will keep looking," Mai said. "As for the infinity symbols—"

I suppressed my gag reflex as Mai gingerly lifted Sonja's head off the table and pulled back the left ear, showing the mark to all in attendance.

"Definitely not a tattoo." Her assessment was made with absolute finality. "Once again there are some of my colleagues who should be fired for laziness."

"How is that even possible?" Stephanie chimed in. "Ten women with the same birthmark? One that seems unnaturally perfect in form to boot."

Mai nodded, her lower lip jutting out.

"I do not know," she stated. "It seems like it is an impossibility. But here it is. No mistake, these symbols contain no ink, only melanin."

"Could one use melanin as a kind of tattoo ink?" I asked.

"Neat idea," she said, "but not possible. The body would absorb the injected melanin as excess. Or worse, reject it."

I sighed; yet another mystery with no viable clues to an answer. Mai gently placed Sonja's head back on the table and turned to me.

"You knew her?" she asked.

"Yes."

"Then I will not take offense," she held up a scalpel, "if you choose to leave for this next part."

"No, I'm staying." I have only been through one other autopsy. Nasty business. These final examinations are hard to stomach. Seeing as two people I knew personally had been taken by this madman, it was only right that I should bear witness to the final words their bodies had to say.

A properly done autopsy takes a considerable amount of time. Most medical examiners do the physical exam in one to four hours, depending on complexity and what samples are requested for testing. Mai spent six hours on Sonja's remains, combing through every little detail of her internal anatomy, periodically holding up an organ for all to see. By the end of the exam, I felt woozy, bile burned my throat, and Mary held a concerned look on her face.

"You okay?" my sidekick asked. "You're looking a bit green."

I narrowed my eyes at her. "And you look like you've done this before."

She chuffed. "I'm a true crime junkie. I've watched more uncensored videos of crime scenes and autopsies than is probably healthy. I got the nausea out of my system in Red Rock."

I took a deep breath, nodding wearily. "Do we know what her cause of death is?"

"I am split on that," Mai said, furrowing her brow. "A few of her injuries bear evidence that she was alive when she sustained them. Blood loss is the most likely. I did not see any evidence of puncture or force-related organ damage."

"So we are still at square one," Agent Allen lamented.

"Not entirely," Mai said. "I found quite a few hairs that did not belong to our victim. Some with the roots intact, so pulling a DNA profile should be possible."

"When did you—"

Agent Allen was cut off by Mai. "Before you showed up."

"And you had us sit through all this because…?"

A mischievous smile crossed the coroner's face, and she let out a high-pitched laugh. "I just like seeing you squirm, big man."

Agent Allen's face went red. Part appeared to be from embarrassment, but I was certain a decent level of rage was included in that shade of crimson. The clock read 4pm, and while my knowledge of human anatomy had been illuminated, we were no closer to finding the identity of the Hatchetman.

"How long for the DNA?" Mary asked.

Mai guffawed. Lifting her eyebrows, our small and round coroner shook her head.

147

"At least two weeks," she said, "and that is only if we can find a lab that is not tied down by red tape."

Four groans simultaneously filled the air as we collectively expressed our frustration. I took a deep breath, trying to calm my disappointment. Crushing silence filled the exam room. A momentary sense of hopelessness.

"Okay." I broke the silence. "I think we have all we can get out of this for now."

Agent Allen regarded me with an inscrutable expression. I couldn't tell if he was pissed that I had taken control or relieved.

"Let's go get ourselves cleaned up and meet back at my hotel room around seven." I felt like I needed a shower. The smell of sanitized death held fast to my nostrils.

Agent Allen gave me an indignant glare, as if to say he didn't need any time to freshen up. Stephanie lifted her forearm to her nose, sniffed, and recoiled in disgust. Scrunching her face, she nodded in agreement. Mary followed suit, letting out a disgusted sigh. Mai laughed at us.

"Why your hotel?" the resistant G-Man demanded.

"You know that techno-wiz you wanted to recruit?" I reminded him. "She'll be making an appearance tonight. You're gonna want to be there, it's like seeing a damn unicorn."

"She's that amazing to see?" Mary asked.

"No clue." I grinned. "No one has ever seen her before."

Chapter 14

Caleb sat in his SUV, binoculars in hand, waiting for the Goddesses to arrive. It was Support Group night. He had learned about this meeting from the Goddess Message Board; there was an entire section on the site devoted to help groups. He knew the names of the four women who would be in attendance, and he knew the gifts three of them possessed. Two of them could serve his purpose. The third was a question mark, her gift unknown to him. The fourth, a Goddess with the ability to control electricity, would be far too dangerous.

A two-story reddish tan structure, the apartment building had large street-facing picture windows that showed off the living rooms of each unit. Two of the three units had curtains drawn. The third was on full display. Caleb could see the back of a woman in the tastefully decorated open-plan room. With light tan and sage furniture, he had a direct line of sight to a couch facing in his direction. A low glass coffee table sat in front of the comfortable-looking seat.

With a stocky build, wearing a bright yellow t-shirt and baggy blue pants, the woman's reddish-brown hair swayed with her movements. She danced as she set up a spread of food. Caleb tried to remember the support group leader's name. Opening his notebook, he turned to the page containing the information.

"Tippy," he said aloud. "Weird name."

According to an instant message conversation he had with one of the support group members, Tippy was the kindest, most gentle, and wisest woman they had ever met. He had been told she was not a member of the Goddess Message Board, a fact that made him wonder how she had become the leader of this local group. Looking through the binoculars, he watched her pick up two silver meditation balls from a table. She rolled them in her hand as she turned toward the window. Caleb felt a twinge of shock run through him as he witnessed her countenance.

"What the fuck," he whispered, disgust permeating his words. "She's a fucking retar—"

His words died on his lips as he watched the silver meditation balls rise from Tippy's hand, circling each other in a dance of levitation.

149

Caleb stared through the binoculars, transfixed by the shining ballet that had commenced.

As they slowly turned, the silver balls spread from each other until there was two feet between them. Stopping equidistant from Tippy's upturned palm, the reflective orbs held for beat then slowly arced upward. Above her head, the metal balls tapped each other, stopped a moment, and began their slow orbit around each other again. As they turned, the sliver globes moved apart, their speed increasing.

At five feet apart, the dancing spheres quickly dropped, appearing as little more than a glinting blur. The balls halted their descent right above the floor, then just as quickly rose to Tippy's head level. The shining orbs came together, stopping directly in front of the woman's childlike smile. Orbiting once again, both balls shot out horizontally. Their paths erratic, the glinting objects flew around the living room at impossibly high speed, deftly weaving around furniture, vases, and standing picture frames.

Watching the display, Caleb had a sudden epiphany. This Goddess wasn't simply playing, she was practicing. She was training for combat. The control she displayed, the defensive and offensive maneuvers that the casual observer would see as an extraordinary juggling act, showed that in spite of her appearance, this woman was a certified badass.

He studied her face through the binoculars. Tippy's broad features, slightly squished face, her flattened nose, full lips, and heavy-lidded eyes, were all hallmarks of Down syndrome. They spoke only of what he considered genetic damage. Something that shouldn't be allowed to live. Caleb's blood ran cold as he took in the totality of her expression. Vertical pupils couched within hazel eyes were looking in his direction, and her face was the portrait of a hardened warrior. Gone was the smile of innocence. Gone was the appearance of childish amusement. The face Caleb saw held lethal purpose, one who would defend her flock to the death.

The arrival of a white van with the words "Accessibility Transport" on the side drew Caleb's attention. With the van parked in front of the apartment complex, his vantage point only allowed him to see the corner of a powered wheelchair being lowered to the sidewalk. Zipping through the tiny resident parking lot, he caught a glimpse of neon pink hair. The sound of the van's side door closing echoed down the block and the uniformed driver quickly hopped into the vehicle, speeding off.

Before Caleb could refocus on the open window, an Uber van pulled up. The grey minivan's driver, a thirty-something woman in blue jeans and a white t-shirt, jumped out. Opening the rear door, she pulled out a pair of crutches and a folded black wheelchair. As she moved to the curb side of the minivan, a blue Honda Accord pulled up behind it. Caleb saw the passenger of the Accord lean over and give the driver a kiss on the cheek. She sprinted from the car to the side of the minivan, a medium-cropped afro bouncing as she went. Moments later the Uber van's driver hopped back into the vehicle, pulling away to reveal three women.

A frail-looking brunette was situated in the foldable wheelchair. Next to her, a sturdy bronze-skinned woman on crutches, her legs bent at uncomfortable angles. The bouncy afro'd woman stood at the helm of the wheelchair. All three waved and smiled at the driver of the Accord as they made their way toward their destination. The Honda sat in front of the apartment building until the women disappeared through the entrance, then slowly pulled away.

Looking back into the unobstructed window, Caleb could see the pink-haired woman in her high-tech wheelchair. She reminded him of the late Stephen Hawking. Her head was pulled back, creating the illusion of a double chin. Her staccato movements showed that she had difficulty with motor control. Checking his notebook, a written backup of his online conversations with the various Goddesses, her bright pink plumage identified her as Maddy Kuntz, twenty-three and electrokinetic when her gift presented.

"Figures," he muttered. "The most crippled of the bunch is the most dangerous."

His attention was drawn to a commotion at the far end of the living room. Tippy greeted each of the three women, hugs and smiles all around. As the women settled into their spots on the couch, Caleb completed his identification.

The frail brunette in the analog wheelchair was Ivory Lydel, twenty-five; her gift appeared to be remote viewing, the ability to see events happening great distances away. The bronze-skinned woman with bent legs was Reina Runningbear, nineteen, with the gift of shapeshifting. A troublesome ability, Caleb thought, but not uncontrollable. The last woman was the wildcard.

With her bouncy, medium length afro, Caleb had little information on Makela Johnson. A smooth, medium brown complexion made her age hard to determine, and none of her online conversations had filled him in on that detail. She could be twenty, she could be sixty. Her gift was also a mystery, as was the fact that she appeared to have no handicap. Despite these questions about her, he thought she was his best target. He didn't need a girl for her gift this time, just a sacrifice to get the Raven's attention.

Watching the feel-good meeting was about as interesting to Caleb as watching paint dry. Ten minutes of silent moving lips and he felt himself falling asleep. Putting the binoculars in his lap, he rubbed his eyes and in one fluid motion smacked his cheeks with both hands. The sting did little to alleviate his boredom-induced fatigue.

He barely registered the old, black Ford Mustang as it took a parking spot on the street. Taking an uninterested look through his binoculars, he watched as the goth driver stood outside the vehicle.

"Cute," he said, a twinge of anger striking him as the word passed his lips.

The young woman pushed black dagger-point locks of hair behind her ears, her purple Bettie Page-style bangs swayed slightly as she moved toward the apartment building. Caleb felt some surprise that he found even a partial attraction to this woman. His desire rested with the pursuit of his own perfection. Sexual desire simply wasn't in him. The moment of lust mutated into resentment. If she turned out to be one of the Goddesses, she could be his sacrifice. At the very least, she needed to be punished for drawing out an inkling of desire from his loins.

Looking back to the group meeting, he watched as the conversation appeared to stop. Tippy rose, headed to the door. From his angle, Caleb could only see Tippy's feet as she backed up and moved to the side. Black combat boots came into view, followed by black jeans and a black leather jacket covering a crimson t-shirt as the Mustang driver came into view. The support group's attendees regarded the woman with adoration the moment they laid eyes on her. In an instant, Caleb knew exactly who this woman was.

"I found you." His sing-song tone reverberated through the SUV. His attraction to her now made sense to him. "Well, every king needs his queen," he said to himself. "Why not…"

Raven stood at the periphery of Tippy's living room feeling unusually self-conscious. The adoring expressions aimed at her, expressions she had seen thousands of times, brought a wave of anxiety. She smiled at the group as Tippy brought out a folding chair for her. Letting out a soft sigh, she took the seat. Tippy remained standing, a shadow at Raven's back in case she was needed.

"I'm glad to see you are all safe," she began, her smile melting into seriousness. "As you've seen on the message board, someone here in Vegas poses a risk to you."

"We've been following the precautions," Reina said, a desire for approval ringing in her voice. "None of us go anywhere without at least three other people."

"Good." Raven regarded the young woman with a wide smile. "Keeping safe is of the utmost importance right now."

Her heart racing, Raven closed her eyes for a moment and drew in a deep breath. She mentally cursed the anxiety-ridden knot in her chest. Four people wasn't a large crowd, but the change was an intimate process. The pain involved, the linking of minds. It wasn't a simple procedure, and it wasn't meant for an audience.

"I don't like to do things this way," she began, regarding the four women with her emerald gaze. Tippy placed her hand on Raven's shoulder. Pausing, Raven took another deep breath.

"Why?" Maddy's digital voice spoke up. Unable to speak, she had been set up with the same computerized voice system used by the likes of Stephen Hawking.

"For one, the process is individual, intimate," Raven said. "You all have a choice. A choice that I don't want influenced by the presence of others."

The women all nodded in understanding.

"This is a no judgment zone," Ivory's thick Southern accent explained. "Whatever choice any of us makes, we all give support." The young lady gave a sly smile. "This is a support group, after all."

Raven chuckled and felt a little foolish. Of course this group would understand and support each other no matter the choice any of them made. The knot of anxiety unraveled as she took a deep, soothing inhale.

"Okay then," Raven smiled, "I want you all to carefully consider what it is you want. You can live a fully human life without your current physical impediments. Everything a human life has to offer will be open to you. Find the job of your dreams, live in peace, maybe even start a family if you want." She took another deep breath. "The tradeoff is that the abilities that occasionally manifest themselves now will be lost. You will be fully human."

The women nodded in contemplation, taking in Raven's words with the utmost seriousness. They understood the gravity of their choice.

"The other option," Raven continued, "is to become fully actualized. The power you only have sporadically will be fully at your control. But you will be sacrificing any semblance of normal life and putting yourselves in harm's way. Keep in mind, the change is permanent. Once it is done, there is no going back."

"I choose to fight," Makela's voice confidently stated. "I've been waiting twenty-four years for this."

Raven studied the woman. Makela appeared to be in her early twenties, though nearly imperceptible strands of grey in her afro hinted she was much older. With no apparent disability, Raven knew they had an uncommon connection.

"You knew Beth," Raven said, referring to the Caretaker who had made her whole. It was a twist of fate that brought Beth into existence seventeen hundred years after the last of the original Caretakers had perished. Or perhaps it was by design. She was born of humans, yet she held one hundred percent of the Caretaker's DNA. The final pure Caretaker, with a destiny to pass the torch to a more prosperous generation.

"When I was sixteen," Makela nodded. "She was searching for you at the time." A note of sadness invaded her tone. "I had been diagnosed with ALS, but Beth took the symptoms away. I have been able to live a fairly normal life, random bouts of telepathy notwithstanding."

"It was a bit ironic," Raven said, "that she, a full-blooded Caretaker, could relieve us half-breeds of these crippling side effects without full conversion, an ability I don't have." A sorrowful smile crossed Raven's face. "Yet making me whole took her life, something I can do for others with no issue."

"And she said you were worth the sacrifice," Tippy interjected.

Raven took a deep breath, nodded.

"I want to be normal," a digital voice spoke up. "I want to be a normal person."

Raven's heart leapt hearing the words Maddy's voice synthesizer conveyed. It was rare for the Waiting to choose the human path. No small amount of envy crossed Raven's heart. A small part of her yearned for a human life. A life free of the Dark Man. A life free from the looming doom she existed to fight against. She smiled at Maddy and nodded.

Tippy walked over to the pink-haired girl in the powered wheelchair and enveloped her in a hug, a smile plastered across her face.

"You're gonna have such a great life." Excitement permeated Tippy's whisper.

Reina and Ivory both gave approving nods and smiles. They had known Maddy wanted nothing more than to be "normal," though even Maddy admitted that "normal" was an illusion. No one was actually normal.

"I want to be whole," Ivory's soft voice floated through the room. "I want to protect my family."

Ivory had spent her life in fear, her brother always coming to her rescue. Two years ago, he was stabbed while stopping a man trying to abduct her. He survived, but guilt had eaten at her ever since. She wanted to be strong. She wanted to take the mantle of protector.

"I choose to fight," Reina stated with finality.

"Okay," Raven said. "Who's first?"

"Maddy," Makela quickly offered without hesitation.

"Maddy," Reina agreed.

"Maddy," Ivory nodded.

"Makela," Maddy's digital voice offered.

"Sorry, sweetie," Makela said, a beatific smile painted across her face. "I can wait a little longer. It's time for you to start the next chapter of your life."

Chapter 15

"I can't get a damn moment to myself."

Less than thirty seconds after I dropped Mary at her hotel, my phone rang. The caller ID showed it was Stephanie. I hit the answer button and her somber voice slid through the Bluetooth car connection.

"Our killer's struck again," she said, "and this time he just left the victim where he killed her."

"You there already?"

"Just pulling up. Maybe he got sloppy." Stephanie voice carried a hint of hope.

"You're gonna miss meeting the legend herself."

"Ugh, I know," the disappointed whine came through the phone. "Say hi to Brianna for me. We'll let you know if we find anything useful."

"Be careful," I said. Stephanie was already gone.

Within five minutes I had parked my car in the Cosmopolitan's underground lot and made the little jog between the public parking elevators and the guest room elevators. Following me into the lift, a pair of bleach-blondes clad in matching white crop-tops and what they probably thought were jean-shorts. To my eyes, they looked like denim thongs. Lost in my head, the low conversation between the girls was little more than mindless background chatter. Until, that is, the elevator doors opened for the pair, and I caught words that haunt me to this day.

"I've never been a farmer," one of the girls exclaimed, "but I'm willing to give castration a try."

Dumbfounded, I stared at the back of the girls as they walked out of the elevator. My mind ran through every possible context I had missed for the comment to make sense, trying to process the statement right up until I entered my hotel room.

Tara looked at me from the bed, her face contorting in disgust. "You smell like a morgue," her words rang out. My wife had the nose of a bloodhound.

"Funny you should say that." I snickered, turning into the bathroom to remove the stench of death.

157

I emerged twenty minutes later. Having scrubbed off the top layer of my skin to remove the morgue perfume, my entire body felt raw. Donning black sweatpants and an old, once-black shirt, I sat on the bed next to my wife. She grabbed her phone off a side table and proceeded to fill me in on her day.

As I hadn't needed remote help while in the morgue, Tara went house hunting. Scrolling through her phone's picture gallery, she showed me every nook and cranny of the homes she had visited. Open floorplans being the trademark of twenty-first century architecture, it came down to bedrooms for our decision to be made. We agreed on a modest-sized, four-bedroom house.

"The next day you don't need me I'll go and buy the place," she said.

Thanks to the payment on this case, we were able to buy a house outright. It was a weird feeling. Our lives were like most people. Forced to finance everything, debt a constant shadow. Thanks to Joseph Handler, by way of Mr. Strickland, we were instantly thrust away from the lifestyle of paying interest on breathing. It felt weird. It felt wrong. An odd sensation in which the stress of making enough money to pay the bills was lifted off our shoulders mixed with the anxiety that everything would come crashing down around us. I let out a long, cleansing exhale. No sense in worrying about the future.

A knock at the door drew our attention. The hotel-provided digital clock read 7pm. I hadn't realized so much time had passed.

"That's probably Mary," I said as I got up. Stopping at the door, I called out, "Who is it?"

"Candygram," an unfamiliar female voice replied. I looked at Tara, who was silently laughing, shaking her head, and rolling her eyes. She motioned for me to open the door.

Opening the portal, I was greeted by a sight that stopped me in my tracks. In a style that could only be described as an anime version of the Blaxploitation character Foxy Brown, five foot seven Brianna Smith stood before me. Beneath a puffed-out, crimson baker boy cap, half-face square lens sunglasses peered at me. A black leather biker-style jacket covered what some might call a shirt. The crimson fabric was skin-tight, with an open void down the middle, the deep brown of her stomach and partially exposed breasts on display. Tight black leather pants paired with crimson combat boots completed the surreal ensemble. The only indication that she was more than an outrageous cosplayer was the leather computer satchel slung over her shoulder.

"You must be the birthday boy," she said with an exaggerated, stripper-esque tone. "Ain't you a tall glass of water."

Brianna threw her arms around me, pulling me in close. She whispered into my ear, "Just go with it."

Walking past me into the room, Brianna let out a loud "Woo-hoo" as she put her computer bag on the couch.

"A'ight," she said. "Are you ready for the night of your life?"

"Um…" To an outside observer, I probably looked uncomfortable with the situation. "Yes?" Truth is, I was desperately trying not to laugh.

Tara got off the bed, walked over to us. Like me, she was trying her damnedest not to roll on the ground in hysterics. She gave Brianna a welcoming nod.

"Oh," Brianna said, "looks like I'm getting the best of both worlds tonight."

She withdrew a laptop, hit the start button, and produced a cylinder that looked like a grey Amazon Alexa. Hooking the cylinder to the computer, she hit a few keys. A circular red light pulsated around the rim of the Alexa-looking device.

"Damn, girl," she said, her eyes locked on the computer screen. "You fine."

Tara opened her mouth to say something, but Brianna held up her hand to stop her. The computer-wiz brought her thumb into her palm. A second later, her index finger. She was counting down.

Four.

"Come on, birthday boy."

Three.

"Let's get this party started."

Two.

"Damn, boy, you work out?"

One.

"Is that a roll of quarters in your pocket or are you—"

Zero.

159

The light on the Alexa-looking device turned green. Brianna sat back, let out a sigh, and took off her sunglasses. She rubbed her luminescent, light brown eyes. Smiling, trying not to laugh, she shook her head.

"I really hate pulling that stupid stripper act," she said. "It's nice to finally meet you, Jonathan."

Tara could no longer hold it in. An explosion of howling laughter bounced off the walls. Brianna and I looked at Tara, amusement plastered on both our faces. Calming herself, my wife took a deep breath.

"What was that about?" she asked.

"Well," Brianna started, "I don't know who might be listening. A standard bug sweep doesn't detect someone using a sonic ear." She gave the cylindrical device a pat. "That's why I built this little guy. It can detect a sonic listening device within eight hundred feet, but it will interfere with any listening device no matter the range."

"So, what's the verdict?" I asked.

Brianna looked at the computer, hit a few keys, and raised her eyebrows. "Well, someone wants to know what ya'll been talking about." She pointed toward the floor. "Got a hit, judging by the distance it's directly under us."

Tara gasped, a look of intense concern crossing her face.

"Should we leave?" I asked. Brianna shook her head.

"I'm guessing it's part of the FBI background investigation your Agent Allen ordered. Apparently, he does not trust you."

"Wouldn't that be an abuse of Bureau resources?" Tara asked.

"I really don't know," Brianna admitted, shrugging. "When I was with the NSA, no one would have batted an eye at such action."

"So—" I started.

"No need to worry," Brianna said as she disconnected the anti-surveillance device from her computer. The green light persisted, indicating it did not require the computer for extended operation. She brought her laptop to a shelf beneath the flat screen television and proceeded to hook up the display.

"Umm," Tara piped up, "why is there no need to worry?"

"Oh, sorry." Brianna realized she forgot to explain herself. "Right now any listening device is only hearing hardcore death metal."

I broke into a full belly laugh.

"That is awesome," I managed to choke out. Taking a deep breath to calm myself, I said, "Okay, let's get down to business."

Brianna nodded, hit a few keys on her keyboard. The TV screen displayed a timeline, each of our victims marked at their estimated time of death. Green lines connected some names to others. I could see a pattern between those with the infinity birthmark and those without. The beginning of the timeline had a red circle, inside it three names with question marks surrounding them.

"So what's the circle about?" I asked.

Brianna smiled, seeming to understand that the rest was self-explanatory to me.

"These three people," she reflexively pointed to the names, "Henry Voss, Patrice Voss, and Therese Tanner, are the only victims that have no connection to those bearing the infinity symbol."

"So you think the birthmarks are his primary targets?" I asked. I did not know if Tara had relayed my suspicions or if Brianna made the connection on her own.

"Wait," she said. "Birthmarks?"

"We're waiting on confirmation," Tara said, "but we believe so."

"Interesting," Brianna said, her chin clasped in her hand. Pausing, her mind seemed to have momentarily relocated. She shook her head.

"Everything okay?" I asked.

"Yeah. Just remembering something. Nothing to do with this case," she stated. "So, Henry and Patrice Voss appear to be our first victims—"

"Our first victims using this particular cutting method," I interjected. Tara and Brianna looked at me blankly.

"I have a theory," I said. Tara narrowed her eyes, dubious at my assertion. "Okay, maybe more like an amorphous concept, that our killer started much earlier. If his methodology in prior kills had been so disparate from what we see now, they would not have been connected to him."

Brianna nodded. Tara's lips scrunched.

"Interesting theory, but not really helpful," Tara stated. I hadn't felt like I had some breakthrough piece of the puzzle, but hearing my wife tell me the concept was effectively useless let some of the wind out of my sails. A thought struck me before my mind could send out invites to a pity party.

"Didn't the police reports say our first victims had a son?"

"Yes," Brianna said as she hit a combination of keys on her laptop. An unofficial stat sheet popped up. "Caleb Voss, nineteen years old but could pass for sixteen. No criminal record."

I looked at the senior high school photo of the young man. He appeared younger than his age. Were he an actor, he could easily be cast in a high school drama with no questions asked. I believed they called it "Eighteen to Look Younger" in the film industry. With piercing green eyes, short-cropped dirty blond hair, his smile held disturbing shades of the serial killer Ted Bundy.

A flush of excitement overtook me. This was our guy. This had to be our guy. If this wasn't our guy, then some other law enforcement agency needs to have him on their radar, because that picture screamed serial killer.

"Is this the only picture we have?" I asked, trying not to let my gut dictate conclusions.

Brianna put her hands on her hips, giving me a look of admonishment. I felt like I was about to be scolded by my mother.

"In this day and age, these ego-driven kids don't know how to keep their pictures off the internet," she said as another clack of typing permeated the room.

A digital filmroll with hundreds, maybe thousands, of pictures popped up. Brianna scrolled through the photos, pausing for a few seconds on each to allow us a moment to gauge their usefulness. Some were family photos, some class photos. One photo stood out to me.

"Hold on that one," I declared.

It was a candid shot, probably taken by either Henry or Patrice. The angle was from his back left, Caleb sitting at a desk, book open, his head resting in his hand.

"Zoom in on his ear," I said.

Brianna slowly zoomed the picture in, her brows raising as she saw what I was seeing. The low quality made clear identification difficult.

"Let me see if I can clean this up a bit," Brianna said. The tapping of keys commenced once again.

In television and movies, this kind of operation produces a perfect, clear image. Television and movies are bullshit. The best one can hope for is something blurry yet identifiable, and that is precisely what we got. Behind Caleb Voss' left ear was what appeared to be a warped infinity symbol.

"Is that distortion because of the image quality?" Tara asked, no small amount of surprise in her voice.

"I don't think so," Brianna said, her face scrunched into a combination of pity and revulsion. "Unlike the victims, that thing is fucked up."

"I wonder—"

My thought was cut off by a knock at the door.

Brianna flinched at the sound. She took a step back, ready to dive for cover.

"Relax," I said, getting up. "That's just going to be Mary."

Walking to the door, I could see my assurance did nothing to calm Brianna. She had spent years hiding from the ubiquitous "They," and her reflexes and reactions were honed to that end. In the years I had known her, I have never asked Brianna who "They" were. My assumption had always been "They" were her former employer, the National Security Agency. Stopping at the locked door, I asked the same sing-song question Brianna had been greeted with.

"Who is it?"

"Candygram," Mary's playful voice returned. My expression could only be summed up by the word "huh."

Mary stood at the threshold, over-dressed in a stylish midnight-blue pant suit, a large manila envelope occupying her hands. Bulky, it seemed to contain some sort of box. "Jonathan Hayes" was written in large black capital letters. No mistaking who the intended recipient was.

"Is this—" I started, thinking it might be the information Mary had promised.

"No," Mary said. "This was left at your door."

163

Walking into the hotel room, Mary handed me the envelope and proceeded to give a vigorous, childlike wave to Tara and Brianna.

"Hi," she said to our tech guru. "I'm Mary Thompson."

Brianna nodded in greeting, her face the portrait of suspicion. She regarded the young woman with the same caution one would use if confronted by a venomous snake.

"Brianna," the Foxy Brown-costumed computer genius replied.

Mary took a seat next to Tara, looked at the television screen with the zoomed-in picture. She put her hand to her mouth, stifling a gasp.

"You found him." It was less of a question and more of a statement.

"We think so," Tara said as I opened the unexpected envelope.

"His name is Caleb Voss, of San Diego," Brianna relayed.

"Oh, before I forget," Mary changed gears, "you should be receiving an email with all the documents I promised. My godfather—"

"I thought you said a friend was helping you out with it," I cut her off. The inconsistency bothered me. I noticed Brianna take a covert picture with her phone. She was planning to give Mary the deep-dive background check treatment.

"I tend to refer to him as a friend. Every time I call him my godfather people think I'm in the mafia."

"What's his name?" Tara asked.

"Mike," Mary responded nonchalantly.

"Mike what?" Brianna asked. I could hear my own doubts in her voice.

"Mike Holvald."

Brianna's eyes widened, mouth agape, and her voice seemed to have taken a vacation. I looked at her, questioning.

"That name mean something to—"

"Are you telling me your godfather is the Penetrator?" Brianna blurted out. A look of shock overcame Mary.

"He's in porn?" I asked.

Brianna and Mary gave matching looks of disapproval. Tara hid a silent snicker behind her hand, not wanting to incur the ocular wrath of the two women in bonding.

"He's one of the best hackers out there," Brianna snapped. "The guy's managed to break into just about every military network on the planet and not get caught."

"How the hell do you know—" Mary started.

"Does the name Nightclaw42 mean anything to you?"

Mary brought her hands to her mouth, her eyes wide. The moment of stunned silence was broken by Mary's explosive, uncontrollable laughter. Brianna, Tara, and I stared at her in confusion.

"He," Mary tried, unsuccessfully, to control her laughter. "He has— He has the— He has the biggest hard-on for you."

Brianna's look of surprise quickly turned to one of seductive satisfaction.

"Maybe you could introduce us one day," she said. Mary, wresting back control of her faculties, nodded.

"I'd love to."

I sighed, shook my head, and smiled. The song "It's a Small World" invaded my mind. Opening the manila envelope Mary had presented me with, I was about to speak when my phone rang. Quickly sliding the answer button, Stephanie's voice came over the line.

"He's devolving," she stated bluntly, her voice flat with a hint of fear.

"I'm putting you on speaker," I said, hitting the hands-free button. "Tara, Mary, and Brianna are here."

"Damnit," Stephanie exclaimed. "I really wanted to meet you, Brianna."

"Another time," Brianna assured her.

"What happened?" I asked, not really wanting the gory details.

"A homeless dude found the body strung up in an abandoned warehouse," she began. "This girl's been sliced up something awful. This looks like torture."

"Do we know who she is?" Brianna interjected.

"Her name is Kelly Talbott," Stephanie answered. "Her driver license and a debit card were in a pocket of her pants. Took a little while to find. Her clothes were piled in a corner, behind a shelving unit. I don't think our killer knew those weren't in her purse, which is not here."

"Why would she have that separ—" I stopped at the sight of three women staring at me like I was an idiot.

"The most likely scenario is that she was going out on the town," Stephanie said. "A lot of girls put their IDs and credit or debit cards in a pocket to cut down on baggage or as a precautionary measure."

The three faces staring at me nodded in unison. Brianna turned her attention back to her laptop and started typing.

"Back to things that matter," Stephanie said. "It looks like our boy done fucked up. Got a full set of bloody prints."

"If it's who we think it is, those prints will be useless," I said.

"Wait." Stephanie was surprised. "You have a suspect? When did this happen?"

"A few minutes ago," Mary chimed in.

"Don't worry, you didn't miss anything," I said, "but he won't be in AFIS."

"His name is Caleb Voss," Tara interjected. "Nineteen, from San Diego—"

"Our vic is from S.D. as well," Stephanie said.

"And," Brianna chimed in as a DMV photograph and basic life statistics of the young blonde victim appeared on the television screen for our edification, "your victim graduated from the same high school as our suspect."

"This leaves only one question for me," I said. "Stephanie, is Agent Allen with you?"

"He's right here, putting you on speaker."

"Allen here," the agent said.

"Agent," I began, "was any effort made to find Caleb Voss?"

"The son of the first two victims," Agent Allen confirmed he knew of the young man. "Yes. We had found voice messages on his mother's phone indicating he had gone on a road trip." The agent paused. "Apparently he was trying to find himself."

"Why didn't he return when he found out his parents were dead?" Tara asked.

"We never managed to contact him," Agent Allen admitted. I thought I detected a hint of guilt in his voice.

"How is that possible?" My voice held an unintended edge.

"My guess," the G-Man countered, "is that the little shit kept his phone off. We just got his voicemail. A few messages were left for him, but no response. No bank activity either. A week before his parents were killed, he pulled five thousand dollars out of his account. We assumed that was around the same time he left on his trip."

"None of this struck you as odd?" I asked. "None of this indicated he was worth closer investigation?"

"Look," the agent snapped, "I was brought in as a consultant, I told SDPD to look into him. As different jurisdictions got involved, I noticed that law enforcement agencies from earlier in the case dropped their investigations. Each time the process to get a warrant to track his phone was started, investigating agencies would quit. I don't know why. They wouldn't say. Just the usual runaround bullshit of resource allocation, budgetary restrictions, and cold trails. Until he crossed into Nevada, I had no authority to press the issue."

"Five grand would probably run out pretty quick. Has anyone checked bank activity on Caleb Voss—"

"Not since November of 2021." Agent Allen's voice expressed our collective epiphany.

"Brianna," I said, urgency permeating her name.

"On it." Her fingers moved in a blur on the laptop keyboard. She stopped momentarily. Her face twisted in disgusted confusion. "Eeeww," she said. "He's staying at the Travelodge on the Strip? Why the hell would he stay there?" After a few keystrokes, she gave her laptop a confused look. "I'm seeing a police dispatch report stating he had been ejected from the motel twenty minutes ago. Apparently, he went apeshit on the room." Shaking her head, she muttered, "Probably improved the look of the place."

"I know where it is," Agent Allen stated. "Stephanie and I will head over now."

"Agent," Tara piped up, "we'll send you a picture of Caleb Voss."

"And I recommend keeping your distance," I said. "We still don't know how he's killing and if he's using a portable device."

"Got it."

"One last thing," I said. "Caleb Voss has an infinity symbol behind his left ear."

"That's very interesting, but it doesn't help us catch him," Agent Allen flatly responded.

"It might," I said. "His birthmark looks like a damn Rorschach test. I think he's targeting the women out of some sort of jealousy. If we can find other women with these birthmarks—"

"I doubt we'll have time to track down anyone. The scene I just saw was an unsub heading into their endgame."

In the background I heard the doors to Agent Allen's Escalade close.

"We can continue this later," he said.

"Jonathan," Stephanie turned off the speakerphone function, "I'll let you know what we find."

"Just be careful," I said. Brianna, Tara, and Mary nodded in a wordless echo of my sentiment.

Hanging up the phone, I turned my attention back to the envelope. It contained a hinged, brushed aluminum box. With all eyes on me, I slid the expensive 4"x4"x2" container from its paper shell. Placing the box on the desk, I carefully opened it.

I looked at the contents in confusion. Held steady by dense grey foam, what appeared to be a dark greenish-grey faceted sphere of graphite sat in the center of the box. The orb was approximately two inches in diameter, its surface cut into large, slightly curved planes like those of an eight-sided die. A small hole appeared to be drilled in the center of each facet. I picked up the strange object, its surface smooth as glass.

"What the hell is this thing?" I blurted out.

Brianna's eyes went wide at the sight of it.

"GET RID OF THAT THING," she screamed, panic permeating every word. "FLUSH IT DOWN THE TOILET!"

Not questioning, I bolted for the bathroom, the sphere held tight in my hand. As I crossed the doorway out of the hotel room's living space, time seemed to slow. I became aware of a hissing noise emanating from the orb. Fiery pain engulfed my hand.

Feeling like someone was trying to drill a hole through my palm, I looked momentarily at the orb. A black gaseous substance was shooting out of the holes in its facets. Without thought, I slammed the bathroom door shut. Holding my breath, I made my way to the toilet and summarily dunked the gas-bomb.

Water in the toilet bowl churned and sputtered, appearing to boil as it turned black. I flushed the roiling black water, evidence of the strange object washing into the great unknown of the Las Vegas sewer. Relieved to be rid of the strange object, I took a deep breath. Big mistake.

In my focus to drown the orb, the basic properties of gas slipped my mind. As I inhaled, I choked on the remnants hanging in the sealed bathroom's air. Coughing, my vision quickly started to blur. Turning on the ventilation fan, I shoved the door open and threw myself out of the gas-filled room.

Tara caught me as I stumbled, and Mary slammed the door behind me. I felt like I was drowning, unable to take in enough air to sustain consciousness. My body convulsed with a prolonged coughing fit as Tara and Mary sat me down on the couch. Fear was splayed across Tara's face. I felt something wet free itself from my mouth. Wiping my lips, I looked to see dark crimson smudged across my palm. I dimly heard Tara's panicked words.

"Call 9-1-1," she instructed Mary, each syllable infused with terror.

"Don't bother," Brianna's voice was calm, despondent. "They can't help him."

"What the fuck, lady?" Mary's anger was palpable.

"He is being judged," Brianna stated. "No one can do anything for him."

As she spoke, my coughing subsided, and my breathing began to ease.

"What the hell does that mean?" Tara yelled. "How can you just stand there—"

I grasped Tara's arm, giving her a meaningful squeeze. She looked at me. Relief shone in her eyes as I took a deep breath. The inhale felt like a thousand shards of glass had been poured down my throat. It was an improvement. The pain lessened with each breath.

For the first time I looked at the hand that held the killer device. I expected to see a gaping hole drilled through it, a mangled mess that resembled ground beef rather than an appendage. To my surprise, the

169

only blemish to my hand appeared to be a quickly healing burn, bits of some black material dissolving into my skin. I sighed in relief.

"You have been judged worthy to live," Brianna said softly.

I looked at her. I was about to ask her meaning when she started shaking. Letting out a stifled sob, Brianna sank to her knees, her breath staggered, her arms trembling. Tara started toward her. Brianna held up a hand to stop her.

"I'm okay," her voice breathless, "just the adrenaline wearing off."

"What did you mean?" I asked. "What did you mean I was ju—"

"Who hired you?" The question was barely audible.

"What?"

"Jonathan," Brianna's voice was measured, controlled, "who…the fuck…hired you?"

Brianna locked her eyes on me. Adjusting uncomfortably in my seat, I furrowed my brow in confusion.

"A man named Joseph Handler," I said. "His daughter is one of our victims."

"No," Brianna said vehemently. "No, no, no, no, no." She hit the floor with each word.

Tara, Mary, and I looked at her, portraits of confusion. We all jumped as she yelled, "FUCK!" Brianna's voice rang out like a shotgun blast. "Twenty-eight years. Twenty-eight years, and this is how that twisted fuck finds me."

"I don't follow," I said, hesitation guiding my words.

"Joseph Handler doesn't have a daughter," she stated. "He doesn't have kids, he doesn't have a family."

"It's the Zabos Cartel incident all over again," I said under my breath, remembering the last time I took a proxy hire.

"I'm not sure he's even human."

"Okay," Mary chimed in. "Back up here. How do you know this guy?"

Pausing, Brianna appeared to have an internal debate, unsure how much she should say. With a resigned sigh, she made her choice.

"In 1991 I was working for the NSA," Brianna said. "I was assigned as a tech to a small town being built in California's central valley called Bedlam." She sighed, and I got the impression this was a story she had never told anyone. "Don't bother looking it up. The town has been redacted. Its existence wiped so cleanly off the earth that even the most ardent conspiracy theorists have never heard whispers of it."

Like children listening to a campfire story, Tara, Mary, and I leaned forward. Brianna brought her legs around, crossing them on the floor.

"I know the place was there. I helped set it up, and I was there when it all went to shit."

"What was her name?" I asked, interrupting Brianna's revelations. "Her full name?"

Brianna sighed, her face a mixture of sadness, sympathy, and contrition. She obviously knew where this was going to lead.

"Atsuko Takanashi," she said. "She was eleven in the brief time I knew her."

"You knew." I felt my face flush with anger. "Five years ago—"

Brianna nodded, understanding my frustration with the case that had killed three of our own, and sent a fourth running to the wind. "Nothing I knew could've helped Darkstone or the others. He's the one who brought me in to DA. When he went into isolation it was a gut punch to me as well."

"Do you know where he is?" I asked, futile hope in my voice.

Brianna shook her head solemnly, an apology splashed across her features. I could feel my heart drop. I made the mistake of hoping I might speak to my mentor again.

"So," Mary brought us back on track, "this pretend sleep study in a government town?"

"Not the government," Brianna said. "They are best described as an extra-governmental agency. They call themselves The Office, and Joseph Handler calls the shots. They use governments all over the world, obtaining resources from them but never answering to anyone."

"So what happened?" I asked.

"They call the substance you were exposed to Black Rock," Brianna said. "And someone spiked Bedlam's water supply with it." She pointed

171

at me. "You were exposed to a weaponized version, one that either kills or has…beneficial physical and/or mental side effects."

I cocked my eyebrow.

"I'm using the term 'beneficial' loosely here," she said. "In the end, Handler gave the order to cleanse the town. No survivors. The Office personnel mowed down everyone. Civilians, government workers like me, soldiers on loan from the U.S. Army…everyone."

"How the hell did they get away with that?" Tara asked.

"If no one's left to complain…" Mary said, her thought trailing off.

"Basically," Brianna said. "The fact that I'm here… I'd say it was a miracle, but it has been more like a waking nightmare."

"How did you get out?" I asked.

"In the rush to get out of the research complex, I ran across Atsuko. An Army private was trying to get her out. We wound up in an elevator, hit the button, and nothing happened." Brianna took a deep breath, "Five soldiers, all members of The Office, had guns trained on us and ready to fire. It was Joseph Handler that stopped their trigger fingers." Brianna chuffed at the memory. "We actually thought he was going to spare us. The elevator started working, and as the doors closed Handler tossed one of those orbs in."

Brianna closed her eyes, a pained look crossing her face. This clearly was a memory she did not want.

"When the gas started filling the elevator, I grabbed Atsuko. I guess I thought I could somehow keep the air away from her." Brianna took in a deep breath, hissing on exhales. "I still hear that young Army private's screams, the image of his skin bubbling and melting away is seared into my mind. I could feel it too, the burning in my lungs and on my skin. I was sure we were all dead."

The three of us were silent. I could tell we all wished for words of comfort, magical words to make Brianna's trauma disappear. None of us knew such a spell.

"When the elevator doors opened, all that was left of that brave soldier was his uniform. His body was a puddle on the floor. Atsuko was still and silent in my arms. I thought for a moment she had died too." Another deep breath came from Brianna. "Silently she turned away from me, heading to the building exit. Heading toward sounds of explosions and gunfire. I called after her, tried to keep her away, get her to turn around. She was able to shove me aside like I was nothing. A scrawny eleven-year-old walked right through me."

Pursing her lips, once again Brianna seemed to have an internal debate.

"If you're worried that we won't believe you," I said, "just remember that I evict ghosts."

She chuckled at that, nodded.

"Outside the research facility, fire and smoke ruled the streets, along with silhouettes of twisted things that were once human. I tried to get Atsuko to leave, but she began to change. This weird, black, beetle-like armor seemed to grow from her body, her legs gained an extra joint. Her hands morphed into massive claws, and before this transformation consumed her face, she said one last thing to me."

Brianna's body shook with an apparent chill.

"She said, 'You have been judged worthy to live, I have been judged worthy to fight. Now run.'" Brianna's face fell. "Whatever she had become, it ran toward the fire. Toward the fight. I got outta there. Spent the last twenty-eight years staying off Joseph Handler's radar."

We all sat in silence, processing the information. My mind reeled with the images. Her description of Atsuko's transformation tugged at something in my mind, some epiphany waiting to reveal itself. Taking a deep breath, I broke the silent contemplation of the room.

"You mentioned side effects from the Black Rock," I reminded her.

"Well," she began, "I told you of Atsuko's. It took a little while for me to notice, but I'm not a great hacker by skill alone. I can see the code and intuit interaction histories. I don't hack a site so much as use credentials I divine by looking at the log-in prompt."

"So it enhances your natural abilities?" Mary asked.

"More like it enhances your basic nature," Brianna responded. "Though nothing is a guarantee."

"How do you know so much about this Black Rock?" Tara asked.

"Because," Brianna said with a mischievous gleam in her eye, "I hacked The Office's mainframe and snagged a copy of their entire research library. A lot of disturbing stuff in there. Handler has no qualms about human experimentation."

173

"Did everyone in Bedlam exhibit unusual abilities?" I asked.

"No, they were exposed to the raw form of the substance. From what I've seen in the research files, it is the weaponized form that can have what they term as enhancements."

"Okay, so what does—"

Brianna cut me off. "There is one effect common to everyone. The dream." Looking me dead in the eyes, her face took on an air of deadly seriousness. "When the dreams start, stay away from the grassy knoll." I could see desperation in Brianna's eyes. "Stay away from the Dark Man."

Chapter 16

Caleb's SUV sat in the empty parking lot, the space bathed in the sickly yellow pallor of a sodium-vapor streetlight. He sat motionless in the driver's seat, fists clenched tight in his lap. Rage couldn't begin to describe his emotional state. Everything was going wrong.

Earlier in the day he had gone to clean up the mess he had made with Kelly Talbott. Little did he know his kill room had already been discovered by a homeless man seeking shelter. Caleb was greeted by police tape and cop cars.

"I had a nice spot picked out and everything for that bitch," he muttered to himself. He growled, the low guttural noise filling the vehicle.

Caleb knew the police now had his fingerprints and DNA. He cursed himself for his laziness. He had gone to the Travelodge to take a nap on a real bed with the intent to come back, clean the scene, and load the pieces of Kelly for disposal. Seeing the police presence, he had considered simply taking them all out. The impulse had taunted him, daring him to let go of his self-control. To act on impulse would have been imperfect, even a raging god must have control over his actions. Being incomplete, Caleb knew he still had vulnerabilities. One sharp cop could take him out.

Exiting the SUV, Caleb regarded the empty industrial building that stood before him with mild interest. A large sign on the white, two-story cube advertised the space was for lease. Square, wire mesh-covered windows were evenly spaced on the second story; the ground floor of the structure was windowless. A near-perfect fortress.

Walking toward the main door, Caleb's mind wandered back in time. He had returned to his room at the Travelodge, anger and anxiety mixing in a toxic mental stew. As soon as he entered the room, Caleb had let loose a primal scream. It didn't help.

Rage does funny things to the mind. Once the red takes hold, memory becomes spotty. It's as though the recording mechanism in the brain starts skipping. Caleb could remember images and short snippets,

175

but not the whole rampage. He wasn't even sure of the order in which he destroyed the room.

He was fairly certain his first act of wanton destruction had been smashing an ugly, round-backed chair on the circular wood table in the front corner of the room. The image of a broken chair leg shattering one of the nightstand lamps entered his mind. Was that before or after he had punched the bathroom mirror into oblivion?

The industrial building's nondescript metal front door was locked. Caleb studied the door for a minute, deciding on where to cut. He knew this kind of door would have moving pylons that locked into holes at both the top and bottom. Raising his hand, two swift motions and the *ting* of splitting metal heralded the door's freedom from the metal rods. All that remained was the center latch bolt. He still wanted a functional door. Having the metal rectangle swaying open was equivalent to putting up a flag for the police.

Taking a moment to consider his options, Caleb's mind wound back to Kelly Talbott. The wretched girl had almost escaped. When he stirred from his "meeting" with the Dark Man, he found Kelly had managed to get one hand free from her binding. With such a large puddle of blood at her feet, Caleb had been pleasantly surprised to find her still breathing. The effort to free her hand had clearly taken its toll. She had the pallor of a corpse, and her lips held a light blue tint. He could not just let her slip from her mortal coil without being punished for trying to flee her god. A sadistic smile crossed his face at the memory.

After he had secured her hand back in its Velcro prison, Caleb lightly tapped on Kelly's cheek until she stirred. It filled him with joy to see her face fall into complete despair as she realized her attempt to escape was a failure. As punishment, he had decided to try something new. His memory focused on Kelly's wide eyes as she felt her hand being forced backward. He had created an air-pressure pocket centered on her palm. Slowly, methodically, he ramped up the intensity. She had tried to resist, tried to keep her hand from collapsing back. As her strength failed, her hand relented to the pressure. At ninety degrees, Kelly felt the resistance of her flesh, the point at which natural motion could go no further. She tried to scream. She tried to beg for mercy. Her voice was silent. A sickly wheezing was all the sound she could muster as Caleb applied more pressure. The crunch of cartilage and bone and the slow ripping of flesh accompanied her hand's new orientation. Her knuckles had been pressed flush to the back of her forearm. He had to admit that he was pleasantly surprised the pain hadn't sent the young woman back into unconsciousness. There was more practice to be done.

The memory gave Caleb an idea. Instead of cutting the door latch, he increased the air pressure in the area he assumed the latch to be. A high-pitched squeak followed by a quiet metallic scraping confirmed his guess. Slowly increasing the pressure, the scraping became a loud *ping* as the latch was forced into the door. He quickly pulled on the handle. Access granted.

His mind wandered back to the Travelodge. At some point in his rage-induced frenzy, the hotel room's flat screen television went sailing through the window next to the front door. Just as security personnel arrived, he grabbed his always-ready-to-go suitcase. Pushing his way past the rent-a-cops, he got into his SUV and tore out of the Travelodge like a bat out of hell. Caleb congratulated himself for not killing anyone. The police might have his prints and DNA from the kill room, but they didn't have anything to compare it to. He wasn't in any database. Since vandalism investigations weren't in-depth, he thought it was unlikely that his fingerprints would be collected from the Travelodge. They had his identifying information at the front desk of the motel; however, connecting him to Kelly's corpse wouldn't happen.

Entering the industrial building, Caleb was surprised that the lights of a small reception area were turned on. In some disrepair, the fifteen-by-fifteen-foot white-walled room had dark wood accents throughout. A centered, beat-up receptionist desk mirrored the wood trim. Two hallways split from the entry room, one to his left, one to his right. What he assumed were office doors appeared to line one side of each hallway, spaced about fifteen feet apart.

His heart skipped a beat as he noticed a wall-mounted alarm control panel behind the reception desk. The white plastic rectangle's LCD screen was dark, indicator lights off. The whole control panel appeared dead. Caleb let out a relieved chuckle.

"Odd," he said to himself, momentarily wondering why the building's owner would pay for electricity but not security.

Looking down the hallway to his right, Caleb noticed a fire map affixed to the wall. It showed the hallways ran in one contiguous path, a large rectangle around a central room. According to the map, this central room had three points of entry, one of which was about ten feet down the hall. Finding the door unlocked, Caleb walked through the rectangular portal into a large warehouse space.

Flicking a light switch to the immediate right of the doorway, Caleb found himself standing on a small concrete platform. Chipped green paint covered a waist-high metal railing, a hand-hold for the five cement steps leading to the warehouse's sunken floor. The room itself was a fifty-foot by fifty-foot cube, the high ceiling lined with hanging florescent shop lights. No trace of former tenants could be found. The previous occupants had taken all their toys with them. Another set of concrete steps mirrored Caleb's entry point. At the back of the room, a metal roll-up door covered most of the wall, while a standard door sat next to the industrial portal. As his gaze fell upon the center of the room, Caleb's lips curled into a perverse smile.

Two large rectangular columns sprang from the floor. Spaced ten feet apart, the load-bearing structures were supported by a pair of cross beams forming a large X between them. Caleb checked the structural integrity of the ready-made crucifix by pulling himself up on it, bouncing as he hung. The steel bar remained motionless under his weight. Each I-beam was four inches in diameter, bolt-welded at a central cross-joint.

"This makes things a bit easier," His voice echoed in the large room as he spoke to himself. "Must be providence. Just a few modifications."

Turning toward the door, Caleb pulled out his notebook and flipped to his homemade directory of resident Las Vegas Goddesses.

"So, who's still available?" he asked the pages. "Oh, I know."

His smile widened as he stopped on a name. This particular girl had been eager to divulge her entire life in the direct messages he had with her on the Goddess website. Name, age, home address, schedule. She had done everything security experts say not to do online. That was not surprising, however. The Goddess site was supposed to be a safe space. And fourteen-year-olds make bad decisions.

Denise Olay sat in her 1996 Honda Civic staring at the single-story home of Maddy Kuntz. She had been tasked with protecting the now fully human woman until the current danger had passed. She didn't mind the tedium of the stakeout. She found the calmness of it meditative, an exercise in awareness without ego. With her eyes locked on the house, her ears took in the rest of her surroundings. Crickets chirped. A cat on a late-night kitty mission darted from bush to bush down the street. An owl's nearly silent flight glided over two houses and made a dive for an unlucky mouse. Raven's footsteps approached the car.

Denise didn't take her eyes off the house when the passenger-side door opened, nor when the car jostled as Raven sat in the seat next to her. Hearing the door close and the lock engage, she turned to greet her friend.

"How did it go?" Raven asked.

"Amazing." Denise's voice held a hint of envy. "Her parents accepted Maddy's sudden change as a miracle from God. They both just wrapped their arms around her and cried."

Raven smiled, nodded, and let out a long breath.

"Good. I was worried they might reject her."

"People seriously do that?" Denise asked.

"Yes," Raven said solemnly. "More often than I'd like. Few have chosen the route of a fully human life. The physical hardships may have been removed, but they get replaced by emotional and relational hardships."

Denise nodded. Her parents had died in a car accident when she was fifteen. Diagnosed with peripheral neuropathy, none of her extended family was willing to take care of a teen with extensive mobility issues. She became a ward of the state, with all the neglect and unloving care the position had to offer. Raven came on her nineteenth birthday. Denise saw no purpose in choosing a fully human life. Those who had shown her love and caring were dead. In her mind, joining the fight required no sacrifice. It was the opposite. She had gained a family. She had found those who cared.

"The sudden change is hard for some parents to accept." Raven looked toward the house. "Maddy's lucky. Do you know Olga Uzencko?"

"She's heading the Big Bear safehouse now, isn't she?" Denise asked.

"Yup, she's the one. She chose the human road." Raven's voice seemed distant as she spoke. "When I came to her, she was bedridden. Hadn't been out of her bed for three years at that point. She desperately wanted to have a relationship with her parents that didn't center around them caring for her. She wanted to repay their kindness, but their kindness ran out the moment she walked into their living room and spoke."

Denise thought she saw a flash of anger and disgust in Raven's face. A rare moment of pure hatred.

"They screamed at her, called her a demon, said it was the devil's work. Her father even picked up a fire poker and swung it at her. I managed to step in before he could make contact."

"So you took her in," Denise stated. Raven nodded.

"Everyone deserves to have support. Everyone deserves to be loved." Raven gave a heavy sigh. "But some forfeit what they deserve, their actions prove they are unworthy." She gritted her teeth. "I discovered that, for all their religiosity and self-righteousness, Olga's parents wanted their daughter to be disabled. They wanted her infirm."

"What the fuck?" Denise blurted out.

"She was a cash-cow for them. In removing her disability, they were going to be deprived of government income." Raven shrugged. "It's not uncommon. They didn't really care about her, they cared about what they could get from her."

Denise let out a disgusted groan, shaking her head. "That's fucked up."

"Yeah," Raven flatly stated. "It most certainly is. And it's all too common. Most of our safehouses are run by the rejected."

Raven smiled, putting the pain she carried for the rejected back into the mental lockbox she kept it in. The memories served to motivate her when needed.

"I am overjoyed to hear Maddy won't be needing us. She's one of the lucky few."

Denise turned her watchful eyes back to the house.

"Mai stopped by." She pointed at the glovebox. "She left some pictures for you."

Raven popped open the glovebox, pulled out a teal file folder with the name Sonja Verztuk printed on the tab. Four eight-by-ten photographs were enclosed. Raven pulled them out.

"You already look at these?"

"Yeah," Denise responded. "Some freaky shit."

Raven found Mai's ability as fascinating as it was morbid. A combination of psychometry, thoughtography, and telepathy, Mai was able to retrieve the final memories of the deceased and produce photographs of them. The process had a high "ick" factor, as it required Mai to place her hand on the exposed brain of her subject. Her position as a coroner made her skills useful, though in conventional cases she was forced to find more subtle ways of disseminating her discoveries. Providing investigators with such photos would lead to some very uncomfortable questions.

Photo number one showed an extreme close-up of a head. Off-angle, a hand pulled an ear forward. Raven let out a wordless, "That figures." Front and center in the photo was a misshapen infinity symbol birthmark, its edges uneven and ill-defined, its color mottled and blotchy.

"Abomination."

Denise furrowed her brow, unfamiliar with the word in this context. "What do you mean?"

"As you know, all the Caretakers that have been activated are female," Raven said.

"I have wondered about that. There's been a lot of speculation."

"Unfortunately, we weren't left with an owner's manual," Raven stated flatly. "Beth, the one who made me whole, was the last of the pure Caretakers. Her existence was something of a miracle itself, as she was born human, but with the full genetic set of our ancestors."

"All the power, none of the weaknesses," Denise said.

"Other way around," Raven corrected. "For all their power, they couldn't escape extinction. But three thousand years ago, a twist of fate taught the last of them that Caretakers and humans had enough genetic compatibility to produce children."

Denise's brows raised.

"There's a lot we still don't know about ourselves and our origins. The Elder has filled me in on what he knows. But his knowledge is limited to his personal experience and what our ancestors told him."

"Okay. So what is an Abomination?"

"Well, as you have lived through it, you know the Caretaker genetics wreak havoc with the human body," Raven stated. "The effect on us, on those born women, is clear."

"All the symptoms of debilitating conditions, no effective treatment or relief." Denise nodded as she spoke.

"Yes," Raven stared at the photograph as she spoke, "the severity appears to be connected to how much of the Caretaker genome is carried by an individual."

Once again Denise raised her eyebrows. "So Maddy—"

"Maddy's DNA carried seventy percent of our ancestor's genome." A sad smile crossed Raven's face. "It is one of the reasons I was happy she chose a human life. With that high a percentage, the possibility of inhuman physical attributes permanently visible was extremely high."

"Like Nexus," Denise stated to convey her understanding.

"Yes," Raven began, "she is the only one who I have made an age exception for. She has eighty-five percent of the Caretaker genome. At thirteen she was dying, puberty having initiated her body's rejection of the additional DNA. The result of the change is that Halloween is the only day she can freely move about in the world."

"That's a hard hand to be dealt."

"Don't feel sorry for the girl." Raven chuckled. "She's a happy, spunky, obnoxious teenager right now. The girl is quite possibly the most powerful of us to boot."

"You're rambling." Denise cut Raven a bemused look.

"The effect for men is different," Raven stated. "It appears to do with the chromosomal difference, something about the Y chromosome acting as a buffer as far as any physical impact is concerned. The downside is that the effects are almost always mental."

"They lose their minds?"

"To some degree or another." Raven nodded. "The real issue comes with their abilities. Before I am able to lock in the genetics, our abilities turn on and off like a child flicking a light switch. Upon puberty, the abilities of males appear to just turn on and stay on."

"Why haven't we seen more of them?" Denise asked. "I mean, there's literally thousands of us."

Raven smiled. It was the million-dollar question.

"I don't know. For some reason they appear to be exceedingly rare. All things considered, I have to be thankful for that." Raven took in a breath. "On occasion the Dark Man manages to find one of these males. They become Abominations, servants to him in life and nearly unstoppable in death." She looked down at the photo of their killer's misshapen birthmark. "I need to be very careful handling this one." She slid the picture back into the folder.

The next photograph revealed the deranged smile of a face that looked to be sixteen or seventeen. That he shared green eyes with her made Raven shudder, as did the desperation shining from within them. She quickly shoved the picture into the folder.

The hair on Raven's arms stood up. Her eyes went wide as she took in the third picture. Quickly flipping to the remaining picture, her mouth began twitching. Hands shaking, she placed the photographs on her lap. Letting out a long exhale, Raven was suddenly aware that she had been holding her breath.

"Holy shit," she whispered.

"What—" Denise began, then noticed what pictures Raven was looking at. "Yeah, those are a bit freaky."

Raven smiled wide. She looked through the pictures again. The first was of Sonja's killer on the ground, back against the wall, fear plastered over his face. Sonja's arm stretched into the frame of the picture. Raven studied the POV image.

Where the young woman's hand should have been, a diffuse blue mist with the vague shape of a hand reached toward the teenage face of her murderer. The second picture showed Sonja's decapitated body.

183

From the angle of the photo, Raven surmised that the poor girl's head was resting on the ground. Pinning her killer against the wall, Sonja's headless body appeared to be kneeling, the strange blue mist forming limbs that had been severed. Where her head had once been, the blue mist formed a distorted oval with what appeared to be a snout.

"Oh my god," Raven blurted out.

Denise looked at Raven's rapidly twitching smile. Her face contorted in confusion, not understanding why Raven would be smiling at such macabre images.

"What am I missing here?"

"The explanation is a bit long," Raven said, "but in a nutshell, one of our ancestors took control of Sonja's body after her soul vacated it."

Shock replaced the confusion on Denise's face.

"Okay, homegirl, you're gonna have to explain that."

Raven took a deep breath. A silent chuckle convulsed through her body.

"We live as paradoxical beings," she began with the cadence of a professor. "We are individuals, yet we are connected to a kind of shared consciousness. In a sense it is a hive-mind that we can enjoin ourselves to and detach from at will. Better than using a cell phone for communication."

Denise nodded. It was the standard method of communication between Caretakers.

"Not so different from a cell phone, when we aren't connected a kind of mental ringtone will let any individual know someone wants to contact them," Raven said, knowing this was information Denise already knew. "That much is common knowledge for us. Since she is permanently connected, I asked Nexus to investigate the nature and capabilities of this shared mind. Like I said before, no one left us a user manual for our existence. In the grand scheme, we are something new. The first generation."

A passing car drew the women's attention. Bright red taillights shone through the dark as the car pulled to a stop in front of Maddy's neighbor. Denise closed her eyes, her ears giving her sight.

"It's a first date," she told Raven. "Didn't go well. She's trying to let him down easy and…the prick thinks he's entitled to a blowjob 'cuz he paid for dinner." Denise gave a humorless laugh. "And there's the slap. Good for you, girl. Don't put up with that kinda shit."

Raven laughed as she looked toward the parked car. The passenger-side door opened. Even in silhouette, Raven could see aggravation in the woman's movement as she slammed the car door. Walking toward her house, the woman stopped halfway, her attention drawn back to the car. A few obscene gestures later, the woman resumed walking toward her home. Denise winced as the vehicle screeched out of its parking space and disappeared into the night.

"Okay, back to what you're saying." Denise shifted her focus back to Raven.

"According to what Nexus has found so far, this shared consciousness is layered. We have just been using the surface level."

"What's below that?"

"Somehow our ancestors figured out a way to preserve their individual consciousnesses," Raven stated. "Think of it like digitizing a person. Their memories, skills, their complete personality are put into a computer. You could speak with them, gain knowledge from them. They would be, in effect, immortal."

"Our ancestors," Denise began. "All of our ancestors—"

"Not all of them as far as Nexus can tell," Raven said. "Though there appears to be a mind-boggling number. Nexus made contact with the first one last year. Since then, she has communicated with well over a thousand. Unlike a digitized image of a person, these consciousnesses appear to be fully aware of their situation. And aware of our situation."

Denise raised an eyebrow. The concept that disembodied minds seemingly trapped inside a non-corporeal network were aware of what is happening outside their environment seemed counterintuitive to her. Raven nodded, understanding the question.

"This top layer which we have been confined to is monitored by them." Raven raised a finger to stop the inevitable question. "They are unable to directly access the living shared consciousness, the living must contact them. Sadly, it does seem that Nexus is the only one of us with that ability...or so I had thought." Raven looked back down at the two photographs in her lap. "I think this is one of those preserved individuals."

Denise looked at Raven's hands. The image of Sonja's body kneeling, a hand of blue mist holding her killer by the throat, a distinctly inhuman-shaped head made up of the same blue mist. The gothy-girl tapped her index finger on the photo.

"I think Sonja broke through the barrier in her final moments," she said. "And I think one of our ancestors was fed up with being unable to act on our behalf."

"Are they trapped souls?"

"No." Raven's words held finality. "Their souls have long since moved on. What we're looking at is a kind of imitation soul. Manifested energy from sheer force of will."

"Why did our ancestor let this fucker live?"

"Because," Raven looked into Denise's questioning hazel eyes, "it knew that this degenerate is far more dangerous dead than alive."

Chapter 17

I stood in a sea of waist-high grass, their stalks swaying in a pleasant breeze. The world around me was a verdant ocean. Wispy white clouds lazily made their way across a brilliant azure sky. The soft rustle of the flowing landscape was hypnotic. Warm, gardenia-scented air triggered sense-memories of twilight summers when I was a child. I felt at peace here. Was this what the ancient Greeks envisioned the Elysian Fields to be? A land of endless calm, fertile and inviting?

I knew that I was dreaming. Lucid dreams were a fact of my life. Something was different here. The texture of the dream was real. Too real. I tested my usual ability to alter a dream. I tried to materialize a mug of beer in my hand. Nothing. Make a flower bloom at the top of a swaying stalk. Nothing. I jumped. Just as I would in the waking world, I landed after getting about a foot off the ground. I could feel the impact as my feet hit the soft dirt underfoot. No, this was no normal dream. This wasn't even a normal lucid dream. I began to question whether I was dreaming at all.

Off in the distance I saw four hills rising above the grassy ocean. They looked like a pleasant place to lie back and take in the sky. Moving toward them, my palms ran over the top of the grass. Pleasant tingles from the light whips of each stalk brought me further into relaxation. As I approached, the four hills appeared to merge into one. Still a little way ahead, I could see a figure standing atop this grassy knoll. Deep black, without any discernable features, the figure atop the hill looked like a shadow that had been ripped from the ground and given the freedom to move about on its own. A featureless arm appeared to beacon me, calling me over to say hello. The words of Brianna Smith came screaming through my mind as I took one more step toward the dark figure.

"Stay away from the grassy knoll," she had told me. "Stay away from the Dark Man."

My trance had broken and the world around me seemed even more real. Underlying the calming warm breeze, an amorphous threat, undefined and easily overlooked. I cocked my head to the side, staring at the beaconing shadow-man. I raised my arm and gave him a one-finger salute. From behind me I heard a soft laugh. The sound was familiar. It was a laugh I had heard a million times before. I turned and came face to face with me.

The other me held a smile of mischief and knowing. Cocking his head in the same way I do, he winked and let out another little laugh.

"You are…" My question trailed off.

The other me shook his head as if to say, "Don't you know who I am?" He held up his hand, index finger raised, shaking it in the air. His expression melted into one of solemnity, his smile one of sadness. My heart raced. Anxiety welled within me, some unknown terror taunting the edges of my consciousness.

"Say something." A nameless fear echoed in my words, a desperation I could not identify. "Talk to me."

Casting sorrow-filled eyes toward the ground, his shoulders slumped. I could feel trepidation radiating from his body expressing an unwillingness to speak. An unwillingness to move forward.

"Please, say something," I implored him. "Why are you here?"

I felt my chest tighten. The sound of blood pounded in my ears. After a long moment his head lifted and, with a resigned sigh, met my gaze.

"Hello, Darkstone," he said. "You've been asleep for long enough. It's time to wake up."

Sweating and unsteady, I bolted from the bed, across the hotel room's living space, and into the bathroom. I could feel my stomach churning, its contents desperate to escape. Reaching the toilet, I shoved my head down and promptly threw up. To say I was a mess would have been an understatement. With each expulsion of my stomach's contents, my entire body convulsed. Sobs choked each inhale between the bouts of vomiting. Tears streamed from my eyes, liquified snot ran from my nose, and when nothing was left in my stomach, chaotic retching sent burning acid into my throat. As the convulsions subsided, I leaned back against the bathroom wall. Using the rough, single-ply hotel toilet paper to stymie my tears, I blew my nose. I held my eyes wide, not wanting to blink. Not wanting to see the images that lay behind my eyelids.

Another wracking sob shuddered through me as the fugue state I had lived in for the past five years crumbled. The night that I lost my closest friends, the night I lost myself, came back to me in disjointed images of terrifying clarity. In my dissociative state I remembered the human trafficking case, our search for the woman named Atsuko Takanashi. I remembered that the four founding members of Darkstone's Asylum had been brought in by an LAPD detective to assist in the investigation. My mind had mercifully pushed aside the fatal confrontation that had killed that case, and my friends.

Now it all came rushing back in sporadic chunks. A run-down warehouse east of downtown Los Angeles. Police officers clearing the building. Rooms with dirty mattresses. Putrescence in the air from buckets that had been used as toilets. A muffled gunshot had my compatriots and I running toward the back of the building and through a large steel door. As soon as we had entered the room, the door shut and locked us in.

It felt like a scene from a horror movie. The twenty-foot by twenty-foot room was dimly lit by two dying florescent shop lights, each periodically flickering. At the center of the room, a young uniformed officer bent over the body of a grungy looking man. A gun lay on the ground close to him. Checking the man for a pulse, the young officer had turned to us, letting us know the man was dead.

Memory became disjointed. Fragmented. Sound was the only aspect that remained clear. The crunch of breaking bone. The wet tear of ripping flesh. Sloshing movement of some unidentifiable thing. A momentary scream. A loud crack. Silence.

My mind resisted receiving the contents of this event. I did not want to see it. I did not want to remember. The totality of my being screamed in defiance. Adrenaline surged through me. My heart pounded. I couldn't breathe. My body convulsed. An explosive sob escaped my lips as the recollection tore through my mind in crystal-clear focus.

It looked like a massive talon. Slick with some unknown black putrescence. Tearing through the head of the young officer, his teeth, blood, and brains sprayed across the room. Supporting the killing

189

instrument was a chitinous, segmented appendage. Sprouting from the dead man's shoulder blade, it resembled the leg of a spider that had grown to monstrous proportions. Fear paralyzed the four of us as we watched this macabre transformation of the dead.

A strange black substance oozed from the corpse as it convulsed. The sound of insectile chittering accompanied the body's anatomical rearrangement. A second spider leg burst forth from the opposing shoulder blade. The oozing black liquid hardened into armored segments on the corpse's back. Overlayed plates of wet black armor. His lifeless head lifting off the ground, the former human's lower jaw stretched open. The sickly sound of tearing skin and muscle echoed through the room. With a fleshy thud, his lower jaw fell to the floor. Black sick covered what remained of his face, leaving a featureless mockery of a human visage. Two segmented mandibles capped with massive fangs sprang from where the lower jaw once hinged to the dead man's head. His tongue, freed from its bondage of the frenum, whipped around in a frenzy. Muscles in the corpse's arms appeared to bulge as the sickly ooze covered them. The fingers of his hands fused, black ichor hardening them into hoof-like structures. Our fear-induced trance was broken when the pelvis of the corpse made a 180-degree rotation. A visceral shotgun blast of ripping flesh and splintering bones.

Mike was the first to open fire, his .38 Special echoing through the room. Myra followed suit with her .44 caliber hand cannon. Both were trained in combat. Mike was a former LAPD detective, Myra a former Army Ranger. Clair and I had our training in spiritual combat. Though we dealt in the occult, we did bring some ranged backup for dealing with the mundane. Clair pumped an entire clip of her 9mm Beretta into the burgeoning monster. I got off one shot from my own weapon before a searing pain hit the left side of my abdomen. Looking down, one of the grotesque creature's spider claws had pierced my side. A body-wrenching shock of pain felled me as the thing freed its talon from my body. I felt the hot wet of my own blood spurting from the wound. Clair immediately dropped to my side, tore off a large swath of my shirt and used it to stymie the bleeding. For a moment I saw terror and hopelessness in her hazel eyes. Then her head fell to my chest and rolled to the ground, her decapitated body slumping to the side, lying beside me. Blood poured from the ragged tear where her head had once been. I hadn't seen the strike that killed her.

From my vantage point, useless and on the ground, I watched as Mike's body was split open, groin to crown. His entire body cavity emptied onto the floor. His eyes, an extra inch apart, registered surprise. I heard Myra scream hate and despair as she reloaded. The boom of her gun drowned out her cries. I watched helplessly as Myra's gun silenced. The right half of her face exploded into a mess of blood, mucus, and grey matter. Her body took a mindless stumble backward into the wall and slowly sank to the floor.

I had no strength. Shock had robbed my body of warmth. With blurring vision, I used everything I had left in me to raise my gun. Hand trembling under its weight, I let loose a single worthless shot. The insectile thing turned its attention to me. An inhuman, blood-curdling keening escaped its jawless maw. The two spider-leg scythes came down on each side of my head; the creature used them to pull itself toward me. Through my fear I had prepared myself for death. Never seeing my wife again was my only regret.

Death never came. As the thing bore down on me, fetid black ooze exploded from its featureless countenance. What appeared to be a steel shaft had penetrated its head. I heard a grunt. In my shock-induced haze, I thought the sound had come from me. The dark room became darker. My vision flickered in and out, my eyelids heavy. When I saw him, I thought I was hallucinating…or that the Grim Reaper was a real thing.

Clad in multiple layers of dark, tattered robes with a cowl pulled so far over his face it was a wonder he could see where he was going, the strange figure knelt next to me. Even kneeling I could tell he was tall. Impossibly tall. Seven feet at least. What I had thought was a steel rod was a steel and brass staff. The shaft was intricately engraved, and a Celtic-style dragon head sat atop the melee weapon. I felt his hand upon my wound. A sudden hit of pain cut through my shock-induced numbness. I could feel blood vessels repairing themselves, muscles stitching back together. I could feel death's icy hand retreating. And then the figure stopped short. The grinding screech of metal being cut grabbed his attention. An ancient-sounding voice penetrated the

191

shambling mass of cloth. He spoke with an odd accent that sounded like a mashup of Irish, Scottish, and Welsh.

"You're not done yet, child," the figure said. "There's still much for you to do."

I could almost hear sympathy from the hooded giant. A melancholy that told me his words were not predicting a future filled with happiness, rainbows, and sunshine.

"They'll be here soon." He nodded toward the locked door as brilliant yellow sparks of molten steel suddenly blasted across the room. "I leave you to the care of your own."

With those words, the stranger vanished, seeming to blink out of existence. My body still wracked with pain, I waited for the rescuers to enter the room, with only the mangled corpses of my friends to keep me company.

When the EMTs set me on a gurney to be wheeled out, I took stock of the room. What was left of my comrades had blessedly been covered by white sheets. The remains of the thing that had killed them were nowhere to be seen. In the spot I assumed its body should have been, only a puddle of rancid black ichor remained.

My arms shook as I propped myself up at the bathroom sink. Filling the basin with cold water, I took a deep breath and dived face first into the cleansing liquid. A shudder ran through me, this time the result of the cold water.

Looking into the mirror, I felt as though I was seeing myself for the first time. My receding hair was punctuated by grey creeping into the sides of my head, my nose had a slight crook. The bags under my reddened eyes, puffy from an extended bout of crying, held more creases than I thought. Blue-grey eyes staring back at me, those were the same. Pushing myself to stand straight, I was struck by how my sight had spent five years stuck within an illusion.

In my fugue state, my mind had constructed the fantasy of a pulled abdominal muscle. Reality revealed a massive, ragged scar covering my left flank. My upper left arm was covered by a tattoo, a dragon roaring in mid-flight. On my right shoulder, a family crest resided. Within a yellow shield, the silhouettes of two rearing lions faced each other; above them, a pair of crossed spears. Pentacles were centered on each of my pecs. I didn't need to see the rest of the set, I could almost feel the Celtic knotwork shields on my back, one over each shoulder blade. Taking a deep breath, my body convulsed on exhale as I struggled against the urge to break down again.

I felt Tara's hands caress my back before they moved to embrace me. Face pressed between my shoulders, her soft breath on my back was calming. I clasped her hands in mine, bringing them up to my lips. I felt her face move as she spoke.

"You remember, don't you?" Her voice was soft, compassionate, with a hint of sadness.

"Yes," my voice trembled.

"I wasn't sure I wanted that," she said. "At least Jonathan wasn't burdened by what you had seen. What you survived."

I turned to face her. Gently holding Tara's chin, I looked deep into the bottomless blue of her eyes. Within them shone her love for me, no matter who I thought I was.

"A—" she began. Placing my finger on her lips, I cut her off and shook my head.

"For whatever reason, everyone believes the man known as Darkstone is missing," I said. "Of those who knew him, you are the only person who seems to remember what he looked like. I have to think there is a reason for that."

Tara's face scrunched, something she did when a memory cropped up.

"I was so concerned with you," she said. "It didn't even register. But—" She paused.

"But what?"

"The moment you signed your discharge papers at the hospital, the doctor and nurses who had been treating you appeared to have no idea who you were." A question crossed her face. "Why didn't I forget?"

"Because whomever or whatever did this knew I'd need you when I remembered."

Tara nodded, considering the idea.

"So what do you want to do?" she asked.

"Leave Darkstone to the stuff of myths and legends," I said. "There's a reason I was erased from memory, that I became an unreachable man who retreated from the world. I will remain Jonathan Hayes."

"The man that never was," Tara said jokingly.

"Thank the gods my brain gave me the same life experiences." Letting out a slow breath, I felt my emotional state stabilize. "Don't know how I'd cope having to figure out which memory belongs to which identity."

"So did you have the dream Brianna mentioned?"

"I think so."

"How was it?"

"Kinda nice until I decided to be an asshole to myself."

Tara cocked an eyebrow but said nothing.

"I did get a look at this Dark Man," I told her. "It was from a distance, but he appeared to be the most terrifying shadow person I've ever seen. Kept trying to wave me over to him."

"What did you do?" There was a hint of surprise in her voice.

"I flipped him off."

Tara let loose a booming laugh. I couldn't help but join her. For a moment I thought that this was why she remembered. Someone to ground me. Someone to pull me back from the abyss of all-consuming despair. She turned, walked out of the bathroom. I took a step to follow and stopped. A strange sensation registered in my mind. It felt like I was flexing a muscle. Checking my body, nothing seemed out of place.

Walking out of the bathroom, I called out to her.

"Hey, hun." She turned to look at me. Tara's jaw dropped, her face the portrait of amazed, fearful confusion. "What?" I asked.

"Look in the mirror," she said, pointing to the full body mirror on the back of the bathroom door.

Looking at the mirror, I, too, was stunned. The blue-grey of my eyes now shone a bright luminescent blue. My irises appeared to generate their own light. I thought back to what Brianna had said about Black Rock enhancing the core of what an individual was. What was I at my core?

Without a thought, my lips began to move as the old incantation returned to me, an affirmation of power Darkstone used when working a paranormal case.

"I stand between the darkness and the light. I stand between peace and the fight. I am a god of old reborn. I am the rock that stands to face the storm."

As I spoke, the flexing in my mind clenched. I felt an instinctive connection to it, a base knowledge of what this feeling and physiological manifestation was. Turning back to Tara, I pointed to a stapler sitting on the desk of the room.

"Take the stapler and throw it at me as hard as you can," I said.

"What?" she exclaimed. "I am not throwing anything—"

"Please just do it," I asked. "If you hurt me, I won't hold it against you."

She picked up the stapler, bounced it a few times in her hand checking its weight. In one deft movement, her arm swung. The stapler sped through the air…straight at my head. Time seemed to slow as I saw the projectile's trajectory. I saw the look of horror on Tara's face as she realized her aim was off, the flying paper-binder seeking a point of maximum damage. For years I had told my wife that any aerial object headed in my direction always used my face as a stopping point. Basketballs, softballs, baseballs, tennis balls, a flying shar pei. The objects inevitably aimed for my face. It was a law of nature.

The stapler exploded two feet in front of my nose, shattering as if hitting an invisible wall. Tara yelped in surprise. Seeing me unharmed, and always quick on the uptake, she laughed.

"Let's try another one." Her tone was far too giddy for my liking.

Before I could get in a word, a barrage of uncapped pens and sharpened pencils, their tips poised for impalement, bounced and shattered before me. Tara's laugh echoed through our hotel room.

"Now try a pillow," I said.

Tara grabbed a pillow off the bed and flung it at me. Her laughter stopped when the white, fluffy headrest landed its target. Holding momentarily to my face, the pillow dropped from its point of impact in a comical manner.

"Oh my god," she exclaimed. "Are you alright? I didn't think—"

"I figured that would happen."

She looked at me confused, the question "Why?" etched into her expression.

"The pillow wasn't a threat," I explained. "I'm not entirely sure, but I think whatever this is will only react to the threat of injury. Fluffy things don't count."

I had my answer. What am I at my core? I am the guy who stands between a child and the things going bump in the night, I am one runs toward the gunfire, I am the one who takes the blows so others may find safety. I am a protector. At my core, I am a shield.

Chapter 18

Caleb hated many things. Right here, right now, taking orders topped that list. Especially when the orders came from a non-corporeal entity that could only speak to him in a dream. Being a spectator was number two. But here he was, uncomfortably prone, lying on steel rafters almost three stories above a dark, long-abandoned dance floor. He had no idea why the Dark Man wanted him here. His egomaniacal Master told him this was an intelligence-gathering task, a chance to learn. The faceless void gave explicit instructions on where to position himself. What he was supposed to learn while his legs cramped thirty feet off the ground was beyond him. The Boy let out a quiet sigh.

"Fucking asshole," he said under his breath.

He twitched as a loud *clack* heralded the arrival of light. Moving spotlights painted slowly drifting, multicolored dots on the rough wooden floor as Johann Strauss' "The Blue Danube" broke out through the long-forgotten sound system of the abandoned club. Caleb's heart momentarily paused when he noticed people sitting at tables that flanked the dance floor. At least, in the shadows they looked like people. The decaying speakers distorted the music, the waltz sounded like a horror movie soundtrack. Caleb's attention was grabbed by a slowly rotating pair of figures. One of them he recognized.

With a plume of neon green hair and his best purple suit, Scott Boyd lazily spun with his partner into the center of the dance floor. From his vantage point, Caleb could not identify the installation artist's other half. Long blonde hair swayed as the strange couple slowly twirled in time to the distorted music. The woman's body was stiff, lifeless. Making a full circle around the rotten dance floor, Scott and his companion moved to the center of the formerly dedicated space. Dipping his dance partner, her face was revealed to Caleb.

"Fucking psycho," Caleb muttered under his breath, trying to silently readjust a leg that had fallen asleep.

Even in the dim light and thirty feet away he could identify the latex imitation of life. A mask covered the head of the mannequin, its arms frozen in a pose perfect for a dance partner. Scott's neon green pompadour shook as the sound of unhinged giggling overtook the music. Caleb's face scrunched in disgust as he watched the imitation Joker plant a long kiss on the plastic girl.

Slinging the mannequin over his shoulder, Scott carried her out of Caleb's sight. The prone Boy breathed a quiet sigh of relief, giving thanks that the psychological torture was over. He rolled his eyes at Scott Boyd's return to the dance floor.

"What did you think of my moves?" Scott asked loudly.

Caleb froze in response to the question. His mind raced, trying to determine if he had given himself away or if the crazy bastard was taking a shot in the dark.

"I know you're there." The green-haired nightmare's voice held a sing-song admonishment, "He said you'd be here as a witness."

Caleb groaned. Yet another thing his master failed to mention.

"A witness to what?"

"Ah, there you are," Scott said, looking up. "A witness to my ascension, of course."

His eyebrows raised. Again, something he had been kept in the dark about. How was he supposed to become a perfect god if information was systematically withheld from him? His face flushed with annoyance.

"Explain," Caleb yelled to the green-haired weirdo.

"He really doesn't tell you anything," Scott said with a sigh. "I have been promised a position as general of his demonic legions!"

Caleb rolled his eyes. As far as he could tell, the Dark Man kept no company, demonic or otherwise. He stood upon a mountain of the dead. He didn't command them, he just crushed them.

"All I have to do is kill a man."

This piqued the Boy's interest. "Who do you have to kill?"

Snickering, his green pompadour bouncing from barely restrained excitement, Scott shrugged.

"You'll see."

Caleb watched Scott scurry about. With his limited view, the prone killer could only see the green-haired man periodically cross the dance floor as he manically moved chairs, pushed a cart full of drinking glasses, dragged a heavy stanchion to destinations unknown. Echoes of unseen movement rang in his ears. Then, silence.

For thirty minutes Caleb lay in a deafening aural void. Icy pins and needles of sleeping appendages clawed at his impatient mind. Anger enveloped him. Too much waiting, too much observing. He needed action, he needed movement, he needed...

A slow scraping filled the decrepit club, accompanied by stumbling footsteps. Swaying and weaving, Scott pulled a wooden chair to the center of the dance floor and gracelessly poured himself onto its seat. Caleb spied a half-drunk bottle of what looked to be whiskey in the faux-Joker's hand. Scott belched loudly, hiccupped, and brought the bottle to his lips. Turning the whiskey container to the sky, the drunk parrot-haired psycho downed the remaining half of the bottle in one go.

"Wh— why," Scott's slurred, drunken words echoed. "Why aren't they—" A hiccup interrupted his train of thought. "Why aren't they here, man?"

Drunken sobbing filled the air as Scott dropped the bottle, put his head in his hands. Caleb felt sorry for the guy. He understood the disappointment of putting forth so much effort just to have people let you down. Sympathy—real sympathy—was a rare thing for him. Caleb felt it now. On one hand the Boy felt little more than homicidal annoyance toward Scott Boyd. The man was an insect, an imposter, a false god. He had tried to imitate Caleb's divinity, his near perfection. In this moment, Caleb felt a twisted comradery with the weeping serial killer.

"It's okay, dude," Caleb shouted down.

Scott jerked, looking around. "Jesus? Jesus, is that you?"

"No, ya drunk fuck."

The inebriated man looked up. With blurred vision he could see Caleb in the rafters. The Boy was squirming his way toward a ladder bolted to the far wall. Scott pointed at him, letting out a sloppy laugh.

"Oh yeah," he said. "I— I forgot you was here."

Caleb reached the ladder. His body burned cold, the stabbing pins and needles of waking limbs forcing his mind into a state of hyper-awareness. Properly positioning himself for the climb down, the requisite twisting had exacerbated his discomfort and made his bad mood worse. Once on the ladder, he paused. A bead of sweat traced its way down his back, sending a shudder through him. The cold abandoned him as raging fire scorched his nerves, his appendages fully awakened from their circulatory slumber. He sucked in a breath as waves of pain washed over him.

"I don't get it, man," Scott drunkenly continued. "I mean… I put this whole thing together." He waved his hands dramatically. "I called the cops and told them where I was."

As the pain dissipated, Caleb reached the second floor. Looking down at the pathetic would-be showman in the center of the dance floor below, he sighed. Fatigue weighed on him; he hadn't realized how much energy it took to lay still for a few hours. He was done being here. He had plans of his own to enact. *Dark Man's orders be damned*, Caleb told himself.

"Where—" Another hiccup punctuated Scott's drunken pity party. "Where did I go wrong?"

Caleb shook his head as he slowly walked toward the stairs. Dealing with a whiney, drunken, green-haired freak wasn't in his repertoire of situational strategies.

"Dude, it's going to work out," Caleb snapped. "But you gotta sober up here. What kind of a show are you going to put on if you're just falling down and puking on yourself?"

With the spotlights painting multicolored dots across Scott and the dance floor, the entire scene reminded Caleb of the old song "Send in the Clowns."

"Yeah." The word was slurred to unintelligibility. "Guess I jus slep it…" Scott's words drifted off as he slid out of his chair into unconsciousness.

Caleb shook his head at the pathetic sight. It wouldn't surprise him if the police did show up while the idiot was sleeping on the floor. He chuckled at the irony such an end would be as he noiselessly slipped down the stairs and exited the defunct club.

Raven lay in her hotel room staring at the ceiling. She mentally obsessed over the images Mai had provided. The idea that one of her ancestors could take control of Sonja's deceased body threw her mind into chaos. A strange emotion raged within her, a combination of hope and extreme anxiety. The idea that she could speak with her ancestors both excited and terrified her. What were they like?

Beth, the last pure Caretaker, had told Raven that her ancestors were…a bit full of themselves. The name "Caretaker" was one they had given to themselves. While their actions were designed to aid others, their motivation was for the sole purpose of being remembered once they were gone. They had felt their existence was far too important to just be another forgotten extinct species.

Raven's rambling thoughts were interrupted by an incessant pinging. The mental noise had the feel of a child rapidly, and annoyingly, hitting a doorbell. She knew exactly who was trying to contact her. Taking a deep breath, Raven answered the psychic call. Instant regret.

"O-M-G, you're never gonna guess what I discovered," the high-pitched, hyperactive voice of Nexus echoed through Raven's head.

A few months away from her eighteenth birthday, Maureen Dunloff, now known as Nexus, was the youngest among the Caretakers. She was also the most powerful, having the highest percentage of Caretaker DNA. Raven found so much power in the hands of the overzealous girl a terrifying proposition. Thankfully, Nexus put that insane energy to work, researching the shared consciousness connecting all of them.

"What do you have for me?" Raven replied.

"Oh, oh, oh, this is sooo cool."

"What is?" Raven sighed, rolled her eyes. Getting an answer out of Nexus was like pulling teeth. The girl liked to draw everything out.

"Are you sitting down?"

Raven did not like that question.

"I'm lying on the bed," Raven responded.

"Perfect," Nexus said. "Check this shit out."

"Language," Raven admonished. Her body went limp on the bed.

An infinite expanse of black greeted Raven as she tried to get her bearings. She felt weightless, yet grounded. As her sight adjusted, she saw cascading dim light shining up from below. The source of the light was not defined, the floor of this dark place appeared to be covered in silent water that rippled, sparkled, and cast multicolored light with every movement Raven made. Suddenly a line of pure white light shot through

201

the waters. It persisted, pulsated. Another line shot through the water. At first glance it appeared to bisect the first line. Raven noticed a three-dimensionality within the waters. The second line of light ran under the first line.

"The top line is a conversation between Holly Langstead and Denise Olay," the annoyingly chipper voice came from behind Raven. "The other is Harriet Brown and Ling Tam. Pretty cool, ain't it?"

"What is this place?"

"Everywhere," the voice responded, "and nowhere."

"Nexus," Raven's tone was that of a scolding mother, "do not start with shitty riddle-speak."

Raven could feel the girl's age through the overly dramatic sigh Nexus used as a response.

"Fine," the girl relented. "This is our shared consciousness. I'd like to call it the Matrix, but that seems a bit derivative."

Raven was almost impressed by the girl's use of a word larger than two syllables.

"More like a blatant rip-off," Raven quipped.

"Well, we're gonna have to call it something," Nexus stated. "Shared Consciousness just isn't catchy."

"While I get your point," Raven said as she turned to face the girl, "we're not going to be turning this place into an amusement park. Now how the fuck did you pull me in he—" Raven face-palmed as she saw the hyper teen doing the Running Man dance.

Nexus was rare among Caretakers; her appearance made it clear she was not wholly human. If her snow white, slightly iridescent skin wasn't a giveaway, her large golden eyes with their permanent vertical pupils would scream of her inhuman heritage. A bright pink mane adorned the energetic girl's head. Large, sharply tapered ears pierced her 1980s glam-rock hair style. A loose-fitting green shirt covered the girl's lithe body, a matching green skirt came to her knees. Her legs held a structure like that of a dog's haunches. With her ankles raised a few inches off the ground, her legs appeared to have a third joint. She stood on the pads of her three elongated toes, each digit capped with dangerous-looking talons. Her hands similarly held three talon-capped fingers and a thumb. A three foot long tail with a pink pom of hair sprouting from its tip bounced as she danced, accentuating the fact that the girl had to cut holes in every piece of clothing she owned to account for the extra appendage. As she moved, pale pink seemed to glide over her skin, the iridescence catching what light bounced in the telepathic meeting grounds. Raven felt the name *Sakura*, the Japanese word for "cherry blossom," would have fit the girl perfectly.

Every Halloween Nexus would venture out into the world. Every Halloween she would receive compliments on her costume. Where other teens might find an appearance so divergent from the norm to be mentally crushing and ostracizing, Nexus loved her look.

The iridescent girl smiled wide at Raven, exposing sharp, oversized canine teeth. Her smile faltered at Raven's lethal stare, bringing her dancing to an end. Shrugging her shoulders, another exaggerated sigh escaped her.

"Well, I discovered something new," Nexus said, answering Raven's question. "I seem to be a switchboard of sorts. It used to be more like a telephone network, all mental audio."

"And now?"

"Welcome to the Caretaker Virtual Reality," she said, spreading her arms wide. "We can do face to face meetings now!"

"That still doesn't explain how—"

"I'm basically the system administrator," Nexus explained. "I can pull in anyone that connects to me."

Raven let out a sigh. As annoyed as she was, she was also deeply impressed.

"Never without permission," she stated.

"Gotcha, boss." The shimmering girl gave a salute. Raven groaned.

"So do you want to meet him?" Nexus asked.

"Meet who?"

"The one who took control of that poor girl's corpse."

Raven's eyes widened. The idea that she could speak with one of their ancestors filled her with alternating excitement and trepidation. Her virtual self swallowed hard.

"Yes."

Nexus placed an open hand, palm down, over the ground of dark waters to her right. A dot of light appeared under the surface of the silently undulating ground. Growing larger and brighter, the intensity became difficult for Raven to look at as the light passed above the surface of the water. Before her eyes, the intense light took shape. Arms, legs, an oddly shaped head. A material appearance grew over the light. The solid image left Raven speechless.

"Raven," Nexus said, "I'd like you to meet Anubis."

The imposing figure stood tall. He appeared to be a statue of the ancient Egyptian god brought to life. Short back fur covered the jackal head, his eyes a luminescent red with vertical slit pupils. An expensive-looking, dark grey three-piece fitted suit adorned the human body of Raven's ancestor. She cocked an eyebrow at his high fashion sense.

"Anubis," Nexus continued with her introduction, "this is my mom, Raven."

Raven's heart simultaneously dropped and fluttered at the title of "Mom." The jackal-headed man nodded in acknowledgment.

"Nexus," Raven said, her voice soft with a tinge of sadness, "I'm—"

"You are my mom." Nexus' voice held a rare seriousness. "The thing that birthed me and abandoned me to hospitals was not my family. Nurses and doctors were the only people showing me compassion, but they all went to their own homes. Their own families. Then you came." Nexus pointed a clawed finger at Raven. "You saved my life. You taught me that I was worth being loved. Even with this appearance, you proved that I was worth accepting. You gave me love. You gave me a family. If that's not being a mom, I don't know what is."

Raven gave an embarrassed nod. Nexus was right, and she did treat the girl like a daughter. A soft chuckle drew her attention to the enigmatic jackal-headed figure standing next to the overzealous teen. Raven frowned.

"Why do you look like that?" Raven asked. "I know that is not your natural appearance."

"I like this form," Anubis answered in a deep, calming voice. "I think it is," he looked to Nexus, "cool."

Nexus smiled, nodding at her ancestor using a word that clearly wasn't in his normal lexicon.

"And the suit?"

"Oh," Nexus said, "that was my suggestion."

Raven cocked an eyebrow as Nexus placed her hand palm up. What appeared to be a webpage from a men's fashion magazine appeared above it, a suave-looking model wearing the same suit leaned leisurely against a marble stand.

"Now, you can probably do this too," Nexus stated. "It looks like we can display images contained within our memories like this."

"I see," Raven said, giving Anubis a smile.

Anubis gestured to Nexus. "She said I would look…hot in this."

Raven groaned, then chuckled as she shook her head.

"Aww, come on," Nexus pleaded, then pointed to the model in the image. "Although, I wouldn't kick this guy out of bed without those clothes on." She gave a mischievous grin.

A sadness once again stung at Raven's heart, one her face could not help but betray.

"Don't look at me like that," Nexus said, rolling her eyes.

"Like what?"

"That look of pity," she said. "I can get a guy."

Something in Raven told her that, despite Nexus' appearance, she probably could.

"All I need," Nexus continued, "is to find a guy with a monster-girl fetish." She shrugged. "Or a girl, I'm not picky."

Raven cocked an eyebrow to that. "Well, there's probably a few of us—"

"Eeew." Nexus cut Raven's thought off. "That'd be like sleeping with my sister."

Observing the exchange, a smile crept into Anubis' jackal countenance. He raised his eyebrows as if to say, "She has a point." Raven let out a soft sigh.

"Besides," a large smile crossed Nexus' face, "according to the comments on my Instagram and TikTok pages, there's a lot of guys and girls who think I'm hot." With the last words, Nexus raised her head in a show of confidence.

Raven's eyes went wide for a moment, "You are posting on—" She cut herself short, closing her eyes as she pinched the bridge of her nose. "Who am I kidding? Of course you'd be posting pics of yourself online."

"Everyone thinks I'm wearing some really obscure cosplay," Nexus said. "But it's this form," she gestured to her body, "that they find attractive."

Raven nodded, a smile crossing her face. Nexus was drawing some confidence from her online interactions, and she was having some semblance of a social life in the process. She could think of no viable reason to admonish the teen for it.

"Just be safe with your online interactions," Raven said.

"Always," Nexus said with a huge smile plastered on her face, her entire body bouncing up and down.

A deep laugh erupted from the business-suited Egyptian God of the Dead; with it, a strange emotion invaded Raven and Nexus. A mixture of humor, relief, sadness, and regret permeated their entire beings. Raven looked to the shadow of her ancestor, questioning and slightly irritated.

"Relax, child," he said, a deep sympathetic voice that seemed to emanate from his whole being. "What both of you have just shown has reminded me of our past failure."

"What failure?" Raven asked.

"Calling ourselves Caretakers," Anubis stated. "Allowing our arrogance to dictate our end."

"I don't follow," Nexus said.

Anubis sighed. Raven realized the conflicted emotions she felt stemmed from the jackal-headed afterimage. Before she could speak, Nexus turned to her.

"Communication here also comes in the form of emotional transmission." Nexus was feeling the same thing from Anubis. "It is impossible to lie when fully immersed."

Anubis' jackal head gave a single nod.

"We found ourselves at our evolutionary end," Anubis explained to his descendants. "No longer able to procreate. Our lives were so long we appeared to be immortal to younger species."

Raven and Nexus looked to the once God of the Dead. Raven had learned some from Beth, the Caretaker that had made her whole. Even Beth, who had been born to human parents, didn't know the full story. A story that spanned almost the entire history of the universe.

"Death found us one by one," Anubis stated, "and in our fear and sense of self-importance we declared ourselves the Caretakers of all life in the universe. We set out among the stars, following the *Teach Anam*, the House of Souls, to every world it went. We took it upon ourselves to teach the native species of every world about Souls, about the Gauntlet, about the Dark Man. We were an army against the void, tipping the scales in favor of the Avatar of Life. And more often than not, we made a mess of things."

"It sounds like you had your heart in the right place," Raven said.

"Our hearts were in fear," Anubis stated flatly, a frustration behind his words. "Our hearts existed in a state of pure hubris. We wanted to ensure the memory of our existence would live on beyond us. It was our only motivation. We believed we were that important. We crossed oceans of darkness just to interfere with the lives of others for our own sake."

"To be fair, you were important," Nexus chimed in. "You're still important. It seems that many are probably still alive because of your actions."

Anubis chuffed. "I am speaking to you now because of that fear of death and extinction. We had discovered a way to record our consciousness, preserve our knowledge and the minds of our people."

Raven's eyebrows lifted, a comforting smile crossed her face.

"That seems like a good thing," she said. "We could use your guidance."

A smile crossed the jackal-headed Caretaker's face.

"Now that you have one who can reach us," he gestured to Nexus, "I would agree. Understand that all of us here in the Hive are but soulless shadows of the race we once were. While we have become more than simple recordings of the dead, we are not truly alive."

"How did you control Sonja's body?" Raven blurted out.

Anubis laughed. His laughter was cold, without humor. It was the laughter of one whose failure was catastrophic.

"I wanted to save her," Anubis said. "I wanted to save all of them. I was unable to bridge the divide, the mental blockade generated by human DNA. In her last moments, Sonja's fear transfigured into mind-bending anger. A righteous anger. An anger that spawns vengeance as

207

justice. The intensity of that ethereal scream granted me a connection, but it was too late for me to save her. In her last moments, she handed her body to me, allowed me to take control."

A sneer crossed Anubis' face as he recounted the incident.

"That's when I saw him for what he was," Anubis growled. "Abomination. I could not kill him, not without unleashing something worse into the world."

Raven nodded in agreement. "That was my assessment as well." She could feel the frustration of her ancestor, and an all-consuming guilt. "You did all you could," she said.

"You do not understand," Anubis growled. "He is my responsibility. You are all my responsibility."

"What do you—"

"I was the last," he stated, sorrow emanating from him. "I am the one all of you come from. You are all my responsibility."

Chapter 19

I am not a morning person. I have never been a morning person. I will never be a morning person. This is an indelible fact almost everyone knows about me, especially the smiling, oversized leprechaun that sat on the couch in my hotel room. Stephanie's peace offering of coffee did little to assuage my aggravation. Sitting next to her, Agent Allen looked comical, the couch appearing miniscule beneath his massive frame. I frowned at the pair, groaning my disapproval.

"What is so important that it couldn't wait for normal business hours?" I did my best to keep the grumpiness out of my voice. I failed miserably.

"It's 8:30," Agent Allen stated, as if stating the time somehow altered my reality.

"Yeah," I snapped, "business hours start at 11am."

The giant G-Man shook his head, his face one of admonishment.

"The day starts at 8am," he said sternly. "Or earlier if a call comes in."

"You forget, I don't work for you." My face felt hot, I could feel annoyance turning to frustrated anger. This was not how I wanted to start my day.

"And you forget that I can revoke your clearance and bar you from this case."

Stephanie's head bobbed between us, her expression that of pure amusement. Our collective attention was drawn to Tara as she walked into the room. Upon Stephanie and Agent Allan's arrival, she had grabbed her clothes and bolted into the bathroom. Now she stood before us in a fuzzy, light pink long-sleeve sweater and black stretch-pants, hand on her hip and a scowl on her face. She wasn't a morning person either.

"Both of you, cut it out." Tara's voice cut through the air, a verbal dagger promising unknowable punishment for disobedience.

I shut my mouth. Challenging Tara when she was in this state was ego suicide. One thing I both love and fear about my wife is her ability to emotionally eviscerate people. Hilarious to watch when used against an egotistical jackass, not so much fun when I'm on that rare receiving end. Agent Allen opened his mouth to speak. A loud slap heralded Stephanie's hand sealing the G-Man's mouth.

"Don't be stupid," she told him.

"Okay," Tara said. "It's early…"

Agent Allen raised an eyebrow at the temporal declaration.

"For us it's early." The sarcasm in Tara's clarification was palpable. "So please enlighten me as to why I had to speed-run my morning routine."

Agent Allen's stone face faltered. A moment of apologetic regret shone through his hardline visage.

"I apologize for the surprise intrusion, ma'am," Agent Allen said.

Stephanie and I looked at Tara in bewilderment. And then it hit me.

"You two haven't been properly introduced," I said.

"We haven't actually been introduced at all," Tara spat back. "And my first impression," she looked that FBI agent dead in the eye, "is you're an oversized walking ego who is one 'little dick' joke away from a mental meltdown. So, if you'd be so kind as to stow the alpha male crap, it would make my morning slightly less annoying."

I couldn't help but snicker at the sight of my wife putting an FBI agent twice her size in his place. She glared at me.

"That goes for you too." Her finger hit my chest. "Enough of the pissing contest."

I sighed and nodded. Holding my open hand toward Agent Allen, I made the introduction.

"Tara, this is Special Agent Brock Allen of the Las Vegas FBI Field Office." I looked to the agent. "Agent Allen, this is my wife and DA operations manager, Tara."

"Again, I'd like to apologize, Mrs. Hayes," Agent Allen said meekly.

"Call me Tara," she said, sitting down on the short end of the L-shaped couch. "So why are you here?"

"I don't know if you really want to hear—"

"I'm backend support for Jonathan," she cut off the agent. "I've seen and heard everything going on with the case so far. And I hate to be out of the loop."

"Okay then," Agent Allen stated. "Mai worked on the body of Kelly Talbott overnight. Aside from our killer leaving a very messy crime scene with his fingerprints, shoes prints, and DNA all over the place, the condition of the body was different."

I felt a momentary sinking in my stomach. "Please don't tell me we have another psycho," I said.

"No," Stephanie interjected. "This is our guy. He's just losing control."

"How do you know that?" Tara asked.

"He didn't fully dismember her," Agent Allen stated. "Some of her fingers and toes had been amputated, her right wrist looked as though it had been put through a hydraulic press, her left leg was split at the knee. There were slices all over her body penetrating down to the muscle, but not all the way through. One of her breasts had been bisected and—" The agent hesitated.

"And what?" I asked.

Agent Allen looked uncharacteristically uncomfortable.

"I'm not quite sure how to say this without sounding purposefully crass—"

"Mai said Talbott's genitals looked as if they'd been run through a deli meat slicer," Stephanie interjected.

I heard Tara suck in a hissing breath as the image hit her mind. "Jesus," she exclaimed.

"One other strange thing was a series of small cuts running from just below her breasts to her pubic bone," Agent Allen continued, more confident about relaying this information. "When Mai cleaned the blood off, it turned out to be writing."

"What did it say?" I asked.

Agent Allen pulled a notepad from his jacket pocket, flipped through to his desired page.

"I have no master. He gives orders in dreams. He has no power over the waking," Agent Allen read.

I could see on his face that Agent Allen had a theory about the meaning of the message. I did as well, though I was pretty sure the FBI agent would have me committed if I spoke about my dream, seeing the threatening figure of the Dark Man in the distance. I already received strange looks from the man every time my dealings in the paranormal came up.

"I don't think he's devolving or losing control here," I said.

Stephanie and Agent Allen looked incredulously at me.

"What makes you say that?" Stephanie asked.

"What you have described is someone testing out new techniques," I informed them. "To use whatever tool he has been using for dismemberment to inflict less than lethal injuries. As for the scene, there's a decent chance he simply hadn't cleaned up yet."

Stephanie and Agent Allen nodded.

"I had considered the possibility," Stephanie said. "After all, this is the first kill room that anyone has found."

"How certain are you of that assessment?" Agent Allen asked as he pulled a series of crime scene photos from a folder. I hadn't even noticed he had brought anything with him.

The eight-by-ten photos appeared miniscule in Agent Allen's hand as he held them out to me. My stomach protested the visual assault of the photographic content. To characterize the scene as a mess would be like calling Godzilla a large iguana. Crossing a picture of two bloody handprints, my brow crooked.

"I assume these are the prints you mentioned," I said, holding the photo toward Stephanie.

"Yup."

"Where were they in relation to our vic?"

"About fifteen feet away from her," Stephanie responded. "There was also a strange man-sized, blood-soaked mud puddle next to the prints. Should be the next pic."

As predicted, the next picture was of slick crimson mud, about the size of a human.

"He bathed in blood?" Tara asked, leaning into me to look at the photograph in my hand.

"Why does it still look wet?" I asked.

"Both good questions," Agent Allen stated. "And no answer for either. It's been sent for testing."

I sighed. The breath spoke of my impatience. As a general rule, investigations are slow. Research takes time. Testing takes time.

Gathering intelligence takes time. I've spent thousands of hours in libraries or on a computer slogging through research. Thousands more combing neighborhoods. But this wasn't some simple missing person's case. Time is always the enemy. However, on this case, time was a combatant. Time cost people their lives. Agent Allen gave me a nod.

"I understand your aggravation," he said in an oddly sympathetic tone. "Welcome to my world."

I opened my mouth to respond, but rapid-fire pounding on the hotel door cut me off. Agent Allen was on his feet, gun in hand, before answering the door was even a thought in my head. I put my hand up, waved for the giant to take a seat.

"I have a feeling I know who that is."

Walking to the door, I glanced at my phone. I had sent Mary a text to come over as soon as Stephanie and Agent Allen arrived. I figured she just came right over rather than wasting her time on a reply.

"Who is it?" I asked in a playful, sing-song voice.

"The four horsemen of the fucking apocalypse," Brianna Smith's voice returned from beyond the door. "Now open the damn door, Jonathan."

Surprised, I acquiesced to her request and was greeted by the sight of one very haggard-looking hacker. Last night's revelation of my client's identity had hit her hard, but by the time she left, Brianna's confidence had returned. Our parting was with hugs and smiles. Gone now was the bravado and high spirits she had just hours earlier. Her 1970s Blaxploitation style replaced by worn purple sweatpants and a faded maroon hoodie. Brianna's afro was bunched at the back, a black topknot of tight curly hair with grey racing stripes flanking her temples. She looked tired, angry, and scared all at the same time. I ushered her into the room.

This time she didn't pull out her anti-listening device. She made no show of trying to mask her presence to any outside observers. She nodded a greeting to Tara, who scooted left on the couch to give Brianna a place to sit. She eyed Stephanie and Agent Allen suspiciously.

"Stephanie," I began the introductions, "Agent Allen, this is Brianna Smith."

Stephanie gasped, a smile painting itself across her face. She turned into a teenager confronted by her celebrity crush.

"H— Hi," Stephanie stuttered. "It's an honor to finally meet you."

Brianna's posture relaxed a little. The idea that she was among friends put her at ease.

"It is a pleasure to meet you," Agent Allen's deep voice seemed to come from everywhere, its volume uncontrolled. Somehow his "indoor voice" decided to take a vacation.

"Likewise," Brianna meekly whispered.

I squatted in front of her. Looking into her eyes, I could not read what was there. A jumble of rapidly changing emotions.

"What the hell happened?" I asked her.

She pulled out a thumb drive from her computer bag, tapped it on the back of her left hand.

"This was taped to my hotel room door when I got home last night," she started. "I've just learned that I spent twenty-eight years of my life looking over my shoulder for nothing."

"So," Agent Allen's voice bounced off the hotel room walls, "you're telling me this Office has been engaged in just about every crime against humanity, and the U.S. government is footing the bill?"

Brianna let out a frustrated sigh. Over the course of an hour, she had regained much of her composure, confidence, and humor. Filling Stephanie and Agent Allen in on the previous night's revelations was starting to bring back her impatience.

"No," she spoke to the agent as she would to a five-year-old, "the U.S. government loaned them resources, land, and personnel. They have agreements with eighty-five countries who act in the same manner."

"And what does this have to do with our case?" Agent Allen asked.

Brianna looked at me, then Tara. "Do you remember that I said I had snagged the Office's research data?"

Tara and I nodded.

"I started going through the information with a more discerning eye," she said. "I'm only about fifteen percent through the database—"

"Is it really that big?" Agent Allen asked.

Brianna gave the agent an exaggerated look that asked, "Are you stupid?"

"It's fifty years' worth of research," Brianna stated. "Sixty petabytes of data."

"What is a petabyte?" the agent asked. He had never heard the term before, nor had I.

"It's next in line up from a terabyte," she explained. "Where one terabyte is the equivalent of one thousand gigabytes, a petabyte is equal to one thousand terabytes." Brianna gave a little chuckle. "Basically, I have sixty thousand terabytes of data to sift through. And because I don't have narrow enough parameters for a search, I have to look at everything."

"Oh," Agent Allen said.

"I also went ahead and did another snooping run into their system." I lifted an eyebrow in surprise.

"They didn't learn their lesson the first time?"

"They tried to bury server access this time." Brianna smirked. "But they failed."

"What did you find?" Stephanie asked.

Brianna turned to me. "Does this word mean anything to you?" She showed me a piece of paper with the word *Dorchaméaróg* written on it.

"Gaelic. I think it's pronounced Doo-r-cha-maow-ro-gh," I said, quite familiar with the word in written form. I've never been certain if my pronunciation was correct, though no Irish person has ever corrected me on it. "It was Darkstone's alternate screen name."

I had used the Irish word when my own moniker was taken. Over the years I discovered quite a few websites with users having taken my name.

"The grammar is…questionable from a Gaelic standpoint, and the literal translation is 'Dark Pebble.'"

"Well, there's almost a hundred gigs of data collected on Darkstone," Brianna stated flatly, "going back to 2004."

My brows raised. The idea that I have unknowingly been under investigation for the better part of two decades made me feel a wee bit inadequate as an investigator.

215

"When Darkstone took off, their investigation turned to you," she said. "The exorcism technique you both used appears to have been their primary interest."

"I prefer the term 'spiritual eviction,'" I said.

"For all their might they couldn't find Darkstone either?" Stephanie asked.

Brianna shook her head. I was thankful that whatever had wiped the memory of Darkstone's appearance shielded me from the Office to some extent. The look on Tara's face indicated she felt the same.

"I ran a search on the infinity symbol birthmark," Brianna said. "In my snooping last night, I found a list of about fifteen thousand names across six continents of men and women with the birthmark." She sucked in a breath. "They were marked as priority subjects for experimentation."

Agent Allen gritted his teeth hearing this. I could see a subdued anger percolating under his stoic façade. "Are they involved with Caleb Voss?"

Brianna looked at him. She understood the angle he was getting at.

"His name is on their list for experimentation," she stated. "He's not working for them."

A collective nod greeted the information.

"I think the Office was trying to kill two birds with one stone." Brianna's voice had a resigned quality. "There's no record that they ever used any other PI firms." She gestured toward me. "That's why the paperwork you were given appeared incomplete and incompetent."

"Let me get this straight," Agent Allen chimed in. "These guys have Jonathan targeted, but decided to use him to find Caleb Voss, another person they're targeting but can't find?"

"Makes sense," I said. "They put me in a position that gave them access without exposure."

"Why would they have risked killing you before getting Voss' location?" Tara asked.

"Our involvement," Agent Allen said. "With other investigators involved, losing one of their targets wouldn't materially affect their desired outcome. It appears that they have limited resources, otherwise they wouldn't have any need for governmental personnel and equipment in large scale endeavors. If they are global, manpower is an issue for them. They can't simply put surveillance on everyone. So, from a strategic and pragmatic point, combining objectives that will efficiently open additional doors with minimal resources is the smart call."

"So they get the results of whatever test they wanted to perform on me," I said, nodding, "and if I died, they would have secured a third party to locate Caleb Voss at no additional cost."

"They had also expected you to lead them to Darkstone," Brianna said. "They know that you normally avoid taking murder cases. They probably figured this would be a case that would prompt you to reach out to him for guidance. Get him to expose himself."

"They didn't realize that no one, not even me, knows where he went." It was more of a statement than a question.

"Yes."

"If it's the technique that both Jonathan and Darkstone use that is of interest," Stephanie began, "why the focus on Darkstone? Jonathan's technique is pretty much identical. Darkstone trained him."

"According to the Office investigation," Brianna answered, "Darkstone's capabilities are stronger and more precise."

I lifted an eyebrow. In the fugue, my capabilities hadn't changed. That the Office investigation thought Jonathan Hayes was somehow weaker was laughable. It did point toward fallibility in their intelligence gathering. These people were not as well informed as they thought they were. A point that could be exploited if necessary.

How does one quantify a paranormal ability? Psychics and Witches are gauged by their effectiveness. Did a psychic lead you to the abducted kid? Did a Witch's spell bring about the desired outcome? Can these effects be repeated consistently? Spiritual effects require hard proof of spiritual existence. I could talk until I'm blue in the face about my experiences, about the number of times some unseen force tried to maim me, kill me, or tickle my toes. It's proof to me, but only to me. To everyone else they are stories. Even photographic and video evidence is questionable due to the large number of hoaxes and student projects showing readily available computer software can simulate just about anything. I know my effectiveness. More families than I can count also know my effectiveness. None of that is quantifiable, none of that is currently provable by our primitive scientific capacity.

"So, what's on the thumb drive?" I asked.

Brianna sighed. Hints of trepidation crept into her face.

"A video." Her words caught in her throat for a moment. "A video message from Joseph Handler."

I felt a flush of…something. I couldn't quite tell if I was getting angry or anxious. My eyes narrowed. I wanted to see the face of the man who had made a mess of Brianna's life, the man who had altered my body and mind, and the guy who could have killed my wife with his little "experiment."

"If you're willing, I want to see it."

Brianna pulled her laptop from her bag and connected the display to the TV just as she had done last night. The flat-screen television mirrored her computer desktop. She inserted the thumb drive. A window opened showing a single video file as the content of the tiny hard drive. Clicking on it, the screen filled with the most unnerving face I had ever seen.

"Jonathan," Brianna said, "Tara, Stephanie, Agent Allen. Meet Joseph Handler."

Tight, waxy-looking skin stretched over the bald man's skull. He looked to be in his seventies. Deep wrinkles were carved into the taut skin covering his face, eyes open so wide that he appeared to be without eyelids. Against a deep purple background, he struck me as familiar. Something pulled at my memory, as though I had seen this video still before. Then it clicked.

"He looks like Marshall Applewhite."

Tara, Brianna, and Stephanie looked at me, confusion written all over their faces.

"The leader of the Heaven's Gate cult," Agent Allen clarified for the trio. I nodded my confirmation.

"Yeah," I said. "In 1997, he and almost forty of his followers killed themselves believing they would be brought to an alien mothership hiding in comet Hale-Bopp's tail."

"I remember that," Tara said. "The guy was a nutball. I can see the resemblance."

Brianna laughed, nodding. "Thank you," she said. "I've spent years trying to put a finger on who he reminded me of."

Brianna looked at the screen, moved to hit the play button. Before she touched her laptop, the screen glitched. Chromatic aberration cut across the display, then returned to normal.

"Shit," Brianna said, looking at her laptop. "Someone just tried to access my computer."

"Not tried." The strange, monotone voice coming from the TV set startled everyone. "Succeeded."

The face on the screen had barely changed. Minute ticks in the aged countenance were the only indication this was a live stream.

"I see we have almost everyone in attendance," Joseph Handler said. "Jonathan, Tara, Stephanie, Brianna, and the dogged FBI agent."

I knew the tactic Handler was using. A show of information as a point of intimidation. It was pointless. We all knew that he had our names, we all knew he had our location. It struck me as a poorly thought-out angle.

"And your intrepid sidekick," the corpse-like face emotionlessly continued, "is currently in her hotel room listening to music and using language not fit for man or God while attempting to figure out why the information she promised you is not emailing properly."

Joseph's strange face attempted what I thought might be a smirk. Or was he constipated? The jury's still out on that. I gave the television a questioning look.

"I just thought you might like to know why she has not responded to your text yet."

"Oh shit," Brianna exclaimed. "He's looking through my laptop camera."

"That took longer than expected," Handler said, a hint of annoyance creeping into his lackluster voice. "A Judged One must be quicker on the uptake."

"Judged One?" I asked.

"Yes," Joseph stated. "As you have been judged worthy, and Ms. Smith has failed to mention it to you, I thought I would give you a quick primer on your new status and responsibilities."

I felt all eyes on me, and a flash of anger toward my client. With staccato movements of his head, I could see why Brianna had stated her suspicion that the man wasn't human. Joseph Handler moved as if he was not accustomed to working a physical body. My initial diagnosis as a paranormal investigator would be that the man was possessed, an assessment I had only made once before in my career as both Jonathan Hayes and Darkstone. My eyes narrowed.

"What are you?"

As much as it was possible, Joseph Handler's face registered surprise at the question. It was not a response he anticipated.

"That is neither here nor there," he said. "I established the Office to preserve humanity. To give mankind a fighting chance when the Gauntlet begins, and to prevent the Dark Man from succeeding."

Out of the corner of my eye I noticed Agent Allen's eyes widen.

"Ah," Handler said, "I see our good agent has met the void."

Brianna and I gave Agent Allen a hard stare.

"Is this true?" I asked.

"Have you had the dream?" Brianna clarified my question, fear permeating her voice.

"Yes," Agent Allen responded nonchalantly. "The guy's an insufferable douche."

"You talked to him?" Brianna's voice suddenly filled with alarm. "Are you fucking crazy?"

Agent Brock Allen looked surprised by Brianna's alarm. It was an odd expression, one that didn't suit his hard face.

"What's the big deal?" he said. "It's not like this Dark Man has said anything my subconscious hasn't told me before."

"Such as?" I questioned.

"Standard cop crap," he said. "Stay on the job long enough and occasional thoughts of suicide crop up." The agent spoke with such casualness one might think he was discussing fast food. "Urges to execute suspects we know are guilty, take out suspects who game the system and escape justice in trial." He paused. "Dark fantasies of violence and retribution. Our job can get frustrating, it can be emotionally taxing. These kinds of fantasies are a small outlet for that."

"He tries to capitalize on that," Brianna stated.

"Yes." Agent Allen nodded. "He's tried to convince me many times to kill myself...or go full vigilante. He's tried to promise me wealth in exchange for lives. He's promised me peace in exchange for my life."

"And you have denied him," Handler's monotonous voice droned through the TV. "Not something most people can do."

"Really? It was pretty easy." The G-Man seemed genuinely confused. "That thing has less charisma than a used-car salesman."

Joseph Handler appeared to regard the agent with clinical interest. Behind his unblinking eyes I could see a desire for experimentation, a desire to see how far he could push the agent, and no compunction about killing Agent Allen in the process.

"Back to your updated position," Handler began.

"That is going to require a new contract," Tara piped up, her voice professional and no-nonsense. "You specifically hired Jonathan, and Darkstone's Asylum by extension, to identify and locate a killer. Any changes must be agreed to and committed to writing."

"The only change I am asking for is the location of the man you call Darkstone," Handler stated.

I held my face, not allowing my surprise to register. Joseph Handler clearly had us all under surveillance, he knew the Black Rock had some effect on me. His surveillance failed to identify me as Darkstone.

"No," I said flatly. "You are my client, not my boss."

Handler's face contorted into what appeared to be an expression of annoyance.

"Understand," he countered, "you now exist by virtue of my benevolence. Should you choose not to comply, you will be deemed a threat and eliminated."

"Well, that escalated quickly," Stephanie muttered.

In spite of Handler's droning, emotionless voice, the threat was real. He may look like a crazy cult leader, but he was far more dangerous. I couldn't reconcile his statement about saving humanity with this man who appeared devoid of humanity.

"Your primary mission has not changed," Handler stated. "I want this Caleb Voss. All you need to do is locate him, my people will take care of the rest."

"Okay." I nodded. Acquiescence seemed the best tactic for now. I had two killers to find. Buying time to strategize was simple pragmatism.

"Before I go," Handler appeared to turn his creepy gaze toward Brianna, "Brianna, your sniffer software is quite impressive. However, you do need to fine tune the voice recognition to decipher the effects of alcohol on speech."

A file upload notification briefly appeared on her laptop. The resulting audio file held the title "9-1-1 Boyd."

"Consider that as my gift to you."

The screen flickered as Handler cut his connection, settling on the mirror of Brianna's computer desktop. Silence permeated the room. Tara, Stephanie, Agent Allen, and I mulled over the virtual encounter. Brianna whipped out her Alexa-looking anti-surveillance device, her face the portrait of anger.

"Fuck you, Handler," she blurted out. "You hear me, you corpse-looking motherfucker?"

She plugged her device into the computer. A three-dimensional display of our surroundings popped up. As the red ring of light pulsated on the cylindrical device, red, blue, and green dots appeared in multiple areas of the 3D hotel map. Two blue dots appeared to be in our room. Agent Allen opened his mouth to speak, but Brianna stopped him with an index finger over her lips. As the red pulsating light on the grey cylinder turned green, the blue dots in our room disappeared.

"Gotcha, fucker," Brianna muttered.

I gave her a questioning look. A broad, mischievous smile erased all evidence of the anger that held sway a moment ago.

"Countermeasures to countermeasures," she said, "and here is my countermeasure to their countermeasure countermeasures."

"I hate that that makes sense," Tara said.

Brianna hit a key on her laptop. The solid green light on her anti-surveillance device pulsated at high speed.

Two pops cut through the silence. A small string of black smoke rose from under one of the bedside lamps, a larger mist of black sprung from the hotel room's high mounted air-conditioning vent. Brianna's smile widened.

"Assholes thought turning their devices off when I ran my sweeper would leave them undetectable."

"What did you do?" Tara asked.

"Because they couldn't shut them down fast enough, I was able to grab the frequency and overload it."

"A targeted EMP," Agent Allen said. "Impressive."

"Basically, but unlike an electromagnetic pulse, I don't fry the electronics. I just cause them to overexert till failure," Brianna clarified. "It's a hardware version of a hacker's brute-force cracking technique."

I walked over to the bedside lamp and lifted it off its nightstand. A radiating soot smudge emanated from a small disk the size of a watch battery. I pulled the disabled listening device from the bottom of the lamp. Wafer thin, the device was clearly custom.

"Well, that's one dead bug," I said.

Agent Allen was at the A/C vent, folding knife in hand. Using the back of the small knife blade, he managed to unscrew the bolts without damaging the vent cover. Peering into the uncovered unit, the agent let out an aggravated sigh. Removing something that had been mounted with an X of black thread, he handed an object to me.

The mini camera was also a custom device. With a lipstick-sized lens housing, a small box on the back end held a mini-SD memory card and a short, paperclip-thin antenna. I pulled the memory card from its housing.

"Any chance this thing hasn't been destroyed?" I asked, handing the small plastic rectangle to Brianna.

Brianna popped it into a slot on the side of her laptop. The computer registered the storage device. Opening the SD drive, five video files were present.

"I'm guessing the end of each file is when the camera was remotely switched off," Brianna said.

Our tech guru opened the first file. Video showed a man in a maintenance uniform looking into the camera, the timestamp one hour before Tara and I had arrived. Brianna fast-forwarded the video. At a superhuman speed the fake maintenance man secured the air-conditioner vent, placed the listening device under the bedside lamp, and left the room. A loud mechanical *click*, and the opening of the room's door let

223

us know that audio was also recorded on the video. To say this made me nervous would be an understatement. Had they seen and heard the overnight revelations? Did Handler seriously try to task me with finding myself knowing full well I am the person he's searching for?

"Can we see last night?" I asked Brianna. "Around 1am?"

"Can do, boss," she said, trying to inject a little levity into my clearly tense demeanor.

The camera angle showed Tara and I in bed, sleeping. I was thankful that we kept the room cold enough to be fully covered, as neither of us wore anything to sleep in. The sound of what could only be described as a bear having sex with a donkey periodically blasted through the room. I heard Stephanie chuckle behind me and could feel Tara's eyes boring through the back of my head.

"And that," Tara exclaimed, "is what I have to deal with every night."

I felt a flush of red in my face.

"Sorry," I said meekly.

After a moment the video distorted, chromatic aberration making the picture hard to discern. I could see myself tossing about, some words were being spoken but the audio also appeared corrupted. In the video I could make out when I woke and sat up, then white noise filled the screen.

"Did the file get damaged?" Tara asked. I could hear my anxiety mirrored in her voice. Maybe we should have done this without an audience.

Brianna fast-forwarded the video. Registering almost an hour of video snow, the chromatic aberration returned. I could make out Tara leaving the bathroom; I followed shortly after and stopped. The video interference looked like a scrambled cable channel from the 1980s. Suddenly the picture came into crystal focus. My face was covered momentarily by a pillow, which dropped in the manner of a Bugs Bunny gag.

"A pillow fight?" Stephanie broke the silence. "Really?"

I laughed, Tara laughed, Agent Allen grunted, and Brianna let out a concerned "Hmm."

"Okay, that'll bear investigation later," I said. "Just wanted to make sure the whole file hadn't been corrupted. On to this 9-1-1 call."

Brianna agreed. I noticed the time was pushing noon. None of us had realized how long we had been at this. Closing out the video player, Brianna pulled up the audio recording Joseph Handler had sent. Having taken a seat once again, Agent Allen sat forward, elbows on his knees, his head rested on his hands. Tara and Stephanie leaned forward looking like schoolgirls about to hear their favorite teacher tell them a story. I stood by Brianna, my body tense. Another wave of anxiety hit me, this time in anticipation of what this call would reveal. Brianna hit the play button.

"9-1-1, what's your emergency?" a man's voice asked.

"Heeeey, thish ish Shcott Boydee," a very drunk voice slurred. "Ya'll're lookin' fer meh."

"Sir," the 9-1-1 operator responded, "are you drunk?"

"Yeaaaah." The voice drew out the word, a giggle behind the vocalization. "I'sh over at de Ish Club. Ya knew thee one, on Harmo—" A retching sound cut the voice off.

"Ish Club?" I questioned.

"The ICE Club, now defunct and empty," Agent Allen stated, a hint of building aggravation seeping into his words.

"Come an git may," the voice said. "I's got three bisches strung up an waitin. Tells 'em tah br'ng dat Pryevate Dish."

"Sir, this number is for emergency services only," the operator arrogantly stated the obvious. "Prank calls are a violation of the law."

"Show's killin' workin' bisches. Show git some piggiesh doewn heer an catsch meh, fukher."

"Sir, I really think you need to drink some water and sleep it off." The operator's voice was infused with annoyance. "I'm trying to be nice here. Drunk dialing Emergency Services can land you in a lot of trouble."

A click indicated the 9-1-1 operator had hung up.

"FUCKING MORON!" Agent Allen's voice exploded, a sonic shotgun blast ricocheting throughout the hotel room. "Someone needs to fire that dumbass."

The surly agent pulled out his cell phone. His tan skin had darkened in his anger, the scar across his face made more prominent by the increased blood flow. A pulsating vein revealed itself in the man's forehead. For a moment I expected the giant to have a heart attack. He hit a button on his phone, placed it to his ear.

"This is S.A. Brock Allen, I need a surveillance unit for the old ICE Club, 200 East Harmon Road. Murder suspect Scott Boyd is believed to be hiding at the location." He paused a second, listening. "It's empty, has been for years. Reach out to the current owners about permission to enter." He paused again. "Coordinate with LVPD to have a breech unit available as soon as confirmation comes in." He paused again. "His own dumb ass told us where he was, that's how I know. And 9-1-1 dropped the ball by not informing us. Get it done."

Agent Allen ended the call, sat back, and let loose a frustrated growling sigh. All eyes on him, he stood and began pacing around the room. Brianna broke the silence.

"Guess I'm gonna have to tweak my software to account for drunk-as-shit speech," she said.

I gritted my teeth, the anxiety turning to frustrated anger.

"Two fucking blocks," I said quietly.

"What?" Tara asked.

"He's been two fucking blocks away this whole time."

Chapter 20

Parked across from a brown and tan single-family home, Caleb impatiently fidgeted. Built fifteen years ago, the house was constructed during the first phase of a planned community in Henderson. Construction of these communities had been steadily ramping up to accommodate the mass of Californian's fleeing their state's high cost of living. Wispy clouds in the bright afternoon sky spoke of darker clouds to come, the weather forecast predicting thunderstorms by midday tomorrow. With modern landscaping sensibilities, most of the neighborhood front yards were filled with the flora of the desert. It was a water-saving measure that eliminated the entire concept of a front lawn.

Opening his trusty notebook, Caleb checked the address for the eighth time since he arrived. Impatience was giving way to anxiety, not a feeling he was accustomed to. In his neat script, the name Sara Lopez was written at the top of a page, her stats and notes from his direct messages with her filling almost two pages. At this moment, the information of his concern was her abilities as a Goddess. Perfection requires accuracy, accuracy equates to success in all endeavors. According to his, or rather "Rita's," conversations with the girl, she had healing abilities. The short exchange he had written in his notebook contained a story about her healing her German shepherd's broken leg. While Caleb had no compunction about disassembling humans, dogs were sacred to him. He would have to make sure he kept her dog safe when he took her.

The Boy's gaze fell upon the SUV's clock. It read 4:30pm. Closing the notebook, Caleb's mind began to wander. His ascension to perfection was nigh: the Raven would come to exact revenge for the death of this girl, and he would take her. She would make him whole, make him perfect, and in return he would… He didn't really know what he would do. He found some attraction to the gothic Goddess. The Dark Man clearly wanted her dead, the rebellious streak in Caleb wanted to keep her alive out of spite. Then there was this desire that had invaded him. He was starting to become accustomed to his mind and body's want for her. Caleb had spent most of his teen years existing in an asexual state. He never felt any sexual desire for women or men; rather, he felt the desire to brutalize both, to make them hurt. But the Raven, the Queen of the Goddesses... He wanted to feel her under his body, to be inside her. Something about the gothy girl turned him on, something he could not place.

Caleb snapped to attention as a blue, 4-door Honda Civic pulled in front of Sara Lopez's house. The rear passenger-side door flung open, and a short girl with jet-black hair exited the vehicle. Followed by an identical girl. The driver and front seat passenger spent a moment saying something to the girls that Caleb could not hear. The twin girls responded with a flurry of hand gestures. Sign language. Sara had said she was born mute, it made sense that her hands would be her voice. It also meant Caleb wouldn't need to worry about a screaming captive. Thankfully he didn't need her to tell him anything, he just needed her to call the Raven to him. He only needed her to die.

The girls watched as the Honda pulled away from the curb and down the street. To Caleb's eyes they looked identical. Standing around four feet, ten inches, the girls seemed small for fourteen-year-olds. Each had the same broad face, big eyes, small nose, straight black hair, and olive complexion. Wearing school uniforms consisting of baby-blue blouses and navy-blue skirts, Caleb thought they looked like a Hispanic version of the creepy twins from *The Shining*. One of the girls unceremoniously smacked the back of her sister's head. Holding the back of her head in a gesture of exaggerated pain, the victim of the sibling assault gave her sister a nasty look. The assailant ran toward the front door of the house, her sister hot on her heels.

"Well fuck. How the hell am I supposed to know which one is Sara?"

His face felt hot, flush with frustration at this unforeseen turn. He knew he couldn't take both. He could kill the one that wasn't a Goddess. What if they both were Goddesses? With their inability to speak, and with his sign-language illiteracy, what was he to do? Caleb picked up his notebook, leafing through the names of Las Vegas Goddesses he had collected. Most had reported abilities that would put him in a dangerous position, their offensive capabilities a potential match to his own. Caleb let out a disgruntled sigh. He had come this far, his target within reach, his goals standing on the precipice of success. And he was being defeated by a goddamn doppelganger.

"Fuck it," he said, and slapped his notebook shut.

Caleb crossed the street, making a beeline toward the front door of the Lopez house. He paid no attention to the lack of a direct path from the street to the door, crossing the desert landscaping, swerving only to avoid the spikes of a barrel cactus that served as the front yard's centerpiece. His plan was simple: knock them both out, flip a coin for who to take and who to kill. In his frustration-borne haste, Caleb forgot a simple rule of life. Nothing ever goes according to plan.

A dark brown piece of wood stood between Caleb and the girls inside the house. He fought the impulse to simply shred the door and storm in. However, his aim was to draw the Raven to him, not the Las Vegas Police Department. Once she made him perfect, he could deal with the police. Caleb was a little surprised that there was no doorbell camera. It seemed this family liked to live dangerously. A white button situated inside a large, flat brass disk protruded from the wall to the left of the door. He hit the button and heard a muffled door chime come from inside the home.

The muffled sound of feet scrambling about came to him as he waited.

And waited.

And waited.

He hit the doorbell again, followed by a firm yet polite knock. Light footsteps approached the door. Caleb heard the deadbolt unlatch and the knob turned. Cracking open, a small face appeared from behind the door.

"Is Sara home?" Caleb asked, his voice sweet, his boyish charisma put into full effect.

The girl held up a finger to indicate he should wait while she completed his request. Maybe he wouldn't need to flip a coin. Maybe Sara would identify herself. The door closed and footsteps retreated. He noticed the deadbolt had not been reengaged. Tapping his finger on his thigh, Caleb counted out sixty seconds. No sound. No returning teen. He reached out, turned the doorknob. Quietly opening the door, Caleb entered the home.

The twins stood, waiting for him at the end of a short entrance hallway. One of them, he thought it might have been the girl who had opened the door, turned to her sister, hands a flurry of conversation. Caleb didn't know what she was saying, but he did not like how this situation was unfolding. Though he was unable to understand sign language, the last gesture the girl made seemed quite clear to him. With her fingers clenched, her thumb outstretched, the girl made a horizontal swipe across her throat.

"You little bitch," he said, deciding that randomly killing one and taking the other was perfectly acceptable. He began to raise his arm. One of the sisters pulled out a sheet of paper.

Five words stopped him dead in his tracks. Large block letters uttered the simple phrase, "There is no Sara, asshole."

Shock radiated from his face. Upon the real Rita Vineland's death, the administrator of the Caretaker online forums had sent a warning to all members. Rita's account was the only one that did not receive the alert. He had spoken to Sara many times, entirely unaware that Sara had been the twin girls before him. He had been catfished. They might only be teenagers, but these teens weren't entirely stupid.

Caleb felt the flush of heat in his face as mindless rage engulfed him. His hands shook, his vision tunneled. These girls had played him for a fool, a crime for which the penalty was death. He lashed out wildly as the first twin ran behind the kitchen island. His strike sliced into the top of a black leather couch. Raising his hand above his head, he prepared for a second strike. He froze, his tunnel vision focused on the unmoving girl before him. Her large, light brown eyes were those of a Goddess, her pupils the trademark vertical slits of a Caretaker. A menacing smile was fixed upon her face. A shiver ran down his spine. A wave of fear washed over him. He felt an unspoken threat and realized that the other sister had distracted him just long enough for his advantage to be lost.

The girl's smile widened to reveal crimson-streaked teeth. A trickle of blood escaped her mouth, running from the edge of her lips and down her chin. To Caleb, the girl appeared to move in slow motion. Opening her mouth, he saw that she had bitten her tongue, ripped into it with her teeth. The pain and damage had caused her abilities as a Goddess to manifest. He moved to strike at her. He failed. The speed of his movements could not compete with the speed of sound.

Evidence suggested the girls were honest about being mute. That she and her sister communicated in sign language attested to that. Their response to the doorbell confirmed they were not deaf. With her Goddess abilities active, this girl had a voice. A voice that could kill.

Caleb didn't hear the girl as much as he felt the pressure of her scream. The noise was a deafening, high-pitched shriek. He felt as if his heart had momentarily stopped. Pain radiated from his chest as his lungs emptied of air, refusing to refill. He felt his feet lift from the ground. The sensation of flying. A part of him was thankful he had left the front door open as his body was flung through the home's entryway. He instinctively created a buffer of air pressure around his body, his subconscious preparing to strike an immovable object.

Impact. The sound of straining metal and crunching plastic shot into his ears as he collided with the rear side of his SUV.

On the ground, disoriented, ears ringing, panting, he looked toward the house. The girl stood in the open doorway, her bloody smile on full display and her middle finger extended as a message to him. He stumbled in his attempt to stand up. The world was spinning. Clumsily he dug the SUV key from the pocket of his pants. A sudden spike of adrenaline sharpened his focus. Glancing back at the smiling girl, the animal instinct to flee took hold. Caleb had the SUV started and in motion before he had the door shut.

Anger took hold of him again. He had been the fool. Gripping the steering wheel with both hands, he winced as a burning pain tore through him. A bump in the center of his forearm had swelled. Pulling to the side of the road, he poked the spot. Searing pain wracked him, his body convulsed with the unfamiliar sensation. Gritting his teeth, he stifled the urge to scream.

"Fuck," Caleb hissed. "That little bitch."

He thought that, at best, his forearm was fractured. If he had been perfect, this would not have happened. If he were perfect, he would have the power to heal the break on his own. The swelling seemed to worsen by the second. Hissing out a reluctant sigh, Caleb decided a hospital would at least be able to give him proper pain medication and check how bad the damage really was. Going up against the Raven like this, trying to force her to make him perfect, was never going to happen if he was showing weakness. Pulling out his phone, Caleb ran a quick search for the nearest emergency room.

As with all things on the outskirts of Las Vegas, it was going to be a fifteen-minute drive to a location aptly named ER at Green Valley Ranch. He let out a frustrated grunt as he hit the navigation button on his cell phone. Putting the SUV back into drive, Caleb pulled onto the road and headed toward the emergency room.

Raven stood between the light, unseen inside the elevator. Periodic beeps ticked down the passing of each hotel floor. Her target was standing in a military-style "At Ease" pose before the elevator doors, feet shoulder-width apart and hands clasped in front of him. She had noticed him while drinking coffee at the Starbucks off New York-New York's casino floor. Slender, dressed in black jeans and a black hoodie, he would have blended into the casino crowd were it not for a vertical, four-inch keloid scar. Running from the base of his nose, crossing his lips, and ending below his chin, she recognized the scar more than the man. He had been included in some intelligence the Caretakers had managed to obtain. This man was in the employ of the Office. Raven's distaste for Joseph Handler and his organization bordered on homicidal. She wondered what a member of the Office was doing in her hotel, and why he had appeared to be looking for someone.

A chime indicated the elevator had reached the man's floor. Raven followed him down a twisting hallway. Reaching his destination, the man gave a "Shave and a Haircut" knock before unlocking a door. Looking at the room number, Raven realized this man was staying directly under her room. She felt a twinge of anger that the Office would dare place any of their agents so close to her. As he entered the room, she followed, narrowly avoiding the fast-closing door.

The room was barely recognizable as hotel accommodations. Two queen-sized beds were turned on their sides, resting against the wall. A long fold-out table had been placed in the center of the room. Black boxes with wires spewing from innumerable ports cluttered the imported tabletop, a series of antennae creating a metal and plastic forest atop them. Two laptops occupied the hotel-provided desk, one of them connected to what appeared to be a clear satellite dish with a directional microphone in the center. Raven recognized the sonic ear. An older man in blue jeans and a green t-shirt sat at the desk, headphones wrapped around his neck. His shoulder holster sported the butt of a very large gun.

"Did you find blondie?" The seated man's voice was rough.

"No," the standing man said. "Don't know where she went."

"My guess would be with her friends at the Cosmo," the older man offered. "Word is Handler managed to recruit the PI."

The younger man offered a skeptical look.

"Johnson's team has been ordered to step back." The older man removed the headphones from his neck, placing them on the table.

"No surveillance on them?" the younger man asked.

"Apparently Smith took out the in-room devices." The older man chuckled. "I told Johnson his on-off strategy wouldn't work with her."

"So what now?"

"Now you assholes can pack your shit and go," Raven said.

Startled, both men looked around the room, guns drawn. Raven stepped out from between the light. Her sudden appearance out of thin air clearly shocked the men. Reflexively, the man with the scar fired a round at her, the bang of the gun causing the older man to put a hand to his ear, wincing in pain.

"Goddammit, Howie!" The older man's exclamation came with the shaking of his finger in his ear.

Howie was frozen, wide-eyed and staring into the nonplussed, green cat-like eyes of Raven. Annoyance filled her as she looked down to see a hole in her shirt at her right clavicle. A flattened bullet protruded from the torn cloth. Pulling the slug out, both men visibly shuddered with the revelation that the cartridge failed to penetrate her skin.

"That hurt." Raven's voice was flat, controlled. She fought the urge to respond with violence. These men were no threat to her. "You may want this back," she said as she tossed the flattened bullet to the younger man. Frozen, Howie made no move to catch the spent round, which bounced off his chest and quietly came to rest on the carpeted floor.

"Put your gun away, Howie," the older man said, sliding his own piece back into its holster. "You're going to get yourself killed."

"Wha—" Fear permeated Howie's voice. "What the fuck are you?"

Raven cocked her head to the side, wondering if any answer would penetrate the clear terror this man was in. She opened her mouth to speak as the older man pushed Howie's gun to point toward the floor.

"I'm—"

"She's one of them half-breeds," the older man cut her off.

As soon as he finished his sentence, the older man's feet left the floor. Raven held him up, her hand wrapped around his neck. Shock and fear were plastered across his face. Anger and hatred radiated from hers. In his fear, Raven's green eyes struck him as the cold, hungry stare of a serpent. He felt a wetness in his pants, heard the dripping of liquid as his bladder involuntary emptied.

"There is only one who gets to call us that," Raven hissed through clenched teeth, "and that's only because he doesn't have lips I can sew shut."

"I—" the older man squeaked out. "I'm sorry! I meant no offense." The man's body began to tremble as tears came. "Please don't eat me."

Confusion washed over Raven's face. She dropped the man into his puddle of urine and stepped back.

"What kind of bullshit has Handler been feeding you idiots?"

"There's stories," Howie, standing as if he had been nailed to the floor, cautiously said. "Guys who were found chewed up, partially eaten."

Raven sighed. Caretakers had found bodies in the same condition.

"We were told you people did it," the older man offered, "because you have powers without being judged, you're on his side."

Raven felt her face flush with anger. The idea that Caretakers would be in bed with the Dark Man was abhorrent to her. That these gullible morons believed such shoddy reasoning was equally galling. She balled her fists, stiffened her arms. These men were soldiers, their words an echo of Handler's propaganda. As insulting as it was, she knew they did not deserve to be beaten for being simple-minded, ignorant tools. She would save this feeling for the thing that fed them the lie.

"You've been lied to," she stated, her voice controlled. "We fight against him. Our aim is to protect life."

The older man let out a relieved sigh, nodding his head. "Yeah, I thought that might be the case." There was a measure of defeat in his words. "Why don't you join us?"

"Because we don't believe the ends justify the means," Raven said. "Unlike Joseph Handler, we will not commit mass murder in the name of the greater good."

The older man's face darkened. He suddenly appeared so small to Raven, like an abused child. As he spoke, she could hear a crushing guilt in him, a guilt that had been kept at bay by carefully crafted denial. A guilt he dared not face.

"There is no good or evil," he began, reciting the mission of the Office, "there is no right or wrong." With each word, the older man's resolve seemed to return to him, his walls of self-denial fortified. "One dead is better than one thousand." The man picked himself up off the floor. "One thousand dead is better than one million. Our mission is the survival of mankind. To that end, no individual life is sacred."

The older man's change of demeanor was religious, his stance one she had seen in ecclesiastical zealots. Words were futile against such deep-seated belief. A resolve of her own held fast.

"Be careful not to become the very evil you seek to destroy," Raven said.

Howie opened his mouth to respond. Raven held up a hand.

"Tell your superiors to get your people out of Vegas." Confidence infused Raven's voice. "We know where every surveillance and strike team you have is located. If they aren't out of the city in four hours, being eaten will be the least of their worries."

It was a bluff. Caretakers kept an eye on the Office but had not devoted the resources for intensive and ongoing surveillance of their activities. The older man's words had changed that. Raven felt something needed to be done about them. That would have to wait. The Abomination was her top priority. Getting the Office out of the city just removed a wildcard.

The older man considered Raven for a moment, trying to divine the veracity of her claim. Letting out a sigh, he made his decision.

"Howie," the man said slowly, "get on the horn and let HQ know our operation has been compromised."

Howie nodded but stayed glued to his spot. Raven gestured to the mountain of communication equipment, inviting the scarred man to comply with his orders. Moving quickly, Howie rounded the tech-loaded table and grabbed a CB mic. He spit out a series of call signs and pseudo-military jargon. An affirmative response crackled through the radio, followed shortly by a blanket recall order.

"Thank you." Raven smiled wide, a paradoxical mixture of sweet and threatening. "Now, if you gentlemen would kindly pack up and get the fuck out of town, it would be greatly appreciated."

Chapter 21

The defunct ICE nightclub was bathed in the soft blue glow of the bright Las Vegas night. A notice of demolition was attached to a chain-link fence that enclosed the property. The end of the old building was just a few days away. Its darkened façade felt foreboding, as though some preternatural force inhabited the structure and was eager to share its fate with any who dared to enter.

From the northeast corner of Harmon and Koval, Stephanie, Mary, and I watched a very animated discussion between Agent Allen and a member of the Las Vegas SWAT unit. Every time the FBI agent said something, the officer shook his head. Each time I could see the massive agent's body language getting more and more agitated. Agent Allen pressed his finger into the policeman's armored chest, made a proclamation, and headed toward us.

"So," Stephanie said as the lumbering giant approached, "what's the verdict?"

"I had to pull rank," Agent Allen stated, an underlying aggravation evident in his words. "It appears all the exit doors have been sealed. Only one way in and one way out. SWAT was trying to exclude us from the breech, saying it would be too dangerous."

"Kinda sounds like it is," Mary said. "From what I've seen on cop shows, this seems like we're not really following proced—"

Agent Allen shot her a stern look that clamped her mouth shut. Gesturing to both Mary and me, he raised his eyebrows. "You guys packing?"

As she was his former partner, Agent Allen knew Stephanie was packing her signature Desert Eagle. The gun was more cannon than pistol. Mary, dressed in loose-fitting black jeans, combat boots, and a black hoodie, nodded. Pulling up her sweater, she revealed a 9mm pistol in a paddle holster attached to her belt.

"I have my concealed carry paperwork if you need it," she told Agent Allen.

"It's fine." Hhe waved her off. "Just don't fire unless absolutely necessary. I don't want to deal with that paperwork."

I opened my coat to reveal my double shoulder holster. As per usual, twin knives occupied leather sheaths in place of guns. Agent Allen pinched his nose as he let out a disapproving exhale.

"Fifteen feet," I said, referencing the fact that within fifteen feet a blade has a combat advantage over a gun. It's the reason cops will use lethal force against someone with a knife.

The giant gave an understanding, albeit disapproving, nod. "Fine." Resignation permeated the word. "Just stay behind me."

Agent Allen motioned for us to follow him. We joined five heavily armed and armored SWAT officers standing at the edge of the parking lot. Even through their gear I could tell they were tense. Unlike me, they were ready for action.

We quickly made our way across the empty lot, jumped a low railing that once served to control incoming club patrons, and spread out as much as the small space allowed. I warily eyed the faded green double-door club entrance. In my tense state I half-expected Scott Boyd to burst through the doors shooting at everyone. Little did I know, that would have been the best-case scenario.

In front of the twin doors, the five SWAT officers made a semicircle, keeping the four of us at their backs.

"I don't like this," Stephanie muttered under her breath. "I really don't like this."

Agent Allen grunted in agreement as one of the policemen tested the doors. They were open. Two of the SWAT members positioned themselves at each side, holding the handles and ready to open the doors for the remaining three. The lead officer gave the signal.

The breech unit slowly opened the doors, opting for stealth rather than a speedy incursion into the unknown. Three officers, rifles raised, moved quietly into the building. A glint caught my attention. For a moment I stared at the wire attached to the top of the left door. Frowning, my mind simply could not reconcile the sight. Why would a club have fishing line attached to the top of the front door? It pulled taut, then snapped as the door hit maximum rotation. In an instant the answer hit me. I yelled out a fruitless warning.

"TRIPWIRE!"

The officers manning the doors reflexively flattened themselves against the walls. The three inside the doorway were on the floor in a flash. Agent Allen, Stephanie, and Mary all dove to the sides, avoiding a direct line with the club entrance. Like an idiot, I stood there staring into the doorway, waiting for the big boom. There was no big boom.

After a few seconds the SWAT officers picked themselves up off the floor, raising their guns in a defensive formation. The two holding the doors moved into the doorway. With a quick examination, the officer on the left reached up and pulled on the thin piece of fishing line still attached to the door.

"Looks like a dud," he said.

"I don't think so," I countered, pointing down the hall to the club's interior.

Multicolored flashing lights had sprung up, and the deep *thump* of a song started playing.

"Early warning system?" Mary asked.

"More like an invitation," I said. "He's been waiting for us."

"Let's not disappoint the bastard," Agent Allen said through gritted teeth.

We entered behind the three SWAT point men. As the song playing over the old sound system became clear, I groaned. Hearing a digital female voice proclaim, "This is motherfucking torture," followed by a heavy bassline hit, I rolled my eyes and growled. Agent Allen noticed my aggravation. He mistook it as a sign of some important observation.

"What is it?" His deep voice somehow cut through the increasing volume of the music.

"'Glowstix, Neon and Blood,'" I said.

To be honest, the look of utter confusion on his face was one of the best things I'd seen in a while. Was my amusement appropriate in the situation? Hell no. Did I need something to take my nerves down a peg? Absolutely. Somehow, the G-Man's confused expression actually induced a state of calm within me.

"What the—" he started.

"The song," I clarified. "It's called 'Glowstix, Neon and Blood' by the band Incubite."

I frowned. The calm I felt was quickly replaced by annoyance as the totality of the situation came into focus.

"And I need to beat this asshole for ruining a perfectly good aggro-tech song for me."

Agent Allen clasped the bridge of his nose, shaking his head.

Clearing the hallway, we were greeted with what appeared to be a decently populated club. Blinding strobe lights limited our field of vision, and with the music's aural assault I was momentarily put off balance. What looked to be patrons sat at booths and low tables that lined the edges of the dance floor. A blonde in a skimpy black dress held her arm up in greeting from a raised VIP platform. Bartenders stood waiting for customers. In the strobing light, these people appeared to be moving. Taking a moment to stare at one of these patrons, I realized the place was populated by mannequins. The SWAT officers seemed to have realized this as well, not reacting to the plastic people.

The SWAT team split, two securing the left side, two to the right. The fifth stayed with us, his body language displaying annoyance of the highest order as Agent Allen walked straight toward the middle of the dance floor. Instinctively we fanned out: Agent Allen in the center, Stephanie to his left, the SWAT officer capping the left flank, Mary to the agent's right, and I sealed the right flank. In retrospect, we were lined up to be gunned down like targets in a carnival game. My only consolation was that Scott Boyd had not been known to utilize firearms.

The music abruptly paused, and the strobe lights ceased as we reached the center of the club. An overhead spotlight encompassed our little team. I could see the two flanking SWAT teams making their way toward a darkened stage in front of the DJ booth. I heard movement coming from inside the booth. Crackling, the old speakers roared to life with the voice of Scott Boyd doing a carnival barker impression.

"Ladies and gentlemen!" his voice blared. "Boys and girls! Welcome!"

"CUT THE SHIT, BOYD!" Agent Allen's voice boomed louder than the speakers.

"Oh, come now, big guy." Scott's words were infused with a syrupy malevolence. "He's not very happy with you, you know."

Agent Allen opened his mouth to speak, but no words came out.

"All of his offers, and what do you do?" An underlying note of crazy punctuated the question. "You throw his generosity back in his face! You cannot deny him. No one can deny the will of the Dark Man. Obey or die is the name of the game."

Agent Allen's face darkened. His lips twisted into a paradoxical smirk.

"And Jonathan—"

A freezing chill shot down my spine. How did this madman know my name? Did the Dark Man convey it to him? That the Dark Man might know my name even though I had not spoken to him chilled me even further. What else did that featureless void know about me? Did it know who I actually am? How was it getting this information? The questions ran through my head at light speed. Boyd's voice forced them aside.

"Jonny-boy," the booming voice came from all around us. "He really didn't appreciate that finger you gave him. I'm afraid I'll have to cut it off as punishment."

I gritted my teeth. My hands reflexively pulled the knives from their sheaths. Out of the corner of my eye I saw Agent Allen put his gun away and produce a taser. Pulling a radio from a belt clip, he addressed the SWAT team.

"Tasers only," Agent Allen said through clenched teeth. "I repeat, tasers only. Use of lethal force is no longer authorized." The SWAT officers made no move to comply with the order.

"But first," the music slowly faded in behind Boyd's voice, "enjoy the show! Welcome to the Dance Macabre!"

Multicolored lights flashed to the rhythm of the music. The illusion of life returned to the plastic club patrons. With three loud *clacks*, spotlights lit the stage before us. The scene turned from creepy to chilling.

Revealed on the stage were three naked women in a familiar physical state. A redhead, a brunette, and a blonde, their features plasticized in permanent expressions of terror. Each of their limbs had been dismembered, wooden joints used to re-connect the arms and legs. Like those Boyd had crucified, the heads had been affixed to the torsos with wooden dowels. Thin cables were attached to each limb. Motors

241

high above each of the three bodies moved the cables like an automated puppeteer. Green glow sticks were attached to each woman's hands, giving them a *Rave of the Dead* vibe, with dance moves like low-rent Disney animatronics.

As the heavy thump of the bass and high-treble aggressive synth music played, Scott Boyd revealed himself. With his bouncing green pompadour and purple, twin-tailed tuxedo, his Joker theme assaulted the eyes with unmistakable reference. Glow sticks in hand, Boyd danced and gyrated, weaving between his jerking victims in an apparent dance of victory.

The killer's slim frame pirouetted between two of the dancing corpses. Center stage, his arms extended from behind the poor dead brunette, giving her the appearance of a four-armed pagan goddess. Doing what I could only describe as the Electric Slide, Scott Boyd glided around the redhead stage left, stopping behind the human-mannequin hybrid to give the dead, jerking body a pelvic thrust. Over the loud, aggressive electronic music, I could hear the man's insane laughter at his act of faux-necrophiliac violation. Bouncing side to side, his glow stick-laden hands winding around each other in a popular Rave-style dance, he made one last winding lap between his handiwork. As the song wrapped, his hands still winding in a figure eight around each other, the lunatic Joker-wannabe shuffled his legs down, bending at the knees, in a controlled descent to the stage floor. Lying on his back, only his glow stick-occupied hands were visible. With the final beat of the music, Boyd launched himself off the stage floor into the air. Landing at the platform's edge in a kneeling position with arms outstretched, a crazed smile was plastered on his face. Silence momentarily filled the musty, defunct club.

"Ta-da!"

Boyd paused, waiting for the clapping to start. When none came, his smile faltered, and his brow furrowed.

"What?" he angrily exclaimed. "You guys didn't like my fucking dancing? I don't do this shit for everyone, you know."

"Your dancing's shit," I barked out. I wanted to punch the man, though I wasn't entire certain if it was due to the smile on his face, the girls he had killed, his ruining a perfectly good song for me, or dancing to it with glow sticks. I momentarily contemplated how sociopathic my own thought process seemed.

"Well fuck you too, Jonny-boy." His grin seemed to widen. "Looks like I'll have to take more than that finger."

Boyd jumped down from the stage to face the five of us. I could see the two-man SWAT teams hiding in the shadows to each side of us, their rifles trained on the faux-Joker. In unison we all backed up. Agent Allen maintained taser range but was poised to bolt if necessary. I couldn't help but wonder what he knew that the rest of us didn't.

"For fucks sake, I said tasers only!" The G-Man's booming voice cut the silence.

Boyd's face dropped at Agent Allen's order. The psychotic bastard wanted to die.

None of the SWAT members moved to swap armament. Stephanie and Mary holstered their guns, stepping farther back as they did so.

"Come now, Agent." The killer's tone was aggressive, malevolence dripping from every word. "Don't beat around the bush. You have to shoot me."

"No," Agent Allen responded, an eerie calm in his voice, "I don't."

"Yeah," Boyd said, producing a five-inch knife from his tuxedo sleeve, "you do."

A hit of adrenaline slowed the world for me. Boyd raised his arm to throw the knife, Agent Allen pulled the trigger on his taser. The taser prongs hit their mark, along with a bullet from our SWAT member. As expected from a specially trained marksman, the shot hit Boyd in the heart. Instant death. His lifeless body jolted for a moment as the taser's electrical current coursed through it. Agent Allen let out a screaming growl, one part angry, one part scared shitless. He turned toward the SWAT member standing next to Stephanie.

"What did you do?" Agent Allen yelled, fear slowly creeping into his face. "Get out! Everyone, get out!" Dropping the spent taser, he drew his gun, backing toward the building entrance.

Stephanie, Mary, and I started backing up with him. The SWAT officers weren't so smart. As I watched the five heavily armed men approach Scott Boyd's still corpse, it dawned on me why Agent Allen wanted to clear the room. My eyes wide, a feeling of déjà vu overtook me. I renewed the mental flex that assured me the preternatural shield I had developed was active.

The crunch of bone and wet tearing of flesh echoed through the quiet club. From my vantage point, all I could see were the dark shapes of the SWAT members standing over Scott Boyd's body.

"Not again." The whisper passed my lips without a thought.

"HOLY SHIT!" one of the officers exclaimed as his comrade was split, groin to crown, each half falling to the ground with a wet splat. The remaining four SWAT members began backing up and unloading their firearms. The gunfire was deafening in the enclosed space. A backlit silhouette of a spider-like appendage whipped around, taking the head off another officer.

Sounds of breaking bone, ripping flesh, and some undefinable wet squishing; I knew the sounds of the metamorphosis, for they had been etched into my psyche two times over. Frozen in fear, I watched the dark form that used to be Scott Boyd lift itself from the ground on two massive, segmented legs that sprouted from its back. The glistening black of its wet chitinous armor periodically sparked as bullets ricocheted off it.

One of the SWAT members managed to pull back to our position near the front entrance, laying down what he thought was cover fire for his two remaining teammates. A gurgling scream erupted from another SWAT member as his chest was pierced by the talon-tipped leg of the Boyd-thing. His jerking body lifted off the ground and was summarily flung into a group of mannequin spectators. The final escaping SWAT member made it to us, and he kept running right out of the building without stopping.

"What the fuck is that thing?" our SWAT officer demanded, reloading his gun.

The flexing in my head clenched as I felt my fear subside. The faces of my mutilated comrades returned to me. In place of the fear and grief I had felt when my fugue ended, red-hot rage coursed through me.

"All of you," I commanded. "Get. Out."

"What the hell do you think you're doing?" Stephanie demanded.

"I got a bone to pick with this thing."

My hands clenched my ritual knives, the meat of my fingers digging into the metal studs at the center of each finger groove. Something in my mind changed, the clench became fluid, dynamic, as though the energy of my body had connected to a greater circuit. A blue light caught my attention. Looking down, the gems embedded in the knives glowed. An epiphany hit me. These weren't simple ritual knives. They were conduits. In the right hands, these knives were real weapons. Looking at the Boyd-thing, I felt one corner of my mouth lift into a lopsided, maniacal smirk.

I half turned to make sure everyone headed toward the exit. When Agent Allen, Stephanie, Mary, and the remaining SWAT team member reached the exit hallway, I turned my attention back to the Scott-thing. Standing silently in the center of the dance floor, the dark mass waited motionless for its next dance partner. I could feel blades of invisible energy extend two feet from each blade. I clenched my teeth and ran at the black mass.

Closing the distance, I could make out the details of what Scott Boyd had become. The man's spine had extended forward, creating a snake-like neck covered in slimy black plates. An armored plate obscured half his face. His insane smile was all that remained of his lunatic visage. His arms were covered in the same wet, black plating, hands morphed into three-fingered talons. Boyd's body had compressed into an almost serpentine funnel that extended into a long tail. The remnants of his intestines dangled from a gaping hole in his abdomen, twitching tendrils dripping blood and black sick. Triple-hinged legs capped by three-toed talons completed his transformation into a streamlined killing machine.

As I closed the distance, I heard what sounded like a mash-up between Boyd's insane laughter and the cackling of a hyena. A flash of movement caught my eye. One of the spider-like legs swept in on me. Arcing my left hand toward the incoming strike, I could feel my invisible blade make contact. No damage, but enough force to redirect the Boyd-thing's strike away from me. Another flash of movement forced me to stop my advance. I swung my right arm to parry a blow from the creature's other segmented appendage. This time I saw a scoring cut in the talon. I felt a surge of confidence. I could do this. I had the strength to take this monster down. A swipe of a clawed arm bounced off the invisible shield of energy surrounding me.

Rearing its smiling head, the creature reminded me of a snake about to strike. I braced myself for the attack. I was concentrating on the wrong body part.

An untenable roar erupted from the Boyd-thing, and its head sped toward me. Inexplicably it stopped a few feet from impact and let out a noxious exhale. The smile etched into the lower half of what used to be Scott Boyd's face seemed to widen. Its clawed arms lashed out, raking against my unseen armor in a flurry of speed that I could not keep up with.

I was stuck on the defensive. Directing all my energy into the shield, the clenching in my mind became a charley horse. My body cramped. Sweat poured from my brow. I felt fatigue setting in. That this ability would come with the drawback of draining me had failed to cross my mind. I saw a blur of movement as one of the spider legs smashed into my side, the impact sending me through the air. I landed a few feet away from the exit hallway. Every inch of me hurt.

Looking up, I discovered Agent Allen, Stephanie, and Mary still standing there. They probably thought they could help if things went sideways. The result of their aid would just be a repeat of five years ago. I wasn't willing to lose any more comrades to another of these things.

Panting, sweating like a racehorse, and bruised from hitting the floor at high speed, I picked myself up. My defenses had gone down, the gems in my knives were dark. Taking a deep breath, I renewed my focus. The wet, monstrous thing's twisted laughter filled the room, its chitin-covered arms calling in a challenge. Clawed hands beckoned, saying, "Come at me, bro." It occurred to me that this was not some mindless killing machine. Whether the mind of Scott Boyd still resided in this abominable chimera or if it was the Dark Man himself who had taken control… There was no time to debate that. Gritting my teeth, I prepared myself for another round when Mary's voice rang out.

"Back off, this fucker's mine."

My mind couldn't reconcile what I was seeing. Mary's blonde hair darkened to jet black, its shoulder length quickly restyling itself. Shortening in the back, her hairline angled down to chin-level dagger points. As she darted past me, I saw purple Bettie Page-style bangs had appeared. A curving branch pattern of eyeliner sprouted from the corner of her left eye. Her eyes had transmuted from hazel to emerald-green. I felt my heart skip a beat when I noticed her pupils. Vertical, reptilian black lines tracked me for a moment, a predatory gleam held within them. Mary was definitely smirking, and I was fairly certain she winked at me as she sped toward the monstrosity on the dance floor.

I felt helpless and utterly confused. My mind had an easier time processing the transformation of Scott Boyd into a spider-snake beast than the idea that my innocent-looking and determined sidekick was a shapeshifting goth. Watching Mary, she held her right arm down, slightly out, with her fingers pressed together in what martial artists refer to as a "knife" position. The deep contrast between the dance floor lightshow and the shadows made it hard to see details. From my vantage point, it appeared that Mary's fingers fused together, her fingernails extended into a solid three foot long, double-edged blade of keratin.

Maniacal laughing echoed through the club at Mary's approach. The Boyd-thing swung a segmented leg toward her, talon tip poised to impale. Her organic blade held out perpendicular to the ground, she twirled in a 360 spin. A cross between a scream, laugh, and yelp came from the creature as Mary's blade sliced through its attack, splitting the talon in two. Whipping her blade around, she relieved the thing of its clawed hands. Halfway through another spin, Mary's blade cleaved a vertical cut through the thing's smiling visage. She severed the head from its obscene body as she completed the turn.

The Boyd-monster collapsed to the floor. Mary's silhouette stood triumphant, backlit by the dance floor lights. I willed myself to move. On my slow approach, I heard a hissing sound, like air leaking from a tire. I realized that the thing that had killed three SWAT officers and made a mockery of my attempt to take it down was dissolving. A flash of memory brought me back to the killing room my friends had died in. Their corpses had remained, but only a black puddle of goo where the thing that had killed them stood. This was why. As I closed the distance to Mary, the last of Scott Boyd dissolved. A slick of black, rancid ichor was all that remained of him.

Stopping in front of the purple-banged goth girl, my mind feverishly tried to find words. Her stance was calm, as if killing monsters was part of her daily routine, and a hint of amusement radiated from her expression. Gone were the serpentine eyes that I had seen moments ago. For a moment I wondered if my eyes had been playing tricks on me. I had no idea what to say to her. On one hand, I was grateful for her saving our lives; on the other hand, I was a bit miffed at her for deceiving me. Then there was the matter of why she let three of LVPD's finest die by that thing's talons. Standing for a moment, my index finger rocking between us, I finally found my voice.

"Mary, you and I need to have a talk about honesty."

"Call me Raven," she said, cocking her head to the side, her smile widening.

"A bit stereotypical, don't you think?"

"Yeah." She brushed off the comment. "I get that a lot."

Mary— Raven began to walk past me toward the exit hallway. She stopped at my side, her hand on my shoulder. She spoke in a whisper.

"Welcome to the war, Darkstone."

In her expression I could see that the shock I felt was written all over my face. The girl now called Raven smirked and turned to walk toward the exit.

"I'll be in the car," she said.

As my shock wore off, the olfactory assault began. What was left of the Boyd-monstrosity emitted an indescribable smell. Decaying flesh, excrement, and almost every other putrid smell seemed to be rolled into one. Suppressing the urge to vomit, I backed away, heading toward Agent Allen and Stephanie. Raven's voice echoed through the empty club.

"Agent Allen," her voice commanded, "get a hazmat team in here to clean this up. And nobody touch that shit. It'll give you nightmares."

Chapter 22

Caleb found himself squirming to get comfortable on the hospital bed. The mattress felt like rock beneath him. He wondered how anyone could sleep on these things. The answer, he realized, was simple. Drugs. Lots and lots of drugs. Sadly, the drugs he had been given only served to dull the pain he felt in his left forearm.

Held in a white and powder-blue sling, his arm was swollen from the tips of his fingers to his elbow. The damaged appendage had taken on a reddish-purple hue. He tried to remember what would have granted him this injury. Besides knocking the wind out of him, he felt nothing when he impacted his car. Caleb realized that being ambushed by a couple fourteen-year-olds might have messed with his memory. He concluded that his arm must have caught the edge of the girl's open front door as he was vaulted out of that house.

The cream-colored walls of the small, eight-by-ten room were sparsely populated. A pair of large, white placards announced the patient's rights in no less than four languages. Each language had its own color, as if people could not distinguish English from Chinese. A three-foot-by-three-foot painting to the side of the small room's door demanded his attention. Something about it just wasn't right.

The painting was an impressionist-style depiction of a desert sunset. In Caleb's eyes it was superbly rendered. Muted tans, browns, and greens in the landscape caused the brilliant yellow, orange, and red of the sky to pop. It should have been a calming, serene image. But something about it felt…wrong. Deep crimson swaths of color careened across the top of the canvas, specks of dark brown and black holding fast within the brush strokes. The same color was sparingly used in the shadows of the landscape. Caleb stood to get a closer look, wincing as pain shot up his injured arm.

Upon close inspection, Caleb saw the source of unease. Atop a distant hill a small figure painted in the same deep crimson stood, frozen in time. Its featureless form left Caleb no doubt about its identity. He sneered, taking a sharp breath, and stopped cold. The room was infused with the scent of antiseptics and industrial-grade cleaning solutions.

Caleb detected something else. The smell of dried, decaying blood. For a moment he considered that he was in a hospital emergency room. This was a place steeped in spilt blood, after all.

He put his face to the painting and took a deep sniff. The deep crimson, that particular red turning brown and black, was blood. He stepped back, hitting the edge of the hospital bed, and lost his footing. Caleb's butt landed squarely on the hard mattress. The jostling sent waves of pain through his arm. He felt hot, sweat formed on his brow. The drugs were wearing off. A shiver ran through him as a cold bead of sweat made its way down his back.

Caleb wondered who the artist of that painting was and why the Dark Man seemed so ubiquitous, yet the masses appeared to be so ignorant of him. Since their first introduction, Caleb had seen images of the Dark Man everywhere. Company logos, religious iconography, film and television shows. The void was always lurking in the background. That dark, faceless figure innocuously on display for the subconscious of all to see. And yet the Dark Man was ignored. A threat no one would speak aloud. A threat no one would consciously acknowledge.

Most of mankind seemed to prefer cute villains, like Michael Myers, Jason Voorhees, or Satan. The Dark Man was a true menace, a real threat. An unbeatable villain. Untouchable. Unkillable. And those he had snagged were helpless against his will. Art and pain, it seemed, granted Caleb a moment of clarity. Comprehension devoid of ego. A knock at the private ER room door brought Caleb out of his own head, his moment of clarity melted into oblivion.

Opening the door, an auburn-haired woman entered the room. Standing five feet, four inches, the doctor held a digital tablet with Caleb's chart on it. Her brown eyes scanned the information. He thought she looked to be of Mediterranean descent and around forty years old, though he couldn't fathom why he bothered putting any thought into it at all. Her hair was pulled back into a neat, professional bun. She looked at him as he sat on the bed attempting to appear patient.

"I'm Doctor Jordan." The woman's voice was soothing, as if her typical patients were children. "I'm very sorry for the wait," she said. "I understand you've been here for a few hours."

"Three," he quickly said, managing to keep the aggravation out of his voice. "Been here three hours, two of those have been me waiting in this room after they took X-rays."

"You're kidding." Doctor Jordan's face dropped. She pinched her nose and groaned. Caleb got the impression that this was a common, and unnecessary, occurrence at this ER.

"So, what's the verdict? Do I get to keep my arm?" The joke rolled out of him with expert charm, his eyes flashing humor.

"You're going to be just fine," the doctor chuckled. "You do have one hell of a hematoma going," she said, looking at his X-ray pictures on her tablet. "No bone fracture, but from the looks of it you managed to dent both the ulna and radius."

Caleb gave her a nod. He had no formal knowledge of human anatomy, everything he knew came from deconstructing people. He knew where to hit for maximum damage, for maximum pain. However, he could not give the medical names for any of those places, bones or organs. He assumed by way of context that the ulna and radius were the bones in his forearm.

"The swelling is what I find concerning. I think we should drain your arm."

"Will that help?"

"It will prevent secondary damage from being done," she stated. "It's a simple procedure. Same principle as liposuction, really. Just a needle to pull the excess fluid from your arm. The results are instantaneous. However, I am going to prescribe some heavy painkillers. Right now, the swelling is choking some of your pain receptors. You're not feeling the full effect of the damage. Once we drain your forearm, it's going to hit you like a ton of bricks."

"I appreciate the honesty," Caleb said, knowing full well the propensity for doctors to play down the amount of pain any procedure will cause. "How long until my arm is back to normal?"

"I'd say about four to six weeks until the bone is back to normal. You should have full mobility with minimal pain within two weeks."

Caleb groaned as anger shot through him. He promised himself that there were fourteen-year-old twins with a painful death in their future.

As he stewed for a moment, Doctor Jordan sat on a stool that brought her to examination height.

"Let's take a look at that arm."

Caleb slipped the white canvas strap off his shoulder, letting the sling fall across his lap. Doctor Jordan gently held his swollen appendage, lightly pressing. Each press into his flesh left a pale dent that slowly rose, turning back into the weird reddish-purple. A knock at the door drew the doctor's attention.

"Yes?"

A young nurse nervously leaned into the room. With her head turned, Caleb's heart skipped a beat. Behind Doctor Jordan's left ear, on full display for everyone to see, was an infinity symbol. He ran through the chances that she was one of the Goddesses or if she was just another sheep following the infinity symbol tattoo trend. He saw no evidence that she had any sort of disability. Had the Raven already visited her? He had exchanged messages with older Goddesses who had their physical impairments fixed by someone named Beth, but they were waiting for the Raven to make them whole. Was the good doctor one of those women? And like the girl whose ambush landed him in this ER, was she put on alert by the Goddess Message Boards? The flurry of questions and doubt paralyzed him.

"I just wanted to let you know that Doctor Callahan has decided to show up for his shift," the young nurse softly said.

Doctor Jordan frowned at such a characterization in front of a patient.

"Martha." Doctor Jordan's warning tone caused the nurse to appear even more nervous.

"Sorry," the young girl's eyes widened as she realized the situation, "I just wanted you to know that you won't have to cover his shift again."

The door closed quickly, Nurse Martha fleeing any further admonishment. Doctor Jordan sighed and turned her attention back to Caleb's arm. As she continued her gentle prodding, Caleb made up his mind on a course of action.

"So," he said casually, "do you post on the message boards?"

Doctor Jordan froze in place. Her eyes slowly rose to meet his. She was greeted by a warm smile. He tipped his head down, moving it to the right to present his left ear to her. The doctor reached out, pulled his ear forward to reveal his distorted birthmark. Her eyes widened at the sight.

"Looks kinda fucked, doesn't it?" he said with a nervous laugh. "Not nearly as perfect as yours."

"I've never met a male with the mark before." Her words were infused with amazement. "But no, I'm not a regular member of the message boards. I got an invite seven years ago. I checked it out for a while, but I didn't feel there was anything there for me." She chuckled. "Guess I should pop back in and see what's going on if guys are starting to crop up."

A wide smile crossed Caleb's face. An internal sigh of relief permeated his mind.

"Have you been—" Caleb began, trying to probe without appearing to be pumping her for information.

"No," Doctor Jordan said. "I'm a sort of in-between person. Have you heard of Beth?"

Caleb nodded. He didn't know much about this Beth person beyond the fact that she had gone about removing the disabilities of the incomplete Goddesses starting in 1994. She seemed to have disappeared in 2009.

"I was born with a severe condition that caused cysts and tumors to grow uncontrollably over my body," Doctor Jordan offered, unsure why she felt compelled to tell not only a stranger, but a patient, her life story. "In 1999, Beth came to me. She said that she was repairing the chaos their genes were causing. I was told that I would have to wait for one she called 'the Key' to come and reconcile the genetic disparity."

"I see," Caleb said. He barely understood half of what she was saying. With the doctor under his gaze, he wondered if this Beth person had also blocked the abilities of those she helped. Would that mean the Raven could not track them?

Doctor Jordan fell silent for a moment. Furious thinking shone in her eyes. Smirking, she let out a little sigh. "Want to see something really cool?"

"Sure," Caleb responded, unnerved by the odd look of excitement on the doctor's face.

Out of her lab coat pocket, Doctor Jordan produced a metal item. It appeared to be a series of metal plates designed to sheathe a finger with a small spike at the tip. Sliding the device over her left index finger, she grinned at Caleb.

"I usually reserve this for extreme cases," she said, "but I'll make an exception for a fellow mark bearer."

Fingers quickly curling themselves into a fist, the spike on the armor ring pierced the base of the doctor's palm. Her grin turned to a pained grimace as she pressed the instrument harder into her flesh. Caleb watched as Doctor Jordan's pupils dilated, appearing to consume the brown of her irises, then snapping into vertical lines.

Right hand on his arm, Doctor Jordan focused on the damage. A pleasant warmth washed over his forearm, followed by an indescribable sensation. He could feel the bones in his arm, pinpoint where they had sustained injury. There was no pain, just an odd feeling that the dents in the bone were being repaired, pounded back into place as one would do with a dented car door. Caleb pulled in a deep breath, overcome by a wave of lightheadedness. Awestruck, he stared as his swollen arm shrank, slowly returning to its pale, cream-colored hue.

Doctor Jordan released the Boy's arm and took off her finger armor. She healed the puncture in her left palm and blinked. Pupils back to their round, human state, she smiled at Caleb, satisfied with a job well done. Testing the movement of his arm, flexing his fingers, Caleb gave the brown-eyed physician a million-dollar smile.

"That is incredible," he said, a rare moment of honesty in his voice. "You are amazing."

"It's not something I do often. Last thing I need is for word to get around. The ability also has its limits."

Caleb raised an eyebrow.

"Genetic issues are beyond me," she explained. "Which kills me when I have a child patient who's suffering from a genetic disease, and I can do nothing."

Caleb nodded, sympathy washing over his face. Behind his eyes he felt impatience and aggravation. She was still talking. Why was she still talking? He got what he wanted. He was done. No. Not quite. An idea struck him.

"Would you like to grab a coffee after your shift is over?" Caleb blurted out.

Doctor Jordan gave a soft chuckle, shaking her head slightly. "I'm a little old for you."

"Oh," his face flushed, "no, no. Not like that. You're just the first person I have met with the birthmark and—"

"You want to talk with someone that isn't hiding behind a computer?"

"Yes," he said, injecting some meekness into the word as he tried his best to look shy and harmless.

"Okay," Doctor Jordan said. "We can meet at the Peppermill tomorrow. Say, noon?" She stood.

He smiled, nodded in agreement. "I'll see you there."

"I'm not saying it's aliens," Raven said, channeling the presenter of the TV show *Ancient Aliens*, "but it's aliens."

An audible slap echoed through the hotel room. Jonathan's hand landed squarely on his balding head. Taking off his glasses, the man in black pulled his hand down his face, stretching every inch of skin.

"This is dumb."

Raven gave the PI a hard stare, one which he returned.

"The exorcist thinks aliens are a step too far?" She cocked a sarcastic eyebrow.

Jonathan let out a resigned sigh. "Touché."

"Okay," Agent Allen spoke up. "So you're an alien."

Raven let out a sputtering laugh. "No," she said, "one of my ancestors was. In fact, he was so prolific that the majority of humans have at least a small portion of his DNA."

Tara's eye's narrowed at the assertion. "Why haven't researchers discovered this?"

"The Human Genome Project has designated those bits of extra DNA as junk DNA," Raven stated. "Not surprising since there is little genetic material available without the Caretaker DNA to compare to."

"Caretaker?" Stephanie piped up.

"That's what my ancestors called themselves. A name we, their heirs, have chosen to continue using."

"A bit presumptuous, don't you think?" Jonathan stated.

"They were dying," Raven began. "A species that had hit an evolutionary dead-end. But their pride, their egos, would not let them simply slip into the darkness with no one to remember them. The Caretakers took to the stars to help younger species facing the Gauntlet, an act designed solely to ensure they would not be forgotten."

"Going need some definitions here," Agent Allen said. "What is the Gauntlet?"

Raven sighed. She had forgotten that she was speaking with a group completely ignorant of their own situation.

"The Gauntlet is what we call it. It is a kind of test which can either propel a species into a prosperous future or secure its extinction." Raven's face darkened as she spoke. "The CliffsNotes version is that two are born, one an Avatar of Life, the other an Avatar of Anti-Life—"

"You mean death," Stephanie said. A sharp look from Raven quickly shut her up.

"Death is a natural part of life, a necessity for the continuation and evolution of species." Raven paused, trying to find simple terms the group before her could understand. "Think of Life as matter, and Anti-Life as anti-matter. What happens when a particle of matter comes into contact with a particle of anti-matter?"

"Mutually assured destruction," the black-clad PI stated.

"Exactly," Raven said. "The same goes for Life and Anti-Life. Thankfully these two are separated in the universe, direct contact is effectively impossible."

"Effectively?" Agent Allen asked.

"The only interaction between Life and Anti-Life is an entity we call the Dark Man."

A visible shudder struck Jonathan and Agent Allen simultaneously.

"So, he's this Anti-Life given consciousness?" Jonathan wondered.

"In a nutshell," Raven replied. "The evolution of any high-level sentient species such as humans is initiated by what my ancestors called the *Teach Anam*'s arrival on a world."

"How do you spell that?" Agent Allan asked. Raven noticed the large man was taking notes.

With an impatient sigh, Raven spoke slowly, "T-E-A-C-H A-N-A-M."

The G-Man raised an eyebrow. "But it's pronounced Ch-ach Ah-naam? Who the fuck made up that spelling?"

"It's Gaelic," Jonathan answered. "Understanding Gaelic spelling is…annoying. I believe it translates to House of Souls."

"Very good," Raven said. "And this House of Souls is limited in capacity. Once a population exceeds the available number of souls, what we call *Nianam*, or Soulless, are born. And everything starts to go to shit from there."

"You're telling me that souls are a real thing?" Agent Allen's incredulity spewed forth from his words.

Jonathan, Tara, and Stephanie looked at the giant G-Man in surprise. It dawned on all of them that this man was not a member of Darkstone's Asylum. His interaction with anything even close to paranormal was likely busting a fake psychic or two. Stephanie and Tara had enough interaction with inexplicable occurrences to believe the possibility of the soul and spirits was fairly high. Jonathan's experience granted him the knowledge of spiritual entities as fact, and the soul almost a certainty. The concept of people without souls walking around, that was a hard pill for any of them to swallow.

Raven stood, walked over to the suited behemoth. Looking up at the man, she motioned for him to bend over.

"Shall I illuminate you?" she asked.

"And how would you do that?" the FBI agent asked as he bent, putting himself at Raven's eye level.

Raven cupped his face with her right hand, her thumb hovering above his left eye. The hair on his arms stood in warning. Her touch was gentle, her hands cool and soothing. Yet something about her unnerved Agent Allen. She smirked at the very uncomfortable-looking G-Man.

"See as we see," Raven said.

A small electrical discharge flashed between the pad of Raven's thumb and Agent Allen's pupil. Jerking up, he blinked furiously, feeling as though a grain of sand were stuck in his eye.

"What the hell was—" Agent Allen's words fell silent.

Standing before him was a being of pure light. He could see hints of Raven's facial features within the luminous figure. His gaze turned to Stephanie, Tara, and Jonathan. He saw similar figures of bright light staring at him. Agent Allen noticed Jonathan seemed different than the others; a pulsating white outline enclosed the totality of his being, almost like his soul had a shield surrounding it. Blinking, the tall man's vision slowly returned to normal. He stood silent, unable to find words.

"It's like that sometimes," Raven said.

"What is?" Tara asked.

"Some people have a hard time reconciling what they see with what they believe," Raven said. "Our good agent here is trying to figure out whether he can accept a new piece of reality or fall into cognitive dissonance. Time will tell."

Raven returned to her seat. "Now where was I?"

"*Nianam* and everything going to shit," Jonathan reminded her.

"Ah," Raven said, "so when the population of *Nianam* starts to outnumber the available souls, the Dark Man begins to awaken. His aim is to destroy all the souls, ensuring a species will obliterate itself. The fastest way for that to happen is for the Avatar of Anti-Life to find and destroy the *Teach Anam*. Thankfully that's never happened. His other option is to kill the Avatar of Life, forcing the *Teach Anam* to move to a different world. Apparently, that has happened a few times over the eons."

"Kill the good guy," Tara said, making sure she understood, "and everything goes to hell."

"How do we win?" Agent Allen asked, his shock abated. "If this song and dance has played itself out time and time again over millions of years with other species surviving, there must be a way to beat the Dark Man. Put that asshole back to sleep or something."

Raven regarded the tall agent with a look that had the stoic man blushing.

"That," she said, "is the right question."

Jonathan, Tara, and Stephanie leaned forward in anticipation of the answer. Agent Allen stood like a statue as he tried to quell the embarrassment of his reaction to Raven. Hard knocking at the door startled the bunch. Jonathan stood, moving toward the entryway.

"And who might you be?" His voice echoed through the room.

"The Queen of Sheba," Brianna's voice returned through the door.

Brianna's bright smile greeted Jonathan. He noticed that her style had once again changed. With feet clad in maroon Doc Martin combat boots, black trip-pants, and a faded Megadeth hoodie, her hair style of choice was what Jonathan judged to be an adorable set of afro puffs. Stepping aside, he ushered her into the room. Giving a nod of acknowledgement to Agent Allen, Stephanie, and Tara in turn, she stopped when her eyes came to rest on Raven. With a sigh she pursed her lips, jerking them to the side.

"Mike mentioned you'd be coming out of the closet."

Raven snorted, stifling a laugh. The rest of the room looked to Brianna in disbelief, their faces asking the question, "How long have you known?"

"Relax, people," Brianna said. "I just found out an hour ago."

"You spoke with the Penetrator?" Jonathan could not keep the mocking tone out of his voice as he said Mike Holvald's hacker moniker. Tara snickered. Stephanie and Agent Allen both wondered why Brianna would be getting information from someone who sounded like a porn actor.

"Yes," Brianna said, "I spoke with Mike." She emphasized his name. "And I received all the information Mary... I mean, Raven, had promised us. He gave me the rundown of what is going on."

"I'm going to have a talk with Mike about keeping his mouth shut," Raven muttered.

"Don't be too hard on the guy," Brianna said. "He worries about you. Wanted to make sure we were keeping you safe."

Raven grunted, throwing herself back into the couch with a teenage-style expression of exasperated disapproval.

"The man still treats me like I'm a kid," she groaned. "I'm thirty-three for fucks sake."

For all her emotional command, her ability to take charge, kick ass, and the fact that she wasn't wholly human, Jonathan found some comfort in Raven's all-too human display of emotional aggravation and personal bonds.

"I'm sorry," Tara interjected. "You're thirty-three? You look nineteen or twenty."

"I was twenty when I was activated," Raven said. "Aging seems to work differently for us than normal humans. Our ancestors had lifespans so long many assumed they were immortal. That was one of the reasons why many cultures deified them. We are something new. I have no idea what our average lifespan is, but it does appear that the aging process is significantly slowed for us."

"Looks like that *Ancient Aliens* TV show is onto something," Brianna stated as she moved to hook her laptop up to the television.

Ignoring the comment, Jonathan turned his attention to their gothy messenger of doom.

"How do we win?" He reiterated Agent Allen's question.

"The Avatar of Life must take the *Teach Anam*, he must become the House of Souls," Raven said. "And I ain't gonna lie, I've met humanity's champion. I don't have a whole lot of hope here."

"So, this Gauntlet has already started?" Stephanie's voice held a hint of alarm.

"At 12:48am, on March 20th of 1990, fraternal twins were born," Raven began. "One was a sickly child, he seemed to be perpetually on death's door; the other was strong and healthy, sickness never touching him. Their mother died due to complications from childbirth, their father was murdered in 2000. Damien, the sickly one, displayed psychopathic tendencies right from the start. Darren was the type to throw himself in harm's way to save a puppy."

"At least who's who was clear," Jonathan said.

"True," Raven responded, "but Darren isn't one for taking advice, listening to wiser or more knowledgeable voices, and manages to go off half-cocked, making a mess of everything." Raven's aggravation was worn on her sleeve. "He had the chance to wait until old age would have made Damien weaker when he fully became the Avatar of Anti-Life. But no. The dumbass had to go and activate the bastard."

"Did you say March 20th, 1990?" Agent Allen's deep voice held an unusual apprehension.

"Yes," Raven stated flatly, as though she already knew what he was going to say.

"The night of screams and laughter," the G-Man muttered.

"What was that?" Jonathan asked.

"The first and only serial killer interview I had done with the Behavioral Analysis Unit," the FBI agent began. "A child killer and cannibal who had been locked up for sixty years. His first words to me were, 'Do you remember the night of screams and laughter?'"

"Do you?" Stephanie asked him.

"Almost no one does," Raven stated flatly. "With the birth of the twins came the full awakening of the Dark Man. The souls of man cried out, screaming in terror. The *Nianam* laughed, welcoming their savior. Most people don't remember it because of the mental trauma associated with the event."

"That interview is why I only spent a week in the BAU," Agent Allen said. "The dream started the night of that interview. I haven't had a good night's sleep since."

Raven nodded in a moment of contemplation.

"So back to how this winning part works," Tara said, bringing the group back into focus.

"Yes," Raven began, "the Avatar of Life—"

"Since we have a name here," Jonathan interrupted, "can we just call the guy Darren from now on? This Avatar of this, Avatar of that, feels kinda cheesy."

Raven snorted a laugh, nodding as though she had felt the same way.

"Okay, Darren needs a device called the Spear of Destiny."

"Like in the Bible?" Agent Allen asked.

"No," Raven stated. "Same name, vastly different items. The Spear of Destiny I'm talking about is real."

Stephanie chuffed, looking slightly offended.

"You're a believer?" Jonathan seemed surprised.

The tall redhead produced a small gold cross on a necklace from behind her shirt collar. Raven looked at Stephanie and smiled warmly.

"I grew up going to church," Raven said. "I'd probably be a believer too if the clergy hadn't declared me a demon in need of killing. If what I have to say offends your religious beliefs, I apologize, but reality and personal truths are often incongruous."

Letting out a sigh, Stephanie silently conceded the point.

"This Spear of Destiny is actually more of a key, and it consists of forty-two pieces," Raven resumed. "Twelve of those are accounted for, including two that are in this room."

The team of investigators looked to each other, questioningly.

"Those knives of yours, Jonathan," Raven said. "They are pieces of a larger whole. Put together and in Darren's hands, the device will permanently transfer the *Teach Anam* to Darren. For humanity, he will become the House of Souls. As a result of a living body, new souls will be born and the *Nianam* will eventually cease to exist." Raven's tone turned deadly serious. "Should Damien get a hold of the Spear of Destiny, he can obliterate the *Teach Anam*. Not only will the souls of humanity be cast into the untamed wild of spiritual chaos, unable to continue providing souls to the newly born, but no new sentient life will ever evolve in the universe again."

"Okay," Jonathan's tone tried to bring some levity to the situation, "so we're stuck in a battle for our very existence. No pressure."

Stephanie gave a little chuckle, Tara rolled her eyes, Agent Allen groaned, and Brianna gave her best "I'm not impressed" face.

"Was Scott Boyd one of these *Nianam*?" Jonathan asked, serious interest returning to him.

"No," Raven's voice was flat. "He was what we call *Nephilim*."

"Again with the biblical terms," Stephanie said.

"The writers of the Bible got the word from my ancestors," Raven stated. "They just didn't understand what it fully meant."

"And what does it mean?" Agent Allen asked.

"Where a *Nianam* is a person born with no soul, *Nephilim* are the result of those whose actions kill their soul," Raven said. "The soul is both robust and fragile. It provides the capacity, desire, and drive to overcome the base instinct where individual survival is paramount. They lead us toward cooperation, group survival, and bonding. Psychopaths, the most blatant examples of *Nianam*, lack this capability." Raven paused, checking to see that everyone was on the same page. "When one rejects the nature of the soul, when one acts in a manner antithetical to its nature, such as committing acts of cruelty or murder, the soul itself begins to die. Those who have allowed the Dark Man into their lives have granted him access to the void left in place of their soul. With each act of callousness, his hold on them gets stronger. If their soul has been completely destroyed, the Dark Man can use their corpse as a proxy to invade our world of life. It is a method that keeps him safe from that mutually assured destruction. He can mold the corpse into any configuration he chooses, and he has access to all capabilities the body held in life."

"This all sounds overly complicated to be natural," Agent Allen said.

"Definitely not what I learned in Sunday school." Stephanie paused in momentary contemplation. "Your ancestors," she addressed Raven, "did they believe in God?"

Raven raised an eyebrow at the question. She had asked the afterimage that called himself Anubis the same thing. From a philosophical standpoint, it was a logical question. One of the great questions in human history.

"In their eons of evolution and experience, they never found any evidence to support the existence of any being resembling what we would call God," Raven stated.

Stephanie frowned. Raven could see a mass of apologetics arguments running behind the sturdy woman's eyes.

"Isn't the Test of Faith to believe without proof?" Raven asked her.

"Well," Stephanie said, "yes."

"Then it doesn't matter." Raven smiled. "If I could give you hard evidence that the God you believe in exists, faith would become irrelevant as you would have knowledge and fact. In that case, the whole concept of faith becomes moot. If you have faith in your God, if it brings you strength and comfort, then go for it."

"I just wonder," Stephanie began. "Because this whole system seems unnecessarily cruel as well."

"Have you read the Old Testament?" Jonathan asked.

Stephanie smiled, nodded in understanding. While the group before her did not share her beliefs, they clearly had no desire to break the faith of one who found comfort and strength in believing.

"The people you refer to as your charge," Agent Allen shifted the subject, an odd disapproval underlying his tone. "Why do you let them live for so long with these mimics of disability? Why let them suffer when you can do something about that?"

"If a ten-year-old tells you they want to be a policeman or policewoman, do you hold them to that for the rest of their lives?" Raven countered.

"Well, no," the agent stated.

"My capability to alleviate their symptoms is a binary choice. Join the fight or become fully human. It is a permanent alteration of their DNA," Raven stated. "Each person needs to grow, to have enough life experience to make the choice from an informed perspective. As such, I will not make the choice for them, and I will not ask them to make that choice before their eighteenth birthday." A twinge of sadness entered her voice. "I have broken that rule once, and I question whether or not I chose wisely."

"Is she not happy with the choice you made?" Jonathan asked, his eyebrows raised.

"Oh," Raven said, "she's happy, all right. To the point of being annoying." Raven cast her eyes downward. "She was thirteen, her body was shutting down. I had to make a choice…"

"If she's happy, then you made the right call," Tara said.

Raven smiled. A melancholy born of self-doubt glimmered in her eyes. Taking a moment, the goth girl let out a sigh.

"There's another reason I don't simply put my charge through the change so early. It might sound somewhat callous." Raven looked a bit apprehensive. "People in this world that live their lives with disabilities have a unique perspective, one that comes from how they are treated by others. They are privy to some of the worst inclinations humanity has to offer, but also get to see some of the best." Raven let a slight smile slip. "They get to see what humanity could be."

"I think I get it," Brianna piped up. "Where most of us 'able-bodied' people learn compassion through our upbringing, they're learning it through a kind of trial by fire. A method that is a bit risky. Easy to fall into a state of misanthropy that way."

"Yes, it is a risk," Raven said. "Possibly one other people would consider inexcusable."

"Considering your options, the methodology makes sense," Jonathan said, a comforting smile crossing his face.

Raven nodded, composing herself. A posture of commanding confidence returned to her. The group remained silent, each member of the team lost in contemplative thought. Jonathan sat back in his chair, letting out a slight chuckle. Raven raised a questioning eyebrow to the sound.

"What do you know about a man named Joseph Handler?"

Chapter 23

Questions. My mind raced with nothing but questions. As the blonde cheerleader turned goth queen sat before me, all I wanted to do was ask wave after wave of questions. I forced myself to perform a kind of mental triage with my curiosity. With the basics out of the way, I turned my attention back to the case at hand. We took down one killer. We still had one even more dangerous killer out there. And then there was this Office, a group that had brought me into this mess under false pretense and wished to assert control over my life now that I survived their "judgement."

"What do you know about a man named Joseph Handler?" I asked. Raven's emerald-green eyes darkened at the sound of the name, a sneer forming on her lips.

"He's a walking corpse, for starters," she stated. I thought she was being facetious.

"Yeah," Brianna chimed in. "The guy looks like the walking dead."

"You misunderstand," Raven said. "He's *literally* a walking corpse."

I raised my brows. A thought teased me, hiding just beyond reach. Some shrouded epiphany that refused to come into the light. Raven sat, staring into my eyes, waiting for the conclusion to arrive. I hate to admit that it took way too long for me to figure it out.

"He's possessed?"

"Bingo!" Raven clapped her hands together. "Someone give this man a cookie."

"Are we talking demons now?" Agent Allen's voice oozed incredulity.

"These things you call demons, poltergeists, and ghosts," Raven said, "are simply life-forms comprised of coherent energy. In typical fashion, humans over the millennia have assigned oversimplified religious and supernatural explanations for them."

"Please don't tell me Scientology got something right," Tara groaned.

Grimacing, Raven looked at my wife.

"Yeah, about that," she said. "One could oversimplify the entity possessing Handler's body as the ghost of an alien."

I let out another groan. I wanted to take this seriously. I needed to take this seriously. I couldn't take this seriously. An uncontrollable fit of laughter erupted from the pit of my stomach. The room looked at me like I had lost my mind. I tried to calm myself. Catching Raven's glowering stare, I managed to bring myself back to the moment.

"You done?" Raven asked, a deadly seriousness to her voice.

"Yes."

"What occupies the corpse calling itself Joseph Handler is a remnant of the second sentient species to have ever evolved in the universe," Raven stated. "They managed to survive the Gauntlet by finding a way to become beings of pure energy. Souls with no need of a physical body. The *Nianam* of their race perished in an orgy of self-destructive violence."

"So they're pretty good to go," I said. "His people don't need to worry about any of this."

"True," Raven nodded, "but Handler appears to have become unhinged. He viewed the demise of my ancestors as the beginning of the end for all life."

"Guess that tells us how much he trusts humanity to get through this," Stephanie stated.

"To be fair," Tara said, "in our current state, humanity's kind of screwed."

Raven let out a snorting laugh, nodding in agreement.

"The problem is that Handler has taken it upon himself to be the replacement back-up." Contempt radiated from Raven's voice. "His methods are untenable, and he believes any means will be justified in the end. Including experimentation on humans. Including experimentation on children. His goal is to win, but his methods blur the lines between humanity and the Dark Man. If a disembodied soul could become a *Nephilim*, it would be him. Thankfully, that borrowed body of his isn't linked to him. If that body is destroyed, he'll just find himself a new one."

"This all makes sense from what I saw." Memories of the forced video conference with the weird man played back through my mind.

"And the guy seems to have a suspicious preoccupation with finding my old mentor."

"He even devoted resources into tracking Darkstone up until his disappearance," Brianna offered. "Then turned his attention to Jonathan."

"I'm not surprised," Raven said. "It's because of that particular method both of you use in dealing with spiritual entities."

I knew that Raven was aware of my full identity. I was thankful she had the wherewithal to continue distinguishing Darkstone as a different person.

"To put it bluntly," Raven said, "you and Darkstone are the only known people who could actually kill him."

"Well," I said, shifting uncomfortably, "that does put a target on our backs."

"Hold up," Brianna interjected. "You said that what we call ghosts are life-forms? Not the remnants of the deceased?"

"For the most part, yes," Raven stated flatly, "though on occasion a person's soul can resist being called back to the *Teach Anam* for a time, but that is extremely rare."

"Our souls don't go to Heaven?" Stephanie sounded like someone just kicked her puppy.

"All we know is that souls return to the *Teach Anam*, then cycle back into another human," Raven said. "No one knows what happens inside the House of Souls. Perhaps the brief period of time within could be perceived as Heaven. I simply don't have the answer to that."

Stephanie cast her gaze down, considering the prospect. While I had never known she was religious in any way, I could understand the impact of having one's beliefs challenged by a countermanding reality. I had seen it many times before. On more than one occasion I had been hired for spiritual eviction only to wind up debunking what some deeply religious folks believed were demons stalking them. Two furnaces in need of repair, one plumbing system on the verge of collapse, and a series of other mundane causes. Each instance resulted in a face-to-face display of cognitive dissonance and religiously inspired cussing. Being the messenger that provokes a crisis of faith is never a position one wants to be in. The more religious the person, the more likely they are to get violent with said messenger. While interesting information, none of it was of help in finding the killer named Caleb Voss. The where, why, and how Raven knew what she knew on this subject would have to wait for another time.

"We need to get onto the more pressing matter of Caleb Voss." Agent Allen's voice preempted my own redirect.

A sneer once again graced Raven's gothic countenance. She let loose an angry sigh.

"If I had it my way," Raven said, "I'd keep all of you out of it. He's a Caretaker problem."

"So he is one of yours?" Tara asked.

Raven gave a derisive snort, shaking her head.

"He is what we call an Abomination," Raven began. "It happens with males, though usually not this bad."

We all looked at Raven, questioning expressions plastered on our faces. Her eyes lingered on us for a moment and soon realized we were missing a chunk of information.

"Oh," she said. "Well, Caretakers are almost entirely female. We don't know why this is. As we discussed, the birthmark denoting our heritage comes with what is best described as genetic interference which mimics a wide range of disabilities and diseases. For some reason, males born with the Caretaker's mark do not suffer physical affects, but rather it impacts their mental state. More often than not, the abilities our shared ancestry provides become permanently active during puberty. As far as any of us can tell, the Y chromosome appears to alter the effects Caretaker DNA has on the body."

"Is there anything you are able to do for the males?" I wondered if she was capable of doing for the males what she could do for the females.

"Not really," Raven said, a note of sadness in her voice. "I tried a full activation on a young man once. The poor thing's mind had shattered, and I thought activating the DNA would help heal his mental fracture." Raven let out a long sigh. "It didn't. In a matter of minutes, he spiraled out of control, becoming a danger to everyone and everything around him. I had to…"

Raven didn't need to complete the sentence for all of us to understand the end result. She took a deep breath and continued.

"With the males there are three options." Her voice was flat, emotionless. "Turn them completely human and hope for the best, kill them, or, in the odd instance that the dude's not a danger, leave them be."

"So, Caleb Voss is on the death list," Stephanie absentmindedly said.

"NO!" The word rang out, all of us speaking in unison. Stephanie jerked as though shaken awake.

"Did you not see what Scott Boyd turned into?" I asked, no small amount of alarm in my voice.

"As I said," Raven gave Stephanie a hard look, "Caleb is an Abomination. There is likely nothing left of his soul at this point. Kill him and what we get is a *Nephilim* with his ability. Scott Boyd was child's play by comparison."

"What is Caleb's ability?" Brianna spoke up.

"He's an Airbender." The reference to the tv show *Avatar: The Last Airbender* passed my lips without a thought. Brianna's chuckling, as well as the disapproving stares of Raven, Tara, and Stephanie, brought a flush of embarrassment. I could feel Agent Allen trying to bore a hole in the back of my head with his eyes.

"Well," I thought I detected an underlying amusement in Raven's voice, "Jonathan's not entirely wrong. Caleb can manipulate air. It's how he has been cutting through his victims, and why no one can determine the tool being used. It also makes him extremely dangerous."

"We're going to need a very careful plan of attack," Agent Allen said.

"Quite," Raven stated. Her tone told me that the takedown of Caleb Voss would be done without the agent in attendance.

An earth-shattering yawn blasted from Stephanie, grabbing everyone's attention. The tall redhead's face turned a bright shade of crimson.

"And that's the bell," Agent Allen's voice commanded. "It's late and I'm tired. We can pick this up tomorrow."

Stephanie and Tara both nodded eagerly in agreement. I felt bone weary. With the sheer amount of adrenaline we had all experienced, it was a miracle any of us were still standing. A beeping from Brianna's laptop computer caught the room's collective attention. Hitting a few keys, she brought up what appeared to be a police report onto the flat-screen TV.

"This is interesting," Brianna said. "Agent Allen, I think I have an assignment for you."

The agent's eyebrows raised.

"A police report was taken at 6pm," Brianna began. "Clair and Therese Guavera, fourteen-year-old twins, had a man bearing Caleb Voss' description enter their house. According to the report, this was an attempted abduction."

"Attempted?" Agent Allen's voice was incredulous. "This guy doesn't appear to do attempted."

"Well," Brianna stretched the word out, "a neighbor saw Caleb fly out of the house and into a silver SUV."

"He ran?" I asked.

"No. According to the witness, he was literally airborne."

A resounding "Huh" escaped the lips of Agent Allen, Stephanie, Tara, and me. Raven sat back, a satisfied grin on her face.

"Good for them," Raven stated.

"Do you know them?" Tara queried.

"I haven't met them," Raven stated, "but I know their names and where they are, like all of the Waiting. As I said before, I have an age limit on who I am willing to approach for their choice."

"You know where they all are?" Stephanie chimed in.

"Yes. Of the Waiting, I know their names, I know their exact locations, but that is all that I know." Raven's voice held a tint of disappointment. "With those who have become fully active Caretakers, we all know each other's names, locations, we can stream our thoughts, emotions, and even what we are seeing to each other. For those not yet activated, I am the only one with knowledge of them, and that knowledge is limited."

"Okay," Agent Allen said, "I'd like to have you with me tomorrow when I interview these twins."

271

Raven let out a sigh. "Fine, I'll come."

"Is there a problem?"

"I try not to show myself until they are ready to make the choice. I dislike disappointing my charge." A touch of concern resonated in Raven's words. "But I will be there. Not sure how much they would be willing to tell a scary man like you." A wide grin crossed the goth girl's face.

Stephanie snorted, stifling a laugh as she walked toward the door. Agent Allen shot her an enigmatic look I assumed was disapproval.

"I'll text you details in the morning," he said to Raven. "Keep your phone on."

With all the manners of a toddler, Agent Allen let the heavy door slam shut, the shotgun blast echoing in my ears. Tara, Brianna, and Raven winced at the sound. I turned to Brianna.

"At least you didn't completely waste your time coming here." I felt a little guilty having her come to the room and have nothing for her to do.

Brianna waved off my concern. "Learning new things is never a waste of time, especially when the survival of the species is on the line."

I nodded in agreement. Brianna stretched her arms above her head, letting out a yawn of her own in the process. Tara returned the involuntary call to sleep. I laughed. I hadn't really noticed my own fatigue until now, my thoughts fuzzy around the edges.

"I guess we're all going to have to follow Stephanie and Agent Allen's example," I said.

"Yeah," Brianna said as she let out another yawn, this time her hand moved to cover her mouth. "I'ma leave my set up here this time," she said. "No point in taking it down if I'll be back here in the morning."

"Can you make it noon?" Tara asked, a yawn distorting her words. Brianna smiled and nodded.

"Before we break for the night," I said, turning my attention to Raven, "there is one thing I need to know."

The question had been bouncing around in my head for the past day with no answer forthcoming. Raven seemed to be in a position to know.

"The dream. I have had lucid dreams before. I've experienced the kind of dream-bleed that comes with sleep paralysis. But the dream, that field, it's different."

Raven nodded her head, her face in expectation of a question she anticipated.

"It's not really a dream, is it?"

"No. It is all too real."

I nodded. I could feel epiphany on the edge of my thoughts. All it needed was a little nudge.

"What is the dream…and where is that field?"

A light breeze wafted through the verdant fields, the air filled with the scent of earth and grass. Looking around, all I felt was serenity. Every worry melted away. The azure sky was dotted with whisps of white. I felt myself drifting through the softly undulating sea of waist-high grass, light caresses from their stalks bringing my mind into a state of complete relaxation. The last time I was here I did not have the time to let go, to enjoy this respite from the reality of murderers and monsters. It was also part of my own plan, a test designed to affirm myself.

I had asked Raven the what and where of this place. Her answer was genuine if not a bit cryptic. This was the borderland, a place where the encompassing energy of Life butted heads with its twin of Anti-Life. It is everywhere, and nowhere. Looking across the fields, my inner peace faded slightly. Standing in the distance I saw the grassy knoll, and the contemptible thing that stood at its peak. Raven told me about the marshlands at the base of the Dark Man's hill. It was a kind of buffer, a place between Life and Anti-Life. In some ways it was like a meeting hall where two warring factions could engage in talks. In the case of the Dark Man, it was where he managed to convince those who stood before him to commit acts of evil, cruelty, and depravity. Agent Allen said he had spoken with the Dark Man. What tricks he had used to emerge uninfluenced was beyond me. Raven stated that she, too, had engaged the Dark Man. She credited the Caretaker lineage for her resilience to the promises and offers the conscious void presented to her. I had my own ideas.

This was not a dream, but it wasn't reality as I knew it either. Given enough time and investigation, I could probably figure out the how of it. Some quantum connection, the Jungian concept of the collective subconscious given form. Brianna had said her first encounter in this place was with herself. I could relate. In here one was able access parts of the mind normally barred to consciousness, subtle influences being the only evidence of their existence.

Like me, Brianna's first experience in this place was reflexive. Where the other her stopped Brianna from engaging with the Dark Man, my other self had ended the fugue I had been mired in. These experiences had given me an idea, a means of being able to get a close look at the Dark Man with minimal danger. The question was if I could do it on command, and if the result would be what I hoped.

I drew in a deep breath and closed my eyes. The scent of my surroundings brought back that totality of calm. I let my mind drift on the currents of indirection, sliding with no destination. The feeling was indescribable, a moment where nothing existed but the calm.

No worries.

No anxieties.

No fears.

No ego.

Only the bare substance of what I was remained.

I stood still, sailing in smooth mnemonic waters. In developing my occult techniques to deal with spiritual entities, this level of calm was the goal. A place where all energy was at my command and all interfering ego had been shed. I had reached it. Bringing direction to my mind, I could feel the barrier between my consciousness and subconscious dissolve.

"You can't win against him, you know," a sullen voice came from behind me.

Opening my eyes, I turned around. A face I hadn't seen in twenty years stared back at me. Momentary nostalgia gripped me as I looked at the image of my younger self. In prime shape, hair parted on the left, a sweep of bangs rested above his right eye. I missed having a full head of hair. He looked tired and beaten down, his skin pallid and corpse-like. Dark circles rimmed his eyes. Eyes through which his cocky arrogance was visible, as were the doubts and fears he carried.

"My aim isn't to win," I told my other self. "My aim is to show him he's not going to win."

A sardonic laugh erupted from the younger me, a hateful sneer crossing his face.

"You're a fool," he said. "You are nothing."

"And you're an asshole."

I could feel the calm still in me, and I could feel the part of myself standing before me trying to break it.

"Why are you here?" My question was more a test than a search for answers.

The other me apathetically shrugged. "You called me here," he offered.

A sly smile crossed my face. He was right, I did.

"And now," he said, "I'm going to tell you that you're a fucking moron."

I raised an unimpressed eyebrow.

"Can you not see reality?" His voice raised. His words came fast and hard. "No one really likes you. Your own wife is just here because she doesn't want to be alone. It's only a matter of time before she finds someone better."

I remembered those words from long ago. I had thought them. Tara had brought the hammer down on that particular fear. Not only with her words. Through her actions I knew them to be lies. Smirking at this younger me, I cocked my head to the side and gestured for him to continue.

"Your parents hated you." His speed increased, feverishly vomiting the words out. "Your dad has to drink just to look at your sorry ass, and mom gave birth to you out of spite. She never wanted you. You're the reason she killed herself."

Again, I remembered these words. All thought during a dark time in my life, a time depression had taken hold of me and told me these very lies. The calm would not break.

275

"You are weak," he continued, frenzied and wild-eyed. "You almost got everyone killed today." A hateful grin passed his lips. "You couldn't do anything to save your friends five years ago. You had to run away, become someone else, just so you wouldn't have to face the guilt of your own impotence."

He wasn't entirely wrong, but I had accepted the reality of the situation. Survivor's guilt was a waste of energy, and second guessing was fatal. That those feelings had passed through my conscious mind and taken residence in my subconscious was unacceptable.

"You should just lay down and die," he said. "Eat a bullet. Take a swan dive off the stratosphere. Give a bus a hug. No one needs you. No one wants you. No one—"

I unceremoniously planted my fist in my younger self's mouth. Reeling back, he wore an expression of narcissistic shock. This visual expression of my own subconscious stared at me in silence.

"You're done." My tone was calm, strong, and commanding. "You have no power over me. You have no home within me."

My younger self moved to strike. A swift feint to the left, his right arm came toward me. I grabbed his right fist mid-punch with my left hand, his throat with my right, and hoisted him off the ground. I looked deep into the tired, angry eyes that once were mine.

"You think you have power," he choked out the words as his feet dangled, searching for a foothold. "Go ahead, go to him. He will take you like he takes everyone, and I will be the one in control."

A sick smile crossed his face. So much resentment. So much hate. It was time to conclude this therapy session. I tossed the younger me to the ground.

"Do you want to see power?" I asked.

A guttural, unintelligible sound came from the other me. I lazily looked at the bright, sunlit fields of green around us.

"This place would be so much prettier in the moonlight, don't you think?"

Closing my eyes, a sense of euphoria washed over me, and with it, revelation. The environment of this so-called dream was a representation of my life's energy. This place was me. I felt connected to it. I could read the ebb and flow of the gentle breeze. I could detect its boundaries and how my own life force connected to the greater world. Opening my eyes, I smiled at the other, younger me. He sat where I had thrown him, legs crossed and pouting like a child.

The bright azure sky slowly turned to a deep midnight blue. Twilight came and went in a matter of seconds. A large, bright, blueish-white moon rose from the horizon, illuminating the darkened landscape. The shining moon cast light upon the face of my younger self, a face that held an expression of shock. I couldn't help but chuckle.

"How could you possibly be surprised?" I asked in disbelief. "You are me. You know what I know. You knew this was coming."

The younger me snorted in derision.

"What do you say we decorate the place?"

Pulling in a deep breath, I visualized what I wanted. With my exhale, an explosion of white circular moonflowers burst forth from the waist-high grasses covering the land. Moonlight reflected from the flowers, giving the landscape an incandescent sheen. My younger, cynical self let out a short laugh as he stood, pointing past me. Following the line of his finger, I saw the grassy knoll in the distance. It appeared to still be in daylight, the Dark Man still visible on the crown of the hill.

"Your power here is meaningless," he said. "You're not strong enough to face him."

"You don't get it." I smirked. "My power here is absolute. Here is me. He is not within me, and his words shall be given no quarter nor consideration."

"Then why speak to him at all?"

"I am an investigator in the midst of a war," I said. "In order to win, I must know what I'm fighting against. I must feel the reason to fight. It boils down to one very old saying. Know thine enemy."

I watched as the cynical, arrogant, hate-filled version of myself changed before me. The dark circles vanished. The corpse-like appearance filled out. The sardonic smile of cruelty transformed to one of warmth. I knew this version of myself well. I owed a debt to this version of myself. It was he that stayed my hand when I held a blade to my own wrists long ago. It was his voice that had once screamed in my mind, drowning out the lies that had taken root and granting me the will to live. This was my true self.

"I miss that hairline," I said.

"How much hair you have doesn't dictate who you are." He smirked.

"No," I said, "but it'd be nice to have a few more stylistic options."

Snickering, the other me took a deep breath. In my usual fashion, he switched from humorous to serious without skipping a beat.

"What are we going to do about that?" He pointed to the grassy knoll.

"I figure I'll treat him like I treat any other unwanted caller."

"Force him to hang up on us?'

I felt a wide grin form on my face.

"Force him to hang up on us."

Distance in the dream held no meaning. The grassy knoll had looked to be about half a mile from where I held my little therapy session. As soon as I began walking toward it, the hill moved to meet me. The moonlit, flower-filled landscape served to bolster my confidence. I knew what I could do. I knew what I was made of. I knew that humanoid void atop its hill could offer me nothing I wanted.

The hill appeared to be just a few hundred feet from me when the light began to change. A dawning sky had developed without my say-so. The flowers around me vanished, with each step the waist-high grass thinned out, began to wilt. I stopped, looking ahead. Everything appeared consistent, but I knew this to be a lie. A mirage. My mind furiously tried to work out the situation at hand. I had been in a bubble comprised of my own life's energy, a fact that had granted me total control.

So, what was this space? This place in dawning light? I knew it was not the Dark Man's territory. I was certain he could not actually reach into the dream without annihilating himself. He could not touch the stuff of life. Conversely, no one could reach into him without the same happening to them. And he would surely have safeguards to prevent some well-meaning but stupid person from sacrificing themselves for the greater good. This was the place Raven had told me about. This was the buffer. The space where aspects of the two opposing states of existence bled into each other just enough for communication, but not enough to be in direct contact.

I took a step forward and felt my foot sink into something wet. Looking down I could see the ground had become saturated in liquid. I pulled my foot up to find it stained blood red. Bits of crimson and brown mud dripped off the appendage.

"Funky."

I pulled in a deep breath, closed my eyes. I could feel the land behind me, the energy it was made of, how it connected to me. Drawing in another breath, I drew in some of that energy as well. It was yet another technique used in basic occult practice, as well as many psychic and "New Age" circles. Witches called it "Drawing Down the Moon." The result is simply to concentrate as much energy within oneself to be directed at will. Opening my eyes, I tried taking that step forward again.

My foot landed on solid ground. Glancing down, the spot on which I had placed my foot was dry, compacted earth. Crimson-brown, blood-soaked marshland extended in all directions around my clean bit of turf. I smirked, looking toward my enemy. What had been a green, grassy knoll was now a mound of barren dirt. I slowly moved forward, creating patches of dry ground as I walked. With each step, the Dark Man's hill moved closer to me.

A stench crept into the air. It started with a subtle, coppery scent of the blood permeating the ground. With each move toward the Dark Man, the scent changed.

Rotting vegetation, rancid meat.

I tasted bile, stifling the urge to vomit.

Pausing, I examined the hill again. Its surface appeared to move, undulating like a sack of worms. I took a few more steps forward.

Fecal matter, stale urine.

I gagged. My stomach rolled in protest at the olfactory assault.

The hill's surface once again transformed. A pile of writhing, mutilated corpses in varying states of decay. Men, women, and children. Some with skin, others with their underlying musculature exposed.

279

Limbs broke under the pressure of compacted bodies. A sprinkling of dismembered appendages rolled and bounced down the hill, disappearing under the surface of the swamp. Viscous black liquid poured from mouths, nostrils, empty eye sockets…and orifices not fit to mention in polite company. Cascading rivers of blood, waste, and ichor flowed into the death bog at its base. Low, pained, gurgling moans permeated the air, an aural accompaniment to the stench. A figure stood at the base of the corpse mound. Taking a couple more steps, I froze.

A white, ankle-length nightgown hung off the woman's thin frame, blood red creeping up from the hem line that sat in the noxious stew of the ground. Matted long blonde hair obscured the woman's face, though I didn't need to see her features to recognize my own mother. A woman who had eaten the business end of a .44 caliber pistol when I was fourteen. In her hands she gingerly cupped a severed head. The bright green pompadour was all I needed to know about the head's owner. Low keening came from the woman, a mournful sound as she brought the head to her bosom, shaking her head.

"Why?" her raspy voice whispered.

"Because he was a murderous piece of shit," I answered coldly. I knew full well this was not my mother, who was a kind but fragile woman in life. A woman driven over the edge by the alcoholic sperm donor that called itself my father.

My faux-mom chuckled as she looked up. The skin around her eyes had rotted away; in place of tears, black sick trickled from empty sockets. In that moment I was grateful for my love of horror movies. I expected this move. Arms crossed with a look of boredom plastered on my face, my foot tapped impatiently. The wretch smiled, the corners of her mouth tearing open into an ear-to-ear grin. Shrugging, she dropped the head of Scott Boyd into the rotten bog.

"Not working on you, is it?" Her voice changed as she spoke, the beautiful rasp of my mother turning into the mutilated gravel of a five pack-a-day smoker.

"No," I chuffed.

"You're no fun," the thing said, plopping into the mud.

"What do you want?" I had purposefully inserted a tinge of impatience into my words, projecting an air of annoyed boredom.

"Your help," the out of place voice said in earnest. "I need you to deal with a problem I have."

"What's the problem?"

"That Raven bitch." The split-mouth woman sneered at the name. "You can't trust her, you know."

"Why?"

"You're just a normal human. She doesn't care about normies." The rotting visage of my mother nodded to emphasize the point. "She only cares about her own. You're a pawn. She is willing to sacrifice you and everyone around you to get what she wants."

"What does she want?" I kept my voice flat.

"To save humanity from itself!"

"And how would she do that?"

"Her plan," the thing said, "is to raise an army of her own people and take over. Make the whole New World Order thing look like child's play. They will subjugate humanity until nothing is left of humanity. Breeding programs to eliminate normal humans like you."

I glanced over my shoulder. I could still see the landscape of nighttime, the flowers covering the low, rolling hills of my life. *Normal* is hardly what I'd call myself.

"You think I'm normal?"

"Well, yes…and no," it said. "You have the strength of will to do what needs to be done, and a little extra power to help you do it."

"Why would I help you?"

"By helping me, you're helping all of mankind." The grotesque smile returned to the mom-thing.

"Why would I do that?"

A strange expression overcame the rotten face, a look somewhere between surprise and annoyance. This clearly wasn't a question the Dark Man had anticipated.

"Why would I help you?" I was over being here. I realized that I already knew this enemy, I had known him all my life. Single-minded, using shock, awe, and fear to convince the gullible, insecure, stupid, and fearful to act on its behalf. I had inoculated myself against it. I had a lifetime of built-up resistance. The Dark Man would be given no quarter, and no foothold in me.

"You care for your wife and your—"

"On what planet, in what reality," I began, passion working its way into my voice, "would I put ANY effort into what you want? Seriously, why would I help you?"

The face of my faux-mother darkened, emitting a low growl.

"You insolent insect." The voice seemed to come from all around me. "Do you think you can deny me? I offer what you want. The death all your pathetic race craves. Life is a burden which you all want to be freed from, and yet you deny the one offering you salvation?"

"You offer nothing of worth," I said. "You are nothing of worth."

I felt a change in pressure, as if the very air were trying to press me down into the ground. I countered the assault, pressing up against it with the energy I had stored. A shocked look came across the animated corpse. I gave a mischievous grin.

"You have no power over me," I said. "You cannot touch me."

A guttural laugh blasted from all around.

"If she had not been there to save you, I would have ripped you limb from limb," the ubiquitous voice proclaimed, confirming that these things Raven called *Nephilim* are directly controlled by him.

"Next time it won't be an issue." I gave a little shrug. "Feel free to give it another go."

My confidence had the precise effect I had hoped for. An enraged scream permeated the noxious bog. I could feel this thing, this embodiment of annihilation, attempt to press into me, his anger a ramping downward pressure. A vise of rage. Rotted stalks of grass bent under the Dark Man's exertion, mud solidified, blood oozed from the ground as mud was compacted under the pressure. I countered his rage, a bubble of energy surrounding me. The ground I stood upon remained unaffected.

"Awwww." At this point, why not resort to playground tactics? "Is the poor bully getting upset? Do you need your mommy?"

My faux-mom's face contorted, split mouth wide in a scream of all-encompassing anger. From her seated position she sprang up, coming at me in a sprinting lunge. Five feet from me, her sharp-nailed hand, outstretched and ready to do mortal damage, burst into a cloud of dust. Momentum carried her body into the hard line that divided this place. A creation of Anti-Life obliterated by the force of Life. I looked to the featureless figure standing upon his hill of rot.

"What's the matter, asshole?" I yelled. The Dark Man's form twitched. "Having a hard time keeping it up?"

"Be gone, wretched thing," the disembodied voice boomed. "You bore me."

"That's what she sai—"

I found myself sitting upright in bed, Tara staring at me from her pillow.

"What the hell just happened?" she asked, referring to my speedy change in position.

Looking at me wife, her beauty shone through the darkness. A sideways smile crossed my lips, a small chuckle escaped my mouth.

"He hung up on me."

Chapter 24

Sodium-vapor lamps cast a sickly, yellow pallor over the parking lot of the small ER, giving the impression that the car park itself was in need of medical attention. Caleb had no intention of waiting until noon to finally have his bait. The Dark Man had told him to be patient. Patience was never his strong suit. The Boy had been on this path for three years, honing his skills and learning to control his abilities. It wasn't until last August that he finally found one of the Goddesses. She had set his path's direction. The path to perfection. The path to godhood. Now, in spite of having been robbed of one opportunity, fate chose to grant him exactly what he required. It was as if everything had been planned this way.

The humiliation of being bested by a couple fourteen-year-olds earlier in the day had transformed into pure motivation. This gift of a new, unsuspecting target was an opportunity he would not waste. Doctor Jordan's abilities were no threat to him. The ability to heal was one without offensive concern. Keeping her under control would be easy. Thinking back to what the Sonja-thing had told him, he grew anxious. If the Raven required her death to pinpoint the doctor's location, how would he convince the Queen of the Goddesses to do what he wanted? He knew nothing of her power. What abilities the Raven possessed beyond making the Goddesses whole was a mystery to him. He let out a deep sigh.

"Gonna need to grab a second girl," he muttered to himself. "I need a living hostage."

He wearily gazed at the ER's automatic sliding glass doors. This wasn't a particularly busy ER, especially at 3am. All the waiting he had been forced to do since he arrived here made him want to burn the place to the ground.

Flashing red and blue lights caught his attention. A police cruiser pulled to a stop in front of the ER, a black SUV behind it. Disheveled, panic written in his every movement, the driver of the SUV hopped out of the vehicle and ran around to the passenger's side. Caleb couldn't see anyone else in the front of the car. He assumed the source of concern sat in the rear. A police officer bolted out of the patrol car and into the building, reemerging in less than a minute with two nurses pushing a gurney. From his vantage point, Caleb could not see the details of what was happening. He caught sight of a very pregnant woman as the gurney was wheeled back into the ER. The police officer stopped the anxious man from following, indicating that he needed to park his vehicle before joining his companion. In hasty compliance, the SUV driver squealed out of the ER entry drive in search of a spot.

His hands on his hips, the policeman was laughing and shaking his head. Doctor Jordan emerged from the automatic doors just as the officer took a step toward his cruiser. Stopping, he turned to face her. The familiarity between the two was clear. The good doctor cocked her head to the side like a puppy as she spoke with the uniformed man, who reached out to caress her shoulder. From this distance, Caleb could not make out the details of the patrolman. Was this Doctor Jordan's husband? A good friend? A friend with benefits? Perhaps even a patient? Without being able to see any facial cues Caleb could not tell, though it did not matter to him. The Boy felt such interactions were pointless, just a means of wasting time as people waited for death to take them.

With a friendly embrace, the doctor and police officer parted ways. Returning to his patrol car, the officer turned off the red and blue lights, turned on the car's interior light, and began doing some paperwork. Caleb's eyes locked onto Doctor Jordan as she made her way across the sparsely populated, jaundiced parking lot. Not knowing which car was hers, his body was tense with anticipation. His first tail. His first follow-home. She passed a blue BMW SUV, walking by the driver-side door. Caleb's hand instinctively went to the ignition key. He let out a slow breath as Doctor Jordan cleared the BMW. Heart pounding, his anticipation and excitement had quickened his breathing. He was bordering on hyperventilating. Calming himself, he watched the doctor's auburn hair bounce past three more vehicles. Flashing lights on a beige Mercedes at the far end of the lot indicated she had unlocked the car with a remote.

He had thought about grabbing her here. Under cover of darkness, it would have been relatively easy. The infection-yellow light cast from

285

the sodium-vapor lamps did nothing to illuminate the area. The ubiquitous industrial lighting interfered with vision, details blurring in the ochre. For the life of him, Caleb could not understand why anyone still used the outdated lighting system.

The slow pace of the ER meant a very bored security guard might be searching their camera feed for something to do. Stopping an abduction would certainly count as something to do. Not that it would be an issue. If he saw them coming, any security personnel would be in pieces before they could get within a hundred yards of him. Such an action would bring unwanted attention to his location, along with the hassle of police roadblocks and gunfire. He wasn't ready for an all-out battle yet. He still needed her. He still needed the Raven to make him whole. To make him perfect. Once he became a full-fledged god, those pesky bullets would be meaningless to him.

Staring with predatory intent, he watched Doctor Jordan gracefully slide into her car and start the engine. The vehicle's headlights came on after a moment and his target was on the move, slowly navigating the small parking lot's speedbumps. Caleb waited for the Mercedes to get within a hundred feet of the parking lot exit before starting his SUV.

Moving through the lot at a faster pace than Doctor Jordan, he reached the exit just as the good doctor turned left onto Coronado Center Drive. The tires of his vehicle screeched as he made the left in pursuit. He muttered a curse under his breath, something about drawing attention to himself. Tracking the Mercedes, the doctor seemed to be one for going annoyingly slow, her speed a paltry thirty-five miles per hour. Catching up to her was easy. It also made Caleb nervous. At this speed, his tail would be obvious.

His mind spun, working its way through the most efficient abduction scenarios. The goal was to get as much lead time as possible. Police would be notified at some point; delaying that notification as long as possible was of high importance. He wanted to make sure the Raven came to him long before his inevitable and epic battle with the Las Vegas police. A glorious bloodbath that would announce his presence to the world. Caleb also needed another of the Goddesses, one who he could use as leverage to force the Raven to comply with his demands.

Time. He needed time. A public abduction would not do. Grabbing her at home would be more effective, provided the good doctor lived alone. That was not a guarantee. He hadn't noticed any wedding band, or cheater line, when she treated him. But who needed to be married to live together these days? Or she could have a roommate. Caleb watched enough *Grey's Anatomy* to know doctors often roomed together. After all, TV was a reflection of likely real-life possibilities. If he waited until she arrived at her destination, he might lose his chance. A flare of red from the Mercedes' brakelights caught his attention as Doctor Jordan piloted her car into the left turn lane at Eastern Avenue.

Pulling behind the doctor, Caleb scanned the street. At this time of night, few cars were on the road. Unlike the Las Vegas Strip, Henderson was mostly residential. A real city that tourists did not often visit. Here, businesses were not all open twenty-four hours. A closed Applebee's on the far left of the intersection attested to this. He considered using the parking lot of the eatery, force her into the carpark and take Doctor Jordan there.

"Too many cameras," he said with gritted teeth. He also knew her abandoned car would be quickly noticed.

The red arrow turned green, and Doctor Jordan made the left onto Eastern Avenue. He waited a beat, then moved to follow. Caleb had seen enough cop movies to have a basic theory on how to tail someone. Don't be too eager. Don't get too close. Drive casual.

For the next twenty minutes he scanned for a suitable grab point. Business parks and superstores lined the empty street. Parking lots bathed in the sickly yellow light of sodium-vapor lamps. Wide open spaces. All had visible security cameras. No good.

The wide three-lane road eventually reduced to two lanes as businesses gave way to apartment and condo complexes. The road's concrete divider moved from a baren grey block for traffic control to soil-filled, tree-sporting planters. Beige and terracotta-colored walls lined the inner edge of the sidewalks. Everything held a blueish sheen under LED streetlamps.

Eastern Avenue split. One lane diverted to the east, one lane continued south. Sticking with his target, Caleb continued down the single southbound lane. Crossing some invisible socio-economic boundary, he noticed a stark change in the neighborhood. Ivy-covered walls of mottled tan marble slabs spoke of affluence. He could see an estate sign, lit with bright LED spotlights, declaring the area Seven Hills. Doctor Jordan made a right turn onto Grand Hills Drive, passing the sign into its declared neighborhood.

Caleb felt a bead of sweat roll down his neck, sending a shiver through his left arm. He was overcome by a wave of anxiety. Chest tightening, he felt time running out. He needed to act.

Grand Hills Drive was lined with walled communities of massive houses, gates with security guard-manned entryways, and the same ivy-covered marble walls. Doctor Jordan drove past the secured points of entry. At twenty-five miles per hour, Caleb was losing his patience. Aggravation piled onto his anxiety. He wanted to do this right. He wanted to give himself as much lead time as possible. He wanted to kill the slow-ass bitch who didn't seem to understand what an accelerator was for. He wanted all this, and he wanted it now.

Following the Mercedes as it made a right turn, Caleb was too engrossed in his strangling emotional state to notice the street signs. The doctor's car made a left onto a gateless residential street. Houses here were clearly for the affluent, but lacked the ostentatious size of their guarded counterparts.

He was done with this tail. Taking a deep breath, he pushed aside the anxiety that threatened to drag him into a fog of indecision. Risk-assessment flashed through his mind, concluded that now was his best chance. Caleb rolled down his window and stuck his arm out. The motion-generated breeze was cool on his skin, the wind's caress calming. With a controlled move of his wrist, the rear tire of Doctor Jordan's Mercedes blew out.

Caleb had expected a loud pop and an explosion of rubber. A cinematic trail of orange and red sparks illuminating the road as the bare metal of the Mercedes' wheel rim destroyed itself on the asphalt. What he got was a puff of white powder and a barely audible wheeze as the tire's air escaped its prison. Doctor Jordan slowly and efficiently made her way to the curb. He felt the whole situation was disappointingly anti-climactic.

Pulling behind the disabled Mercedes, Caleb turned his SUV off and reached into a center console compartment. He pulled a hypodermic needle from a leather folding case. Low illumination of sparse streetlights gave the liquid held within the syringe a black tint.

Body shaking in anticipation, he waited for the good doctor to exit her vehicle. He could see her shadow moving about in the cabin of the car, appearing to search for something. A loud *thunk* heralded the opening of the Mercedes' trunk, followed by the driver-side door. Doctor Jordan held her cell phone in her hand, its flashlight feature turned on. Leaving the SUV's headlights on, Caleb got out. From her vantage point he appeared as a dark, backlit silhouette. Not wanting to be rude, the doctor kept her flashlight pointed toward the ground.

"Everything okay?" Caleb asked.

Doctor Jordan let out an exasperated sigh as she saw the tear in her tire.

"Yeah," she said with bemoaned acceptance. "Just a flat. Thank you for stopping but I got—"

Words failed her as Caleb's visage came into full view. The hair on her arms stood in warning. She felt cold sweat form on her brow, her heart pounded in her chest. Her knees were shaking. Something wasn't right here.

"Um, hi," she said.

Caleb gave her a wide, warm, charismatic smile.

"What— What are you doing here?" Doctor Jordan kept her voice steady. "Are you following me?"

"I need you," Caleb said, his tone calm and soothing. "I need you to bring her to me."

"What are you talking abo—" Doctor Jordan's words cut off. She began hyperventilating. Her heart kicked, the rushing of blood consumed her ears. She felt like she was drowning. Bending over, she grabbed the side of her car to stabilize herself. The wheezing of her attempts to procure oxygen made the Boy chuckle softly.

"Don't worry," he said, "you're not gonna suffocate. But I need you so she can make me perfect."

Pulling the hypodermic needle's cap off, Caleb rushed the asphyxiating doctor, grabbing her from behind and plunging the drug-delivery device into her neck. As he removed the syringe, the doctor's breathing slowly normalized. He had perfected this technique. Caleb knew the drug took about three minutes to render a person unconscious; he timed his oxygen-denial for about two minutes. By the time Doctor Jordan took in a full breath, she was no longer able to hold herself upright. Moving the small woman to his SUV, Caleb propped her up in the passenger's seat and secured her seatbelt.

Closing the Mercedes' driver door and trunk, Caleb loaded himself behind the wheel of his own vehicle. Looking at the unconscious doctor, he gently moved a strand of her hair from her face, caressed her cheek with his finger.

"I cannot tell you how much this means to me," he said softly, almost lovingly. "Thank you, Doctor."

Raven studied Special Agent Brock Allen as he drove the government-issued Escalade south on Las Vegas Boulevard toward Henderson. Something about the man didn't sit right with her, something she could not put her finger on. To her knowledge, he had been honest with her, as well as the small contingent from Darkstone's Asylum. So what was it about the man that raised a subtle unease within her?

"What?" the agent asked, glancing toward her.

"It's…nothing." Raven mentally cursed her own reticence.

"Okay." Agent Allen drew out the word, a lingering question couched in the sound. His breathing was heavy. Deep inhales and exhales designed to manage stress.

"Are you expecting problems?" Raven's voice held underlying concern. "You seem a bit pent up."

The FBI agent gave her a sideways glance. His intimidating and inscrutable expression would have put the fear of God into lesser people. Raven lifted a questioning eyebrow, unfazed by Agent Allen's glare of death. His eyes back on the road, Raven could see his jaw muscles clench and unclench. He appeared to be working up to a question. The two sat silently for a few minutes. Raven looked out the window of the

SUV as strip malls and gas stations gave way to a short expanse of rocky, brush-filled fields. Land yet to be developed.

"So, you're the leader?" Agent Allen's voice brought Raven's attention back into the car.

"No." Her words were flat, final.

"Who calls the shots?"

Raven chuckled at the question, finding the agent's need to understand hierarchy very human.

"I guess I am a de-facto leader." Raven looked back out the window, not wanting Agent Allen to see the involuntary expression of sadness and doubt crossing her face. "They all look to me, I'm the one who brought them into this mess."

With a raised eyebrow, the agent glanced toward Raven. He was met with a view of the shaved, high-cut hairline on the back of her head.

"I make requests of the others. I don't give orders," she said. "If someone chooses not to accept the request, I cannot force them."

"How often are your requests refused?"

"So far," Raven turned to look at Agent Allen, his eyes firmly fixed on the road, "never."

The agent raised an eyebrow again. In his experience, orders, even those characterized as requests, eventually found at least one challenger. He had butted heads with superiors more times than he could count, a personality flaw that had him reassigned from a cushy D.C. office to Las Vegas. He felt someone must have been protecting him. He didn't end up in Alaska.

"I have a hard time believing that."

Raven smirked. "It's true. There have been times where discussions were held, challenges of a sort, I suppose. One person or another felt the requests didn't make sense or there were concerns. In the end, either my explanations were accepted, or a compromise was reached via consensus. We are bonded on a level that normal humans simply can't understand. We let each other into our minds, and while the information passed between us is controlled, there is still a huge level of trust that must exist to allow even the smallest access. Emotions, intent, subterfuge, obfuscation, these are all things that pass through the filters of control. Lies are nearly impossible."

291

"Nearly?"

"There's one who has managed to get away with lying once." Raven held up a finger, humorous conviction passing her lips. "Once."

Raven chuckled to herself, remembering a time Nexus, in her teenage stupidity, decided she could make a pizza-run wearing a hooded cloak for a disguise. She had tried to tell Raven she was sitting on the toilet for an hour. As it turned out, Nexus had watched the 1990 *Teenage Mutant Ninja Turtles* movie. A scene where one of the turtles leaves the safety of the New York City sewers in a fedora and trench coat gave her the idea. Thankfully, the owner of the pizza parlor happened to be in the Caretaker's loop, but also snitched on the poor girl.

Following the Escalade's navigation instructions, Agent Allen piloted the G-ride into the left turn lane at Saint Rose Parkway. His questions momentarily subsided, Raven absentmindedly studied the M Resort and Casino sitting across the street. Black and tan, the sixteen-story tower mirrored the desert landscape. She had questions of her own for the special agent. For the life of her, she was unable to string them together to form coherent sentences. A green traffic arrow heralded the SUV's acceleration.

"What can you tell me about the Guavera twins?" Agent Allen broke the silence.

"As I said," Raven couldn't help an underlying tone of annoyance in her voice, "I can tell you their names, I can tell you where they are. In extreme circumstances I can tell you if they're in dire distress. Outside of that, nothing."

"Hmmm." Agent Allen appeared to contemplate the information.

"Everyone steers clear of the Waiting," Raven said, "with one exception."

Agent Allen raised his eyebrows.

"Support groups are set up through our online community—"

"The message boards Voss has been using to find his victims."

Raven felt a flush of shame. It was a simple statement of fact, but she felt responsible for making Caleb Voss' ability to find her charge easier than it should have been.

"Yeah." Her voice was flat. "That one. Normally those who have made their choice leave the message boards. Some who chose the human route stay on to provide support and encouragement, set up in-person support groups, and try to help those whose mental health needs that extra love and understanding. Then there's Tippy."

"Tippy?"

"Theresa Freya Sorson, but she insists we all call her Tippy." Raven smiled at the thought of her friend. "That woman has the biggest heart, lives in a world where she sees the joy and wonder that cynicism destroys for most of us. She is one of those people who is truly magical. Simply being in her presence alters your perspective. It's as if, for a short period of time, you can see the world through her eyes. And it is a marvelous thing to behold. That ability has nothing to do with her being a Caretaker, however. She's—"

"She is a Down's kid," Agent Allen stated. "What you're describing is the effect those born with Down syndrome have on the people around them." Agent Allen took a beat, then amended, "Well, those who aren't mired in a mentality of hate and self-loathing."

Raven nodded her head in agreement. Like her, Tippy was something different. A being possessed of old magic and new power. "You've known a few people with Down's, I assume?"

"Three cousins," Agent Allen began, "and more victims than I'd like to remember. There's a lot that can get me worked up, but nothing brings me to violence faster than some asshole talking shit about a Down's kid."

A wide grin crossed Raven's face. This was the first time she had heard any semblance of honest, personal passion enter the giant agent's deep voice. Whatever the cause of her unease with the man, his character, his trustworthiness, wasn't in question.

"You'll like Tippy," Raven said. "She's a hoot, wise beyond her years, and she took it upon herself to run one of the support groups. She's also the only Caretaker that didn't need me to activate her."

Agent Allen's eyebrows raised once again. Taking notice of his own persistent expression of questioning, he thought he should just keep his eyebrows up until they were done talking.

"She was born with her DNA fully active," Raven stated. "I'm not sure why. Possibly the chromosomal deviation just had that portion of her genetics locked in place." She shook her head. "I don't know, and it really doesn't matter. She's sweet, amazing, kind, generous…and if you threaten her friends, she makes a raging mama bear look like a fucking hamster."

Agent Allen let out a laugh. A real laugh. A laugh that, for just a moment, transformed him from a hardened, emotionally walled-off purveyor of the law into a genuine, vulnerable human being. Raven thought she saw a momentary look of embarrassment in the man's deep tan as he caught himself, plastered inscrutability back onto his face. She felt one part of her unease with him had been answered. He wore a mask. A mask that he desperately clung to. The person she saw beneath for a moment, a laugh that showed an underpinning of real emotion…she wanted to meet that person.

Raven was jolted from her thoughts as the car swung hard to the right, pressing her into the door. "Sorry," Agent Allen said. "Almost missed our turn."

"It's fine." Raven smirked. "Gonna have to do a lot more than that to hurt me."

Agent Allen snorted, a controlled expression of humor.

"So," he began another round of inquiry, "how do you propose to defeat the Dark Man? Won't this Damien character have entire armies at his disposal? According to the records Mrs. Smith grabbed from the Office, there's only about fifteen thousand Caretakers worldwide."

"Fifteen thousand the Office has identified," Raven stated, a taunting tone ringing in her voice. "I am connected to a hell of a lot more than those bastards know about."

"How many are we talking here?"

"Oh," Raven drew out the word, "twenty-three million, give or take."

The Escalade made a sudden swerve as the number hit Agent Allen like a ton of bricks. Raven reflexively grabbed the "Oh Shit" bar above the passenger-side window. The agent appeared to be hyperventilating as Raven looked at him.

"You okay?"

The agent smoothed out the Escalade's path down the road, his foot suddenly acting as though a lead weight were attached to it. Raven watched the speedometer as they surpassed one hundred miles per hour. Fast approaching, she could see a roundabout in their path. Barren trees and low scrub sprouted from the rocky planter that served as a traffic guide.

"Um, Agent," Raven said cautiously. "If we crash at this speed, I'm going to walk away just fine. You probably won't."

She felt Agent Allen's foot let up, the SUV quickly dropping speed as friction and gravity took control. He braked, navigating the roundabout at a slower than necessary speed, and headed east on Bicentennial Parkway.

"You wanna talk about it?" Concern permeated Raven's question.

"I—" Agent Allen's voice wavered. "I just— I don't. I'm relieved."

"Suicidal acceleration is your way of expressing relief?"

The FBI agent drew in a long breath, let it out in a slow and measured exhale.

"I figured he might have actually been telling the truth for once," Agent Allen said. "When the Dark Man told me there simply weren't enough of you to help us, enough of you to stand against him."

"It's a funny thing about him," Raven said. "He's a pathological liar. That thing once tried to convince me that the soul of my father was with him. It was all in the style of the *Exorcist* movies." Raven mimicked a demonic growling voice. "Your daddy's here with us, don't you want to be with your daddy?" She chuckled at the notion. "If he wasn't the very embodiment of annihilation, the Dark Man might make a good comedian. He wasn't too keen on the idea when I suggested it to him though."

Agent Allen snorted, a sound Raven interpreted to be a stifled laugh.

"So, what can we expect here?" the giant G-Man asked as he piloted the Escalade left onto a residential entrance.

A concrete, landscaped center divider held a sign announcing the name of the housing tract, the word "Inspirada" in bold blue, a stylized blue bird flying above the title. Raven could see three preset architectural designs made up the planned community. Tan, terracotta, and browns reflected the desert housing color scheme of newer developments.

"I'm guessing two teenage girls and one or two parents," Raven stated unironically.

Agent Allen chuffed derisively. "Is that all?"

"I told you, all I know are names and locations." Annoyance permeated her words. "I know their ages due to their involvement in our online community. But that's it. We don't stalk our own." Raven snorted. "We're not the FBI."

Agent Allen gave an unintelligible sound in response. Raven couldn't tell if he was amused by her comment, angered by it, or hungry. With a slow right turn, the agent brought the Escalade to a halt in front of a two-story brown and tan house. Raven looked at the dwelling, its cookie-cutter appearance pleasing yet forgettable. Exiting the SUV, she took in the desert-themed front yard.

"Either these folks are really water conscious, or their HOA has a hard-on for cacti." She chuckled to herself. An odd snicker from Agent Allen told her he thought the same.

Walking up the short front driveway, Agent Allen and Raven looked like something out of the world's strangest buddy-cop movie. A gargantuan, suited FBI agent side by side with a comparatively tiny goth. An L-shaped path led to the front door. Rounding the corner of the pathway, the two found an aggravated-looking short man in a grey sweatsuit standing at the front doorway. Agent Allen pulled his badge from the inside of his jacket.

"Mr. Guavera?" Agent Allen's voice was firm yet welcoming.

"Yes," the short man briskly answered. Standing at five feet, five inches, Mario Guavera sported a lean build, slicked back black hair, and a black goatee. His brown eyes held an unspecified anger. Cutting through dark olive skin, deep frown lines gave the man a ferocious appearance.

"I'm Special Agent Brock Allen of the FBI. This is my colleague—" Agent Allen realized he had no idea how to introduce Raven to anyone.

"Mary Thompson," Raven stated, using the name her parents had given her.

"The FBI's got a goth squad or something?"

Agent Allen lifted a disapproving eyebrow. Raven snorted a laugh. Stepping forward, she turned her head and pulled her left ear forward. The little man's eyes went wide as he saw the infinity symbol birthmark. In an instant his demeanor went from agitated to deflated, a sadness crossing the father's face as he pulled the door completely open and gestured for the odd couple to enter. Agent Allen noticed a dent on the door's inside edge as they entered.

A short hallway led to the home's open-plan living room and kitchen area. Framed family photographs sat on floating shelves that had been arranged in a random step pattern. A large flat-screen TV was attached to the kitchen-facing wall. Barstools lined one side of a granite-top kitchen island. The outcropping served as the dividing line between the cooking and living spaces. A three-piece, black leather living room set was centered around the TV. In the center of the seating arrangement, a medium-sized glass coffee table was covered in textbooks and what appeared to be someone's homework.

Raven ran her finger over a slice in the back of a short couch. Her eyes traced the line of trajectory and saw no other damage in the room. She looked to Agent Allen, calling attention to the cut.

"Definitely our guy," she said with certainty.

Agent Allen grunted in agreement. Mario Guavera looked between the two questioningly. His face told the story of calm, but his eyes spoke of fear. Fear for his daughters.

"Please don't take them from me." Mario's voice strained to maintain composure and his hands trembled as he addressed Raven. "My wife and I, we can't—"

"I'm not here to take them." Raven's voice was soft, reassuring. "I'm here to make sure they remain safe." She sighed. "And to chastise them for being so stupid."

A relived sigh caught in a laugh as the frightened father placed his hand to his chest. Smiling, he gestured for Agent Allen and Raven to sit.

"Can I get either of you anything to drink?"

"I'm good," Raven said, waving her hand.

"Thank you for the offer, but that won't be necessary," Agent Allen stated. "We just want to go over a few things with you and your daughters if possible."

"Seeing the leftover damage, I think we can throw out a few of those questions," Raven added. "I'm pretty damn sure this was our guy."

"That's what Therese and Claire said," Mr. Guavera relayed. "They had told me a few weeks ago that a warning had gone out on that message board your people use."

Raven snorted at the characterization. "They're your people too," she admonished.

Mario Guavera's face reddened with embarrassment. "Yes, I'm sorry." the words came through anxious breaths. "When the girls told me the warning had been updated to specifically include Las Vegas, I got worried."

"Did you have any reason to believe they would be targets?" Agent Allen held a small notepad and pen in his hands.

"I had no reason to believe they weren't in danger."

The FBI agent gave a relenting nod. Raven nodded in agreement with the father.

"They told me they were taking precautions," Mario continued. "No real names, no giving out our address."

"And you believed them?" Raven snorted in disbelief.

"Well," Mr. Guavera shrugged, "I try to maintain trust with my children. We talk about everything. My wife and I are blunt about everything."

"You just believed them when they told you about what they are?" Incredulity seeped from Agent Allen's tone.

"When your mute children suddenly sport the eyes of a snake and start talking, you've got two options," Mario snapped at the agent. "Either they're possessed or telling the truth."

"How did you choose truth?" Raven asked.

"The day they told us, we had found an injured pigeon," Mario began. "Its wing had been broken and the poor thing was in a bad way. We put it in a shoebox, placed it in the back yard, and started feeding it, trying to nurse the little guy back to health. It wasn't working." Mario suddenly seemed far away, as if the memory had pulled him from the present. He paused, letting the past play through his mind.

"And then?" Agent Allen gently prompted.

"Therese and Claire said they had something they needed to tell us, to show us, and they brought us to the dying bird." Tthe father gave an odd chuckle. "Theresa smiled at me before biting down on her tongue so hard blood came out of her mouth. Naturally her mother and I started to freak out. Then we saw the change, her eyes turned to that strange lizard look."

"Funny," Raven said, "most people seem to find them closer to the eyes of a cat."

Mario cocked his head to the side, considering this. "I've never owned a cat, so I couldn't really say."

"So, her eyes changed, then what happened?" Agent Allen said, trying to keep the conversation from derailing into pointless dead-end tangents.

"We freaked out." Mario let out a laugh. "We weren't sure if we should call the doctor or a priest. Then she spoke. For the first time, we heard Therese's voice. It was stunning."

"What did she say?" Raven asked.

"She said, 'It's okay, just watch.'"

"Watch what?" Agent Allen asked, though he had a pretty good idea of the answer.

"Therese put her hand over the dying pigeon. In an instant it sprung up, full of energy. Its broken wing had mended." A broad smile crossed Mario's face. "The moment my daughter moved her hands away from it, that bird took off like it just discovered the joy of being alive."

"I take it that was when you figured out she wasn't possessed?" Raven smirked.

Mr. Guavera gave a laugh as he vigorously nodded his head. He tapped the tip of his nose to drive the point home.

"Her voice was angelic," he continued. "And she said, 'I love you,' before falling silent again. Claire had mirrored her sister's transformation but did not show us what she could do. She spoke in a barely audible whisper. Later she told us why."

"I take it she's the one who threw their would-be abductor out of the house?" Raven asked.

Mario looked at her, his eyebrows raised with an unspoken question.

"I had a similar experience when I was eleven," she said. "I was also born without a voice. A man had come to kill me. The moment I saw the barrel of his gun, I found my voice, and it taught him how to fly."

Mario nodded solemnly, yet his eyes held hope. "And now you can talk without—"

"Yes." Raven smiled. "Though my situation was a little different. Be assured, though. Whatever choice they make, you will hear their voices again."

The appearance of two short girls cut the conversation off. One of the girls, dressed in a bright orange sundress, eyed Agent Allen with suspicion. The other wore baggy blue jeans with a dull grey t-shirt, questions written on her face. Agent Allen's size hid Raven from the girls.

"Therese, Claire," Mario said. "Come meet our guests."

Therese and Claire made their way around one of the couches. The twins stopped, eyes wide and mouths open at the sight of Raven.

"*It's you,*" the girl in the orange dress signed, her hands moving with purpose. Her face appeared to be in an awestruck daze.

Raven smiled warmly at the girls and the familiar refrain of recognition. Why these women who Raven had never met and who had never seen her always recognized her was a great mystery. A bit rusty from disuse, the gothy woman on the couch raised her hands, slowly forming words. In another life, long ago, she had been able to speed-talk with her hands. Now she was slow and deliberate. She knew these girls could hear. The point of the silent speech was one of connection.

"*Yes. I have come to talk with you.*"

Mario watched the short exchange, a subconscious smile gracing his countenance. Patting the seat, his daughters' spell was broken. Sitting, one on each side of him, the girls appeared to be mirror images of each other. One with a clear, feminine flair, the other going for the tomboy look. Matching pensive and pursed lips were locked in place as they both stared at Raven.

"Agent Allen, Ms. Thompson, these are my daughters," Mr. Guavera said. "This is Claire," gesturing to the girl in the sundress to his right, "and this is Therese," Mario gestured to the tomboy on his left.

"It is very nice to meet you," Agent Allen said. He attempted to sound cordial. He failed.

"Don't mind him," Raven signed to the girls. *"He's socially inept."*

The two girls snickered. Mario smiled, obviously holding in a laugh. Agent Allen raised his now signature eyebrow of questioning and disapproval. He couldn't read sign language, but he knew when something was said at his expense. Grunting, he put on a smile. Opening his mouth to speak, Raven cut the large man off.

"How did you learn to activate your abilities?" Raven was curious. She knew that moments of distress and danger could trigger the dormant Caretaker DNA. She had learned herself that emotional and physical stressors quickly brought that inhuman part of the Waiting to the forefront. Doing it on command, that was a novel idea.

"They said it was—" Mario began.

"Let them speak, please," Agent Allen cut him off.

"Our doctor showed us how," Claire signed.

"She's one of us," Therese added. *"She told us that pain would let us control our power."*

"Your doctor?" Raven couldn't hide her surprise.

"A doctor taught them how to do that?" Agent Allen interjected.

"Doctor Adriana Jordan," Mario said. "She's been their pediatrician since they were born. I think the girls were her first patients when she started her own practice."

Raven nodded. In her mind she could see the psychic tether that led to Doctor Jordan. She was currently on the northeast side of Las Vegas. Raven assumed the doctor's office must be located there.

"I'd like to speak with her," Agent Allen said.

"No," Raven countered, giving the FBI agent a hard look. "If she has nothing to do with this case, I won't let you bother her."

Anger flashed in Agent Allen's eyes. To be reprimanded by a civilian on his case would require a short discussion away from the prying eyes of interviewees.

"Are you going to take us away?" Therese's hands trembled with the words, barely able to form the signs to ask the question.

Raven felt her heart sink. This was why she stayed away from the Waiting. This was an anxiety she tried to avoid imparting on those not

301

ready. A deep sigh escaped her as she put on the most comforting smile she could manage. She reverted to sign language. This was not a conversation for Agent Allen to listen in on.

"*No, sweetie.*" Raven looked between the two girls. "*It's not time yet.*"

A look of relief crossed the girls' faces. Twin exhales released their anxious thoughts.

"*When the time comes, it will be your choice,*" Raven signed to the girls. "*It's like choosing a career for your life. You can come and join me, or you can live free of the power you now have and able to choose all human life has to offer.*" She wasn't sure if her message was clear to the girls.

"*Will we still be able to see our mom and dad?*" Claire asked.

"*Yes,*" Raven said. "*There's no reason you couldn't.*"

While Raven's words were true, Caretakers rarely visited their parents. Not because they were discouraged. Many felt their presence would bring danger to their families. Raven's family was all but gone. Her father had died before she underwent her change. Mike Holvald, a man who had become her guardian and protector when her life was threatened by misguided zealots, was all the human family she had left. Fate forced Mike into this fight, he chose to stay when the opportunity to exit was presented to him. The man wasn't necessarily a "Nice Guy," but he was a good guy.

Raven gestured to the two girls, pointing behind her own left ear, then signed, "*Can I see?*"

The girls nodded in unison. Therese moved her head to the side, pulling her ear forward. Like all female Caretakers, her birthmark was a perfect infinity symbol. And like all Caretakers, perfectly circular freckle-like points, or pips, were in the vicinity of the primary symbol.

A theory had been under investigation recommended by Raven. The pips appeared to have different configurations. Raven hypothesized that these parts of the birthmark denoted genetic markers that defined what abilities each Caretaker had inherited. With enough active Caretakers to make viable comparisons, this did appear to be the case, though they had yet to decipher all the varieties and combinations.

Therese had three pips. One at a forty-five-degree angle from the center of her infinity symbol, two in a straight line toward the back of her head. The angled pip was consistent with healing abilities, the other two were currently unknown. Raven gave the girl a nod, a smile, and a kiss on her forehead. Claire, following her sister's example, moved her head to the side and pulled her left ear forward. Raven expected to find her birthmark to be a carbon copy of her identical twin sister's.

Raven's heart stopped at the sight of Claire's birthmark. It was an exact match to her own. Two pips vertically equidistant on the centerline of the infinity symbol. An indication that, like Raven, Claire had a perfect fifty-fifty genetic percentage. Also like Raven, she would be able to perform the same genetic manipulation to transform one of the Waiting into a Caretaker or make them completely human. A sense of hope overtook her at the sight.

Twenty-three million of the Waiting spread across the globe was an impossible task for Raven alone. If Claire chose the Caretaker route, Raven would have help. Statistics being what they are, she thought it likely that others would be found who could help the Waiting as well. As she had done with Therese, Raven gave Claire a nod, smile, and kiss on the forehead. Returning to her seat, Raven addressed the sisters.

"Think about what you want," Raven signed. *"But not too much. Just live your lives and be happy. For now, there is no reason to dwell on the future."*

The twins leaned forward, looked at each other across their father. Some mystical ability only twins possess appeared to be at work. No words passed their hands, no communication of any sort. And yet…

"Mr. Guavera," Agent Allen redirected the conversation, "I noticed a rather pronounced dent on the edge of your front door."

The father gave a little chuckle. "Yeah," he said, "apparently that douche took some damage on his way out."

Agent Allen smiled at the news. A look of concern crossed Raven's face.

"Guess we should check with the ERs," Agent Allen said to himself.

"There's an emergency room about a mile from here, over by Saint Rose Parkway and Colorado Center Drive," Mario offered. "If he just went by a Google search, that would be the closest."

Agent Allen nodded a "thank you" as he wrote the information in his notepad.

"Mr. Guavera." Trepidation infused Raven's voice. "Mario, how long have you lived here?"

"We've been in this house for about a year," he said. "Before this we were living in a small two-bedroom apartment on Green Valley Parkway. We were there for—" Mario looked to the ceiling, trying to find the right number, "fifteen years, I think. The girls were born about two years after my wife and I moved in there."

"I see," she said. "Why would you take your kids to a doctor who is on the other end of the city?"

Mario regarded Raven with a look of pure confusion. "What do you mean? Her office is only two miles away from here."

Raven felt a spike of anxiety. She thought it unlikely that the doctor would be taking time out of her practice on a Thursday to take a thirty-mile round trip. Sighing, Raven reminded herself that she really didn't know anything about Adriana Jordan, her business or habits.

"Guess you'll be getting that chance to talk with the good doctor," Raven said to Agent Allen. "Because right now she is nowhere near Henderson. And that is making me nervous."

Claire and Therese shared an anxious look.

"How would he have found her?" Agent Allen asked.

"I don't know." Unease swelled around Raven's words.

"I think I might," Mr. Guavera said, his face the portrait of concern. "Doctor Jordan volunteers at the ER I mentioned."

Raven and Agent Allen gave the small man a surprised look. The FBI agent opened his mouth to ask how the father knew this, but decided the information wasn't of importance. Raven no longer wondered what Adriana Jordan was doing in the northeast of Las Vegas. She knew why the doctor was there. Abruptly standing, Raven put on as calm and confident a face as she could muster. Putting his notebook and pen back in his coat pocket, Agent Allen followed suit.

"Thank you for your time," Agent Allen said, extending his hand to Mario Guavera. The short man stood, shaking the offered appendage.

"*You two remember what we talked about,*" Raven signed to the twins. The girls smiled in response, concern tainting their expressions.

"You don't need to worry," Raven said aloud, "Doctor Jordan will be just fine." Raven hoped her declaration was the truth.

The goth queen turned to Mario, shook his hand, and smiled at him. Worry permeated his face, and Raven had a good idea of where that worry came from.

"You can relax," she told the fearful father. "I have someone on their way here now. We'll keep watch until this monster is no longer a threat."

The little man seemed to relax at this news, his shoulders dropping in relief. Mario hadn't even realized his entire body had been in a state of anxiety-induced tension until this moment. With a calming breath, the rest of his body let go. He had feared the man would come back to take his girls, or worse, take revenge for their injuring him. Now he felt secure knowing a bodyguard with more stopping power than a tank would be watching over them.

Raven gave a little wave to the twins. The girls jumped up from their seats, ran around their father, and embraced her. The Caretaker ran her hands over the girls' heads, smiling. She knelt to look both of the undersized fourteen-year-olds in the eye.

"You two remember what we talked about." Raven's voice was calm and soothing. "And don't do anything stupid. I don't want to have to come back here to scold you. I want our next meeting to be a happy one."

Claire and Therese vigorously nodded their heads in agreement. Following Agent Allen, she walked out the front door and into the sunlit desert.

"Make a call to Jonathan and Stephanie," Raven said to Agent Allen as they made their way to the Escalade. "We need to meet back at the hotel."

Agent Allen pulled the SUV's key fob from his pocket, hitting the remote unlock button. "Why do I have to make the call?" His annoyance was unmistakable.

As she walked past him, Raven grabbed the Escalade's key out of the giant's hand. "You have to make the call because I'm driving."

Chapter 25

From the parking lot of the medical examiner's office, I could see dark thunderclouds on the horizon, poised like a massing army preparing for invasion. A warm wind rustled my coat. Lifting my head to the sky, I closed my eyes. The building standing before me held nothing but death. Some had exited this world in peace, some wasted away, some left in fear, and some in abject terror. Here and now, I felt only calm. The sun gently warmed my face as currents of air soothingly slid over my skin. This was the feeling of life. A momentary existence in a blip of time on a small, insignificant speck of dust we call Earth. And in this moment in time, our unfathomable insignificance had become the front line in a war humanity had forgotten to prepare for. We are now, in this moment, the only thing of importance. None of us could see them, those eyes focused on our tiny, primitive world from across the stars. We cannot see them, but I know they're there. I can feel them on us.

"You ready?" Stephanie's voice broke my trance. "She's waiting."

My compatriot's hair did not absorb the same calm from the wind that I had. A mane of frizzy red doing the Halem Shake. In the car, her hair had been flat-ironed and straight. Along with her suit and mirrored aviator sunglasses, Stephanie had reacquired the imposing air of the FBI agent she had once been. Humidity and wind now gave her the look of a haggard chauffeur. I couldn't help but snicker at the sight.

"Yeah," I said, trying to hold on to the calm. "After you."

Flashing our credentials at the door, we made our way toward Mai's exam room. Initially she had requested Agent Allen's presence. I got the distinct impression his unavailability was to her liking. I was curious how she, an independent coroner from Hong Kong, managed to get wrapped up with Agent Allen. From what I could tell, the two seemed to have a long history, and they didn't appear to like each other very much. Well, maybe that wasn't quite right. Mai liked teasing Agent Allen. Agent Allen liked Mai's capabilities as a coroner.

Rounding a corner, I saw Mai speaking with a grumpy-looking round man in a rumpled brown suit. A Clark County Sherrif's

Department badge hung from a chain around the man's neck. Apparently he assumed it was a good replacement for a tie. His hair was black. Too black. The kind of dyed black that made hair look like plastic. With his pitiful looking combover, he had the appearance of a supporting character on some gritty TV police drama. From his demeanor, and the exasperated "Oh shit" sigh Stephanie let out, I deduced this man was one Detective Marcus Hanson. He had been the homicide detective assigned to the Nevada leg of the Hatchetman case prior to Agent Allen asserting jurisdiction. With the theory that two killers were on the loose, Detective Hanson had claimed the FBI had no authority over the exhibition murders. Much to my chagrin, the angry meatball had been correct.

Considering Hanson had been so eager to take back a portion of the case, I couldn't help but wonder where the hell the man had been. Our copycat murders were solved, the perpetrator dead. From where I stood, the man was a deserter at best, a failed detective at worst. I'd recommend he be put back on patrol, but from the looks of him the guy would probably have a heart attack if he was forced to run five feet.

The conversation between Mai and the rotund detective appeared quite animated, hands flailing angrily from both sides. At just the right angle, it looked like they were engaged in a slap fight. On our approach, Detective Hanson noticed Stephanie and me. It appeared he had recently discovered his theory about two killers was correct.

"Look," his voice was rough, "just give me what you have on the dead hookers. It's my case, you had no right to examine my evidence." He pointed a finger at Mai, stopping just short of contact. "You don't work for the county, and your involvement probably fucked up my chance of getting a conviction."

"You want to put Scott Boyd on trial?" Stephanie's face was scrunched in confusion as she asked the question.

Detective Hanson turned an angry glare toward us. Stephanie and I just held up our FBI consultant credentials to cut off the obvious question.

"Who the hell is Scott Boyd?" For a seasoned detective, Hanson really wasn't much for detecting.

307

"The perp who killed those young ladies," Stephanie responded, emphasizing the word "ladies."

"Did you actually do any work on this case?" I asked. "You may not have gotten the memo, but we managed to identify your perpetrator, track him down, and, unfortunately, he was killed in the process of trying to arrest him. You no longer have to worry about going to trial." I looked the fuming detective dead in the eye. "You're welcome."

"Why didn't anyone tell me?" Hanson's voice was the low, measured tone of a man on the edge of rage.

"I left five messages for you on your cell phone." Mai returned the finger Detective Hanson pointed at her. "If you are not going to pick up your phone or check your messages, maybe you should find a job that does not include the need for communication."

The detective's building anger did not abate at the revelation of his own incompetence.

"You should have tried harder, you dumb chink." Hanson's face had turned beet red.

There are few things that instantly cause my blood to boil. One is bullying the defenseless, the other is the use of racial slurs. Balling my fists, I took a deep breath, reminding myself that turning a victimizer into a victim would be counterproductive.

"You need to leave," I told the detective. "Right. Now."

"Don't tell me what to—"

"There are cameras in this hallway." Stephanie smirked. "They also record audio."

Detective Hanson stopped short. Looking around, he caught sight of the security cameras populating the ceiling of the hallway. Grumbling unintelligibly, he pushed Mai out of his way. Stephanie and I stepped to the side, giving the angry man his out.

"That is assault," Mai said.

Detective Hanson stopped, turned his head. "Actually, it's battery." Stomping off like a child sent to their room, the detective turned a corner and disappeared.

"Fucking *Nianam*," Mai muttered, shaking her head. "Can never take responsibility for their own failings."

I raised an eyebrow at the word. Raven had given us no names of Caretakers or those who work with them.

"Are you—" Stephanie began to ask.

Mai turned her head, cocked slightly to the right. We were greeted by a warm smile and vertical pupils. She chuckled at the shocked expression on Stephanie's face.

"Raven did not tell you." Her smile widened. "Let us take this out of the hall."

Indicating an examination room to our right, Mai pulled the door open and gestured for us to enter.

"Don't we need to suit up?" Stephanie asked, recalling the abruptness of our first visit. I was wondering the same.

"No need today," Mai responded. "The dead are in their drawers."

Shuffling into the room, I wasn't sure why we had been called for an in-person visit if there was nothing on the bodies to show us.

Mai sat on a rolling stool, Stephanie and I stood facing a darkened lightbox on the exam room wall. The lightbox was usually used to view X-rays. Today a grainy photograph was held in place by metal clips sprouting from the fixture's aluminum frame. The photo appeared to have been taken in low light. The central figure, a thin and threatening person, stood over a slumped body. What I thought was a pool of blood emanated from the prone figure. The colors of the photo were strangely muted and slightly off.

"What are we looking at here?" I asked.

"Sonja Verztuk's last moment of freedom," Mai flatly stated. "This was the last thing she saw before the Abomination took her."

"How the hell did you get that?" Stephanie blurted out in shock.

"Well," Mai began, "it is kind of gross."

Stephanie's eyebrows lifted in anticipation. I could see her hidden interest in the gross and creepy bubbling to the surface. She may not like to be in the presence of slimy and disgusting things, but the tall redhead loved hearing about it. I, on the other hand, loved horror movies. But there was a limit to the gore and disgusting side of things I could tolerate. The dream, that Bog of Death I had walked in just a few hours ago, with its putrid stench and mountain of writhing corpses. That was pushing the limit for me.

"By touching the brain of the deceased, I can access memories," Mai stated. "Using a piece of photo paper, I can transfer those images, creating what I call a mnemonic photograph. The closer to death the memory, the clearer the image." Mai pointed to the photo. "As you can see, this image is not very clear. Part of that is likely due to Ms. Verztuk's emotional state, the other factor is that the memory was created almost a full twenty-four hours before her death."

"Do you have any photos right before her death?" I was curious to see what the poor girl's last moments were. Morbidly curious. And I knew that seeing such a sight would serve to bolster my determination to find this Caleb Voss and bring a well-deserved pain hammer down on his ass. While initially my job was simply to locate and report his location, nothing in my contract said the killer had to be in one piece when the Office took possession of the man. And nothing said I had to keep the bastard away from anyone else looking for him.

"Yes," Mai said, a note of apology in her voice. "Raven currently has the rest of the photographs."

"Is that Madame Toulah on the ground?" Stephanie asked, a lump in her throat.

"Yes."

Stephanie and I let out controlled sighs. As far as I could tell, my compatriot was wading through the same sorrowful anxiety spike I was having. From my pocket I pulled out my cigarette case.

"No smoking," Mai said sternly.

Opening the case, I showed her the neatly arranged sticks of cinnamon. Mai's face scrunched in confusion. Pulling one of the reddish-brown sticks from its home, I placed the spice in my mouth, angling it to the side as though it were a cigarette. Her eyes narrowed, a question dangled on her lips.

"Quitting smoking sucks," I said flatly, the stick of spice held between my teeth. "Been trying for the better part of a decade. This is one method a family friend showed me."

"Is it working?" Mai asked.

I pulled the cinnamon stick from my mouth, held it between my index and middle finger. "Meh," I said. "It does taste and smell a hell of a lot better, but I've been jonesing for a cig since this whole shitstorm landed in my lap."

Stephanie snorted. Mai sagely nodded her head in understanding.

"Now," I turned the subject back to the photo, "I know you didn't call us here just to show off your talents."

"No." Mai smirked. "That is not my style."

She turned on the lightbox, illuminating the photo. Backlighting the photo increased its contrast. Dark shapes became crisper, blurred edges came into focus. Mai pointed to the dark figure's right hand.

"This is what I called you in for," she said. I could see what appeared to be the hint of a syringe in the figure's hand. Mai clipped another photograph to the lightbox. The photo was taken during the autopsy, close-up on Sonja's neck just above the point of severance. A small, almost imperceptible dot of red sat less than a tenth of an inch above the plane of decapitation.

"A puncture mark?" Stephanie asked, though she knew the answer.

Mai nodded, pulled out another photograph. This time it was the neck of Janet Gert, the first of the Waiting in Las Vegas that Caleb Voss had murdered. The photograph focused on a point within the slice. A small, straight laceration gouged through the tissue.

"I almost missed the one on the first girl," Mai said. "That thing made his cut straight through his injection point. I'm guessing these would be found on all the Waiting he has killed."

"That explains how he kept the girls compliant during transport," Stephanie said.

"I ran the toxicology screening again, this time looking for sedatives."

"Do we have results?" I asked.

Mai cocked her head, scowling at the query. My face flushed with embarrassment, realizing the foolishness of my question.

"Midazolam," she stated. "It is in the benzodiazepine family, generally used as an anesthetic and amnestic. It generally lasts only twenty-four hours in the system, but our killer finished his work before the drug could cycle out of the blood."

"Where the hell did he get his hands on that?" Stephanie asked. "And why didn't it show up on any other tox screening?"

311

Mai shrugged. "No one was looking for it," she said. "While I would love to blame the clear incompetence of the other coroners who have worked on this case, in this instance I cannot." Mai let out a sigh. "This Abomination did a decent job of making his methodology difficult to discern. The normal humans he killed were done in a straightforward fashion. No tying up, no knocking out, just a straight up slice and dice. His last victim, Ms. Talbott, being a notable exception of course."

The characterization was…less than tactful, but it made her point.

"I also have to think," Mai continued, "his supply of midazolam must be limited."

"It's a controlled substance, I would think," I said. Mai nodded. "Where did he get it? And how much does he have?"

Stephanie stroked her chin, thinking on this. Mai appeared to be considering the question as well.

"What did his parents do for a living?" Mai asked.

Stephanie let out an explosive "I should have thought of that" sigh.

"I'm guessing no one bothered to catalogue Patrice Voss' medicine cabinet," she said, thinking back to the blatant incompetence displayed in Henry and Patrice Voss' homicide investigation. "Caleb Voss' mother was an anesthesiologist."

"Why would she have midazolam in her home?" Mai asked.

"Why was Michael Jackson being administered propofol when he wasn't going through any medical procedures?" I countered with the rhetorical question, referencing the King of Pop's drug habit that had killed him. Mai gave a light grunt of understanding.

"So," Stephanie began, "we have answered the question of victim transport. Not really helpful." She let out a sigh. "There's no way this guy could possibly be tried by our legal system."

Mai simultaneously nodded and shook her head. I pondered the thought for a moment. He could feasibly be tried for the murders, but the wisdom of doing so was shaky. Even if stripped of his powers, the entire tale of how Caleb Voss came into police custody would be written off as delusional. I turned to Mai.

"Do you have anything that might help us track his current location?"

It was a desperate question. Mai Xaio dealt with the dead, the aftermath of tragedy. Even with her superhuman abilities, she was not equipped to track down a suspect.

"No," Mai confirmed. "If I had a body with some evidence of his location, I might be able to help. From what I gathered between the bodies of Sonja and Janet, he does not use the same kill room twice."

"Damn," Stephanie let slip.

"It's okay," I said. "It isn't your job to find him, it's ours."

"Does not make it any less frustrating for me." Mai's voice held a hint of anger. She took a deep breath, opened her mouth to say something. Pausing, Mai reconsidered adding anything else.

The silence of an autopsy room is specific. It's not quite deafening silence; one isn't overtaken by the sound of blood rushing through their ears. It's not the oppressive silence of a pitch-black, unfamiliar bedroom in the middle of the night. There is something calm about the silence, if one puts the purpose of the room out of one's mind. Had the room held a purpose other than housing and cutting into the dead, it would make a great place for meditation. We stood in the silence of this room. I felt oddly calm in spite of being front and center in a murder investigation, one in which people I knew personally were among the victims. It was as though the universe itself was telling me this would all be over soon, there was nothing to worry about anymore. And then the silence was shattered.

Blaring from my pockets, a heavy guitar riff caused me to jump. Not in the metaphorical sense, not a flinching jump scare. I literally jumped backward. I quickly fished my phone from my pocket before the whole damn song could blast through the echoing room.

"Jonathan speaking," I said, having answered the call so quickly I didn't look at the caller ID.

"This is Agent Allen," the deep voice on the other end announced. "Grab Stephanie and meet us back at your hotel room."

"What's going on?"

I heard Raven's voice in the background, but it was too low for me to understand what she had said. Whatever it was, Agent Allen disagreed with her. One word made him relent.

"You'll find out once you get there, but make it quick. We have a clock running." A click heralded the end of the phone call.

"Who was that?" Stephanie asked.

"Everybody's favorite FBI Agent," I stated. "We need to go. Apparently there's been a development."

Mai's eyes widened, questioning.

"Sorry," I said to her. "He didn't specify. If it's what I suspect, this whole case might be over very soon."

Mai just nodded and smiled.

"You two be careful then," she said. "Do not get dead."

Tara, Raven, Brianna, and Agent Allen were engaged in a heated discussion when Stephanie and I walked into the hotel room. A map of northeastern Las Vegas was displayed on the flat-screen TV. From my vantage point in the small entry hallway, it appeared to be a three against one argument. The FBI Agent stood alone against the women who, in all likelihood, were right in whatever the issue was. I groaned at the sight.

"Look," Raven said to Agent Allen, "I'm trying to keep you from getting killed."

"And I am telling you that this is my suspect, this is my case, and I run the show."

Brianna gripped the bridge of her nose and squeezed her eyes shut in a look of pure, exasperated frustration.

Rolling her eyes, Tara asked, "You're not seriously pulling that juris-my-diction crap, are you?"

"You didn't seriously quote almost every shitty cop movie ever made, did you?" he countered. I could see instant regret on his face as Tara's searing death stare bore into him.

"We know this guy can slice people into tiny parts," Brianna said. "We know he can do it at a distance. Since his weapon is the very air we breathe, he can probably do more. Do you really want to send in a team who won't even get close enough to see his face before they're beheaded or suffocated?"

It was time for me to chime in.

"The ladies are right," I said. Agent Allen glared at me. "It is way too dangerous for you, or any other team you could send in."

"If we go in with heavy armor—"

"Dude," Raven cut him off. "A blade of air traveling way above the speed of sound will render any armor you have worthless."

"Then we set up a sniper and lure him out—"

"I'm trying to help you here." The exasperation in Raven's voice bordered on desperate. "I don't want to have to pull rank on you."

Agent Allen let out a loud, sardonic laugh. Tara, Stephanie, Brianna, and I looked at the goth in confusion. Raven took a calming breath, holding up a finger to let us know we should wait for a moment.

Round pupils stretched into vertical slits. Where I had seen them as feline before, they now struck me as serpentine. Raven appeared to stop for a moment, frozen like a statue, her eyes glazed over. She blinked, her eyes returned to their human, round-pupil state, and she looked at Agent Allen, cocking a mischievous smile.

"Answer your phone," Raven stated, an ambiguous humor in her tone.

Agent Allen looked at her in confusion for a moment. I saw a near imperceptible flinching of his entire body when his phone rang.

"Agent Allen here—"

I could hear the muffled, rather angry voice of whomever was on the other end of that call. Agent Allen's face betrayed nothing, but minute changes to his body language told me the poor guy was getting chewed out by someone he couldn't argue with. He nodded at something that was said, a gesture I tend to do myself despite knowing the person on the other end of the call cannot see the non-verbal response.

"Yes. Yes, sir," the agent said with deference.

We all looked at Agent Allen as he took what I assumed to be a verbal haircut. Something about him seemed to diminish over the short phone call.

"I understand," Agent Allen said with finality. He ended the call and glared at Raven. "How. The. Ever loving. Fuck—"

Raven held up her hand, cutting off the angry FBI agent.

"Dana Hardy," she stated.

Agent Allen's face dropped, his appearance that of a little boy whose favorite toy had been taken away from him.

"Who is Dana Hardy?" I asked.

Agent Allen's voice held an odd air of defeat. "She's the assistant to Jeremy Schwartz." Agent Allen held up a hand to cut off the obvious next question. "And he is the assistant special agent in charge of the Las Vegas field office. My boss."

"So that was her on the phone?" Tara questioned.

"No." Agent Allen nodded his head. "That was ASAC Schwartz telling me to back the fuck off." He let loose an explosive, angry exhale as he sat on the couch.

"I understand you're frustrated," Raven calmly said.

"Do you?" Honest anger exploded from the FBI agent. "Do you really? I've been tracking this piece of shit for almost ten months, most of that time having to contend with the fact that I was just a consultant to a bunch of fucking Keystone Cops who couldn't find their own assholes with both hands in a room full of mirrors."

We all stood silent, listening to Agent Allen. He had been at this way too long. I could understand the frustration he felt, the hopelessness every time another body was found. An unspoken agreement to give the man time to vent kept our collective mouths shut.

"And then there's the missing evidence."

His statement brought me back to Tara, her attempts to find the missing pieces of the investigation. She was told by various police departments that they no longer had information on the case. I assumed all the evidence had been moved to FBI custody. I was wrong.

Agent Allen took in a long, calming breath. "I have felt like someone has been fighting me on this since day one, keeping this piece of shit hidden away from me."

Raven sat next to the frustrated man. She placed her hand on his shoulder, her face imbued with understanding.

"Someone has been hiding him," she said.

A resounding look of shock simultaneously appeared on everyone's face. I had considered the Office might have been responsible for the missing case files and evidence. Brianna had found nothing to support that notion, though it seemed they had a hacker who rivaled the capabilities of our own techno wiz.

"Who?" I asked.

Raven shook her head. "We don't know. And it's not the first time an investigation of ours has run across this kind of missing information. There is someone out there helping people like Caleb Voss from the shadows. Subtle enough to go unnoticed by the overall organizations and departments, devious enough to get individual investigators to drop their inquiries."

Agent Allen sighed, understanding.

"Look," Raven said to him, "I am trying to keep you alive here. You'll get your hero moment, and the work you've done has not been in vain."

"I don't care about being a hero."

"Too bad, 'cuz it's gonna happen," Raven said. "You, my dear agent, are about to be the public face of this operation."

Agent Allen raised an eyebrow. I pulled a cinnamon stick from my cigarette holder. Brianna took a seat in the chair she had pulled in front of her laptop. Tara and Stephanie sat on the short end of the L-shaped couch. From the outside we must've looked like a group of children settling down to listen to a tale. Raven took notice of this and chuckled.

"Jonathan," Raven began, "I need you in on this."

A look of alarm flashed across Tara's face. "No," she said. Her adamance took Raven by surprise. "I almost lost him with that Scott Boyd raid..." Her words trailed off, holding back that it was the second time she had almost lost me.

"I'll be fine," I said, putting my hand on her shoulder. I squatted down to eye level with my seated wife and pulled the cinnamon stick from my mouth. "I'm harder to kill than you give me credit for." I smirked at her worried face.

"I don't want you to do this."

I felt horrible defying her feelings. The last thing I wanted was for my wife to feel unimportant. Hell, I didn't really want to do this. I had zero interest in winding up in another room surrounded by butchered corpses or stuck in a hospital bed fighting for my life...or losing my life. But this was a matter of saving more than just one person.

317

"I don't particularly want to do this myself," I told her.

Tara let out a sigh. In her face I watched as she went through fear, worry, resistance, and finally acquiescence. She understood what doing nothing meant. She understood there was a reason I was being chosen for this. She reached out, cupping my face with both her hands. Her touch was gentle, hands cool. Smiling, she looked into my eyes and tightened her grip.

"If you die," Tara said through clenched teeth, "I will kill you."

I smirked, pulled her lips to mine. Pulling back, I looked into her eyes. Those beautiful blue oceans I could get lost in for days on end.

"I love you," I said. She smiled. We kissed one last time before remembering that there were other people in the room. The magic my wife commanded was her ability to make me feel like I'm the only person that exists. I could only hope I make her feel the same.

Standing, I turned back to Raven. All eyes had been on the display of worry and affection shared between Tara and me. I felt a momentary flush of embarrassment.

"Okay, so what's the plan?"

Chapter 26

Cold. Every inch of Doctor Jordan's body felt cold. Her mind was hazy, memories hard to access. Thoughts spun in fragments, a mass of mental disorder. But the cold. The cold was there. Solid, all encompassing. Her eyelids felt heavy, energy drained. Despite her waking consciousness, the doctor longed for sleep. But the cold. She tried to move, to find a blanket, a sweater, something to warm her. She couldn't move. Something was stopping her. Something was holding her in place.

"Holy shit," a voice came to her. It was familiar. She had heard the voice somewhere before. "Are you going to sleep all fucking day?"

A fog seemed to cover her memories. Every time she tried to remember, the cold interrupted. As her mind filtered through fragments, the cold became more distinct. Where were her clothes? Why couldn't she feel the fabric against her skin?

"WAKE UP!" the familiar voice yelled at her. Her eyelids were still too heavy, lead weights not wanting to budge.

An image came to her. A tire on her car. It looked like it had been slashed. She felt the cold again, but it was different. It was two distinct kinds of cold. She could feel cold metal at her mid-back pressing into her skin, a sharply defined X. The cold metal was also at the back of her forearms and a portion of her calves.

"JESUS FUCKING CHRIST!" The voice seemed to be echoing from all around her. "I DON'T HAVE ALL DAY!"

Driving. She remembered driving. Where was she going? Currents of cold air hit her skin, breaking the thought. Lolling her head, her eyelids felt lighter as she struggled to open them.

Home. She was heading home. The memory of hearing a *pop* from her car, the car becoming hard to steer.

"STOP IGNORING ME," the voice demanded, its agitation echoing.

A boy... No, a young man. He had hurt his arm, came to see her in the ER. Green eyes. She remembered green eyes and a distorted infinity birthmark. He wanted to talk about the power they shared. What was his name?

"Oh my god," the exasperated voice came again, this time with the sound of approaching footsteps.

A dark figure approaching her as she looked at the flat tire. Walking toward her. Did he try to help?

"Yo, Doc." The voice was close now. "You in there?"

Adriana felt a finger poke her forehead. It was an odd sensation, as though the poking finger was miles away from her. The image of the dark figure came into the light. The green-eyed young man stood before her. What was his name?

"I need you to wake up." The agitated voice held an underlying desperation. "I can't have you taking a coma break when I'm so close."

She had thought it strange her patient was at the side of the road with her. Had he followed her? His smile seemed warm and inviting. What was his name?

"Damnit, you stupid bitch." The voice had returned to anger. "WAKE THE FUCK UP ALREADY!"

The kindness of those green eyes had vanished in a flash. She couldn't breathe. He had stolen her breath. The young man moved quickly, injected her with something. What the hell was his name?

"Okay, I guess we're doing this the hard way." The voice seemed resigned to some unknown course of action.

Doctor Jordan's fragmented thoughts were interrupted by a hand forcefully making its way across her cheek. The crack of the slap seemed distant in her foggy state, but the pain brought alertness and clarity. Her eyes snapped open.

"Caleb," she exclaimed. The sting of the strike lingered on her cheek.

"That's my name," Caleb said, standing before her with his arms wide. "Took you long enough to wake up. I thought I might have given you too much."

Doctor Jordan shivered. Looking down confirmed her suspicion that she was completely bare. With an instinctual reaction to cover herself, she tried to move her arms. Feeling the restraints, the doctor's eyes fell upon her Velcro-bound wrists attached to steel beams. The hair on the back of her neck stood on end as she found her ankles in a similar bind. A chill ran down her spine. The good doctor could not tell if it was from fright or the cold metal on her skin…or both. Fear pushed aside the drug-induced haze that had clouded her mind.

"Wha— What do you want from me?" It was a question she wasn't sure she wanted to know the answer to. Binding a naked woman usually had only one purpose.

Reading her expression, Caleb let out an exasperated sigh.

"No," his tone exaggerated his words, "I'm not going to rape you. Why that's the first thing you all think of I will never understand."

Doctor Jordan's fear momentarily gave way to disbelief.

"Really?" Incredulity and confusion permeated her words. "I mean— Really? You really don't understand why a woman you drugged, stripped, and bound would have rape as their first thought?"

"Not really," Caleb stated, a total lack of comprehension reflected in his eyes. "I'm a god, therefore supplication is in order."

"A god?" The remnants of Doctor Jordan's fear evaporated at the insanity of his words. "You're fucking delusional. Who the hell fed you the idea that you were a god?"

"My master." Caleb spit the title out as though he had bitten down on cancer. "The Dark Man. Have you not met him? I would think he would have come to a Goddess such as yourself. He wants us all."

"Eh, no," Doctor Jordan said. "I don't know who this Dark Man is. He sounds like a comic book villain."

In defiance of her expectation, Caleb snorted a laugh and gave a slight nod. His expression had morphed into one of pure charismatic charm, his smile warm and eyes empathetic.

"Well, he hasn't told anyone his name." Caleb shrugged in a charming, paradoxical manner. "Calling him the Dark Man just seems to be…right."

Adriana's eyes darted around the room, taking in her surroundings as she spoke. She hoped the lunacy of Caleb Voss would prevent him from noticing, or prevent him from caring. About fifteen feet behind the crazy Boy, waist-high concrete appeared to denote the foundation of the building she was in, white corrugated sheet-metal provided the sunken room's walls. Two short staircases on either side of the room led to doors she presumed landed on the main floor. With only a few lights in operation, it appeared whatever was behind her dissolved into darkness.

321

"Please understand," he continued, his tone pleasant, almost soothing, "your sacrifice will not be in vain. You will serve to bring me to my full, perfect glory. A living god to rule over mankind. It is an honor of the highest order."

She couldn't tell if the warm, wide smile of appreciation he flashed her was genuine, or simply to keep her from screaming. Her heart pounded in her chest. She gently pulled at her Velcro bindings, testing them. They were lock-tight. A fear-filled convulsion ran through her.

Smiling and shaking his head, Caleb walked toward the back of the room, situated himself between the staircases, and turned to face her. "Those restraints are pretty solid," he said, leaning against the concrete portion of the wall. "Not as good as leather restraints. I mean, you can't really compare Velcro to a full-on stitched and riveted buckle system, but they're a hell of a lot cheaper and still get the job done."

Doctor Jordan felt a bead of sweat slide down her cheek. "What do you want from me?"

"Well," Caleb's voice echoed through the large room, "I need you to bring the Raven to me."

"And—" She took in a deep breath. "And how do I do that?"

"By dying."

A chill passed through Adriana Jordan's entire body, the feeling that someone was in the process of digging her grave. She didn't fully understand what was going on, but she did presume that the Raven must be the one she and all the other mark bearers were waiting for.

"Why do I have to die?"

"I was told that at the moment of your death she will know where you are. She will come here, and she will make me whole. She will make me perfect. She will make me a true god."

Doctor Jordan let slip a soft laugh.

"This is stupid," she said. "You think she'll help you if you kill me?"

"Oh, I'll be going to grab some insurance in a few minutes."

"Insurance?"

"Well, you're right about her likely not willing to help me with your corpse hanging there and all." His tone was as nonchalant as if he were discussing the weather. "But I think I can persuade her." He winked at Adriana, his charming smile still plastered in place.

"How are you—"

Flashing her a sneer of annoyance, Caleb chastised, "If you'd shut up and listen, I'm getting to that."

He took in a calming breath, putting his smile back on. Doctor Jordan noticed the smile had changed; it now looked like he was trying to be charming. Caleb's natural charisma was fading, his façade crumbling.

"The little bitch that sent me to you." Caleb's teeth were clenched as he spoke. "She'll be my insurance. Or it will be her sister." He shook his head. "I can't tell the two cunts apart."

He paused, hand moving to his chin in momentary contemplation.

"Or maybe she'll be the sacrifice and you can be the insurance." His smile widened. "How does that sound to you?"

"Who— Who sent you to me?"

"Some little fourteen-year-old that needs to be taught a lesson." Caleb sneered as the humiliation of his defeat flashed through his mind.

"You would kill a child?" Adriana's voice was steeped in disbelief and horror.

"The bitch is gonna die anyway. Don't you want to live?"

It occurred to Doctor Jordan that she knew nothing of what this Boy could do. She did know he could cut off her air supply. She remembered that much. What else was he capable of? She needed to know. If nothing else, maybe she could get this Raven person here before he could grab another victim. She was a doctor. She had made it her mission in life to help the injured and sick. If her life was the price to stop this creature, the price to save a child, she would gladly pay it.

Adriana took in a deep breath, let out a cleansing exhale. She could feel the mental fracture forming, a crack in her sanity just large enough to let go of her own survival instincts. She accepted whatever her fate may be.

"You're pathetic," Doctor Jordan blurted out.

Caleb furrowed his brow. Her words erased his unsteady smile. The corner of the Boy's lip convulsed in rapidfire sneers.

"Shut your—"

323

"Are you fucking insane? I mean, seriously, you're trash." Adriana infused her words with as much vitriol as she could muster. "I bet the only reason you don't rape me is 'cuz you can't get it up."

Caleb let loose a low growl. "I said shut—"

"Oh, that's it, isn't it?" Doctor Jordan let a cruel laugh slip. "Or is your junk just as deformed as that birthmark—"

Blood exploded from her shoulder, a deep cut slicing to the bone. Caleb stood, finger pointed at her, his face contorted in rage. A wave of pain overtook her. Adriana's jaw clenched as she let out a hissing exhale. She could feel the activation of her birthright, a strange sense that her mind had shifted, her birthmark crawling on her skin. So long as Caleb didn't hit anything that would cause instant death, she knew he could cut her over and over again. She would simply heal. She could keep him there for days.

Sadistic glee shone in Caleb's eyes as he watched Doctor Jordan's pupils form the vertical slits that denoted her heritage. A sick smile formed on his lips. It felt good to inflict pain. It felt good to prove his superiority. He was a god, and even Goddesses needed to be taught a lesson for disrespecting him. Goddesses needed to know their place.

"Physician," he hissed, "heal thyself."

Doctor Jordan matched his sadistic smile with a smile of defiance. The wound in her shoulder quickly stitched itself together. In a matter of seconds, a trail of blood was the only evidence left that she had sustained any injury. Caleb let out an echoing laugh.

"Oh," he said, "this is gonna be fun."

Raven stood between the light. Photons that glided across her skin tingled, demanding attention she would not give them. Her mind was focused elsewhere.

She examined the two-story, white office building from across the street. A single, silver SUV was parked in the small lot at the front of the building. Thanks to Agent Allen, traffic had been shut down for three blocks in every direction. The post office on the north side of the enemy's lair had been evacuated. What looked like a mass of shrubs, weeds, and trees stood to the south. Brianna had shut down every traffic-monitoring camera and online camera in the area, which only left CCTV and people with cell phones looking out their windows to be concerned about. All said and done, Raven could not take Caleb Voss down out on the streets, but she did need him to come out of the building.

The plan was simple. Get the Abomination outside and distracted long enough for Jonathan to slip in and rescue Adriana. Once Caleb was forced back into the building, Raven could take him down. Simple plans are the best. Not because they work, but because when the plan inevitably doesn't go as expected, changes are easier to make.

Raven had to run under a single assumption: Caleb needed a living hostage to get what he wanted. The message delivered through Sonja Verztuk's animated corpse indicated as much. Anubis stated he had told Caleb that Raven could only find him upon the death of the Waiting. It seemed like a good idea at the time. If he were running under such an assumption, if he wanted to force her to fully activate him, he needed a bargaining chip. And he wouldn't be able to kill the doctor until he had that second hostage. At least, she hoped he wouldn't. Insanity isn't prone to rational thinking.

She could feel a desperate, intense urgency flowing through the psychic tether connecting her to Doctor Jordan. A preternatural scream that could not be ignored. Whatever was happening within that building had put her charge in severe distress. This wasn't the simple "I need you, bad things are happening" urgency she had felt from Rachel Hawkins a few days ago. This was active pain. Active terror. And it had been going on for almost half an hour. The strength of the connection tore through Raven's mind. And then it stopped.

The sudden silence shot adrenaline through Raven's body. A shudder of fear gripped her. Calming herself, letting the echoes of Doctor Jordan's terror purge from her mind, she felt the connection was still there. Adriana Jordan was still alive. Raven breathed a tentative sigh of relief. She waited.

A city street deprived of traffic has a texture to the quiet. Only the sound of a light wind flowed through the streets, rustling trees, and shrubs. Warm humidity and the slight scent of wet desert within spoke

325

of the impending storm sailing through the skies. The silence was broken by the squeak of metal rattling through the deserted street.

Raven watched as one of the white steel doors opened slowly. Dirty blond hair was the first thing to poke from behind the armored hatch, followed by the rest of Caleb Voss' head. She felt as though she were watching an episode of *Scooby-Doo* as he peered around with an exaggerated—and highly suspicious—attempt to make sure the coast was clear. Confident he was alone, the Boy quickly made his way to the SUV. With mechanical efficiency, he climbed into the driver's seat and started the engine. As he pulled the vehicle onto the empty roadway, Raven inserted earplugs she retrieved from her pocket.

A sonic boom enveloped the street. In a state of adrenaline-fueled slow motion, Raven watched the windows of Caleb's SUV explode. The front end of his vehicle broke apart as if it had been hit by an invisible truck. Lurching on two wheels, the SUV spun a full 360 degrees and came to a jarring halt. The remnants of the engine spewed smoke, oil, coolant, and gasoline. The mutilated driver's door wrenched open, and a dazed Caleb Voss stumbled out. Weaving like a drunk man, the Boy took a few steps away from his car. He swayed, turning his head toward the car.

"What the fuck was that?"

Another sonic boom sounded. Caleb fell to his knees, hands covering his ears. Raven saw a metallic flash and the SUV was explosively lifted into the air, spun on its horizontal axis three times before crashing to the ground upside down. Its roof caved on impact. Terror occupied Caleb's face. Fear of the unknown was written upon his youthful countenance. Past the scared killer, Raven watched as a black-clad figure made a stealthy entrance into the office building. Somehow Jonathan managed to prevent the doors from shrieking as they opened.

Stepping from the mini forest on the south end of the office building, what appeared to be a sparking blur walked to the middle of the street. The silhouette of a bulky figure was visible through the shimmering air.

"What do you want?" Caleb screamed at the figure. "Who are you?"

The blurred figure came into sharp focus as six two-inch metallic balls slowed their revolutions around her. A very angry Tippy Sorson glared death at the frightened psychopath. Clad in oversized jeans and a baggy blue t-shirt, normally she was a happy girl who looked unassuming and harmless. Caleb recognized the woman. He remembered her as a simple-minded, mentally deficient creature he had watched through a window. Though he had recognized her combat capacity, the prospect that she could be a lethal force, he had written this off. He did not believe she had the intellect for such action.

Her smooth brow was now furrowed. Vertical pupils situated in her heavy-lidded eyes were locked on Caleb. Tippy's mouth twitched. Happiness and joy were her default emotions. Anger was something she could not sustain for long. But the sight of this man, knowing what he had done to her sisters in waiting, this fueled a fire she had trouble controlling. A sneer of loathing defaced her countenance.

"You need to be gone," she said. "You need to be no more."

Caleb gritted his teeth. This thing was an abomination in his eyes. No Goddess could ever be from such poor genetic stock. Regaining his sense of balance, the loathsome Boy stood.

"You need to die, you fucking retard." Vehemence, the need for retaliation, infused his every word.

Tippy's expression darkened. She'd had run-ins with those who were verbally abusive toward her. Normally she would simply turn her back on them, though some occasions were so bad that she wound up crying in her mom's arms. She would cycle out the bad emotions and return to her happy self, not allowing those who looked down on her any place in her mind. But this time... This one... This thing that had hurt and killed. Raven had given her blessing to teach this one a lesson.

Another sonic boom exploded in the street as the six metallic balls lazily revolving around Tippy suddenly accelerated, exceeding the speed of sound. Her form blurred once again. Concussive force shoved Caleb back into the overturned remains of his SUV, his hands once again going to his ears.

Pulling his hands down, he saw a crimson smear on his left palm. Touching his left ear, he found a trickle of blood. The sonic blast had ruptured his ear drum. Caleb's face contorted, rage screaming from every cell in his body.

"You fucking bitch!" He swiped his arm, sending a blade of air to cut the blurred girl into pieces. He failed.

A low crack sounded as Tippy's shield of whirling metal increased in speed. Gale-force wind surrounded her, a tempest adding to her protection. Protection that Caleb's invisible blade could not penetrate. He let out a guttural, growling scream. A different tactic came to him. He could surely still deprive her of breath. A smile of dark intent took possession of the Boy's face.

Raising his hand toward his target, he uttered a single word: "Die."

A shot of pain radiated through him. Caleb's hand went limp, bones pulverized and hanging uselessly from his forearm. He hadn't seen what hit him. Taking a step back, his body shuddered from the pain. He felt this entire fight was unfair. He was a god. He should be able to overpower some mentally challenged twit without any issue. If only he was perfect. The thought of his perfection granted a moment of realization. She was here. She had to be here.

"Where is she?" he screamed at the blurred, whirling dervish. "Where is the Raven?"

Tippy took a step toward him, no answer forthcoming. She couldn't understand why he hadn't run away. She would have. She thought he might need... Oh, what did Raven call it? More motivation.

He caught sight of a reflective flash. One of Tippy's metal balls slammed into his right shoulder. He felt the joint dislocate, adding to the pain from his flopping, unusable hand. A moment of awe grabbed him as he comprehended the level of control Tippy had over her weapon of choice. She could have easily taken his entire arm off.

Caleb was certain the Raven was here, and his hostage was still alive. He backed toward the building. His legs shook from the pain that tore through his body with each step. He refused to be taken down by such a trivial thing when his ascension to perfection was at hand. The blurred figure stood in place. He could see the silhouette of her head tracking him as he put distance between them. If he turned around, would she send one of her death orbs to take his head off? He had to chance it. Wincing as he held his right arm, Caleb turned and ran back into the office building.

Standing in the road, Tippy brought the speed of her metal spheres down to that of a lazy river. With a meditative gait, the six balls made three winding helixes around her body before coming to a stop a foot away from her chest. One by one the balls formed a line before her. Tippy reached out, taking hold of each metal ball, reverently placing them into the pockets of her baggy jeans.

"Well done." Raven's voice seemed to come from nowhere.

Tippy felt a gentle hand on her shoulder. She turned her head to see Raven materializing as though reality were a curtain being drawn back to reveal the green-eyed Caretaker behind it. Flashing her a smile, Raven gave Tippy a light kiss on her temple. The young woman beamed.

"Thank you," Raven said. "Go wait with Agent Allen and the others. This won't take long."

"Okay," Tippy said cheerfully. Her tone turned serious for a moment. "Be careful. He's dangerous."

Raven smiled, nodded. "I will. Don't you worry."

"He's also a fucking asshole," Tippy muttered as she turned toward the staging area down the street.

Eyes wide, Raven stood watching Tippy in disbelief. She had never heard her long-time friend use such language. One thing she knew, however: If Tippy Sorson thought you were an asshole, then you are indeed an asshole. Chuckling to herself, Raven turned toward the building.

Letting out a sigh, she said, "I hope you and Adriana have gotten out of there, Jonathan." Walking toward the white steel door, Raven cloaked herself inside the light, disappearing from sight.

Chapter 27

In 1789, Benjamin Franklin wrote, "Nothing is certain except death and taxes." I'm certain the man had never tried to enact a plan, because I can say with absolute certainty that no plan ever goes according to plan. Our plan was simple. Get Caleb Voss to come outside, I slip in behind him, grab the girl, and Raven takes the douchebag down. Easy-peezy.

We made the educated guess that Voss would need a second hostage. According to Raven, this "ghost" of her ancestor calling itself Anubis—I was both amused and unnerved that he would own the name of the ancient Egyptian God of Death—had taken over the corpse of Sonja Verztuk. Through her he had told Caleb Voss it was the moment of death that drew Raven. It was, in my humble opinion, a poorly thought-out scare tactic. I was confident that our killer knew Raven would not simply help him if he asked nicely. At least, not after the number of people he had killed. So he would need a living hostage to convince her. Pretty basic psychology here.

We decided that waiting for him to come out was our best option. The boyish-looking young man made his appearance as expected, and the diversion was on. I was momentarily captivated by Raven's friend Tippy. Her ability to raise an SUV off the ground and spin it using a two-inch meditation ball was, in a word, mind-blowing. As soon as the car hit the ground, I slipped into the empty office building. A symphony of destruction drowned out the screech of the building's door, a noise that no amount of cautious movement could entirely silence.

Brianna had provided schematics for the building. I knew the first floor held a warehouse space at its center, one doorway situated off the main hallway to the right of the building's lobby. The other door required one to go down the hallway to the left, turning the corner at the end. Our killer seemed to be obsessed with warehouses and storage spaces. Through an industrial office rental website, we were able to see what the space looked like. The first thing I had noticed was the X crossbeam support in the storage space. This place came with its own crucifix.

I quietly made my way to the warehouse entrance to my right and slipped inside. Cold air hit me the moment I entered. It was the kind of chill one would expect from a refrigerated room. A few stairs landed me on the sunken concrete floor. The sight before me stole my breath. Illuminating the front half of the room, an old bank of shop lights flickered intermittently. Receding darkness granted the storage space an appearance of infinite depth and the foreboding impression of staring into the abyss. As if she stood sentry to this gateway into hell, a bound woman hung from the steel crucifix situated between two square columns.

Doctor Adriana Jordan's naked body hung limp, held up by black wrist restraints attached to the steel beams. Her legs were held apart by similar restraints wrapped around her ankles. Despite the cold, beads of sweat slid down my forehead. My heart pounded, the sound of rushing blood filled my ears as I slowly moved toward her. I feared I was too late. Crimson covered almost every inch of her body. A wash of red that made the immortal image of the blood-covered prom queen in the movie *Carrie* seem like the result of a paper cut. Spatter and pools of coagulating blood surrounded her still body. I could not fathom how anyone could survive this level of blood loss. In the flickering low light, I could not tell if she was breathing.

Placing my fingers on Doctor Jordan's neck, I searched for a pulse. To my surprise and relief, her heartbeat was strong and steady. I sucked in a deep breath. Taking a moment, I was able to see a small rise and fall in her chest. I patted her lightly on the cheek, trying to rouse my intended target of rescue.

"Doctor Jordan." I kept my voice low. "Doctor Jordan, wake up. It's time to go."

Anxiety gripped me, my chest tightened. The adrenaline coursing through my system amplified the sense of urgency I felt. Caleb Voss was being pushed to come back here. We needed to vacate before his arrival. Doctor Jordan's head lolled from side to side, she let out a pained moan.

"I for—" she said weakly. "I forgot— I forgot pain."

I felt confused. *Pain?*

"What about pain?" I asked.

The doctor raised her head, her brown eyes seemed to look through me. "I couldn't stop the pain."

This was a matter to be discussed in a safer environment. We needed to get out. We needed to get out now. I placed my hand gingerly on her cheek.

"Doctor," I said firmly, "I need you to focus. I'm going to get you out of here, but I need you to focus."

Without warning, Adriana snapped her head away from me, fear splayed across her face. Taking a deep breath, she stifled a scream. Eyes instantly alert and focused, she recognized that I was not her torturer.

"Who— Who are you?"

"I'm the guy getting you out of here."

Doctor Jordan nodded. Shakily she said, "Get my wrists. I'll get my legs."

I had the impression that, even in this desperate situation, her nudity was on her mind. Where I stood, I couldn't see much beyond her head. I readily agreed. Quickly, I reached up and pulled one of her wrist restraints open. The zip of the Velcro was loud enough to echo through the large room. Undoing the second restraint, I backed up and turned my head to give her some modicum of privacy as she bent over to free her legs. I handed her my coat.

The sound of a door slamming blasted through the warehouse. Doctor Jordan gasped, her eyes wide with fear. I turned to see the medium-sized killer gripping his right arm, his boyish features contorted in pain. Clearly Tippy had done a number on this guy. His shoulder was obviously dislocated, and his right hand flopped about as if all the bones had been removed.

"WHO THE FUCK ARE YOU?"

I looked at Caleb Voss, cocking my head sideways. In one fluid motion I pulled my knives from their homes under my arms. I felt the mental flex that heralded the unseen armor I had been gifted, or possibly cursed with. I just hoped that I would be able to stave off an attack from this creature long enough for Raven to, once again, save my ass.

"I'm the guy who's taking this nice lady and leaving with her." As I spoke, the gemstones embedded in the knife blades illuminated.

Caleb sneered, cocked an eyebrow. "Are you a god?"

I paused. The question struck me as oddly familiar.

"No," I answered. Bringing my knives up in front of me, I crossed the blades to create a focal point for my energy.

"Then," Caleb said as he swung his left arm toward me, "die!"

My body shuddered. I felt the unseen force strike my invisible shield with a booming crack. For a moment I had thought my abilities were up to the task of defending both myself and Doctor Jordan against Caleb Voss' lethal air. Then the pain hit. Gritting my teeth, I saw deep slices on both my hands. I had been partially successful. I was still breathing, and my fingers were still attached. But the unseen barrier was not strong enough to prevent me from getting cut. This did not bode well.

Doctor Jordan laid her hand on my back. I felt a strange sense of warmth, felt the wounds on my hands close.

"If someone asks if you are a god," she whispered, "you say yes."

The realization hit me. "Ah, *Ghostbusters*," I blurted out. "I'm gonna have to watch that when I get back to the hotel. Great movie."

Caleb stared at me as though I had just grown a second head and it was spouting gibberish.

"I take it you've never seen it," I said to the momentarily stunned killer.

Caleb's face flushed. A loud growl accompanied another swing of his left arm. Another booming crack as his blade of air struck my shield. I heard a short, pained cry. It took me a moment to realize that I had made the sound. It felt as though the scar on my abdomen had ruptured. White hot fire burned my nerves, my knees shook.

The warm sensation returned. The pain abated. I was momentarily back in the killing room with that strange cloaked figure healing what should have been a fatal wound. Though Doctor Jordan's healing took less than a second, my mental slip into the past felt like an eternity. I let out a controlled exhale.

"I take it you're not an Ivan Reitman fan?" I gave the enraged killer a sarcastic smile. His rage faltered.

"Are you not taking this seriously?" His tone sounded genuinely confused.

"Is there a reason I should?" I had no way out of this. With my shield and a healer at my back, our best chance was to get this lunatic to screw up. Normally sweet-talking narcissists—and Caleb Voss was most definitely a narcissist—would be the path that could grant an opportunity to strike or escape. In this case, complimenting the Boy wasn't going to get us anywhere. Enraging him into making a mistake was the next best thing.

Caleb's eyes darkened. "Do not mock me."

"Why not?"

A low growl came from the young man.

"All I want," he said, his words slow and controlled, "is to have the Raven make me perfect. Where is she? Where is the Raven?"

I could see his control was tenuous, close to its breaking point. His body shook, though I was not sure if it was from the pain of his injured arm or the effort to maintain some semblance of composure. Probably both. From the corner of my eye, I saw the door to the room slowly and silently opening. I saw no one, but I knew she was there.

"She's—" I stopped. A quick mental analysis of his verbiage made my skin crawl.

Years ago, I had dated a woman who always inserted a V into the word "Colorado." She would say "Colverado," I would repeat the word as "Colorado." She never figured it out, and I never directly called her on it. Just seemed impolite. But it irked me. I'd be lying if I said that her mispronunciation didn't factor into our break-up. And now I'm faced with a megalomaniacal killer with nomenclature issues. The universe hates me.

"I— I'm sorry," I said, incredulity dripping off every word. "Did you just call her THE Raven? Like it's a title?" My knife-filled hands began gesturing erratically as my annoyance grew. "What, you think she's THE fucking Raven of York or some shit?"

There was something cathartic about letting loose. This pet peeve of mine had been tested time and time again. People adding letters to words and names, and my own sense of decency not allowing me to outright correct them on it. I finally had an outlet, and Caleb Voss was getting the pent-up aggravation from a lifetime of dealing with stupid people. The young psychopath stood frozen, a dumbfounded expression on his face.

"Are you stupid? It's a name. Raven. Just Raven." Out of the corner of my eye, I watched the door slowly close. "There's no 'The' included."

Caleb's slack-jawed expression twisted into hate. He bared his teeth like an enraged dog.

"I have spent my whole life dealing with imbecilic, smooth-brained, self-assured fap-masters like you." Sliding my knives back into their sheaths, I threw my arms up. "I can't take it anymore. Your sorry-ass attempt to get perfection, something you're never gonna get by the way, is the quest of a moron! Bacteria has more common sense than you! If you think you can take me down, then have at it! Take your best fucking shot, Quasimodo!"

Caleb raised his left arm above his head. I had chosen to take a calculated risk. Along with the sheathing of my knives, I had also released the mental flex that provided some modicum of protection against this creature. Was it stupid? Yeah. Yeah, it was. But sometimes one needs to trust in the luck of fools. And have faith in their friends.

"How dare you—"

"You want to know where Raven is, Elephant Man?"

Caleb's arm began to come down. It jerked to a stop before he could complete the action. His eyes went wide, fear reflected within them. He could not move.

"I'm right behind you." Raven's words slid through the air over Caleb's shoulder.

The sight has been burned into my mind. Not from the horror of it, but from the awe. It looked as though the very fabric of reality tore open, giving birth to Raven's form. She held the loathsome monster by his neck, her face the portrait of vengeance. A gothic avenging angel. Caleb's lips quivered, and the paralysis he experienced did not stop his bladder from emptying itself. The front of his khaki pants darkened with urine.

"I told you I would find you," Raven said. "I told you that you would suffer." A frightening calmness infused her words. "I told you that you would scream."

Caleb whimpered. In that moment he struck me as a frightened little boy, eyes pleading for mercy and forgiveness. Had a blood-covered

335

woman not stood right behind me, I might have felt some sympathy toward him. I heard the faint sound of sirens from beyond the warehouse walls.

"Shall we begin?" Raven's eyes became luminescent, the green of her irises brightened.

The shriek Caleb let loose was deafening. In the enclosed space, his scream ricocheted off the corrugated steel walls. His entire body shook and jerked like the ghosts depicted in Japanese horror films. Staccato movements that defied physiology. His eyes rolled back into his head as it wrenched upward. Screaming morphed into a strangled gurgling. Then silence. Caleb Voss collapsed, hitting the floor with a quiet thud.

I wanted to ask if he was dead but knew the sheer stupidity of the question. Killing him was never an option, and it would have been letting the Boy off way too easy. Raven had a plan for him. I had chosen to remain ignorant of it. Doctor Jordan moved to my side. She had tied the belt-strap of my trench coat to wear the garment like a bathrobe. I momentarily thought how much of a pain it was going to be to clean all the blood out from the inside of the coat.

Adriana looked at the unconscious Caleb, a mixture of hate and horror on her face. Looking to Raven, a question formed on the doctor's face.

"No," Raven answered the unasked query, "the change doesn't normally feel like that." She smirked at Doctor Jordan. "Gotta be honest though. I put him through the same pain as bad period cramps. Dude's a lightweight."

Adriana Jordan let out a snorting chuckle. I raised an eyebrow.

"What?" Raven said innocuously. "I might only be half human, but I'm still a woman."

That part of her physiology never entered my mind, nor was it something I had any interest in exploring.

"They're almost here," I said. The faint sound of slamming car doors penetrated the walls. "You need to go."

Raven nodded, grabbed Caleb's waistband, and tossed the young man over her shoulder like he was a sack of potatoes. "Wanna see something cool?" she asked.

Doctor Jordan and I nodded in unison. Raven disappeared from sight. It was as though she had blinked out of existence. There one minute, gone the next. The only clue that she was still in the room with us was the unconscious body that appeared to hang in the air.

"I never get to show off." Raven's words came from everywhere and nowhere.

"That's great," I said, hearing movement in the lobby of the building just outside the door. "Now go."

The floating body of Caleb Voss joined Raven in her invisibility just as the doors to the warehouse burst open. Clad in their ubiquitous blue windbreakers, FBI agents with their guns drawn rushed into the room. Agent Allen strolled in behind the breach team, his face the portrait of disappointment. Looking at Doctor Jordan and me, he motioned for us to follow him. Adriana Jordan let out a sigh of relief. It was over.

Emergency vehicles covered the street in front of Caleb's final kill room. Black Escalades, police cruisers, and fire trucks created a wall between us and a line of television reporters. Walking into the sunlight, my vision took a moment to adjust. Almost instantly, EMTs whisked Doctor Jordan toward two waiting ambulances. A paramedic approached me and insisted I get checked out. I vehemently declined.

I felt like I had walked into the middle of an ant hive. Uniformed people moved with purpose. Orders were shouted in sporadic intervals. Radio chatter assaulted my ears from all directions. I was tired, I just wanted to crawl into bed and sleep for a week.

Three people dressed in paramedic uniforms walked by me, one pushing a sheet-covered gurney. I knew these were specially selected agents from the FBI Las Vegas field office. What body, if any, was under that sheet, I did not know. I tracked them as they moved toward the coroner's van. I was surprised to see Mai leaning against the vehicle, arms crossed and a satisfied smile plastered on her face. A hand smacked my shoulder, causing my heart rate to spike.

Agent Allen stood next to me, flashing a rare smile. Behind his eyes I could see the still-smoldering desire to have been able to put Caleb

Voss in handcuffs and perp-walk our killer before the ocean of television reporters clamoring just out of sight. He regarded me with a shake of his head.

"I can't tell if you're brave, stupid, or insane," he stated.

"A bit of each, I suppose." A grin formed on my face. I had wondered the same thing before this whole operation started. "Though my wife would probably lean more toward stupid."

"You're damn right," Tara's voice split the air as she trapped me in a bear-hug. I was fairly certain she cracked one of my ribs. She looked up at me, her eyes blazing relief, worry, and a hint of anger. "You are not doing that again."

Oh, how I hoped she was right.

A booming laugh exploded from the giant FBI agent at my side.

"You two go get some rest, I have to talk to the vultures." Agent Allen gave a final nod and moved toward the chattering sound of journalists shouting questions at anyone who passed by them.

Looking at Tara, I put my hand on her cheek. "I told you I'd be fine." Pulling her lips to mine, I kissed her with all the strength I had left. She tightened her grip around me. I let out a pained groan. Yeah, she definitely cracked one of my ribs. Letting go, she took a step back, an apology crossing her face.

"I think you're going to need to get this cleaned." Stephanie's voice weaved its way through the air. She held my coat. "The good doctor wanted me to give you her thanks and gratitude, and apparently you now have free healthcare for the rest of your life."

I chuckled, hoping that the mental trauma Doctor Jordan had suffered would be something she could come to live with. Healing the body was one thing. Healing the mind is an entirely different animal. And while it could have been worse, it was bad enough. Taking the coat, Tara, Stephanie, and I made our way toward my car.

"Mister Hayes." Mai's voice said my name as if she were stating the answer to a question. We all stopped to look at her. She held a white envelope out to me. "From Raven."

I took the envelope. It contained a short note, starting with a single phrase of absolute truth: "We are all in this together."

Chapter 28

Caleb sat cross-legged in the bloody marsh, head in his hands. The stench of rot he had once enjoyed now filled him with dread. He had become the embodiment of despair. The epitome of self-loathing. His chest felt tight, anxiety wrenching his muscles into a fear-filled knot. The air felt thick and sticky, a humid mass that mercilessly pressed down on him. Tears fell freely from his green eyes. Sobs wracked his body.

Unfair.

This was so unfair.

"What's the matter, son?" The voice was a calm, soothing baritone. Caleb recognized his father's temper and cadence.

Looking up, he saw the man. Henry Voss was tall with a medium build, dressed in his signature white crochet sweater. A full head of white hair topped the man's kindly features. He squatted before his son.

"Hey, kiddo," Henry said. "Chin up. It can't be all that bad."

Caleb straightened, felt the blood-soaked mud he sat in slide and squish as he moved.

"I failed," the Boy croaked. "I'll never be perfect. I'll never be what I am supposed to be."

Henry shook his head, giving Caleb a comforting smile. "That is true." His voice was smooth. "But you were never going to succeed. You've always been a failure."

Dumbfounded, Caleb stared at his father. The man tilted his head slightly to the side, the warm smile plastered in place.

Something clawed at Caleb's mind. Something that he had forgotten. What was it? When was it? Fragmented memory teased him, dangling answers just out of reach. His father was frozen, staring at him with that warm, loving smile. Henry took a deep breath and stood.

"You really are a stupid little shit, aren't you?" Despite the words, Henry's voice continued to have a calm, almost loving tone. "You couldn't even take down one middle-aged, shit-talking PI. Pathetic."

"It's not my fault," Caleb sobbed. "If she just made me perfect—"

"Come now, kiddo." A roughness entered Henry's voice. "You know Raven never had the power to make you perfect."

A bead of black liquid emerged from Henry Voss' eye. The viscous sick slowly wound its way down his cheek. Caleb stared at the foreign substance, a horrific realization emerging from within him.

"Nothing about you is worthy of perfection." Henry's voice grew rougher, like gravel in a dying blender. "She has taken it all from you. The only thing left for you to do is die. At least you can be of use to me that way."

A moment of memory invaded Caleb's mind. His father had been sitting in the living room of their San Diego home. Situated on the cream-colored couch, the old man was reading a novel. Caleb quietly stood at the doorway of the living room. He needed to test his accuracy, he needed to prove his loyalty to the one he thought was a messenger from God.

The Boy had already killed more animals than he could count. Birds, cats, dogs, squirrels, even a couple raccoons were among his early victims. The process had been emotionally eviscerating for him. He loved animals. But just as Abraham was willing to kill his own son at the behest of the Most High, Caleb had to prove his loyalty, his faith, by killing that which was sacred to him. And then it came time to graduate, to grow, in preparation for his perfection. To prepare for his ascension to godhood. A deft flick of his wrist and blood exploded from the side of his father's neck. The man bled out in less than a minute without making a sound.

With tears streaming down his face, Caleb looked at his hands. The appendages were stained in blood. Bits of brown-crimson mud slipped off his fingers as he flexed them, quiet splatters as they hit the boggy ground.

"God," his voice barely a whisper, "what have I done?"

The countenance of Henry Voss scrunched in confusion, pressure from the muscle contractions pushing more of the thick black liquid from the man's eyes. He appeared to be crying mascara. Caleb's eyes widened at the sight. A flush of fear pulsed through him.

"What do you mean? You did exactly as I asked. You proved your loyalty."

The fake Henry smiled wide, baring his teeth. Yellowed with swaths of black rot, they looked like the teeth of a meth addict. Viscous black ichor drooled from the dead man's mouth. Caleb shook violently as a wave of remorse washed over him.

"I'm sorry, Dad," he whispered.

The faux-Henry appeared surprised.

"Is that regret I hear?" The face of Henry Voss was almost entirely covered in wet, black slime. "Is that weakness? What happened to my little god?"

Caleb sneered at the figure before him.

"You're not my father. You're the Dark Man." Hate filled his voice.

Faux-Henry cut a predatory grin at the Boy. A chill ran down Caleb's spine. A momentary, undefinable fear. Then he remembered. Caleb Voss remembered the promises this thing had made.

"I WAS SUPPOSED TO BE PERFECT!" Rage exploded from Caleb, the moment of guilt and fear replaced by self-pity and hatred. "You lied to me. You told me I could be a god, you told me she would make me perfect. You told me—" His voice croaked in a sob.

"I tell many people many things," the Dark Man said. "Sometimes they even get the things promised to them...though, not in the way they thought they would."

With a widening smile, the faux-Henry's body swelled. His sweater tore open as his abdomen split, spewing noxious gas and black sludge. His wet, blackened façade bloated, skin stretching taut, eyes bulging from their sockets. The slime-covered face ruptured, sliding off in ragged pieces to expose rancid, maggot-infested muscle beneath. As the decaying, wet flesh disintegrated, fake Henry's head fell backward, hanging for a moment by the remnants of his spinal cord. It fell into the swamp with a loud, grotesque *splat*.

Caleb watched, shaking. A part of him was disturbed by this horror, another part fascinated, and the last part angered. As the remaining pieces of Henry Voss were devoured by the swamp, the Boy turned his eyes to the figure standing atop his kingdom of corpses.

"You wanted perfection." The voice came from all around Caleb.

"Yes." Caleb's voice was low, meek, as the booming bass of the Dark Man's words penetrated him.

341

"I can make you perfect."

A flash of anger ripped through Caleb's eyes. "Why should I believe you?"

"Oh," a deep chuckle resounded through the bog of death, "it's not the perfection you want."

A dubious scowl crossed Caleb's face.

"Let me put it this way," the ubiquitous voice said. "You don't have a choice. You are mine, and you will do what I say. I will make you perfect... A perfect killing machine."

"Fuck you."

A wave of pressure bared down on Caleb, sending his face into the bloody mud.

"You have no choice."

A freight train of adrenaline hit Caleb, his breath strangled by the fear taking hold of him.

"What do you want me to do?" he whispered, acquiescing to a power he could not fight.

"Die."

Darkness.

All he could see was darkness.

Caleb would have thought himself asleep had he not felt the opening and closing of his eyelids. Sitting up, he moved his hand along the floor. Cold, rough metal covered in a layer of gritty dust. He rose to his hands and knees, feeling for anything in front of him.

"HELLO?" His words ricocheted off unseen walls, amplified into an aural blast that stung his ears.

He continued in one direction, hoping to find the wall that had yelled back at him. Hands outstretched in the darkness, he shuffled for about ten feet. A shudder ran through him as his fingers made painful contact with a smooth metal wall. He hissed out a breath. His fingertips followed a weld line where the floor and wall met. His hands found large rivets spaced six inches apart sitting a foot above the ground. He banged once on the wall, a metallic boom assaulting his ears. Turning himself around, he rested against the unseen wall.

"It's not fair." His voice echoed quietly in the darkness. He could feel tears welling in his eyes, the tightness of sorrow in his chest. "I was supposed to be perfect. I was supposed to be God."

Pulling his knees to his chest, Caleb wrapped his arms around his legs, rocking himself back and forth. Tears came freely as his body was wracked with wave after wave of self-pitying sobs. He missed his home. He missed the comfort and stability. He missed the carefree life of the child he had been before that power had come to him. Before He had come to him.

"Mommy." The word came out in a strangled sob. He could not recall his mother as she had been in life, only the memory of his last look at her remained with him. Pieces of sliced meat tossed into a shallow grave. His body convulsed.

Trying to regain some sense of composure, Caleb struck the metal ground as hard as he could with his right hand. Along with the loud metal boom, a vibrating shockwave traveled up his arm. Pain hit him. He realized his dislocated shoulder and pulverized hand had been healed. Working the fingers, a painful crunching indicated he had just fractured something in that hand. Hissing through his teeth, Caleb froze.

A sound. He was sure he heard a sound. A distant knocking from the other side of the darkness. Using his left hand, Caleb knocked on the wall. Hope filled him when a knock came back in response, this time closer. Again, he knocked on the wall. A voice responded this time. It sounded like the person was right on the other side of the metal barrier.

"Get back," the muffled voice said. "We're going to cut you out."

We? Who is we? Did someone call the fire department to help him? Did the Raven— Did Raven put him in this place just to teach him a lesson? He had no idea how long he'd been in this abyss. Was his time served?

Having shuffled back diagonally from the voice, Caleb peered into the overwhelming darkness. He felt a rush of adrenaline upon hearing the muffled sound of an angle-grinder starting up. Joy enveloped the Boy at the prospect of release from this blind hell. His joy was cut short by the painful, reverberating shriek of metal being cut. Bright orange sparks shot into the darkness, their light dimly illuminating a small portion of the wall, unable to penetrate further into the darkness.

The room acted as an oversized amplifier for the high-pitched grinding. Caleb's hands did little to muffle the banshee shriek threatening to deafen him. The work was slow, with his rescuers taking periodic breaks. A small diagonal slice was made from the top corner of the rescue hole in progress. A thick, triangular wedge of metal fell into the dark prison. A reverberating clang echoed through the darkness.

With the outside world exposed, Caleb thought he would see a beam of light come through the opening, an indication that the sun would shine on him once again. Only a dim illumination came, along with an olfactory explosion. The unmistakable scent of wet desert engulfed the room. He leaned to look through the small opening. From his angle all he could see was deep grey clouds illuminated by distant city lights.

A flash. A bang. Lightning tore through the sky. Booming thunder rocked his metal prison. The top of a black helmet crossed the hole, a bright LED light mounted to the top.

"Just be patient," the helmet said. "We are going to get you out of there. Get back."

Anticipation warped time for him, each second became an eternity. The dangerous sparks of molten metal were symbols of freedom, the periodic flashes of lightning divine fingers reaching to pull him from Purgatory, cracking thunder the voice of God demanding his release. He would be free.

The steel chamber shook with the clap of thunder and keening metal. Caleb saw gloved fingers slide through the hole, gripping the cut segment of the wall. With each tug of the rescuer's hand, he could see the makeshift portal opening, one inch at a time. As the top of the new door cleared the wall's edge, more fingers appeared. Caleb counted the hands of three people. Crawling on his hands and knees toward the exit, his prison shook one final time. A shrieking metallic rip heralded the end of his confinement.

"Watch the edges," the rescuer's voice shouted. "They're gonna be sharp."

Hands reached out. The rescuers held Caleb's arms, stabilizing him as he emerged into the dark desert. Standing, he closed his eyes as he took in the stormy desert scent. Light rain pelted his skin. A cool, moderate wind tussled his hair, and the quiet sound of his clothes rustling brought a moment of peace. Taking in a deep breath, he felt alive.

"Thank you," he said.

Strong hands gripped his wrists and wrenched them behind his back. Caleb's eyes snapped open, fear tore through him. Cold metal and the quiet *snik* of handcuffs locked his arms into place. For the first time he looked at his rescuers.

Five men dressed in black combat gear stood before him. No heraldry was presented on their uniforms, their faces obscured by balaclavas. Two of the men had assault rifles trained on him. Looking down, Caleb saw red dots from laser sights moving across his chest. One of these unknown soldiers held his cuffed wrists.

"Let's go," one of the soldiers said. In his confused, fear-filled state, Caleb wasn't sure who said it.

The ground was uneven. A poorly maintained dirt path circling the cylindrical storage container that had served as Caleb's prison. The twenty foot tall metal structure was situated on the side of a hill. Periodic flashes of lightning granted a clear view of the large tank. A decaying coat of tan paint was giving way to the elements. Large swaths of paint were stripped, chipped, and revealed rusted metal. Light bloomed ahead of him, cast-off illumination from the headlights of multiple cars. Caleb assumed his captors' vehicles were parked at the head of whatever road brought them to the steel storage unit.

"How—" Caleb began as the soldiers pushed him around the parameter of the old storage tank. "How long was I in there?"

Three military-style Humvees came into view as Caleb and his captors cleared the edge of the squat silo. He blinked furiously, the brightness of the lights momentarily blinding him. As his vision normalized, he counted six more soldiers standing sentry by the vehicles.

"About four hours," a voice answered Caleb's question, its owner backlit by the headlights.

The backlit man's movement was strange, a staccato gait, as though walking were unfamiliar to him. Caleb took in his bald head and wide-eyed stare, the man's eyelids seemingly absent. A smile was plastered on the man's face. It was probably supposed to be comforting or inviting. He found the expression disconcerting, almost threatening.

A gloved hand grabbed a bushel of Caleb's hair, forced his head down and to the right. He felt a bare hand pull his left ear forward. The hand quickly let go. His head freed, Caleb looked at the strange man. The skin appeared so tight across the man's face that determining expressions was nearly impossible, but he recognized rage in the man's eyes.

"It's gone," the man said through clenched teeth.

Caleb's heart punched his ribcage. For the first time in his life, he felt panic. He wanted to look in a mirror. He needed to look in a mirror. Every fiber of his being needed to know if it was true.

"The birthmark is gone." Vitriol infused the strange man's words. He let out a frustrated grunt, walked a few feet from Caleb, and turned to look at him.

"What— What does that mean?" Caleb's voice shook.

Taking a deep breath, the strange man calmed himself.

"It just means we'll have to alter the experiments." The threatening smile returned; the Boy's eyes went wide. "You're still a valuable specimen."

"And he's the last one you'll get," a voice from the darkness declared.

The clack of cocking guns filled the air as the soldiers turned toward the voice. Calmly walking into the light, Raven stopped at the edge, standing in the grey where the light met the dark.

"Nice to finally meet you, Joseph."

The soldiers raised their guns in preparation to fire.

"Don't bother," Handler said to his detail. "You're just going to waste the ammo."

"You." Vicious accusation infused Caleb's words. "You did this to me. You took my destiny away from me." Tears rolled down his face, mingling with the beads of rain falling on him.

"Not me," Raven calmly stated. "You did this to yourself."

"WHY DIDN'T YOU KILL ME?" The words exploded out of Caleb. He struggled to break free from the soldier holding him. "YOU FUCKING BITCH! JUST KILL ME!"

"Will someone shut him up?" Handler barked out.

"Please," Caleb sobbed, sinking to his knees, "just kill me."

The butt of a rifle cracked across the Boy's face, rendering him unconscious.

"I told you that you would beg for death." Raven's words were cold. She had a good idea of what awaited him in the company of the Office. It turned her stomach, but it was a fitting punishment for his crimes. She also had an ulterior motive for allowing Joseph Handler to take him.

"Why are you here?" Handler eyed Raven suspiciously.

"To give you an ultimatum," she responded nonchalantly.

Somehow Handler's inscrutable face registered incredulous surprise. "How dare you—"

"2132 Bathesda Street in Bridgeton, New Jersey. Third floor," Raven said. "311 Pike Road, Oskaloosa, Iowa, sub-basement, second level. Douglas, Wyoming, sub-basement level three under the Douglas High School. Do I need to go on?"

Handler excreted something akin to a laugh. He cocked his head at the Caretaker.

"Old sites," he said, boredom seeping into his tone. "Brianna Smith's information isn't entirely up to date."

"Kansas City, Richard Bolling Federal Building, fifth floor."

Handler's demeanor shifted. A subtle change in his near-expressionless face told Raven she had hit a nerve.

"Who told you—"

"Oh," Raven said casually, "in five minutes it won't be under your control anymore."

"What have you done?" The seething words came from Handler with explosive rage.

Raven smirked. "Simply making things right. As we speak, Homeland Security, operating on anonymous information provided to the NSA, is detaining a number of government officials, questioning them about some…questionable choices and involvement in multiple missing persons cases."

347

"How dare you?" Anger flashed in Handler's wide eyes. "I am trying to save humanity—"

"You shouldn't even be here," Raven countered, cutting him off. "This isn't your problem, this isn't your fight."

"With the true Caretakers gone, humanity doesn't stand a chance," Handler said. "*Nianam* have infested this world. I am giving mankind champions that can stem the tide when the Gauntlet begins."

Raven stopped, her incredulity turning to disbelief.

"Did— Did the Elder not tell you?" she asked.

Handler's head jerked to the side, the closest he could get to a questioning expression.

"The Gauntlet began over three decades ago," Raven stated. "And the twins were actualized in 2011."

A look of complete terror managed to grip Handler's tight face. He had been operating under the assumption that the Gauntlet was still decades, if not centuries, away.

"You really need to go back to your people," Raven said, an unspoken threat held in her words. "You have no dog in this fight."

Handler's terror mutated into fanatical resolve.

"The Elder is here," he said. "I know what he has planned. And if he fails, all life, everywhere in the universe, perishes. Including my people."

Raven could see this tactic wasn't going to get her anywhere, and he wasn't going anywhere. Shifting her sight to see within, she looked at the group before her. Of the eleven soldiers, four souls shone bright. Raven figured they must be new recruits, not yet tainted by the evils they would be asked to perform. The souls of five soldiers were pockmarked with black voids, each a different number. Each cancerous pit of oblivion denoting some egregious action, some crime against humanity, that they had committed. Two of the soldiers were vacant voids, light-sucking silhouettes against the Humvee lights. Raven could tell these two were *Nianam*, born without souls. Those whose souls had been consumed by the void had a particular texture to their darkness, a subtle tell they were connected to the Dark Man.

"If you want to help, fine," Raven said. "But you're going to run under my strictures."

Handler let out an explosive laugh.

"Why would I take orders from you? You're nothing but a pale shadow of the true Caretakers, a half-breed with delusions of grandeur."

Raven gave a tight smirk. His terminology brought out the desire to throttle the walking corpse speaking to her.

"My methods can enhance your abilities. I can turn your people into truly strong warriors."

"Your methods create *Nephilim*."

"Yes," Handler admitted, "but the Black Rock allows a person to become a *Nephilim* without having to die. And without being under the control of the Dark Man."

A sardonic laugh escaped Raven. "Are you stupid?" she blurted out.

Handler looked at her in confusion. He could not understand why she didn't want such power.

"I've looked into your so-called Judged Ones," Raven said. "They're weak."

Handler sneered.

"And from the intelligence you appear to have on us, your assessment is simply wrong."

"Is that so?" Handler said. "How about we put that to the test."

A woman exited the lead Humvee. Standing five feet, five inches, she was dressed in a stereotypical FBI-style suit, long black hair pulled into a ponytail. Her face was pretty, but hard. Standing at Handler's side, she regarded Raven with contempt.

"This is Grey," Handler said. "One of our strongest. Four hundred sixty *Nephilim* kills."

Raven's eyebrows raised. A thought formed in her mind. A thought she was not yet ready to voice. One thing at a time.

"Okay," Raven said, "show me what you've got."

Grey stepped forward. As she moved, her body appeared to grow grey armor, her tailored suit disappearing beneath chitinous plating. What stood before Raven looked like an H.R. Giger painting come to life. A biomechanical Grim Reaper with its organic plating styled into what appeared to be bone, pneumatic hosing, and metal. Grey's countenance was that of a jawless skull. Air hoses extended from under her cheekbones and swept back over her shoulders. A tattered grey cloak

349

engulfed the right side of the Reaper visage. Holding out her right hand, a large scythe grew, its shaft a series of interlocked femurs, the blade blue-black iron.

Raven gave a small whistle. She was impressed.

"I love the look," Raven stated honestly. "Now come at me."

Grey lowered the scythe, blade to the ground pointing forward, her legs bent in preparation to rush her opponent. Raven thought it was a pretty basic stance, the move so obvious anyone could dodge it. Grey paused, her head tilting to the side. An air of confusion surrounded her as she took in the fact that Raven's combat stance was putting a hand on her hip, tapping her fingers impatiently.

"Well?" Raven shouted. "Are we doing this or not?"

Her weight momentarily shifted to her back leg, a catapult that launched the Judged One forward. As soon as Grey's foot left the ground, Raven pursed her lips and blew.

The soldiers dropped their guns, hands covering their ears at the screeching sonic blast. Grey flew backward past Handler and into the front end of a Humvee. The force of her impact crumpled the military vehicle's engine, its headlights sputtering into oblivion. Raven still stood with her hand on her hip, disappointment now plastered on her face.

The bio-mechanical visage of Grey melted away, the *Nephilim* transformation reverting to her human state. One of the soldiers rushed over to her, checking the woman's pulse.

"She's just unconscious, sir."

Raven could see a flash of anger in Handler's lidless eyes, his mouth sneering hatred. She smirked at him. Not because anything was actually amusing, just because she knew it would piss the possessed man off even further.

He had not expected this. His intelligence on the Caretaker half-breeds told him they were weaker than the Judged Ones. That they were nothing compared to their ancestors. Not having one of their ancestors to compare to, he realized that the original Caretakers, a species his own people had never met, must have been horrifyingly powerful. It is no wonder early humans deified them.

"Now that we have that out of the way," Raven began, "I'm giving you this one." She gestured to the crumpled, sleeping form of Caleb Voss. "Consider him a peace offering. You paid for his identity and location. As a friend to Jonathan, it is only right that I honor your contract."

"You don't get to tell me—"

"SILENCE!" Raven's voice boomed. "If you would kindly keep your fucking mouth shut." Exasperation infused Raven's words. "The Office now operates by the grace of my benevolence. Clearly you have some people who can hunt and dispatch *Nephilim*. You get to take some of that burden off us."

"There are only twenty-two," Handler said. "We need more."

"No. Your days of human experimentation are done."

Handler gritted his teeth. He thought Raven to be naïve; she had no idea what they would be up against. Even as powerful as she was, in a war of attrition, the modern Caretakers would be overwhelmed. After all, he thought there weren't that many of them.

"We need more," he reiterated. "You cannot hope to fight against an army of billions."

"Oh, ye of little faith." The sing-song tone of Raven's voice irritated Handler.

"We need more." Handler gritted his teeth.

"You will cease your operations," Raven's face darkened, her tone a lethal warning, "or we will tear down the Office piece by piece. Every stronghold you have, every governmental agreement you have made. We will burn it all to the ground."

Handler huffed, derision bleeding from the sound. He had spent over a century constructing the Office, its reach was global. Their presence, approved or not, was in every country. He did not believe she could do it. The Office had identified only a handful of Caretakers that had become fully active, and only fifteen thousand of the Waiting worldwide.

"Really?" A sly smile crossed the undead man's face as he called her bluff. "You and what army?"

Raven stared him dead in the eye. As if waiting for this moment, the sky lit up. Lightning cut a jagged scar across the heavens. Joseph Handler's face fell.

"Don't you know, Handler?" A smile curled at the corners of her mouth, amusement flashing in her green, serpentine eyes.

The illuminating flash revealed a sea of women. Handler could not tell how many there were. Was it hundreds? Thousands? They all silently stood at Raven's back, each poised and ready for war.

"We are Legion," she said, opening her arms. "We are many."

Chapter 29

Adapt or die.

It's a simple phrase. A binary choice at the crux of all life. Everything evolves or fades into extinction on that single simple principle. Businesses, friendships, marriages, even governments are ruled by this simple concept.

Adapt or die.

My compatriots and I started Darkstone's Asylum almost two decades ago. The idea was simple: Help the little guy. Have a network for the independent private investigators. The kind of PIs who were willing to take jobs the big firms deemed beneath them. PIs who would help clients no one else would believe or didn't have the kind of money the big boys charged. We wanted an organization that would provide for those working in the shadows of those large, corporate firms. One that would procure the same benefits for our members, carving out regions to ensure there would be enough work for our PIs, and enough PIs for our clientele. Price controls, ethics guidelines, accountability with the ability to maintain independence. We wanted to be the go-to organization for those in need. Before D.A., my penchant for taking on weird, spiritual, and often unbelievable cases had many traditional private investigators telling me I should be put into an insane asylum. With my friends, I created one. And it has been exhaustingly glorious. Our mission was a success.

Adapt or die.

Thanks to Caleb Voss, a man that media outlets referred to as the Hatchetman, my world and the world of those around me had been forever changed. It felt as though a comforting blindfold had been ripped from my eyes. A blindfold my mind had once desperately tried to keep on after the events of the Atsuko Takanashi case. I had clung to that life of ignorance through an alternate identity, one born of desperate delusion. I— We needed to adapt to this new reality. Darkstone's Asylum needed to adapt to this new reality. The possibility that one of our members could walk into a fatal investigation, an investigation stemming from the Dark Man, had become all too real. That damnable thing placed a target on my back. By association, my colleagues had become targets as well. It was time for a change, and Raven had provided a path for us.

Adapt or die.

Overall, the mission of Darkstone's Asylum changed only slightly. An unprecedented convention of all the regional managers for D.A. was held in Las Vegas. Six hundred twenty-nine managers. Tara and I outlined the changes we were going to make. As Jonathan Hayes was Darkstone's protégé and official successor, my words held some weight. We would be consolidating into a singular organization, all investigators becoming employees as a result. This kind of change traditionally came with a lot of resistance. The naysayers were fewer than I had expected.

Adapt or die.

Operations and command structure for the new incarnation of Darkstone's Asylum would be similar to that used by the FBI. However, investigators would still be available to take private investigation work. In fact, it was encouraged that they do so. We wanted to still operate with the same premise of helping the little guys. The catch was that all managers and investigators would be required to undergo a background check that made the NSA's security look incompetent. This last bit had ninety-six regional managers quit on the spot. I couldn't help wondering what those individuals were hiding. In the end, the changes were put to a vote. All remaining managers voted in favor.

Adapt or die.

There was a purpose to our consolidation beyond simple security. One month after Caleb Voss had gone missing—or was killed by the FBI, if you watch the news—Congress passed a security spending bill. Attached was a rider, an addition to the bill, innocuously called the Public Safety Against Unknown Threats Act. This bill used the laws and legal decisions regarding bounty hunters to deputize two private institutions against "unknown or unexplained threats to public safety and national security." Darkstone's Asylum was one of those named institutions. Over the years, Raven had set up contacts and influence within the U.S. government. It was those players she had enlisted to craft the bill. For the first time in my life, I was glad that most of our lawmakers couldn't be bothered to read the laws they vote on. The

PSAUT Act came with the benefits of solid funding and investigative power. Darkstone's Asylum had become an official force to be reckoned with. An army of light against the consuming darkness.

We had adapted.

My thoughts drifted as I drove down the Las Vegas Strip, heading toward the still-under-construction D.A. National Headquarters. With our first infusion of government funds, we procured an official base of operations. It was the same building where Caleb Voss' quest for perfection and godhood had come to an end. Tara wasn't thrilled by the idea that our offices would be placed in a building where such violence had been committed. She knew Las Vegas history well enough to know that any building older than two years would have a morbid past. As such, she had not protested. Well, not too much.

Three weeks ago, the primary offices were completed. Darkstone's Asylum officially moved in and got to work. Normally I would take the freeway to the office. Today I was feeling a need to slow down, take in my environment. Take a moment to breathe.

At ten o'clock in the morning, the late October temperature was a pleasant eighty-five degrees. "Pleasant" being a relative term. Even though the summer tourist season ended about a month ago, the Las Vegas Strip was busy. Tourists walked in every direction, hopping from casino to casino in search of wealth and free drinks, stopping to watch the water fountain show in front of the Bellagio, making their way through numerous off-shoot alleyway shopping arcades between resorts. Every expression, every emotion, could be seen on the Strip. A microcosm of the human species.

A bewildered Midwestern family gawked at the immense buildings around them, smiles of amazement plastered on their children's faces. Loud hooting and laughing blasted from a group of young women encircling what was clearly a bride-to-be. The tiara and silver sash with the word "Bride" in bold blue letters was a dead giveaway. Two well-dressed twenty-something men carried a properly shit-faced man between them; their night had either been that amazing, that horrible, or they had a serious drinking problem. Three European tourists, I assumed from the copious number of fanny-packs in their possession, were finding out a basic truth about Las Vegas the hard way: Just because you can see a hotel on the Strip doesn't mean it's within walking distance. The poor sweaty trio looked like they were ready to keel over from exhaustion. From their condition, I guessed they were from a country that considered seventy degrees to be worthy of an excessive heat warning. The angry glares two of them directed toward the third said all there was to say about who had made the ill-advised decision to hike.

Lights from each casino glittered in the mid-morning sunlight. The plethora of LED video screens that had replaced the old neon signs shone just as brightly in the day as they did at night. This was the Vegas everyone knew, lit 24-7. A place of fun, a place of debauchery, a place to lose all your money, or, if you were one of the lucky few touched by the gods, to win a fortune.

I took in more of the crowd while stopped at an excessively long red light, poised to turn left toward the freeway. The Wynn Hotel and Casino sat to my right and the Fashion Show Mall to my left. I watched as a mother comforted her child on the sidewalk. The little boy couldn't have been older than six or seven years old and appeared to have taken a tumble. Mouth agape in cries of exaggerated pain, the boy wailed. His mother, squatting to eye level with him, appeared to speak calmly. I have no idea what she said, but with a few words a wide smile of disbelief crossed the child's face. He started smothering his mother with kisses. It was an innocuous moment in time. It was a meaningless moment in time. To that boy, it was the only important moment in time. This is what life is for us. Moments converging, lives intersecting, bonds affirmed, love expressed. It is something worth preserving. It is something worth fighting for.

The sight of downtown Las Vegas from the freeway is only interesting for about the first five visits to the city. The clump of tall buildings with the names of each hotel/casino identifying them did nothing for me anymore. I had become jaded. The scenery had become repetitive. I realized I needed to start taking a different route to work. Pulling off the high-speed road, I uneventfully made my way to the construction site that housed my office.

The exterior shell of the building remained the same. The primary difference was the replacement of the shrieking white steel doors. Now the entrance had twin, half-inch thick bullet proof glass doors with the words "Darkstone's Asylum" and our logo etched into it. Very governmental looking. I wasn't quite sure how I felt about that.

The lobby had been completely redone, enlarged to give about fifteen feet between the front doors and security desk. Four comfortable, dark brown leather chairs were situated on each side of the entrance with their backs against the walls. Bronze plaques etched with staff names hung on the cream-colored walls behind the chairs. A large, carved seal was displayed prominently behind the chestnut-haired woman seated at the security desk. Four brass plaques bracketed the seal, the names of Darkstone's Asylum's founders etched into the polished plates. Some discussion had gone into whether to put pictures of the founders on the wall. Thankfully the metal plaques were chosen. I did not relish the thought of having to find an explanation for why my picture had "Darkstone" below it.

Denise Olay, our front line of security, gave me a welcoming smile. Per Raven's suggestion, every branch of D.A. had at least one Caretaker attached to it. With our enhanced background checks, I discovered there were already twenty-three Caretakers attached to Darkstone's Asylum as investigators in various regions. They were damn good at their jobs too. The inclusion of Caretakers among our ranks was a means of ensuring all situations could be handled. Denise was our dedicated Caretaker. She was the reason we did not have any metal detectors at the front door. Threat assessment was her forte. She had the ability to read intent from any person she could see, her senses sharpened to the point of making listening devices pointless. If we could record her sight, we wouldn't need telephoto cameras either. She was, in essence, a walking security and surveillance system. I had tried to convince her to take a position within our investigative branch. She held the opinion that front door security and receptionists were the gatekeepers, the first line of defense against potential threats. I couldn't argue with that.

A man stood in the lobby looking at the shiny plaques on the wall. He appeared to be in his mid-fifties with short-cropped brown hair, streaks of grey creeping in on the sides. Horn-rimmed glasses framed a kind face. His complexion indicated he did not get along with the sun very well. He had the fidgety appearance of a nervous teen going on a first date, dressed to impress with metallic blue button-down shirt and black slacks. I surmised he had purchased the clothes for just this occasion as a sales tag on his trousers was still attached. The small bouquet of roses he held confirmed he wasn't here for an interview.

"Hi." The man jumped a little at my words. "Are you waiting for someone?"

"Oh," the man smiled, "yes, I'm here to see Brianna Smith." He gave me a quick once-over. "You must be Jonathan."

"How did you know that?" I raised a brow.

"Bri mentioned you always wear all black."

Nodding in concession to the point, I asked, "She actually lets you call her Bri?"

His face flushed, seemingly embarrassed. "We've been talking a lot on the phone and—"

"Wait," I said, his identity striking me, "you're the Pene—"

"Mike," he cut me off quickly. "Mike Holvald. I prefer to leave my handle to the online world…especially since it makes me sound like a porn star."

I gave a little chuckle at this. "Yeah, it kinda does."

"Well, when a large group of people start knowing you by a specific name, no matter how ridiculous it is, you can't simply go about changing it."

I smirked, nodding in agreement. "Quite true. I assume she knows you're here?" Mike gave a nervous nod. I gave him a pat on the shoulder. "Ease up, my man, no need to be so nervous. She already knows what you look like, and she obviously likes you or you wouldn't ever see her in real life."

Mike took in a deep, calming breath. "Good point."

"You got this." I smiled. "I have to get to work, but it was really great to put a face to the name… Well, names."

Mike snorted a chuckle. "It was nice to meet you as well."

I turned toward one of the heavy, electronic security doors that had been installed on each side of the lobby. Denise pressed a button and the door to the right swung itself open.

There had been much debate surrounding where to locate our offices. Most government buildings tend to place their offices on anything other than the ground floor. The second level of our HQ was lined with windows, a potential hazard from my perspective. I had authorized putting in the money to replace those windows with bullet-proof glass, but one nutcase with a .50 caliber sniper cannon would render the enhanced security pointless. Yes, I am paranoid.

The decision was made to convert the ground floor into our offices. The warehouse area where Caleb Voss had held Doctor Adriana Jordan was completely remodeled. The walls were reinforced with quarter-inch steel plating, six large offices and a conference room constructed in the central box that the Hatchetman had intended to use as a kill room. The offices that shared a wall with the building's exterior were cleaned up, had some technical upgrades, but generally were left as we found them.

The first mahogany office door had a removeable nameplate reading "FBI Liaison Special Agent Brock Allen." The look on the giant's face when he was ordered to become a permanent fixture in our ranks was both priceless and pathetic. Tara, Stephanie, and I had spent the better part of the last month trying to convince the man that he was not being punished. Thus far we have been unsuccessful in getting through to him.

My office was the second door on the left with a silver nameplate reading "Investigative Director Jonathan Hayes." The last door in the row held a similar name plate, "Director of Operations Tara Hayes," emblazoned on its dark wood edifice. Stephanie and Brianna were given two of the remaining central offices. Stephanie was given the title of "Lead Investigator." I tried to get Brianna to take the title of "IT Director." She insisted on "Digital Sorceress Supreme." I still had "IT Director" engraved on her name plate, albeit in small letters under her "official" title.

The last office was bequeathed to Mai Xaio after I had offered it to Raven as a base of operations. According to the goth queen, Mai had been adrift for a long time. Though Agent Allen had no problems contacting her, that was just due to the nature of mobile communications. Mai had spent years bouncing from job to job, staying at the various Caretaker safehouses for short stints, never really being stable. Taking her on as a permanent member would give her a place to

359

ground herself. In time she might even consider this place home. I know all too well the toll being adrift in the world can take. And a periodic, uneasy feeling that kept creeping into my stomach told me having a medical expert on staff would prove invaluable. Even if that medical expert's patients were usually dead.

My office was about twice the size of the run-down Los Angeles office I used to work from. Boxes were strewn about the room. Moving in was a slow process. One wall had shelves built into it, a second wall had an integrated filing cabinet. The wall facing my desk had an LCD screen set in a faux-window frame, displays designed to give the illusion that I wasn't trapped in a closed box. I could put on any scenery I wanted, looping videos of the outside world. Today I decided on a nighttime view of New York City.

The old wooden desk at the rear-center of the room had been moved in with most of my old office items. It still retained the dusty wood smell that had permeated my former headquarters, and that smell was infecting the new room. I had procured a new desk chair. The black, high-backed leather monstrosity could fit two people comfortably. I loved it. Sinking into the chair, I felt like some 1980s cartoon villain. All I was missing was a cat. I took a moment to absorb the feel and scent of my surroundings.

I had placed the dark green box on my desk last night. The gold pentagrams on each side glittered slightly in the light of the room. My mind had been mulling over what to do with the Red Hag named Thassa. I promised her I would find her a family. That was two, almost three months ago. I hoped she had slept soundly within the box. Putting aside all mental debate, I opened the hinged box and turned off the electrical current feeding the crystal. Slowly the small green LED light faded. On the client side of my desk, Thassa stood. Looking at me with her deep black eyes, her red hair flowed along unseen currents of energy permeating the room. I pulled my spirit box from a desk drawer, turned it on, and placed it before the beatific spirit. Thassa reached a pointed finger into the box.

"I have a proposition for you," I said. Thassa cocked her head to the side, questioning. "This is the home of my people." I indicated the totality of the building. "We exist to help those in need. Good people are here, they are my family. I want you to become a part of that family."

"You. Want. Me." It was a question, and I could see disbelief on Thassa's face.

"Yes," I said assuredly. "I'll call a meeting to introduce you to everyone, let them know you're here and you are one of us."

The corners of her small mouth pulled into a great, warm smile. "Home." I wished the spirit box had the capability to convey the emotions behind the words, but I could almost feel her joy. "I. Am. Home."

"Yes." I smiled at her. "Yes, you are. Welcome home."

"Look. Around," the electronic voice said.

"Yes, please do." I nodded. "Before you go exploring, I must tell you that a few people here will probably be able to see you just like I can." I thought of Denise at the front desk and Mai in her office. I hadn't bothered to ask, but I was fairly certain Caretakers could see non-human spirits. They could see souls, after all. "If they get startled, please don't be offended."

"I. Good." I interpreted this as she was okay with the possibility of startling people. "Happy."

A wide smile crossed my face. "Good, now go explore your new home."

It is an odd sensation to feel like an inhuman spirit reminds you of an excited teenage girl, but that was how I felt as Thassa nodded, turned, and disappeared through the wall containing my fake window. Closing the lid of Thassa's former sleeping chamber, I placed the spirit stone box into a desk drawer along with the spirit box. I thought for a moment that I should commission the Green Witch of Hawthorne to make enough of these spirit boxes to place one in each office. Thassa didn't just have a new home and a new family, she had a new protectorate. She had just become a part of our security system. Having the ability to communicate with the entire staff would be advisable. I leaned back into my oversized chair, letting out a sigh of satisfaction.

Right here, right now, all was right with the world. And with the buzzing of the office intercom, my zen feeling vanished. I hit the answer button on my old-school, multi-button office phone.

"What's up?" I asked.

Denise's voice was tense. "You need to come out here right now."

"What is it?"

"Just—" She paused. "Just get out here." The urgency in her tone had me out the door expecting the worst.

Denise stood behind her security desk, mouth agape, staring at Thassa. The Red Hag's hand slowly waved a greeting at the dumbfounded Caretaker, her face held a bemused smile. Denise's reaction to the spirit had clearly interrupted Brianna and Mike. The two master hackers had their arms around each other, Mike had lipstick smeared across his mouth. Both held mirroring looks of confusion. I couldn't help but snicker at the scene.

"I guess I should introduce you," I said, holding in my laughter.

"You're damn right," Denise said. Her voice lowered. "What is she?"

A thought struck me. Caretakers may be able to see the things we call spirits, but it doesn't mean they *have* seen them. These entities we call spirits are far less common than TV would have us believe.

"Her name is Thassa. She is a Red Ha—" Catching myself, I chose to finally correct the name of her species. "A Red Lady."

Skepticism and suspicion were written on the Caretaker's face. I heard a throat clearing, and Mike's voice broke into the conversation.

"Wha— What are you guys talking about?" He gestured to Denise. "And what are you looking at?"

I knew Mike and Brianna were unable to see Thassa. From the outside, Denise and I must have looked a little crazy.

"You can't see her?" Denise asked, forcefully gesturing at the floating red-haired woman. From Mike's perspective, she was gesturing at thin air.

Mike lifted an eyebrow. It seemed he just noticed the eyes Denise was sporting. I chuckled, catching Denise's attention. I pointed to my eye, letting her know she had subconsciously activated her inhuman half, her cat-like pupils couched within a frowning face.

"Oh," she said. "Yeah, I forgot about that."

"What—" Mike started.

"It's nothing to worry about, baby," Brianna said, her hand resting gently on Mike's cheek. He rolled his eyes.

"Raven's always trying to keep me in the dark," he said. "She says she's trying to protect me. I'm the one supposed to be protecting her. Please don't start that with me too."

"This is going to take a bit more than a simple introduction," I said under my breath.

Thassa turned to look at the lovers. She appeared to think for a moment, then moved to them. I saw what she was about to do. My hand instinctively covered my mouth to hide the mischievous smile covering my face.

The Red Lady began by caressing Brianna's cheek. Our resident computer goddess jerked back from the unseen hand.

"What the hell?" Alarm permeated her voice. "Mike, I'm kinda in the dark here too."

"No need to be alarmed," I said, still hiding my smile. Brianna shot me a look of confusion. I pointed to Mike's chest.

Thassa made her move. Mike watched in horror as the buttons on his metallic blue shirt were undoing themselves in rapid succession. Brianna could make out the impression of hands gripping each side of his shirt as it was wrenched open, exposing the room to Mike's nearly translucent paleness. His chest hair did nothing to dampen the glow of his reflective skin. Thassa appeared to wince at the sight, despite being a translucent, glowing white herself. The pot was calling the kettle black.

Pulling his shirt closed as quickly as possible, Mike said, "Okay, I get it. You're here."

I could hold back no longer. Laughter erupted from me. Denise, who had done a much better job of hiding her amusement, cracked. Bending over, she let out a howling laugh. Mike glared at both of us. Denise rounded the security desk and walked over to Mike and Brianna, her chest convulsing with laughter.

"Yeah," Mike said. "Yuk it up."

Brianna put her hand under his shirt, rubbing the offended man's chest. "Relax, babe. Find the humor here." Her face told the story of a woman with better self-control than either Denise or myself. Mike let out a long sigh as Denise looked him in the eye.

363

"Do you want to see her?" she asked.

"You—" Mike's words were cut off as Denise removed his glasses and put her hand on the left side of his face. Her thumb covered his left eye.

"See as we see," she said. Mike jerked his head back, blinked as though something had stuck in his eye. His eyelids fluttered furiously, then froze, his eyes wide open in an awe-inspired stare.

"Oh," he said, "hello there."

Thassa nodded her head. She appeared to be giggling. The red-haired spirit gave her customary wave of greeting. Mike's hand slowly moved to return the greeting.

"Now me! Now me!" Teenage excitement appeared to grip Brianna. Denise snorted, then repeated the process.

I could see awe in Brianna's face as she looked at Thassa.

"Wow, you are beautiful," she said. "It's nice to meet you. Welcome."

Thassa's face lit up, an expression of pure bliss. If she had any doubts about having found a home, Brianna had erased them. Thassa looked at me, pointed back toward the rest of the building. A question, a desire to continue her exploration. I smiled.

"Go for it," I said. "This place is all yours."

Denise looked at me, a dubious expression I couldn't quite read.

"Are you sure about this?" she asked.

"Denise, if the shit ever hits the fan, she is the best back-up you could ever ask for."

The Caretaker nodded slowly. She was not entirely convinced.

"Hey," Mike's voice chimed in. He pointed at Denise. "You could have done that this whole time. Why—"

"Because it was funny," Denise said.

"Mike," I pointed at the D.A. logo behind the security desk, "don't forget that you're standing in an asylum. We're all a bit crazy here."

I held my smile of good humor, but I felt that humor wane. While the name had been divined due to other, less tactful "colleagues" making jokes about my sanity, the word Asylum has one other definition. Darkstone's Asylum isn't just an organization employing PIs with a penchant for insane cases. We grant protection for those seeking refuge.

We exist to help those seeking asylum from insanity thrust upon them in this world.

The words crossed my mind as I watched my colleagues, my friends, laugh, argue, and point fingers at each other. Our half-human head of security, a hacker infected by a substance with unknown long-term effects that granted her super-human capabilities, and this new, normal yet extraordinary, human hacker. Though they were just the people standing in front of me, they represented a microcosm of the people that comprised Darkstone's Asylum. That mantra, that binary choice, thrust itself into the forefront of my consciousness. That choice everything boiled down to. Unwanted and unwarranted, the words involuntarily passed my lips in a whisper.

"Adapt or die."

Epilogue

The woman stood unsteadily at the edge of the small parking lot, her eyes having difficulty focusing on the white, two-story office building in front of her. The hood of her sweater was pulled over her head as far as it could go to obscure her identity from prying eyes. The sun beat down mercilessly on her. Summer had lingered longer than normal, refusing to give up its blazing grip. The sweater felt tight. Sweat soaked almost every inch of the garment, causing the material to constrict around her. Fine, jet-black hair was plastered to her face. A combination of sweat and dust created an ad-hoc cement that held strands in sculpturesque rigidity.

A bead of sweat crawled down the side of her face, sending a shiver through her. Cold was creeping in. She knew she was going into shock. Blood had painted her left sleeve bright red, sweat enhancing the color's vibrance. Six smaller, expanding points dotted the neckline and right arm of her hoodie. She dared not look down, but she knew the sticky wetness on her hand wasn't just sweat. A convulsive shiver wracked her body. Focus was failing her. She was running out of time. Swaying like a drunk, she concentrated on putting one foot in front of the other, the laser-etched glass doors on the other side of the parking lot her goal. Salvation. Through those doors was her salvation. Thankfully, the lot was small, but in her condition, it may as well have been the Grand Canyon.

Halfway there. Almost there.

Her sight went in and out of focus with each jarring footstep. She felt her heart racing. Adrenaline hastened the road to her end. Had it not been for her sweat-soaked clothing, she would have bled out six blocks ago. The constricting sweater acted to staunch the flow of blood, though not well enough to prevent the Grim Reaper from following her. A hooded specter hanging just out of sight, like a vulture waiting for her last breath. Her chest felt tight, breathing labored. She felt like she was drowning.

Just a few more steps.

Through the glass doors she could make out four people. Her eyes couldn't focus on them, blurs hidden behind glass. She stumbled, her hand reflexively shooting out, finding the handlebar of the door. She knew that she would not get up if she fell. Breathing hard, she took a moment to ensure her feet were securely under her. She blinked. Her eyelids felt heavy, they wanted to stay shut. She recognized this tiredness, this particular call to sleep. A siren's song to lull her into the deep, endless slumber. She chanced a look at her hand on the door handle. Her grip was slippery, her hand a cavalcade of bright red, darkening crimson, and rivulets of pale skin where sweat had cleaved a path through her blood.

Looking through the door, a moment of focused vision graced her. The four people inside had not noticed her. They were engrossed in some sort of exchange. A man who appeared to be in his mid-fifties was fumbling with the buttons on his metallic blue dress shirt. A pretty Hispanic woman was blowing the man a raspberry. A balding man dressed in black had a bemused, if not introspective, expression on his face. Then there was her.

The woman hadn't seen Brianna Smith since she was a child. Brianna had saved her life once before. She hoped the hacker could do it again. Using all of her strength, the hoodie-clad figure pulled the door open.

She felt a sense of flying as she moved into the lobby of Darkstone's Asylum HQ. Light-headed, she knew her body was on its way to the ground. A part of her didn't care. A part of her wanted the sleep. Wanted the rest death promised her. In her altered state, the fall seemed to take forever. An endless plunge into the abyss. It felt...good.

With lightening quick reflexes, Mike Holvald caught the collapsing figure. He could feel her fast, shallow breathing. Looking at the shocked faces of his companions, he appeared unsure of what to do.

"Denise," Jonathan said, "call an ambulance."

Denise quickly moved toward the security desk.

"No." The word was barely a whisper, but it stopped Denise in her tracks.

Mike gently lowered the woman to the ground, seating himself next to her. Brianna knelt at his side. The face looked familiar to her. Dark circles rimmed the Japanese woman's eyes, her lips held a slight bluish tinge. The rise and fall of her chest was fast. Too fast. Brianna thought she was hyperventilating.

"Sweetie," Brianna said, "I need to you relax. Slow your breathing."

"No ambulance," she responded, attempting to comply with Brianna's request.

"Get Mai out here," Jonathan said. Denise gave him a dumbfounded look. "She's a medical professional. She might usually deal with the dead, but I'm pretty sure she can help with the living."

Denise nodded in understanding.

The woman couldn't tell if Denise was having a seizure or simply rejecting Jonathan's order. The security officer stood still as a statue of a few seconds.

"Mai is on her way," Denise said. "I also contacted Raven. She was going to come here today anyway. She's bringing help. With the way she drives, it should only be about fifteen minutes."

Jonathan cocked an eyebrow as he knelt beside the woman. He looked back to Densie. "Grab me a pair of scissors. We need to get this sweater off her."

The man in black had counted seven spreading points of blood. Two on her right arm, one on each side of her chest, one on her neck, and two on her left arm. With the sleeve of her left arm drenched in blood, he thought there might be more. Denise handed him a pair of orange-handled paper scissors. He looked at them dubiously, raised his eyebrows, and let out a sigh.

"Gotta use what you've got," he said.

The woman's breathing slowed. Her eyelids fluttered.

"Oh no," Brianna said, patting the woman on the cheek. "No sleeping."

With no small effort, Jonathan managed to make a small slice into the sopping sweater sleeve. He gave the scissors a disgusted look, as if they had failed at their only purpose, then tossed them aside. Grabbing the sides of the sliced fabric, he yanked on them. A wet ripping echoed though the lobby as the cotton fiber tore open. Searing pain shot through the woman. She hissed through her clenched teeth.

"Sorry," Jonathan said. "So, tell me," another fleshy rip of fabric resounded, "who are you?"

The woman took a shuddering breath as her sleeve was ripped open to the shoulder. Jonathan could see there were only two wounds. They were ragged gouges, as though someone clawed into her skin to rip something out. One of the wounds was bleeding profusely; Jonathan thought an artery or vein might have been hit. He heard a security door open behind him, heralding Mai's arrival.

"My name is Atsuko Takanashi." She looked at Jonathan's surprised face. "I heard you were looking for me."

A Huge Thank You

I would like to thank all of my family and friends who supported and encouraged me through the process of writing Darkstone's Asylum: The Hatchetman. Your belief in me means more than any of you could ever know.

Music Credits

"Divide" by Assemblage 23 from the album *Failure*. Written and Composed by Tom Shear. ©2001 Metropolis Records.

"Glowstix, Neon and Blood" by Incubite from the album *Toxicum*. Arranged by Neill Oblivion. ©2011 ProNoize.

Online Content Creators
(All can be found on YouTube)

The Trash Taste video podcast: @TrashTaste

Joey "The Anime Man": @TheAnimeMan

Connor A.K.A. "CDawgVA": @CDawgVA

Garnt A.K.A "Gigguk": @gigguk

Printed in Great Britain
by Amazon

44229405R00205